PINK ICING

Alison Hay

To a dear, special friend, Sue Walker,
from Alison Hay (alias Pauline
with love,   Murphy)
                        xxx

*This is the original
publication*

Part 1

Chapter 1

As she entered the park with her daughter, Rose had a good feeling that this lovely, yet ordinary place, with its expanse of grass and its ancient, blossom-laden trees, would shortly become somewhere really special for her and Carla - a place stored forever in their memories. She looked towards the railed-off playground, where squeals of excitement were coming from a toddler being pushed in a bucket swing by a young woman.

'Swings?' Rose suggested. 'Long time since we had swings together.'

There was no response from Carla, skating beside her, so she repeated the suggestion, adding, 'we used to push each other, remember? And we'd sing - like this: *High in the sky as if we can fly. Up, up away, far from today....*'

'Don't. You can't sing, Mum,' said Carla, looking around.

'Embarrassed, are you?' said Rose, smiling. 'Right, I won't sing but we'll still go on the swings. You love them.'

Carla looked up at her mother with an expression close to scorn in her startlingly blue eyes.

'That was when I was little. I'm big now. I don't want swings, I want to skate all round the park.'

'Wait, you'll get hot in that jacket. I said you wouldn't need it. Here, let me....' Rose took hold of Carla's arm but she pulled away.

'It ain't to keep me warm. Auntie Fay told you - it's to stop me getting hurt if I fall over.' She skated away on roller blades she'd had less than two weeks.

'Hang on, I'm coming with you,' called Rose. 'Wait.' Carla didn't respond. 'Bloody roller blades,' Rose muttered. 'Fay's daughter shouldn't have given them to her. I'd have got them if she'd said.'

A woman with a dog had come alongside and was staring at her. Rose scowled. 'What are you looking at?'

The woman gave her a wary look and walked on, quickly.

God, she must have spoken her thoughts out loud! Hadn't done that for ages, or so she hoped. She began to run - something else she hadn't done for even more ages. Her legs wobbled all over the place, out of control.

'Wait, will you,' she yelled, but the effort, combined with running, was too much. She stopped for a moment, gasping for breath and looking around for somewhere to sit. A few yards ahead Carla had also stopped but didn't look around. As Rose, puffing, caught up with her, she glanced sideways and said in a chant,

'Can't run, can't sing, can't remember. What can you do, Mum?' Then she was off again leaving Rose speechless, staring after her.

The tarmac path that Carla was following bordered a huge circular piece of grass. Oh, well, she'd end up where she started. A bench about fifty yards away, on a graveled oasis, backed by a little wooded area, looked inviting. Rose walked to it, her legs still a bit shaky, and sank down. At some distance now Carla was skating steadily. Of course she'd want to practice but she could do that any time. It was so like kids - must do it now, can't wait, never mind what anyone else wants.

That dig 'can't remember' - was Carla meaning her birthday party? She hadn't mentioned it, not a word. If that's what she was getting at it wasn't fair. Rose hadn't forgotten - she did forget things but not that. It wasn't her fault the hospital appointment was on the same day.

She felt in her bag, rummaged, then stopped. Throwing her head back she laughed aloud. She hadn't got any - didn't need any. Thanks to Terry and those patches he'd got her, she wasn't a smoker anymore. She slipped a hand under her jacket and loose shirt and patted her stomach. She was eating again, enjoying her food, but mustn't get fat.

She smiled, picturing Terry. No other man had done as much for her. He'd suggested sending Carla an iced cake. What do kids do on birthdays? Blow out candles. He'd even bought the cake from a posh West End baker, and got them to post it, all beautifully packaged. It was a shame they couldn't have been there. Meeting Terry would have been like an extra present for Carla. And he was dying to meet her, but not today he'd said. She should see her daughter alone to give her the news - news of the best present anyone could ever have. With that thought in her mind Rose looked more kindly at the small, busily skating figure.

Even from this distance she could see Carla's face was as pink as her quilted anorak. Of course she was too hot. And, all bundled up, she looked only about six and so lovable. In a few minutes she was back, sitting just long enough to catch her breath, then was off again without having said a word. Rose called after her,

'Come back, I've got something lovely to tell you.'

If Carla heard she gave no sign. She skated away vigorously. Rose called again, louder, 'Don't go far. I want to talk to you,' and again Carla didn't respond.

Oops, she'd fallen. Rose shifted, reached for her bag, preparing to go to her but she was already sitting up. Tough little trier as always - she'd be okay.

Rose's attention was taken by the sound of laughter coming from the little glade behind her. Half turning, she saw a girl on the path between shrubs, holding a toddler by the hand. A little behind them was a guy pushing a pram, walking with slow, easy steps as if he had all the time in the world. A real family. The girl looked younger than Rose. She was pretty with long brown hair. The guy was tall and lean, dressed in jeans and a leather jacket, and his hair was tied in a ponytail. Rose would have liked to speak to them but they didn't seem to notice her. She closed her eyes and peopled the scene with other figures; she became the girl, holding Carla, and Terry was the pram- pusher. One day that fantasy would be real. It wasn't always going to be other people.

The family passed by, their voices becoming distant. Were they going home to a pretty, neat house with a garden? She should be doing that. It was her right as much as theirs - as much as anyone's.

A picture of her flat came into her mind with its grubby paintwork and slimy walls. Graffiti decorated the staircases:

6

who'd fucked whom, obscenities with threats, and silly kids' slogans, *Jack for Crack* and *Coke for a Poke*. She pushed the unwelcome image away but still it came back; even the smell of sick and shit, with the hateful, bloody force of reality. It wasn't going to hold her for much longer. She had Terry's word for that and he could make things happen.

She opened her eyes and glanced towards Carla. She was still sitting and the dog woman was bending down beside her, handing her something white. A tissue? Hanky? Was Carla upset? Not her big, brave girl, surely? Anyway, she had to fall over sometimes. The woman was looking in her direction; Carla was looking too, and pointing. What was going on - being said? Rose got up but at the same time Carla got to her feet and patted the dog. She seemed to be laughing. No point in going over. No, she was skating again, and it looked as if she was on her way back. Rose sat down.

'Mum, I fell over. Didn't you see?'

'Yes, but it was only once. That's how you learn. Was that a nice dog?'

Carla nodded and sat down on the far end of the bench.

'Be great to have a dog,' said Rose, 'and live near a park.'

'I do live near a park.' Carla's voice was flat.

'I mean properly living somewhere - us together in a house like Auntie Fay's, with a pond in the garden and a little gnome fishing. Be lovely, wouldn't it, sweetie?'

The child stared straight ahead. Rose repeated, 'Wouldn't it?'

Carla looked at her then, her eyes expressionless.

'You're always saying stuff like that.'

'But it could happen - soon.'

'It won't, Mum. It's like wishes that don't come true.'

'What d'you mean?'

She might not have spoken. Carla was looking across the stretch of grass to where the woman with the dog was throwing a ball. She waved and Carla waved back, shifting as if about to get up.

Rose stretched out a detaining hand. 'Never mind her.

Remember, I told you about Terry? Your present was from both of us. You got it, didn't you?'

'Yes, Auntie Fay told you.' Carla didn't push Rose's hand away but she didn't look at her.

'More than I ever had - a birthday cake. Did you have candles?'

'Eight,' said Carla. 'I'm eight now.'

Not a clever question. Mustering a bright voice, Rose said, 'Good thing it didn't get squashed, your lovely iced cake. A pink squidgy mess that would've been.'

Now Carla looked at her and grinned. Rose took a decision. She'd tell her now. They'd laugh and cry together, kiss and hug: real mother and daughter stuff.

'Sweetie, I've got a lovely surprise for you.'

Rose's words elicited no reaction. Carla was again watching the ball-chasing dog. There was no going back. Rose squeezed and stroked her arm through the anorak.

'It's something really, really special, better than anything you could ever wish for. I'm having a baby - a little girl'

Carla's head jerked round. She stared at her mother with an expression that Rose could not describe, then one stark word jumped into her mind – horror.

'Why? Why d'you want one? You've already got a little girl.' Carla threw off Rose's hand and was up and away from the bench like pink lightening, feet going like paddles churning the gravel.

Stunned by her reaction, Rose was motionless for a moment, staring at Carla's retreating figure. She was heading for the gate - the exit to the main road. Scared for her, Rose grabbed her bag and, stumbling on her wedge-heels, ran after her.

People were spilling into the park: children released from school, mums with pushchairs, dog walkers, all cramming through the narrow gate. Carla was through and out of sight while Rose struggled.

'Get outa my way. Let me through, can't you - my daughter's in danger.'

'The big gate's quicker,' said a lumpy-looking girl,

8

complacently.

'I don't want the bloody big gate. My girl went this way.'

Rose pushed the stupid lump out of her way. She trod on a dog's paw; it yelped and the old man, attached to its lead, snarled, 'Clumsy bitch, that's abuse that is.' She half-turned to glare at him and nearly tipped a toddler out of its pushchair. She didn't care - she was through the gate, a kissing gate of all bloody, stupid names. She turned right but was it the right way? Was it the way they'd come? Yes, down to the traffic lights. Had Carla gone across? There was no sign of her. She must have gone across. The lights stayed green interminably. In the end she made a dash for it.

'Silly cow. D'you want to get us all killed?' shouted a driver as he braked and swerved. Children stared out of the side window - one shaking his fist. Rose raised her hand to him, lifting a middle finger.

As she reached the far pavement she stumbled, nearly falling. Her chest was hurting; so were her legs but she had to keep going. There was a road straight ahead but was it the right one? She hadn't noticed the name. Would it lead to Chestnut Close? Would Carla have gone back to Fay's? She might have gone anywhere. At least she hadn't got herself run over - not so far. No sign of her along this road but it looked familiar. No point in asking anyone the way - not this bloody rude lot, all pushing towards the crossing. She'd be swept back if she didn't move.

She heard a funny rasping noise in her chest as she ran. This wasn't doing her any good. She slowed to a fast walk, then a slower one as she saw the sign: Chestnut Close. How could Carla do this to her- and in her condition? Stress would do her no good at all - they'd told her that at the clinic. Just as her legs felt as if they were going to collapse, she arrived at Fay's house.

The front door was open. Fay stood just inside. Gasping for breath, Rose clutched the doorjamb. Fay caught hold of her arm and drew her into the hall.

'Carla's safe, Rose.'

Struggling to get her words out, Rose began, 'She could

– could've got killed - running off....'

Fay stroked her shoulder and said, gently, 'She shouldn't have come back alone but she's upset. She's upstairs. D'you want to go to her?'

Rose stared at her then, with a gasping intake of breath, said, 'What about my upset? D'you think this is good for me?'

Her voice had risen. Fay looked up the stairs then back at Rose.

'You look all in. Better come and sit down. Have a cup of tea. You've had a fright.'

Rose allowed Fay to lead her into the sitting room where she sank into the nearest armchair. With a sob in her voice, she said,

'I was frightened. Anything could have happened to her. There's evil men about. Every day there's a kid missing somewhere, or she could've got run over.'

She blew her nose on a tissue from a box Fay handed to her.

'She's safe, Rose. Just rest while I put the kettle on.' Fay disappeared through an archway into the kitchen.

Rose leaned back against a bulk of cushions and closed her eyes. Carla was safe: she was safe too. Terry would keep her safe. Gradually the heaving of her chest subsided. She stretched her legs out in front of her - they felt less wobbly.

Footsteps sounded on the stairs, going up, then, after a few minutes, coming down. Seconds later Fay put a tea tray on a low table and handed Rose a Harry Potter mug.

'Two sugars, that right?'

Rose should have corrected her - she'd cut down, but she needed that sugar. She nodded, took the mug and drank thirstily.

'Carla won't come down and join us, I'm afraid. Perhaps, when you've rested a bit....'

Rose interrupted: 'What did she say to you when she got back?'

'Nothing really. I asked her why she'd left you and she burst into tears. She said, "Ask Mum," then she scrambled upstairs, somehow, still in her roller blades. I followed her but she clammed up. It's about the baby, I imagine.'

Fay poured tea for herself, gently nudged a black and white cat to budge up a bit and sat down on a sofa opposite Rose.

'I thought she'd be excited,' Rose said. 'Didn't expect her to go off like that. Bloody scared me, she did. Really upset me.' She looked at Fay expecting the reaction she'd received when she'd arrived, panting and feeling sick, but Fay wasn't looking at her. She was looking down into her mug of tea. Had she heard?

'Really upset I was. She didn't think about me.'

'She's a child, Rose. Her feelings still come first. That's the way it is.' Fay's voice was soothing but she was still staring into her mug, holding it with one hand while absently stroking the cat. There was a long silence. Rose sensed criticism and distance.

'She wasn't like that once. Used to care about me - even looked after me. I know that wasn't really right - I've learnt that - but she thought about other people. She's gone really babyish since coming here.'

Fay looked straight at her, unsmiling.

'I think she's needed to be a little girl again. And she's had to adjust to a lot of change, specially being without her mum. She does care about you. When there was that awful storm last week she kept saying, "I hope Mum's all right." She wasn't a bit scared of the thunder, just worried it would be as bad where you live.'

Rose smiled then. 'I've always hated thunder and lightening.' She finished her tea, gulping, finding it hard to swallow. Kids! They could really tear at your heart. 'You sure she'll be all right?'

'She will be. It was a shock. We'll have a talk later. We're going swimming at six -thirty. She won't miss that. More tea?'

Rose nodded.

'I was surprised when you rang me about the baby. I didn't know you had a....' Fay hesitated.

'Bloke,' Rose finished for her, smiling. 'Still can't

11

believe it myself. This wasn't a one-night-stand.' She patted her scarcely noticeable belly. 'He's not my usual sort. He's older and really clever and sorted.'

'What does he do?' asked Fay, pouring more tea and offering biscuits and little iced cakes.

'I will, thanks. Got an appetite since I stopped smoking and drinking. Terry's got a good job – he's a financial something or other - buys and sells all over the world.'

'So he travels?'

'No, he does it over the Net or the 'phone, from a posh office in the
City. But he's been everywhere. Hours and hours he works, sometimes all night.'

'Is that hard for you? Bit disruptive isn't it?'

'No, 'cause he's still got his own place. Safer, he says, so I don't lose my
Benefits. He's got money and he's ever so generous but, as he says, I've got my entitlements. He says we'll set up home together once the baby's come. He can't wait to meet Carla, but he's always so busy. Just think, Fay, soon we'll be a proper family.'

Fay was staring into her mug again. What was she thinking Rose wondered - that she'd heard it all before, from all the parents whose kids she'd fostered over the years? Well, she was wrong this time. It was all going to happen. And what right had she to judge – sitting in her comfy home with everything she could need around her, a husband coming back from work, grown-up kids off her hands. She wouldn't know 'tough' if it bit her in the backside.

Rose finished the cake and biscuits, followed by a gulp of tea, then said, 'Carla's got to get used to the idea of the baby. It's no good her being jealous….'

'Rose,' Fay interrupted, her tone firm and her expression serious, 'jealousy is a normal feeling. You've been her mum for eight years - just hers. She needs time to accept the idea of sharing you.'

'I've cocked it up. Is that what you're saying? Should've left it to you or Liz to tell her. It's what social workers are for

12

- to get all the flack. But we are all going to be together whatever happens. It's my life. I got a right to some happiness.' Rose's voice was as firm as Fay's but with an added note of defiance.

More gently Fay said, 'You did your best but Carla was almost bound to react this way. She's been apart from you for several months.'

Of course she'd bring that up. They were never going to let her forget that Carla had to be taken away - put in a Place of Safety.

'Are you saying that it was my fault? I couldn't help drinking you know. I had to drink to escape. Nobody's helped me like Terry has. We are going to be together, no matter what Carla or anyone else says.'

'I want you to be happy, you and Carla and the new baby but she needs time and lots of reassurance. She's confused. Try to see it from her viewpoint. It won't be just her and you in the future, there'll be a baby and - maybe, Terry.'

What did she mean - maybe? Rose had Terry's word they'd be together. Furious though she was something warned her to say no more. Her future was her business, hers and Terry's. She finished her tea, eyeing Fay over the rim of the mug. She was stroking the cat again, looking down. Her face was a bit flushed. She was angry. She was hiding it, like they all did, these professionals. It was what they didn't say that you had to be wary of. She'd had enough flack for one afternoon; she wasn't staying for this silent criticism.

Fay looked at her suddenly and smiled.

'It hasn't been all bad, this visit. Carla was really pleased that you were meeting her from school. Do it again. You know you can come whenever you like.'

As Fay stopped speaking the clock in the hall chimed the quarter. Rose looked at her watch.

'Thanks for the tea. I gotta go. Give Carla my love

Simultaneously, they stood up.

'Will you go up to say "Goodbye"? I can just check....' Fay put a hand on Rose's arm as if to detain her but she moved away.

13

'No, best get off or I'll miss the bus.' Rose put her jacket on and swung her bag onto her shoulder.

'If you did miss the bus, would it matter? They run until after ten. You could have some supper with us. Come swimming and stay over?'

Christ, didn't the woman ever give up? Inwardly, Rose shuddered. She shook her head and walked into the hall, hesitating at the foot of the stairs then resolutely opening the front door.

'See you,' she said and hurried down the path.

'Fresh Air' it said on the tin. She giggled. Bit different from the sort in the park. Stuff like that you can't catch in a tin. She pressed the button and sent a fine sweet-smelling mist around the room. It tickled her throat, making her cough. She opened a window and quickly closed it again, recoiling from the disgusting cooking smells coming from next door. Terry didn't expect her to cook - he'd ring for a Take Away, but much later. She liked the way he decided things for both of them. It wasn't that he bossed her; he just knew they liked the same things at the same time. They hadn't seen each other for days so she knew what they'd be doing first. Not that they were at it all the time: sometimes they talked. He asked her what she thought about things on the telly, which Soaps she liked, and about her as a little girl. No other man had taken an interest in her except for a lay that was just for his pleasure. She'd always thought, 'How was it for you, darling?' was a joke question - the sort you'd hear in a comedy on the telly - then one day Terry had asked her. If they'd been doing it in bed she'd have fallen out, laughing. He hadn't been cross, and had laughed too when she explained.

Rose looked around her. Was there anything she could improve in the time left? Throwing a cheap, Indian-looking spread over the sofa had hidden its shabbiness a bit, and she'd scrubbed and polished the painted furniture - at least the place was clean. But she'd better have a scrub too and wash her hair so it would go all fluffy, the way he liked it. Then she'd put on the dress he bought her for her birthday. It was smocked all over the bust, giving the impression she had decent-sized tits. He didn't care about her size, he'd said - she was lovely the way she was, tits and all. From the first time he'd undressed her she hadn't instinctively put up her hands to hide them.

He was late - eight he'd said, but it was nearly nine. He was usually a bit late. A man like him, in business, had all kinds of pressures on his time. He always said he was sorry but something had cropped up. She wasn't used to men who apologized. He'd ring her if there were a real problem. Thanks to him she had the phone. He'd paid the last bill, stopping her from asking the Social, who probably would have refused anyway.

She went into the bedroom and stared at her reflection in the glass. Her hair was now like a halo. She rubbed a bit of lipstick above her cheekbones to brighten her face and it seemed to do something to her eyes - show them up. Carla's eyes, she thought, something good I've given her as well as my hair.

She looked at her watch - nine now. He wouldn't let her down. He never had. Done more for her than any of them, but they took the credit: Liz and the others, and the daft Alcoholics' Support Group who'd given her a progress medal last week - what a laugh. She'd managed to accept it with a serious face. They meant well.

She'd check on something while she waited. Grinning, she took a key from a china pot on the dressing table and crossed to a huge, ugly wardrobe. Its long mirror-fronted doors made her look like something in a fun palace. Sometimes, when she had to get up in the night to have a pee, her distorted reflection gave her a fright. She unlocked the left hand door and reached up, standing on tiptoe, feeling for something on the shelf. Her fingers touched glass and followed the reassuring shape of a bottle.

She gave a small laugh, locked the door and replaced the key in its pot. Her secret, the means to oblivion she'd never have to use - certainly not now with the sound of another key turning in the front door.

15

Chapter 2

'Don't need a bath,' said Carla. 'Not after a shower. I like the showers at the swimming baths - real hot.'

'You still need to wash your hands and face and clean your teeth. You do that while I find your nightie,' said Fay, marveling at the child's change of mood. Once she'd entered the water she'd given herself wholeheartedly to her new skill, swimming a width for the first time.

'She's coming along well,' commented a watching mother. 'You must be proud of her.'

Fay had smiled and nodded, waiting for the questions that always pass between mums - how old, any siblings, which school? She dreaded them because they nearly always led to an admission that she was a foster mum. At that point she always clammed up; as politely as possible she deflected the natural curiosity of the questioner. She never told a child's story - it was not hers to tell. And she cringed at the inevitable reaction towards her: how wonderful, how self-sacrificing, wasn't it agony handing them back? She knew a few foster parents who reveled in the kudos. How did they cope with the foster children who told them they were rubbish and only in it for the money? She'd had a few like that over the years: they expressed their hurt and anger by trying to demolish her. Maybe, it was their way of coping with their natural parents' inadequacies.

Thank goodness the woman had walked away to attend to her own child.

Not a word had Carla said about Rose's visit. After her mother left she'd come downstairs carrying her towel and swimsuit and talking about leaving soon and not being late. In the nearly five months Fay had known her she'd had learnt that to probe into Carla's thoughts, however subtly, would send her into herself. Hard though it was she had to hold off and leave her to talk in her own time.

She took a warm, clean nightdress from the airing cupboard on the landing and smiled on hearing gargling and splashing from the bathroom. Carla was becoming proud of her teeth now they'd been scaled and polished. Shame there had to be a filling, but how many children escaped one or two, even with conscientious care, and Carla hadn't been near a dentist in her short life until Fay took her.

The telephone rang. Fay answered it in her bedroom. She hoped it would be Rose but it was a man who sounded as if he were shouting against all the traffic in Delhi. She replaced the receiver after a restrained, 'No thank you'. Why should it have been Rose? She'd never rung before except to say she was visiting, but with Carla being so upset, perhaps, this once....

'Auntie, where are you?' Carla called from the landing.

'Coming. I was on the phone.'

'I didn't know where you were. You won't go out, will you?'

'Of course not. There's always one of us here, me or Uncle Bill. You're never on your own.' Fay walked onto the landing. Carla was standing in the bathroom doorway. She gave a strange little whimper and ran to Fay who hugged her. Effortlessly she lifted her then stood her down on the floor of the bedroom that had housed several foster children over seventeen years.

'Was it Uncle Bill?' Carla asked. Of course she'd know it wouldn't be her mother.

'No. He's playing in his darts' team tonight. It was a salesman.'

Fay noted the books spread out on the duvet and one on the floor, well away from the bed: *My Naughty Little Sister*

'Shall we have a story?'

Carla nodded and Fay slipped the nightdress over her head.

'This one,' said Carla, picking up *The Sheep Pig,* which she knew by heart, word for word. Best of all she loved the books, well thumbed over years by Fay's children, telling of more innocent days.

Smiling, Fay took the book from her. She had always been fascinated by children's reading habits. Plenty of foster children didn't read at all - had never been read to. Some loved the socially realistic stories about dumped babies and unreliable parents, and growing up In Care. Maybe they liked to know that their situation was not unique? Such stories were really important for them but not for Carla - she loved unfamiliar settings, animal characters and humans with strange or special qualities.

Uncharacteristically, Carla roughly pushed the other books off the bed, slipped off her socks and knickers and slid under the duvet. Fay sat on a wicker chair and began to read, glancing at her now and then to gauge her reaction to the familiar story. There was none: she gazed steadfastly at the far wall, her thumb in her mouth. Fay doubted that she was hearing a word.

Terry arrived carrying paper bags, containing cartons of chop suey, sweet and sour pork, spring rolls and two sorts of rice. Eating first was unusual – especially when he hadn't seen her for three days.

'I'm starving,' he said, 'that's why I shopped. Haven't left off work all day. Got to get some fuel inside me so I can rev: up.'

He took charge, warming plates under scalding water, dishing up and waiting on her as if she'd been working. Not that she had any complaints - in a different way her day had been tough too. He didn't mention it – had he forgotten the main purpose of her visit to Carla? She'd bide her time – not say anything that might spoil his good mood. He'd be disappointed with Carla's reaction. Maybe she'd tone it down.

He talked about a friend who'd won a big sum on a horserace and how he'd advised him to invest it but, mainly, he concentrated on eating. Then he made tea, proper China tea, he told her, to wash the food down. That done he began clearing up.

'No you rest,' he said, when she got up to help. 'You'll need to.'

Rose lay on the sofa and closed her eyes, waiting. Water was running now in the bathroom. He was fastidious about being clean and fresh. She liked that. Few of her lovers had been fussy about personal hygiene. Filthy most of them were, stinking of booze and sweat and their last meal. That's how she'd thought of men until she met Terry. And it was such a lucky chance meeting him. If he hadn't collided with her in the shop doorway, causing her to spill her shopping they might never have spoken. She'd seen him a few times - they used the same corner shop. He'd noticed her too. 'You've a little girl,' he'd said, then had gathered up her shopping and carried it home for her. Funny beginning to a relationship - she usually met men in pubs.

'Are you asleep?' His words brought her upright with a laugh, eyes still shut.

'Dreaming,' she said. 'Guess who about?'

'Too easy. Up you come.' He lifted her as if she were a child. Her face rubbed against his chest and she realized he was naked.

'Where are we going?' she asked, opening her eyes.

'Not outside - not giving your neighbours a treat'

He carried her into the bedroom and laid her on a towel spread on the duvet. On the bedside locker were an anglepoise lamp - not hers - and a basin of water, bottle of baby shampoo and a razor.

'What are we going to do? I washed my hair earlier.'

He grinned. 'Depends what you mean by hair.'

She caught on at once and began to giggle. 'You could cut me.'

'Not if you keep still and stop giggling.'

Much later, while he dozed, she lay in his arms reliving every blissful moment. She'd never had sex like it. She thought he was going to devour her once he got going, but not until after the longest foreplay she'd ever known. He'd massaged her with scented oil - not an inch of her body was neglected. Three times she'd come before he even entered her. His mouth alone could bring her to a peak of excitement she'd never imagined possible. But, afterwards as always, insidiously creeping into her mind, nudging the edge of her consciousness, came the doubt. What was she compared with

19

him - a too thin ex. alcoholic, the wrong end of twenty, no great claim to looks, no money? Was it just sex he wanted? He could get that anywhere, couldn't he, with his looks and position? Yet he seemed so sure of their future together. They'd find just the right place and have a proper home.

She forced her mind into the present. The warmth of lying close, the gentle movements of his sleeping body - they were reality, not her silly unsure fancies. He moved his head, rubbed it against hers and murmured something.

'Didn't hear?' she said, leaning up on her elbow.

He opened his eyes, 'What did you say?'

'No, what did you say?'

'I don't know - must have been dreaming. What's the time?' He picked up his watch from the bedside table. 'Three o'clock. Better get moving. Things to do.'

'At this time? Why can't you stay 'til morning - proper morning?'

'I've people I must contact. Dealing worldwide I have to fit in with different time zones. I've told you, I don't finish all my work in office hours.'

'I know but I hate it when you leave. It won't always be like this, will it?'

'Not when we're together in our own place. I'll still work long hours and odd times but we'll be under the same roof. All of us, then - you, me, Carla and my little Sugar.' He splayed his hand on her belly.

'Not Sugar,' Rose said, 'nor Candy. She'll have a proper name like Louise, or Emma, or Emily-Jane.'

'Whatever you say, babe. Shouldn't I be able to feel something - movements, kicking? What did they say at the clinic?'

'Can't remember. I'll ask when I go for a check up. I feel a strange wriggle sometimes but not exactly kicking. Do I look different?'

'Yes. There's more of you.' He cupped her breasts. 'You look lovely.'

She hoped for more but he swung his legs onto the floor and stood up. By the artificial light that penetrated the unlined curtains, she admired his smooth body, not all ape-man hairy like some she'd known. It was a shame the hair on his head was thin – he'd be bald soon but you can't have everything in one man and, apart from that, she had everything in Terry. His movements were long and slow - she couldn't imagine him ever hurrying. Once dressed he said, 'I'll make tea. You'd like that, wouldn't you?'

'Yes, but I should be making it for you – the worker.'

'You conserve your strength,' he told her as she pushed back the duvet, preparing to get up.

She laughed and lay back.

'What?' he asked.

'Nothing - just the things you say, like someone on the telly. I told Fay about you and your work. I think she was impressed.'

'Don't tell her things - not 'til we're together. It's no one's business but ours,' he said.

He didn't sound cross, but firm, like a teacher.

'I wanted her to know we've got plans….' Rose hesitated, wishing she could talk of Carla's joy at the news of the baby. She could pretend, but when Terry met Carla he'd find out the truth and that would show her in a bad light (one of her gran's sayings). No, she'd better tell it as it was. She shifted, half sitting up. 'You see, Carla was…like… upset when I told her about the baby – jealous I s'pose. I talked to Fay about you and our plans so she'd know it was all going to be all right. I thought she could pass it on to Carla sometime – reassure her.'

'Well, don't say anymore. These people have ways of twisting things.'

'But how can they? Fay knows I ain't drinking anymore - still going to the alco's meeting at that awful Community Centre - doing everything right. She knows I'm looking after myself, and so does Liz. She thinks it's all down to them - what they've done for me. I want to tell her it's not them at all, it's you.'

Terry sat on the bed and stroked her hand.

'Let them all think they're wonderful and you're doing

everything they want. That way they can't be critical or they'd be criticizing themselves. You're a good mum. You visit Carla and want her back. They can't stop you now you're not drinking. Play their game, Rose.'

He got up and went to the kitchen. Rose lay pondering on his words. She supposed he was right. He was clever - much cleverer than she was, although he often told her she was bright and didn't think enough of herself. When they were together - really together- she could help him with his work if she wanted to. He was always saying such things.

'Tea with one sugar, not two.'

He put the mug beside her.

'You're bossier than the clinic nurse,' she said, sitting up.

'I've a right to be. Got a vested interest.'

'There you go again. Listening to you is as good as the telly. Ain't you having tea?'

'No babe, must love and leave you.' He kissed her swiftly on the mouth, then shrugged his shoulders into his smart leather jacket and left the bedroom.

'When will you...?' she began, but the sound of the outside door quietly closing silenced her. She drank the tea then slid beneath the duvet, moving into the space he'd left. It was still warm. She closed her eyes and drifted into sleep, smiling.

Nine hours later she was up and shopping in the street market. She walked jauntily, pleased with her pink flared trousers (loose round the waist to accommodate her expanding belly), and the pink and pink and white trainers, both presents from Terry.

' 'Lo darlin',' said Benji at the fruit stall. 'Back again. Got some lovely apples, real English ones, straight up from Somerset. Want some?'

Smiling, Rose nodded. Straight up from Spain more likely, but for all his old flannel, Benji was all right. He weighed a kilo of gleaming red apples and handed them to her in a brown paper bag, saying,

'I don't want to lose your custom darlin', so I'm not

criticizing but you seem to 'ave gone mad on fruit. Good for you, specially them apples, but don't give yourself the runs. That's forty pence to you.'

Walking away she broke into a giggle. She'd never touched fruit if she could help it: now she couldn't stop herself and Terry encouraged her. It was wonderful for her and the baby. She needed to build herself up, fill her body with good things, give it treats it had never experienced.

She liked the market. Bit different from the one in *Eastenders* – well, of course, this being proper East End, people were friendly. "All right, darlin'?" and "Like your barnet, my lovely," were familiar calls from stallholders, even some she never bought from. But like the market on the telly there was plenty of litter about, banana skins, dog ends galore, plastic food boxes. The smells were very mixed, some disgustingly nose wrinkling, but one attracted her strongly and she walked towards it.

Coffee was one thing but - sugarcoated doughnuts too - she was nearly drooling. No, she 'd be firm.

'Rose! How are you? You're looking great.'

She turned to face Ellie Parsons, a large friendly woman whose body seemed to be struggling to get into, or out of, mock leather trousers and a skin-coloured tee shirt. Rose didn't feel she could return the compliment.

'I feel great,' she said. 'Not even throwing up. Well, I s'pose I'm past that stage.'

'You're not…pregnant?' Ellie sounded stunned. 'You don't look it. Always thin as a rail.'

'I am, and it's Terry's, the bloke I told you about.'

'You pleased then? You've kept it quiet.'

'Yeah, really pleased.'

'You going to the next Group?'

'S'pose so. Don't really need it but we're s'posed to keep going, ain't we?'

'Yeah. Let's have a good natter afterwards – make it worthwhile. You can fill me in about this.'

Ellie gently prodded Rose's belly.

'What about now?' said Rose, laughing

23

'Can't – I'm off to see my ma-in-law but see you Thursday.'

'Great.' Rose watched Ellie walk away, buttocks wobbling like twin jellies. A giggle rose in her throat. She had a long way to go before she looked like that, so…. She turned towards the coffee stall, now ogling the huge doughnuts. Oh well, tomorrow she'd be good.

Chapter 3

It was pretty grim, the Community Centre. Some said part of
it was once a public bathhouse, where people paid a few
pence to use a towel and bar of soap; the only way they could
get clean when one cold tap was shared by a whole street.
Rose wrinkled her nose - there was a funny smell. It hit you
even as you walked through the big doors into the open area
that Ellie called 'the foyer'. (She could be a bit like Terry with
big words). It was a soapy, bleachy smell - horrible. Did it
date from the bathhouse days?

'Rose.'

Ellie was pushing her bulk between resistant glass
doors, donated by some benefactor and, to prevent them being
vandalized, set inside huge Victorian wooden doors.

'You'd think they were trying to keep us out, not drag us
in,' Ellie said.
'Glad you've come. Bit of propaganda for them too - us, the
successes.'

Rose giggled. 'You're a success but Dave thinks I'm a bit
fragile. Ain't had a drink for weeks but he don't trust me. It
was the others who voted me for the medal.'

'Cheek,' said Ellie. 'You deserved it. Bit of a mother
hen, our Dave. Wonder if he's got a life outside the Group.
What would he do without us alcos? He'd be needing a job.'

'Like social workers,' said Rose, giggling. 'I reckon they
need us more than we need them.'

'True, in your case. You don't need anyone now you've
got your bloke, and they'll have to return Carla to you now
you're sorted. They should get on with it. I'd make a fuss if I
was you. You don't need them telling you what to do
anymore…Oh, hullo Joe…'

Ellie's attention veered from Rose who moved away to
study the Community Centre's notice board. Offers of Tai Chi
and Kung Fu classes, Colonic Lavage (what the hell was
that?), a bedsitter over the fish and chip shop (ugh!) and jobs -
loads of them, beguiled her. Choices had always confused her,
and she hated any decision that required thinking more than a

day ahead. One day she'd get a job - maybe hotel and catering work, shop assistant, barmaid – no, not that, anything but that! There was a world out there full of offers but would she want any of them? Would she ever have to cope with the demands of bosses and the interchange with fellow workers, funny, bitchy, irritating, gossipy? She hoped she wouldn't have to think seriously about getting a job for ages, maybe years. And for now she had enough to cope with, looking after herself, and that meant looking after the coming baby, and keeping Terry happy. She smiled with relief when her ponderings were interrupted by a male voice calling her name and Ellie's. The caller was Dave, the group leader.

'Come on in, girls, great to see you. We're just starting.'

He ushered them into the meeting room as if they were special guests. A few members acknowledged them. Rose observed there were two newcomers, a man with a beer gut and a tired-looking woman, both middle-aged. Not much of interest there. She sat next to Brad, a nineteen year old. She was amused to see that his shoulder-length hair was streaked with green in addition to last week's bronze. She liked him. He was friendly, unlike some of them there. He turned, twisting in his seat, to look her up and down.

'Nice top,' he said. 'Pretty. Not a bad bottom, either. Quite like what's in between too. Not too proud to mix with us now you're a medal winner?'

She grinned and pretended to punch him.

'Order,' said Joe, an old-stager. 'We got new people to impress.'

'Thank you, Joe,' said Dave, dryly. 'We have got two new members, Rob and Jenny. Welcome, both of you. Now, I'll just go over our few rules then we'll have proper introductions.'

'Why not improper ones?' said Brad, which set Ellie and Rose giggling.

They'd heard it all before - the confidentiality issues. It took five minutes for Dave to explain them in his most pedantic voice. He ended, 'And then there's the strict ruling about not smoking on the premises.'

This was met with groans.

'But we can drink,' said Brad. 'They don't say we can't drink.'

'The last's taken for granted, surely?' said Joe. 'It's bloody well why we're here.'

There were a few laughs, drawing a severe look from Dave.

'Now, Jenny and Rob, welcome again. Would you like to tell us a bit about yourselves, then we'll go round the group. We say as little or as much as we feel comfortable with.'

'Nothing from me,' muttered Brad, closing his eyes and dropping his
chin to his chest.

Rose listened to Jenny's story: widowed unexpectedly, daughter a druggie so no support there, but Rob's lengthy life history nearly sent her to sleep. Brad gave a long snore. Minutes later Dave said,

'Great, Rob, thank you for your openness. Now who'd like to talk?'

'I don't mind,' said Rose, surprising herself. 'I'm Rose and I started drinking in my teens. My mum was an alco so I just copied her. It made me feel big and everything looked rosier...'

'Joke,' said Brad, still with his eyes shut.' Rosier - more of her.'

'Shut up, Brad,' said Rose, giggling. 'Yeah, I felt important. Nothing I couldn't do.'

'So why did you stop if it made you feel good?' asked Rob.

'This time or in the past?'

'Both, if you like.'

'Mostly 'cause I ran out of money. I'd get a job and start again. Then my little girl got taken away from me and I didn't care after that...'

'Didn't care she'd been taken away? Gawd, what sort of a group have I come into?' Rob's tone was contemptuous. Rose flushed.

'Let Rose continue in her own way and time,' said Dave.

27

'All right, Rose? Want to go on?'

'Yes, I bloody do. D'you think I didn't care about my Carla? It was me I didn't care about - end of the line for me. I took some pills and drank but my neighbour got an ambulance. In the hospital they talked about getting dried out and that's why I come here. I ain't had a drink for weeks - right Dave?'

'Yes. Rose has done really well. We gave her a star last time, didn't we? One member's success is everyone's here.'

The group clapped. Even Brad roused himself sufficiently to pat one hand against the other.

'Anyone going to continue?' asked Dave. 'Trev?'

'Yeah. I'm Trevor Hill and I'm an alcoholic,' said the pot-bellied, thirty-something man sitting next to Ellie. 'I started young, like Rose. Couldn't do without it. I'm still struggling. It's friends who don't help. "Come on, Trev, one drink won't hurt you." You gotta learn to say "No" and it's hard when you gotta reputation. You don't want to be a wet…'

'And giving in is really being wet,' interrupted Joe. 'It's much tougher to say "No." I know all about that. Two of my brothers drink like fish and can't see any problem with it. The fact that one's broken up with two wives doesn't seem to matter….'

'Moslem, is he?' asked Brad, suddenly wide awake. 'Or bigamist?'

'Don't be daft. He just wrecks all his fucking relationships and owes money all over London. Then there's my shit of a younger brother…'

'Joe,' interrupted Dave, in a schoolmasterish tone. 'Your brothers aren't members of the group. D'you want to say anymore - about yourself?'

'Yeah, I do. I was only trying to show these new members that you can do it even when everything's stashed against you. You gotta give them some hope, Dave. You don't know what they're struggling with.'

'Shut up, Joe,' said Ellie. 'It ain't your group. You always want to take over.'

'It is my group and it's your group. It belongs to all of

us.' Sounding and looking belligerent, Joe half rose from his seat.

'You're right,' Dave interposed hastily. 'It is everyone's group which is why we have a few rules. But the group belongs to its members, not to outsiders. It's part of the confidentiality agreement that we stick to our own experiences. Now, does anyone want to say anything else on that or shall we move on?'

'No, not yet. The No Smoking rule is fucking torture, and there's something else I want to say'.

So rarely did Brad speak, except to send someone up, he had everyone's attention.

'What if something funny's going on – something connected with a member. We oughta say, didn't we?'

'Is he meaning me? Rose wondered. He'd twisted round in his seat, his knee brushing hers.
'Who are you looking at?' Her tone was jokey but his expression was serious. 'Got something on me, have you?'

'No, not on *you* Rose.'

'On Ellie, then? Don't like me being friends with her? Got a wicked past, has she?'

Several members of the group laughed and made suggestions.

'What are you up to, Ellie?'

'Don't you know? She's got twelve Chinese immigrants living in her shed.'

'That pawnshop stick-up - that was Ellie's work. Her touch written all over it.'

'Let's get on,' said Dave, in a tone of weary disapproval. 'Do I have to go over the confidentiality agreement or are you all clear on it?'

The few nods and murmurs seemed to satisfy him. Brad tipped his baseball cap over his eyes and let out a long and unconvincing snore. By the time the meeting ended he was genuinely asleep.

'Feel like a snack?' asked Ellie as they walked into the street, and into an unseasonably fresh wind. 'My Ron's being fed by his mum tonight. Be nice to have a change - for me, I mean.'

Rose readily agreed. She'd taken to Ellie from when she first joined the group but there never seemed to be time to get to know her really well with Terry turning up at odd times, often without prior warning. She'd stayed at home a lot then, partly because she was afraid of missing his visits and, partly, because she often felt ill due to coming off the drink.

'D'you think Brad's on anything, Rose?' asked Ellie as they sauntered to a café she recommended.

Rose shrugged. 'Could be. Always a bit spaced out. Dangerous though, mixing drugs and drink. I never done that, have you?'

'No. Can't afford to.' Ellie gave a snort of laughter. 'Plenty of things I'd do if I had money. Get out of this place for a start.'

'We're going to, Terry and me. Once the baby's come.'

'Why wait 'til then? Wouldn't it be better to find somewhere now and get settled? I've read that moving with a new baby is one of the most stressful things you can do - next to a death and divorce.'

Rose laughed. 'I ain't doing either of those - yet. Terry's looking for somewhere all the time but he says it's gotta be right.'

'D'you go with him - looking?'

'Not yet. Better to rest and let our little girl grow, he says.'

'Rose, you're pregnant, not suffering a serious illness. He's wrapping you in cotton wool.'

'Yeah, I s'pose he is. Nice though. First time it's ever happened to me.'

'Why are you so sure you're having a girl? Bit soon to tell, ain't it? I was going to ask you the other...ooh, look out, dog shit.' Ellie grabbed Rose's arm and pulled her aside. 'Disgusting, they ought to be shot - not the dogs, the owners.'

Rose grinned. She was slightly out of breath. She gulped in a dose of richly polluted air to answer Ellie's question.

'I was a bit small, and what with the drinking and something a bit funny with my blood, they did a test thing - an amnio....'

'Amniocentesis?' Ellie suggested. Rose stopped and turned to stare at her, impressed. Smiling, Ellie continued: 'I may not be pregnant but I read magazines. I know all about blood pressure and stretch marks too. Just ask. Here we are, darlin', Kev's Kaf.'

They entered the café where the owner greeted Ellie warmly. He came out from behind his counter and gave her a hug, with difficulty: both being more pregnant-shaped than Rose. He asked Ellie, 'Who's your friend?'

'Rose. Rose, this is Kevin.'

Kevin shook her hand. 'Seen you around. Got a lovely little girl.'

Rose smiled and nodded. Kevin's attention moved to an elderly woman getting up to leave, so Ellie led the way to a table by the window and they sat down. Rose looked around the room with its red and white check tablecloths, and a tiny vase on each table with a red carnation - well, pretend carnation. It was something to have proper tablecloths. And the place was clean. There was a smell of cooking but there'd have to be in a café. It was nice - bright and cheerful.

'Thanks Ellie, I like this place, but I was afraid Kevin was going to ask questions.'

'No, he's all right. Not the gossip most people are round here. Anyway, you've got nothing to be ashamed of. You can't help anything, not from what you've told me. Always being taken advantage of.'

'Not any more. I got protection.'

Ellie grinned. 'Sure it ain't over-protection? Go on about the amnio. Everything was all right?'

'Yes. Should be fine. Terry was so excited....'

'With you at the hospital, was he?'

'No. He was working. Been different if I'd been his wife, I expect. Could have asked his boss for the time off.' Rose picked up the menu. 'I'm hungry.'

'There's specials too, on the board,' Ellie told her.

'Made up your minds girls?' called Kevin from behind the counter.

'Egg, sausage, chips and mushies for me, please,' said Ellie, not bothering to glance at the menu or the board. 'Always the same. What about you, Rose.'

Rose studied the board for a minute. 'Omelette and salad - no chips though.'

'What? You won't get fat on that, lovey,' said plump Kevin. 'You sure?'

Rose nodded, grinning.

'Oh, she will, Kev,' said Ellie. 'She'll get fat all right.'

Rose shook her head at Ellie, mouthing, 'Shut it.'

Looking bemused, Kevin disappeared behind a curtain of colourful, plastic strips.

'It's all right. He didn't twig. Nice but dim is Kev,' said Ellie quietly. 'Why the secrecy, Rose? You're pleased, you said.'

'I am pleased. It's Terry who wants it kept quiet 'til we're a proper family - all together.'

'I don't understand. You sure he ain't married?'

'Of course he ain't.'

'Have you asked him?'

'No, there's no need.'

'You been to his place?'

'Not yet.'

'Your food won't be long, girls, Want anything to drink?'

Rose smiled her relief at Kevin's arrival. He set out cutlery and plastic sauce bottles.

'Orange for me,' said Ellie. 'Same for you, Rose? We're both on the wagon.'

Rose nodded, wishing Ellie would curb her tongue. Like most inquisitive people Ellie held nothing back about herself, but she had no right to include Rose. As soon as Kevin moved away, the questioning resumed.

'Where does he live, this Terry?'

'Marlow Court. You know it?'

'I do. Used to be council, and a more rundown, rat infested place you couldn't find. They wouldn't spend anything on it so a property developer bought it. It was a scandal: public housing sold off to benefit some wide boy. He certainly changed the place. Turned it into Fort Knox. I bet half the local mafia live there.'

Rose's desire to challenge Ellie's quip about the mafia had to wait. Kevin arrived with their drinks. By the time he'd fussed over his sole customers and exchanged a few quips with Ellie, she'd simmered down.

'Don't include Terry with them - the Mafia,' she said, managing a smile.

'Someone else we know lives there,' said Ellie. 'Brad.'

'He can't. It's posh.'

'Not that posh.' Ellie laughed. 'I heard Brad's parents and grandparents lived there so he was allowed to stay. Others, like him, accepted a golden handshake and were pleased to go.'

'He fell on his feet then,' said Rose. 'Security gates, intercoms, lifts that work and garages.'

'How d'you know all that if you ain't been there?' asked Ellie.

'Terry's told me all about it. I know we can't live there 'cause it's a one person flat. One bedroom, huge sitting room with balcony, bathroom and kitchen. Not as many rooms as I've got but much bigger. Sounds lovely, except it's always a muddle.'

'Mucky sort is he?' said Ellie, grinning in a knowing way.

'No, not a bit.' Rose's words came out more sharply than she intended. Ellie drew back against her chair, still grinning.

'Sorry. Clumsy me. Don't shoot

The impossibility of being cross with Ellie for more than a second was both endearing and infuriating. Rose opted for the former reaction. She'd picked up the plastic sauce bottle and, now, pointed it at Ellie, who lifted her arms in mock surrender.

'Now then, girls, no firearms allowed in this establishment. It ain't High Noon, it's suppertime.'

Kevin placed loaded plates in front of them.

'I gave you a roll seeing as you didn't want chips,' he

33

said to Rose.

'Lucky you, Rose,' said Ellie. 'Not everyone gets a roll with Kev. He's never offered me one.'

'Get on, you're a respectable married woman,' said Kevin.

'You saying my friend's not respectable, you cheeky thing?'

'No, I'm sure she's as respectable as you. Now, at risk of being misunderstood, is there anything else you ladies fancy? Beside me, that is.'

All three burst into laughter. Recovering first, Rose drained her glass then asked for another orange.'

'Same for me, my favourite tipple,' said Ellie, then, as the plastic curtain closed behind Kevin, added, 'That put him off the scent.'

Rose put aside the bread roll. She'd keep it for her next visit to Carla, for feeding the ducks in the park, unless Ellie wanted it. Ellie shook her head.

'Thought you didn't mind people knowing you drank,' said Rose,

'No, it's admitting it to ourselves that's matters,' said Ellie. 'I couldn't, you know - not for ages. That's Brad's trouble. He sits there, cap over his face, smirking at the rest of us as if he's different.'

'So why does he come?'

Ellie leaned towards Rose, needlessly glanced around at the unoccupied tables, then said in her special, confidential voice, 'He hadn't any choice. It's in his probation order. Told us when he joined the group and pretty sour he was about it. Hasn't said anything since.' Ellie concentrated on chewing for a moment, then continued, 'Not that he ever says much but he did say quite a bit tonight. Funny – as if he was wanting to warn someone. Any idea what that was about?'

'Why should I know?' Rose looked down at her plate. She dug her fork into Kevin's mixed salad, lettuce, tomato and cucumber - not exactly imaginative. Terry made wonderful salads with olives and anchovies and hardboiled eggs. French, they were, he said and told her the name but she'd forgotten it.

She didn't remember much French from the secondary school that she'd hardly attended. What bit she did remember certainly didn't include the names of posh salads.

'All right is it?' asked Ellie, spearing a fat sausage. 'Sure it's enough?
We can always have a sweet to fill the gaps. You could do with a bit of filling.'

'I don't want to get fat,' said Rose. She felt irritated by Ellie's confidence in her own eating habits. Didn't she see the same person in the mirror that the world saw? Thighs like turkey drumsticks in her sheath-like trousers, boobs like balloons squashed into a resisting bag.

'You look a bit frail for an expectant mum,' Ellie persisted. 'And men like something to get hold of. I don't suppose this Terry's any different.'

'He likes me as I am and so do I,' Rose said, defensively. 'And why d'you call him "this Terry"? He's my Terry. He says so.'

'Sorry, sorry. Didn't mean to offend.'

'Everything to your liking?' asked Kevin, reappearing. 'Coffees now, or later?'

'Later,' they replied in unison, which set them giggling.

'What's wrong with us? We're a bit light-headed - as if we'd had a few. Shows we don't need booze to give us a lift, but what d'you do if this -er- your Terry takes you to a posh restaurant: doesn't he want to buy you wine?'

'He just has a glass. He's really firm about it. Helps me, you see, by hardly drinking.'

'Well, he sounds a saint. That's a nice top, Rose. Blue's your colour. Shows your figure - what there is of it. Small but firm, like me.' Ellie jiggled her breasts. 'Terry get it for you?'

'No. It's from the market. Only cheap.' Like me, Rose thought, but was pleased Ellie had noticed. Brad had admired it too, in his way. She didn't mind his remarks. He was a tease and she knew he liked her.

For a few minutes they concentrated on eating. Four youngsters came in, two boys and two girls. Noisily they sat down. One of the boys caught Rose's eye and gave her a

35

suggestive leer. She looked away, cross. He was tattooed on every bit not covered by a tee shirt, that bore the words: *cfuk me - you'll like it*! The girls were half-naked with skirts barely covering their pants, pierced belly buttons on display, and breasts lolling out of crop tops.

All four lit up as Kevin appeared.

'No smoking,' he said. 'It's written on the door. Sorry, but that's a rule.'

'Fuck that,' said the youth who'd eyed Rose. 'No wonder you got no customers 'cept for a couple of tarts.'

Ellie started to get up.

'Who d'you think you're calling a tart? Think you're a man do you? I'll teach you....'

'No need,' interrupted Kevin. 'One press on a buzzer and the cops will be round. You apologize, or get out.'

Spitting expletives the foursome left, turning over a table and two chairs.

'I'm really sorry, girls,' said Kevin, putting the furniture to rights. 'You're the sort I want in here. And Rosie gal, don't judge on what you see now - come chucking out time and we'll be heaving.'

The sound of a phone ringing took him back behind the curtain. Rose wished she felt reassured by his compliment, but she kept seeing the way that horrible guy had looked at her.

'Now that's a decent bloke,' said Ellie. 'Not sinking his principles for trade.'

'He's like my Terry - got principles,' said Rose, brightening. 'Men like that are rare. I'm lucky, Ellie? And my Carla's lucky but she don't know it yet. She's going to get a lovely dad.'

'She's met Terry?'

Rose hesitated. 'Not yet. We don't want to rush her,'

'How long have you known him?'

'Five - nearly six months.'

'And in all that time he's not met Carla? Doesn't he like kids?'

'Course he does. I told you how he feels about the baby. He just wants it all to be perfect. A nice home for us all and not round here.'

'Then shouldn't he be spending this time getting to know Carla? Won't it all be sprung on her all at once - moving, having a new sister and someone to be her dad? Poor little kid.'

'What d'you mean, "poor little kid". Got kids yourself, have you? You're such an expert.'

Rose knew well enough that Ellie was childless. The taunt brought a flush to Ellie's cheeks. She bit her lower lip, looking everywhere but at Rose, who didn't regret her words. How dare Ellie criticize her and Terry. They knew what they were doing.

'Sorry, Rose. Didn't mean to upset you. Just seems an ideal time for you all to get together; so Carla knows what's going to happen. That's all I meant.'

Rose saw the look of genuine regret and concern on Ellie's face. She softened, recognizing that Ellie, beneath the know-it-all bossiness, was as true a friend as she'd ever had.

'Clear your plates, girls? Coffees now?'

Ellie beamed up at Kevin, leaving Rose to reply. He stacked their plates on a tray then reached for the untouched roll.

'No, I want that for my little girl,' Rose said.

'What? Is that what you feed her on? We can do better than that.'

The laughter of all three broke any remaining tension.

'Ducks,' explained Ellie. 'The little girl likes to feed them.'

'I know. I heard you say so,' Kevin said. The girls exchanged guarded looks; how much else had he heard?

An influx of early pub leavers curtailed further talk other than an exchange of banalities with the newcomers, a group of middle-aged men and women. On their walk back to Rose's block, which was the closer of their homes, Ellie moaned about her dull husband in a way that elicited more teasing than sympathy. Shouldn't she be grateful that he was always squashed into his personal armchair, watching the same T.V programme or snoring over the sports page of The

Mirror?

'Ain't there something nice about knowing where he is, what he's doing, what he likes?' suggested Rose.

'Swap Terry for my Ron then, will you?' said Ellie and received a playful punch on the arm. They parted with promises to meet soon and, much as she enjoyed Ellie's company and was often loathe to leave her, Rose ran up the concrete stairs eagerly.

She deftly unlocked the door and rushed to the phone. Terry had set up an answering machine for her but there was no telltale bleep. She pressed 1471. Nobody had called. She rang his number. It was engaged. It often was. He'd be contacting people all over the world, like he'd explained. No wonder he could afford to spoil her. He must earn a mint in overtime.

In bed she shifted and turned, irritated by the light intruding through unlined curtains and the screech of tuned-up engines as local boy racers, out from the pubs, began their nightly pleasure. How she hated them. She'd deal with the ones on motorbikes, if only she had the guts. A thin, steel wire stretched across their route would put paid to them, then she'd snatch it away and run, and who'd be the wiser? Such awful yet pleasurable fantasies entertained her restless mind, interspersed with gentler images of lying beside Terry, then, insidiously, some of Ellie's words crept in like uninvited guests.

'Shouldn't he be spending time getting to know Carla?' 'Why the secrecy, Rose?' 'You sure he's not married?'

She pressed her face into the pillow and almost covered her head with the duvet. She could shut out the light but not the words. Why did Ellie have to spoil things for her? She was a friend: didn't friends give support and encouragement? Wasn't there anyone she could trust? Yes, there was - Terry. Together, they'd show everyone who'd ever doubted them that they were a real couple, a family, and they'd start soon. They wouldn't wait the way Terry wanted. She'd persuade him she didn't need everything to be perfect. It was enough to have him and the baby. They could live anywhere. She didn't care as long as they could be under the same roof and it wasn't this one.

She was calmed by her new resolve. She listened to her steady breathing, thinking of the blood circulating from heart to brain, round all the organs and into her uterus. On the scan she'd seen the placenta, that rich purveyor of all the nutrients her baby needed - the doctor's words. She'd smiled at their formality, then, he'd explained that the baby would take all the best from her blood and she'd need to eat well so she didn't miss out. She'd taken home leaflets about diet. Terry had glanced at them, then brought round books and videos that gave so much detail she felt swamped with information. He meant well, wanting the best for her and the baby. With that thought gently nuzzling into every corner of her mind she slipped, at last, into sleep.

Chapter 4

Liz Allan sank onto the deep, welcoming sofa, wondering
how she'd resist curling her legs up beside her. That was the
trouble with leaving a visit to Fay until late afternoon - it was
the place where she wanted to relax, shed inhibitions, and
even fall asleep. She looked with satisfaction at the floor-to-
ceiling bookshelves; encyclopedias and children's books on
the lower shelves, classics and biographies higher up. There
were board games in much-used boxes and videos whose use,
along with the television, was rationed. The colours in the
room were warm; apricot and cream for curtains and chair
covers, a green carpet and the walls a shade warmer than the
universally loved magnolia.

Photographs nearly covered one wall: Fay's son and
daughter (now grown up), and foster children whose home
this had been for weeks or months. Prominent, were recent
photos of Carla, one on her roller blades and another of her
blowing out the candles on her birthday cake. Fay had sent
Rose a copy - typical of her thoughtfulness.

Liz glanced into the kitchen through the archway that
separated the rooms, yet gave immediate access to distressed
or over-adventurous children. Fay was making tea. Taller than
the average woman and large-boned, hair slightly greying and
pulled back into a short ponytail, her looks belied her nature.
Her usual expression was serious, severe at times, but her
smile told everything about her. It came readily, altering the
contours of her longish face, lighting up her dark blue eyes,
embracing everyone around her.

Liz recalled dropping in some years ago, on a fostering
training session of which. Fay was the course leader.
Unwillingly, she'd overheard two aspiring foster parents
speculating on what Fay might be like with children.

'Bit of a dragon,' said one. 'Scary for little ones.'

'Surprised they took her on,' said her companion. The
course hadn't even started; they were judging solely on looks.
If the wonderful foolproof selection panel accepted them,
Heaven help the mothers they might be dealing with in future.

Liz had walked away grinning, silently admonishing herself for being equally judgmental.

'You look worn out.' Quietly Fay had come into the room carrying a loaded tray. She put it on the coffee table.

'Bit shattered. Thank Heavens it's Friday.'

Fay poured tea for them both and cut two large wedges from a cake, oozing moisture.

'Your lovely lemon drizzle cake.'

Fay smiled. 'More drizzly than usual. Carla's as keen on it as you are. I've just taken some up to her and Sally. They're painting. Sally is next-door's grandchild - same age as Carla. They get on a treat.'

'I've seen such a change in Carla. It was good meeting her from school, seeing how she interacts with other children,' Liz said, and drank her tea slowly with the enjoyment of one who has been deprived too long of comfort and sustenance. She put down her mug with a smile of supreme satisfaction and gently fended Jess, the cat, from jumping onto her knee from where she could reach the scented cake.

'Strange taste for a cat - sweet stuff,' said Fay.

'Discerning. Nobody makes cakes like yours. I cheat and buy mine from the W.I. market.'

'Nothing wrong with that. What time do you get to bake? You still full time?'

'Yes. I was meant just to cover maternity leave, but, though we've heard Jenny's not coming back, they're not rushing to advertise.'

'No, they know when they're well off. When you were part-time you did far more than your share. You'll be late home now.'

'My choice. Carla was keen to go for a walk and I thought it might give her time to open up a bit - talk about the coming baby. I had to nudge her. A bit risky, but it worked. Has she talked to you?'

Fay sighed. 'No, it hasn't changed since I talked to you on the phone. Not a word about the baby since Rose's visit. I really thought she was beginning to trust us.'

'I'm sure she does. I wonder if she thinks you expect her

to look forward to this baby? Look around the room, Fay - photos of babies you've fostered, babies of friends and family. Who could doubt you love babies?'

Fay smiled. 'I see what you're getting at. She's afraid of disappointing me. That's why she hasn't shown her anger to me - not since that day when it was nothing but shock and anger. What should I do, Liz? Probe a bit, too?'

'I think the chance will just come, or you can subtly make it happen.

Perhaps when you're playing together. Poor little thing, she terrified she's going to have to look after her mother *and* the baby.'

'That's why she's looking anxious again. She's been doing so well, behaving more like a little girl - even throwing the odd sulk. And sleeping better - hardly ever having one of those awful nightmares.'

Fay paused and rubbed her right leg, just above the knee, a gesture Liz recognized as indicating she had a concern. She'd noticed it in meetings: Fay's hand would start gently rubbing while she waited for others to finish talking so she could have her say.

'I'm afraid they happen after Rose's visits.' Fay gave a small regretful smile. 'She wants to see her mum - is deeply upset when Rose doesn't turn up but, when she does, there's this reaction. The nightmare's always the same: someone breaking in or is already in. Oh, the harm that wretched burglar caused.'

'And in a futile search for drugs, something Rose has never done. A floor below and he'd have hit the jackpot – that's where the pusher was arrested,' said Liz.

Her thoughts flickered for a second over her experiences of foster parents who, not having Fay's level of tolerance and understanding, wanted parental visits to stop. Whatever support and training they received, they would stick to their own simple philosophy: if the parents caused upset they should be kept away.

'She won't visit her mum,' Fay continued. 'She still says she won't ever go back. I tell her the nasty man is in prison and the doors and windows have new locks but then she gets even more upset. It's as if she thinks I'm trying to persuade her. What chance is there of rehousing?'

'Little. I bring it up regularly but after two rehousings they're hardly top of the list, and Rose isn't agitating because she's anticipating setting up home with Terry. She's told you all about that.'

'Yes. Maybe he will be the answer to her prayers.' Fay sighed and finished her tea. Between her and Liz was an unspoken code: discussion about parents was limited to issues affecting the child or, in current jargon, on a 'need to know' basis. But if clients divulged to foster parents all they told their social worker, then a freer discussion was permissible. Liz saw the professional relationship as one of mutual respect and understanding. Without trust neither could serve the best interests of the child. She knew she was more open with foster parents than some of her colleagues and hoped she had enough sense and experience to know why and when she needed to be.

'I was wondering - it's been over five months....' Fay tailed off, looking a bit sad.

'Don't worry. I'm not going to recommend any drastic changes. We need to see continuing stability for Rose.'

Fay looked relieved. The hall clock chimed six times. Liz put her cup down.

'Let me top you up,' said Fay. 'Hang on 'til the traffic dies down a bit.'

Wearily grateful, Liz succumbed.

'Ring your husband if you like,' suggested Fay, ' but I expect he's used to your being late.'

Liz smiled ruefully. 'He is. I rang him from the park and left a message. I guess he was collecting Jack from school.'

Fay poured the tea. She settled back into her chair and immediately the cat jumped onto her lap.

'Carla loves him. Never had a pet, she says. Just as well. Poor Rose has barely been able to look after herself. Do you think she'll cope with the new baby?'

'If she stays off the drink. And we'll give what support

we can. She must have given Carla basic care as a baby as the health visitors never called us in. It was when she was drinking heavily that the neglect started. And once Carla was at school Rose seemed to think she was off her hands. Even then we had no reports that she was unwashed and always hungry. That came out much later when she'd been absent a lot - as if they noticed her more when she wasn't there.'

'Numbers, I suppose,' said Fay. 'And there was poor little Carla at home mopping up after Rose. No wonder she's had to learn how to be a child.'

A sudden drumming noise attracted their attention. Fay smiled. 'Here they come. You listen - Carla always jumps the last two stairs.'

A thud and giggles followed her words.

One of the best things about not living on top of her job, even if it meant driving for an hour or more to reach home, was the time it gave her to unwind: to switch into Liz, wife and mother, shedding Liz the social worker. Sometimes the switch was hard to make, particularly when a client's life story was as poignant as Rose's. What chance had she to develop into a responsible mother when her family blueprint had been alcoholism and, probably, prostitution? *'Mum's men were never there in the morning – make of that what you will.'* Rose had said this early in their relationship, once her anger had lessened.

'I wonder what you make of it?' Liz had asked and Rose had grinned and said, *'I s'pose she had to live on something – I never remember her working.'* After a pause Rose added, *'Funny –it seems I can tell you anything.'*

These were words Liz had heard many times but they never failed to touch her, and when said by Rose, who'd been let down by nearly everyone in her life, they came close to drawing tears. She couldn't take the trust of clients for granted –all too often they saw their social worker as critical and condemning. The press didn't help – journalists couldn't be ignorant of the code of confidentiality that tongue-tied her profession, while they exploited every grievance, real or invented, voiced by angry clients.

Fay was right - the traffic had thinned. A twenty-minute delay had paid off. Liz drove across Putney Bridge then began to relax as familiar landmarks of her home patch gradually came into view: trees and a glimpse of the common. She seldom neared home without feeling a surge of gratitude to her husband's great aunt who had left them her house – a property they could only have bought with a crippling mortgage.

She turned into the avenue, lined with cars because so many houses were now flats and bed-sitter conversions. She was lucky to have a short driveway to park in. Hugh's car occupied the garage while hers gathered coatings of leaves or blossom overnight, according to the season, and regular splattering of slimy white pigeon excrement, apparently precisely aimed at the windscreen.

The house seemed deserted. She heard no sounds as she let herself in.

'Hugh, I'm home,' she called. 'Sorry to be late.'

'Again,' said a dry voice from the top of the stairs.

'You got my message?' she asked, noting her husband's slow descent and his unsmiling features.

'Yes, but no indication how late you'd be.'

'I'm really sorry but I've been particularly worried about....'

'A foster child no doubt. So - what about your own?'

'What d'you mean? Jack's all right, isn't he? Where is he?'

'In bed.'

'Waiting for a story?'

'Hardly. He's been throwing up most of the day. I had to fetch him from playschool after lunch.'

'Have you called the doctor?' Liz started up the stairs but Hugh put out a detaining hand.

'Hang on; he's just got off to sleep. He's not running a temperature so I haven't called Jill. He's just been really miserable and, like any four year old, wanting his mum.'

Liz shook off his hand and moved past him. 'I shan't

45

disturb him. I just want to check him. Why didn't you ring me? My mobile was switched on.'

'I didn't want you to panic.'

'So you'd rather make me feel guilty for not being here?'

He sighed and walked down to the hall. 'Dinner's nearly ready - when you are.'

Quietly, Liz stood beside her sleeping child, resisting an urge to bundle him up, hold him to her, and press her lips against the soft curve of his sleep-flushed cheek. Overwhelmed with guilt-strewn love, she swallowed hard to combat the threat of tears. She risked a gentle brush of a kiss on his warm forehead then tiptoed out.

Dinner was a subdued meal. After Hugh commented, 'The meat would have been okay if you'd been earlier,' there was no exchange between them beyond the usual requests: 'Pass the salt, please,' and, 'Help yourself, there's plenty more.' Only when she'd eaten did Liz find the strength to talk. Even then she felt constrained. He wouldn't want to hear about her day and she knew enough about his. She commented on an item in the local paper.

'A fair on the common - look. That'll be fun for Jack. It starts tomorrow.'

'And start him throwing up again. I don't think so.'

'Hugh, why are you trying to make me feel guilty? There's no need. I'm capable of feeling it without your help.'

He smiled for the first time since she'd arrived home. 'I'm sorry. It's not you I'm fed up with - it's your bosses. You were supposed to be part-time again weeks ago. You've got to get tough - give them a deadline - next month, next week....'

'I can't. It takes time,'

'They've had time, for God's sake. They knew weeks ago that wretched woman wasn't coming back. Why didn't they advertise immediately? And she didn't have any qualms about resigning, did she? She put her family first.'

'Meaning I don't? That's so unfair. I didn't want to go full-time but they were desperate. That selfish creature took the job knowing she was pregnant and not telling anyone for months.'

'That was their problem, not yours. You don't always have to step into the breach. You're not indispensable. You're damn lucky I work from home....'

'And you are damn lucky I had a reasonably paid and secure job when you were struggling to set up in practice here - your choice, remember? You could have stayed with the firm.'-

'Oh, you'd have loved that. Having to find a good child minder instead of a husband on the spot. Don't tell me you'd have stayed at home and been the dutiful housewife.'

'You've never wanted me to be that. You were willing to look after Jack. You wanted to. You didn't object when I went back to work.'

'I didn't bargain on your going full-time - anymore than your child did.'

'That's ridiculous. Jack's secure and happy. He always has been.'

'Well he didn't seem too happy today.'

'For God's sake, the child was ill and....' She broke off, no longer in control of her voice. Hugh gave her a look that came as close to contempt as she'd ever seen on his face, then he left the kitchen to slam himself into his drawing office.

Liz loaded the dishwasher, cracking a plate and dropping cutlery through the grid so she had to pull out the tray to retrieve it. She pricked her hand on a fork and bled a ridiculous amount. She staunched the flow with kitchen paper then searched for plasters. Surely there were some, somewhere, in the home of a young child. She went upstairs and looked in the bathroom cabinet: none. She felt irritated: it wasn't the sort of thing she'd neglect to replace but she couldn't remember everything. She went to her room and stripped. Maybe a long soak would revive her or, better still, send her to sleep, halting the endless revolution of thoughts that ground through her mind like feet on a treadmill.

She'd have to speak to her manager. Her caseload was unmanageable. No account was ever given to thinking time - time to mull and consider. It was a luxury not afforded in work hours; so it crept insidiously into the precious quiet times when work was the last thing she wanted to dwell on. And at this moment she needed to empty her mind of Hugh's reproaches and her own, and those nagging questions about loyalty and duty that must beset any responsible working mother.

Chapter 5

Since that eight o'clock phone call she'd been busy but there
was a limit to what you could in a two bedroom flat. The third
time she wiped the windowsills with a damp cloth Rose burst
out laughing. There had to be something better to do. But for
the rain, falling like broomsticks, she'd be out of doors,
meeting Ellie perhaps, having coffee, chatting, and enjoying
silly exchanges with Benji and his mates.

Her restlessness wasn't just physical. A plan was going
round in her head that would bring Carla and Terry together,
at last. She'd tell him tonight. He was sorry he hadn't called
yesterday but he'd make it up to her. They'd go to a pub on the
river, he'd said, somewhere in Berkshire.

It hadn't been raining when he phoned. She hoped it
would stop and turn into a perfect summer evening. She'd
wear one of the dresses he'd given her - the one that even had
matching knickers! That was a real laugh. Last time she wore
it was at home - without the knickers as he'd suggested. It was
so short every time she moved he had a glimpse of her and
that was enough to get him going.

He couldn't get enough of her, but he was always like
that. The advantage of being pregnant was she never had to
say 'no'. Not that he fancied it when she was on but she'd
known some men who did. Bit perverted in her view.

It was lovely to get out of London. Just as if her wish had
been answered the weather changed. Only few miles after
they left the M 40 the clouds yielded to the sun's final defiant
burst. Trees were gilded and half-timbered and tile hung
houses seemed to radiate warmth. Rose looked about her,
smiling happily as they drove through villages that scarcely
looked real in their pretty orderliness. The hood of the long,
silver car was down; so country smells, sweet and sour,
assailed her nostrils. The warm breeze tugged gently at her
baby curls but she didn't mind. She could be seen - a proper
girlfriend beside a proper boyfriend, being driven in his posh
car. No more the envious onlooker, standing on a squalid

pavement, wondering what it would be like to be one of the girls in sunglasses and a silk scarf looking neither to left nor right, no doubt disdainful of a district that she'd never need to set foot in.

'We're going to Goring, ' said Terry, 'or near there. Nice pub I know.'

It was, and judging by the numbers of cars in the car park, plenty of other people thought so too.

"Don't worry, I've booked,' Terry said as they walked onto the large verandah that extended even beyond the riverbank. 'I said we'd eat outside if the weather was okay.'

At once a waiter appeared and led them to table, already laid, and with a *Reserved* sign on it. He handed them leather bound menus then pulled out a chair for Rose. She sat down, smiling up at him. Who did he think she was? Someone important?

Rose opened the book of menus. 'What d'you usually have?' she asked, bewildered by the choice. She was relieved that Terry took charge, making selections for her. After the waiter moved away she began to relax. The atmosphere, the setting, the warmth of the perfect evening and the chatter of fellow diners was soporific. The river seemed to slide by as if in no hurry. Swans glided around, hopeful for scraps. One got onto the decking and approached the tables. Flap-flap went its rubbery feet.

'Just like snorkeling flippers,' said Terry, an observation that set her laughing. Someone offered the bird a piece of bread but a waiter, holding a chair shield-like in front of him, shooed it away.

'Not allowed, he said, against protesting murmurs. 'You know - Health and Safety regulations.'

'Ridiculous,' came the response from several diners and echoed by Rose.

'Carla would have loved that swan,' she said. 'We must tell her about it.'

'When? What d'you mean -"we"?' asked Terry. 'Coming home, is she, so I'll meet her at last?'

'No, not home. We don't want that, not to that crappy

flat. There's a show at her school at the end of term. You could come. It's going to be something to do with an old book called *Flower Fairies*. Carla's the May fairy. She's ever so excited.'

'I expect I'll come - work permitting.'

Their waiter appeared and set an array of dishes in front of them. Rose thought she had never been so hungry

Look....' Terry stretched across the table, picked a giant prawn out of her salad and expertly stripped it. 'Pop that in, you'll love it.'

Rose closed her eyes for a second as she chewed.

'I didn't know there was food like this,' she said, 'or places.'

She looked around her, noting the willows and the wildfowl and the little rowing boat tied up on the opposite bank. It was a picture book place, like a scene from one of Carla's favourite new stories, *The Wind in the Willows*. She'd chattered about it on the way to the park - before the upset. No, this wasn't the time or place for such memories.

'You haven't always lived in London. Didn't you live in Kent for a time?'

Rose nodded. 'Gravesend. Bit different from this. That was when Mum was ill and I stayed on at my gran's after she died. Then Gran died when I was eighteen so I came back to London.'

'We're both orphans,' said Terry, 'lost in a storm. I reckon that's why we met. It was destiny.'

'I like that idea,' Rose said. 'That's a lovely thing to say '

Losing his parents must have hurt Terry really badly. He never talked about them and, once when Rose asked him what his childhood was like, he clammed up. Rose's natural curiosity was unsatisfied but now was not a time to probe and risk spoiling a lovely outing.

'Ready for your main course?' The waiter appeared and removed their plates onto a trolley, then placed several more dishes on the table.

'That was lovely,' said Rose, 'but how can I eat any more'

51

She leaned back in the chair and rubbed her stomach.

'You can and will eat more. You need to,' said Terry.

The waiter smiled. 'No one turns our food down.'

'Quite right,' said Terry. 'I'll see she eats up. Thanks, that's great.'

Rose laughed happily. It was good being taken care of even if Terry was a bit bossy. And he was in such a good mood – perhaps now was the moment.

'Terry, when can we all be together? I hate the flat more and more.'

His attention wasn't on her. He was looking upwards. Rose followed his gaze.

'See how the sun's catching the wings of that little plane? Must be lovely up there,' he said.

'Wonder who's in it? Some celebrity I expect. Terry, can't we move in together?'

He looked at her then, unsmiling. 'I've said we will, when we've a decent place. I'm doing my best.'

'I know. I wasn't complaining. Why don't I do the looking? I've got more time than you.'

'No. Be sensible Rose. You need to rest.'

'I'm pregnant, not ill. I've done it before, remember?'

'You were younger then and, maybe, fitter. You must look after yourself.'

'I'm only eight years older than when Carla was born, and that's seven years younger than you. You're the one who should be resting.'

Terry grinned. 'I'm not pregnant. You haven't been able to look after yourself for years; so make the most of it now you can. The result will be a healthy baby.'

'There was nothing wrong with Carla. She was lovely and still is.
You'll see for yourself soon.' Rose's tone was slightly defensive.

'I have seen her - in photos, remember? She is lovely and I can't wait to meet her and be with you both.'

'Then let's make it soon. Carla won't come to the flat; so I shan't get her back while I'm there.'

'They've told you that, have they?'

'No, but it's true. Liz isn't going to push for Carla to come home while she's so frightened. I shan't get them off my back 'til I've got a new place.'

'I can only do my best, Rose. Surely Carla can't stay in foster care if you're proving how much better you are. Suppose I wasn't around to help you, would she be fostered indefinitely because of the situation with the flat? That seems ridiculous.'

'No, that would be silly. I don't know what they'd do if they never found me another place. I know Liz has tried.'

'Not hard enough. So when we find a private rented place you think they'll release Carla?'

Rose laughed. 'Not release – it ain't prison. Yes, if it's okay. Liz thinks it will be much harder for Carla if the baby arrives before she comes back to me.'

'And once you've moved and Carla's back with you, will Social Services be off your back?'

'I s'pose so. Liz talks about support - I don't really know what she means.'

'What support will you need? I'll be around. They're not fucking interfering with my child.'

Terry's voice had risen. Rose glanced to left and right. A middle-aged couple stared at her, then swiftly looked away. They should mind their own bloody business.

'Don't get cross, Terry. Why should they bother us? Once we're in a nice place together it won't be their business. They've plenty to do without interfering with decent families.'

Terry smiled. 'And that's what we'll be. I can't wait to have my own little girl.'

'Come to the clinic next time I go,' said Rose, beaming. 'You might get a glimpse of her.'

'If I can get away. Waiter - another jug of orange juice, please.'

They walked after the meal - something Rose never did for pleasure. Walking was for getting from A to B, a tiresome necessity for people who didn't have cars, or so she'd always thought. Now she was beginning to find there was a lot more to walking than reluctantly putting one foot in front of the other. There was the good feeling it gave her body, probably stirring up her blood and making everything work better. It generated energy instead of tiring her and that was strange.

Her gran used to say, 'Save your legs, girl, never run when you can walk,' as if energy was something you could run out of. She'd be horrified at the advice the midwife gave her granddaughter. Often, as she went about her chores, she'd chant, 'Hardworking people need rest, rest and more rest.' Those words should be inscribed on her gravestone - if she had one. Rose said this to Terry, who added, 'Achieved at last,' which set them both laughing.

The evening held on to its perfection, then dissolved into a sunset that caused Rose to close her eyes. She stumbled. Terry took her arm.

'What are you doing, silly girl?'

'Shutting it in.'

'Shutting what in?'

'The sunset. I used to do this when I was little - making it stay longer.'

Terry pulled her to him, enclosing her with his arms.

'You funny little thing,' he said and started to kiss her. She responded, arching her body against his hardness, small breasts crushed against his chest. If the passengers on a passing steam barge were entertained she didn't care.

He drew away a little after a few minutes. 'Have you ever made love out of doors?'

She shook her head, still regaining breath.

'It's wonderful. Come. I know somewhere.' He led her by the hand along the towpath for several hundred yards. It was quiet, the birds no longer splashing and quacking, the willows seeming to thicken as the light faded. They left the path and, climbing between the strands of a wire fence, entered a copse. Terry held her hand tightly as if afraid she'd stumble again. He seemed so large and safe beside her she feared nothing. He ducked under some low branches and held them away from her protectively.

'Look, a natural bowl,' he said, as they walked into a

small hollow screened by the branches and entwining ivy.

He made a bed with their clothes, laughing away her worries about the dirt. He'd buy her a dozen new dresses. Now she was naked she felt cold and vulnerable. When he laid her down she instinctively closed her eyes and stretched out a hand for a duvet.

'Relax. We're safe here. No one will come - well, except us.' He laughed: she didn't. 'Come on, loosen up. We won't be cold. Nothing like a good fuck to warm you up.'

He'd always said 'lovemaking' before: 'fuck' was what all the others had said. She'd never thought about it until she met Terry. It was part of the familiar language.

She wanted to weep when it was over. He'd hurt her for the first time, and her sudden sharp cry seemed to encourage him to yet more violent thrusting. At last, rolling from her, he said,

'Christ, that was something. Must be the country air. Better get dressed. Work to do.'

It was so different from the outward journey. Enclosed in darkness, without talking, she felt as far from Terry as if he were a minicab driver and she a passenger. As the light pollution of west London obliterated the stars she said,

'I hate going back, don't you?'

Perhaps he hadn't heard her. She didn't try again.

At her flat he saw her indoors, declined her offer of coffee, gave her a quick kiss then left. His mind already on important work, she supposed, as her thanks received a murmured, 'Yes, it was great,' from halfway along the gallery.

She bathed in water that turned grey, as had the water in the bucket when she immersed her discarded clothes. She let the bath empty then showered with, now, tepid water. Vigorously rubbing herself with a rough towel, she restored her circulation and hurried to bed before the shivering could return. It was a warm night, or had been, but the coldness came from within.

In the small hours she awoke feeling extreme pressure just below her ribs. A wave of nausea told her to move - urgently. Getting out of bed she almost fell but, clawing the wall, she made it to the bathroom. A surge of pain twisted her lower gut: should she sit down or bend over? Her legs dictated the former and, seconds later, her bowel exploded. Sweat ran off her yet she shivered. She'd never had such pain, not even with Carla. Could that awful thrusting have hurt the baby? She began to whimper, scared of it getting worse, scared of being alone.

'Carla,' she sobbed, 'I want you with me. I need you.'

There was a terrible smell like rotting food She dropped her head almost onto her knees and wanted to die as a tsunami wave of nausea swept over her, then the remains of her delicious meal landed between and over her bare feet.

Liz turned the file and pushed it across the desk so her manager could read it. She had given it to her three days ago but such were the demands of her job she hadn't had time to open it. Liz struggled to be sympathetic and failed, saying nothing.

This manager of three months standing was a mystery to the team. Appointed in a rush, and from an undisclosed number of candidates but thought to be several, she had shared nothing of her history with them. All they knew was that she had been a Child Care worker in Northumberland, was divorced and childless. Always immaculately turned out in a suit, her dark hair piled up so her neck was revealed as long and very white, like her narrow hands, she could have stepped from the cover of the American magazine, *Management Style*. Liz's colleague, Dan, had a sister in New York who'd sent him a copy after he described his new boss to her.

She sat opposite Liz, looking at her over expensive-looking spectacles. She didn't glance at the file, just expectantly at Liz.

'Is this the case shortly due for review?'

'One of them,' Liz said. 'The mother, Rose, is a recovering alcoholic, doing pretty well. Housing's a problem. Her daughter, Carla, is terrified to return to the flat where a burglar broke in at night when she was alone.'

For the next five minutes Liz outlined the case history. Sheila's response was not inspiring.

'So you need to get onto housing.'

'I have - many times. It'll be a struggle to give Rose priority when there's an enormous waiting list. Most of my colleagues are up against the same thing for a variety of reasons.'

'So we're keeping a child in foster care whose mother is now able to look after her, simply because they can't be rehoused? How long can we stand the cost of that?'

'I know it seems all wrong but Rose has been rehoused twice. I've tried to push them on the psychological needs but they've so many waiting - disabled, elderly, homeless....'

'Yes, so you've said. I am aware of pressures on housing. They aren't peculiar to London.'

Sheila's tone was tinged with sarcasm. Liz hoped she hadn't sounded as if she were *teaching her grandmother to suck eggs,* but if Sheila had even glanced at the file, she'd have seen the many letters to the housing department and housing associations.

Swallowing a sigh, Liz continued, 'There are the other considerations. As I've said Rose has been off the drink for only about three months. She sees her present boyfriend as her saviour but this worries me. She's changed to please *him,* not for her own sake and Carla's, and, given her low self-esteem....'

'Be a bit hopeful,' interrupted Sheila. 'Maybe Rose has chosen right for once.'

'I sincerely hope so,' said Liz, drily.

Sheila stretched and rotated her elegantly shod right foot and rubbed the cuff of her jacket with her right hand, exposing a tiny watch. She glanced at it then at the clock on the wall.

'Sorry, are we running over?' said Liz. She knew she'd had less than the allotted supervision time.

'We're all right but you must have other cases you want to discuss.'

Not really 'want', thought Liz, but said, 'Yes, rather a lot, but I'd just like to finish about Rose. She's still pretty fragile. Rang me on Tuesday to report she'd been ill all night with d and v. Almost called 999 because she thought she might be going to miscarry'

'But didn't - that's a good. We might be moving towards a positive review. Now, let's move on.'

Used to leaving supervision feeling upbeat, having discussed, pondered and often been enlightened, a dispirited Liz returned to her desk just ten minutes later.

'Didn't inspire you with confidence?' said Dan, a recalcitrant forty-something Welshman and dear colleague.

Liz sighed. 'Why did our lovely boss retire before she even needed to?'

'She did need to. Denise had given her all and for what? Seeing the relentless erosion of a job she'd been dedicated to for thirty years? Forms before clients and cover your back. Learn your flowcharts and you'll be a social worker. Don't listen to gut feelings - its just wind.'

Liz burst into laughter 'Are you a bit cynical?'

'No more than you. We're realists, Liz, but carrying the banner of hope against bloody awful management is too....'

'Stop it, Dan,' Liz said, still laughing. 'You're almost shouting. We've got to be fair. We're a pretty close-knit lot. Not easy taking us on.'

'Come off it. If she can't cope with us she shouldn't be in the job. She's damn lucky to get such an experienced team, but does she know it? No, she hasn't bothered to learn a thing about us. Hell...no, leave it, I'll take it.' Dan reached over and picked up Liz's ringing phone. 'Oh hi, yes, she's right here.'

He handed the receiver to her. 'Your hubby.'

Liz said, 'Hullo darling, is anything wrong?'

'No. Why?'

'Great. Only you don't usually ring me at work.'

'I wouldn't bother but your dentist rang. He wants you to confirm your check-up next Thursday. It's for you and Jack. He said you always go on Thursdays.'

'I do, only I'll be working.'

'I thought you said you 'd be sorting that out.' Hugh's tone was even, thank goodness.

'I would have but, with so many cases to discuss, there wasn't time.'

'And your son, not being a case....' His tone had changed.

'Please Hugh, not now. I'll do my best to arrange something.'

'Well, you'd better. I'll see you later, but, please, not too much later.'

His abrupt ringing off was enough to leave Liz in no doubt of the reception she'd get if she were late home. She replaced the receiver and picked up a file distractedly.

'Trouble at mill?' said Dan.

'The usual. I did promise Hugh I'd discuss my hours today. How can I cut down until there's someone else to take over?'

'While they think you can carry on they'll drag their feet. You've got to be ruthless, Liz. Anyway, you must be owed weeks of toil, or d'you think our new boss will interpret that as *time off in the loo?*'

Liz laughed. Thank Heaven for colleagues like Dan. If two desk widths hadn't separated them she'd have hugged him.

'

Chapter 6

Wouldn't it be sensible for Carla to start getting to know the man she was going to live with - the man who would be her first and only proper dad? Since Ellie had voiced her views, Rose was asking herself this question every day but it was one to put to Terry. She hesitated, remembering he wanted to wait until they had something positive to tell Carla, such as a definite moving date, and Terry was a man with firm convictions. He had to be like that to be so successful.

'You don't make something of yourself if you're easily led. You don't want to end up like your mum,' were words that came to her mind. They were Gran's words. Nearly always they were followed by: 'You want to find yourself a good man. That's been your mum's trouble, not finding a good'n.' She'd say that over and over, moving onto how she'd had a good man and had lost him. Her Stan was a soldier and got killed in Korea. She had a photo of him in his uniform. It stood on the shiny dark cabinet that had housed the bone china tea service and mementos of visits to seaside towns.

The strange thing was, after Gran died, she'd found no evidence that there'd been the marriage that was claimed. Gran's surname on her death certificate was the same as on her birth certificate. And if the sainted Stan had been the father of Ruby, her mother, and grandfather of herself, then Ruby would have been born before nineteen fifty four, the date on her birth certificate. Had Gran pretended to be married? She was always addressed as Missus, and neighbours and tradesmen treated her with respect - even deference. Often she'd told Rose how, when Ruby was twelve, she moved to Gravesend from Stepney. This was to give her daughter a better life, away from the riff-raff; so she was furious when Ruby moved straight back to London on leaving school. What good did her efforts do? What thanks did she get? That was the start of the rift between them – a rift only eased when Ruby sought sanctuary with her having been diagnosed with cirrhosis of the liver.

Why was all this old stuff going round and round in her

head? Rose hated thinking about the past. She wanted to close and bolt the door on it. That's what Terry seemed to have done. She'd tried really hard after Gran's death. Shoe boxes of black and white photos, nothing written on their backs, and of people she didn't know, she'd burnt in the tiny back garden along with old clothes and rubbish. The landlord had been furious, raging about acrid smoke and how Rose was turning the place into Kilburn where, he'd heard, Hindu families cremated grannies in their backyards.

The ringing phone, interrupting her memories, came as a relief. She jumped to answer it and felt momentary disappointment when she heard Ellie's voice.

'Come to supper on Saturday - you and Terry. I want to meet this guy. Course, we might not be good enough for him but I can cook a meal fit for a king."

'Ellie, he's not like that. It would be great for us all to meet. I'll ask him.'

They chatted for a few minute then Ellie said, 'Must go - Ron'll be in and wanting his tea any minute. Let me know about Saturday.'

It was confusing - supper, tea, dinner? They could all mean the same meal. When she went out with Terry it was always to dinner. She was sure Ellie would feed them well, though maybe not with the sort of food Terry approved of. Like many overweight people she seemed more interested in food than sex. Sex was all talk with her, Rose was sure. She giggled as she quickly banished a mental picture of Ellie and Ron at IT - the union of two bouncy castles. Once she 'd seen a slogan on an advert for a diet: *Successful Sex is for Slim People*. Oh no, that didn't include her either - well, not for a while.

Silly of Ellie to accuse Terry of being posh. His flat might be posh inside but it wasn't in a posh part, as Ellie well knew. And there was nothing wrong with Ellie's house - spotless she kept it. It would be good to be with another couple. It would demonstrate that they too were a couple, but why did she feel this need with a belly that was beginning to arrive before she did? What more should she need as a statement? The answer came all too insidiously - proof - the sort of proof her poor gran might never have had, and Ruby didn't want - maybe.

She wasn't sure if Terry was coming round so she rang him but the phone was constantly engaged. Finally, she pressed Ring Back and minutes later got a response.

'We're going out on Saturday,' he said, before she could say more than, 'Hello.'
'Friends of mine want to meet you. We'll go to a pub - the Goring one perhaps, or somewhere different. I'll arrange it...'

'Terry,' she interrupted, 'Ellie's asked us over on Saturday evening. She wants to meet you.'

'Nice thought, sweetie, but another time. One of my mates is only passing through on business. He's off to New York on Sunday.'

'Who'll be there?' She felt a strange mixture of excitement and apprehension. This was what she wanted, wasn't it?

'Just a couple - and maybe one other.'
'Shan't I see you tonight, Terry?'
'Sorry, no - piles of work to get through. I'll come over early on Saturday. Only two days away. 'Bye, sweetie.'

Disappointed again she moped through an hour of TV, which didn't impinge at all. She'd have liked to go round to Ellie's but dreaded more questions about Terry. She had an open invitation to go round any time but seldom took it up for that reason. Why should she have to justify Terry to her or anyone? Then she remembered - she had something to tell Ellie that might surprise her – dinner with Terry's friends. Just a pity it had to be on Saturday.

She put on a pink and cream gypsy-style blouse that looked good with her brown Indian cotton skirt. She wouldn't need a jacket; the day had been almost too hot. She repaired her make-up, using a bit more than usual - you never knew who you might bump into but, sadly, it wouldn't be Terry. As she locked her door, the next-door neighbour came out.

'Still on your own, are you?' she asked with a nasty grin. She looked pointedly at Rose's belly. 'Well, not completely alone. When's this one due?'

She locked her door, reaching forward, arms outstretched so her considerable bulk blocked Rose's way. She pocketed her key and still didn't shift.

'Well, when? Or aren't you sure?'

'That's my business,' said Rose, hating her smirking face and wishing she could punch it.

'No it's not. Not if it's treated like the last one.' Giving an unpleasant cackle she walked away along the gallery.

Rose watched her disappear into the stair well, then reappear crossing the yard. Once she was out of sight Rose moved.

Ellie was disappointed that the dinner arrangement had been hijacked by Terry, but pleased for Rose.

'Good you're going to meet some of his friends at last. Can't wait to hear all about it. Have you eaten?'

'It's all right, Ellie. I know you and Ron ate back along.'

'No matter, I'll rustle something up. You gotta keep your strength up. Scrambled   eggs and bacon do you? Plenty of protein - that's what pregnant women need. Sit down, gal.'

'Thanks,' said Rose, grinning. Ellie took two eggs from the fridge and cracked them into a basin. Trust her to know best what a pregnant woman should eat. Pity she didn't attend to her own diet.

'I know I gotta eat well. Might even be able to feed this one myself, like I couldn't with Carla. I wasn't well all along with her: had what they called intermittent bleeds so I didn't know I was pregnant 'til it was – you know – too late…'

A loud blast of cheering sounded from the T.V. in the living room – so loud Ellie closed the kitchen door.

'It's football or the garden with Ron. Now he's got Sky there's football somewhere in the world, night and day,' she said.

'Don't you ever go out together?' asked Rose.

'Yeah, but it's difficult with me on the wagon. Ron loves his pint and won't drink softs, as he calls them - not in the pub with his friends watching, but he will at home.'

'He's stopped drinking too?' Rose was impressed.

'Yeah, but temporarily, he says. Once I've really cracked it he'll start again.'

'Will you mind?'

'No. He's been ever so good. Not reproaching me. Got to let him have some pleasures.'

Ellie whisked the cooking eggs and tended the bacon at the same time. Rose was impressed. She'd never been a confident cook even at the most basic level. She'd have to learn when she was living with Terry - they wouldn't go on having Takeaways -or would they? Funny the way he didn't expect her to cook.

'There you are, ducks.' Ellie put a full plate in front of her.

'Looks good,' said Rose, and seconds later added, 'tastes good too. Thanks Ellie.'

'No problem. Don't like to think of you on your own - probably not eating and worrying about that evil cow next door. How dare she get on at you. She should give you credit for what you've done - giving up fags and booze.'

'Never mind her, I don't s'pose I'll have to put up it much longer. I might put a lump of dog shit through her letterbox when I leave.'

Ellie found this convulsively funny.

'That's the spirit. God you've changed, gal.'

'Got something to change for,' said Rose. 'Easy to stick two fingers up when you've got someone like Terry behind you. Stick with me through thick and thin he will.' She ate for a few minutes. 'I'm really sorry we can't come on Saturday. It's that sort of ordinary thing – I ain't being rude - I mean, like, nice and ordinary, sitting around the kitchen table with friends that I never done. Closest I've come to it has been with you at Kev's.'   Ellie smiled. 'I know what you mean. Who are these friends you're meeting?

'Don't know. Just friends of Terry's. One's on a flying visit from somewhere and just staying one night. That's why we can't make it to you. – can't change Terry's arrangement.'

'There'll be other nights. Let's make sure of that.' Ellie sounded determined. 'Hey, why don't I do your hair for the occasion - give you a bit of a trim and set? You're lucky to still be so fair – no touching up the roots.'

Rose smiled happily. 'That'd be great as long as you don't change me too much. Terry wouldn't like that. I can't remember when I last had my hair done properly. 'Cause it's curly I can get away with chopping it a bit myself.'

Ellie laughed. 'No you can't, gel - not to a professional's eye. I been dying to get my hands on it for ages.'

'Cup of rosie?' called Ron from the door which he'd opened a couple of inches. 'Spect Rose'd like one too.'

Ellie grinned and got up to fill the kettle.

'This is the sort of thing you got to look forward to - never a moment's peace.'

'Can't wait,' said Rose, giggling.

As promised, Terry arrived early on Saturday afternoon. Casually dressed in a blue open neck shirt and grey flannels he looked as good as when in he was in a city suit. Casual, though, wasn't right for Rose. He enthused about her beautiful hair-do then became critical about her choice of clothes. He pushed aside the elastic-waisted jeans, specially designed for pregnant women.

'That's for a size sixteen frump,' he said.

'You know they come from that posh maternity shop in Oxford Street,' she protested. 'You told me to go there.'

'Yeah, well, there's casual and casual. You're not ready for those, anyway - you're still tiny.'

'I don't even know where we're going.'

'Richmond. Pub on the hill. Now try the pink dress on - you should still be able to get into it.'

What was all the fuss about? Pubs were casual places. He was like a bossy sales assistant in a dress shop - the sort she loathed, only he made her laugh, while they intimidated her. After several changes he said she looked wonderful.

In the car, she said 'Tell me about your friends. I don't know much about them.'

'No need – you'll be meeting them. Johnny and Crystal live in Bali - big time businessman, he is. Hotels, clubs, you name it he's got it. They're only stopping over on their way to the States. Not sure if Kenny's coming alone or not. He's in business too.'

'Will they like me - approve of me?' She grinned, not sure if she really cared. As long as she was Terry's girl, mother of his expected child, what the hell did their opinions matter?

'D'you think you'd be here if I had any doubts?' he said. Not quite the answer she'd have liked.

The pub was big and really old. Dark pictures in gilt frames nearly covered the walls, huge brass urns full of dried flowers sat on the windowsills, and there were great beams holding up the ceiling. The waiters were uniformly dressed in white shirts and black trousers but the punters were dressed in anything from smart to sloppy.

'There they are - at least Johnny and Crys are,' said Terry and walked towards a table where a middle-aged man and woman were seated. The woman, blonde and bosomy, wore a multi patterned shiny dress, in shades of blue and yellow. The man, casually dressed in cream trousers and a scarlet shirt, which didn't flatter his florid complexion, saw them and waved. He stood up, shook hands with Rose and introduced Crystal, his wife. He clapped Terry on the back and said,

'Great to see you again, lad. Time you came over to us. And this is your lovely Rose. Sit down my darling. What'll you have to drink?'

'Orange juice, please,' Rose said, and sat down next to Crystal who turned and gave her a friendly smile. Terry leaned over to give Crystal a peck on the cheek, then followed Johnny to the bar.

'So you're expecting,' said Crystal. 'When's she due? Terry did say but ...so much going on, you know.'

Rose smiled. 'I don't always remember myself. October. Terry's ever so thrilled.'

'I know. He e-mailed us as soon as he knew. Five

months now and you're so tiny and neat.'

Rose laughed. 'Clever dressing - thanks to Terry. Are you old friends?'

'Fairly. Terry and Johnny do a lot of business together. J needs to be kept in touch with the London end of things and Terry's his link. Bit above my head - all this financial stuff.'

Rose grinned. 'And mine. What's it like living in...Bali?'

Crystal smiled and began to describe their lifestyle. Rose listened, fascinated. Occasionally her eyes strayed to the two men at the bar who seemed to be having a good time. Johnny had a loud laugh that reached to their table. He caught her looking at him and blew her a kiss. She smiled and looked away, unimpressed. Johnny had a beer gut and a beefy face. Not attractive.

Rose wondered why Terry had fussed about her appearance so much - his friends were nothing special. Crystal was quite pretty but you could scrape the makeup off her, and her considerable cleavage was a bit crepey. The sparklers around her throat and dangling from her ear lobes, and set in her several rings were genuine, Rose supposed as they reflected lots of colours.

By the time the men returned with their drinks, Rose had pictures in her mind of shady palms, silvery beaches and girls swaying along in bright sarongs, sucking milk from fresh coconuts, and Crystal was offering her all of this!

'You and Terry must come to see us and I mean all of you. How old will the baby be at Christmas - oh, two months. Would that be too young?'

'I don't know. If she's strong and healthy it couldn't hurt her, could it? I expect lots of people fly with little babies.'

Rose turned excitedly to Terry, but his attention was on the waiter who had arrived to take their orders. There was a lot of discussion about the choice of wine. Once that was settled the talk was about money markets, to which Crystal contributed despite her earlier claim of ignorance. The food arriving was a relief to Rose. At least they couldn't talk so much and eat at the same time. Then it occurred to her that, off the subject of money, they might ask her about her life and she dreaded that, but they seemed uninterested in anything about her except her pregnancy. She didn't mind talking about that - anything about it - the scan, the amniocentesis. Johnny asked as many questions as Crystal did.

'Have you got children?' Rose asked.

Crystal looked at Johnny and away - a look that said nothing. 'Sadly, no, but we are involved with many. Poverty's rife in Bali; so we do what we can, don't we darling?' She beamed at her husband.

'Oh we do. Crystal and I have put many a kid on the right road out of poverty. If we got it, we share it.'

A phone rang with a familiar jingly tune. Terry drew his mobile out of his hip pocket.

'Sorry. It's Kenny. Hullo mate. Oh, okay. See you.' He snapped the phone closed. 'He's got held up. He'll try to join us for coffee.'

'He's a friend of Terry's who stayed with us last Christmas,' said Crystal to Rose.

'Very useful contact, too,' said Johnny. 'Fingers in several property pies.'

This comment sounded promising to Rose. She cast Terry an enquiring look. His response was just a smile.

When they had made their choices from the sweet trolley and it had been wheeled away, Johnny beamed at Rose and said, 'You've already got a lovely little girl, I hear.'

'Yes, Carla. She's eight.'

'You carry a photo of her, don't you Rose?' said Terry, smiling in a way that made her feel important.

'Yes, of course.' She took it from her wallet - a smaller version of the framed photo of Carla blowing out her candles.

Johnny leaned across and took it from her.

'Goodness. Terry has found himself a bed of roses. Beautiful.' He passed the photo to Crystal who said,

'Sweet. Lovely hair. She's like you, Rose.' She handed it back and Rose put it away. The smile Terry gave her was lovely - warm and approving.

Rose plunged a spoon into a mountainous concoction of meringue, ice cream, cream and strawberries.

'I'll never get through this,' she said to Terry. 'You might have to help me.'

'You will, and I won't,' he said smiling. 'You don't have to worry about your weight. Once little Sugar arrives you'll snap back like a piece of knicker elastic. I'm right, aren't I?' His question was for Johnny and Crystal.

'Lovely size. Not an ounce overweight,' said Johnny. 'Oh, here's our friend ....' He waved to a leather-coated figure approaching their table - a tall, slim man with straight black hair and swarthy colouring. A narrow moustache followed the line of his thin upper lip. He nodded briefly at Rose when Terry introduced them, then he clicked his fingers to a waiter to bring him a chair. Once seated he fell into intense conversation with Johnny as if they were the only two present. Crystal caught Rose's eye and winked.

'High powered stuff. Got to be tolerant. D'you find Terry's the same when he's with his cronies?'

Rose looked at Terry who grinned, and said, 'No fear. I don't mix business and pleasure. We have other things to do, don't we Rose?'

She smiled and nodded, thinking, what d'you call this meeting, business or pleasure?

'You living together?' asked Crystal. 'I hope so as you're soon to be parents.'

Terry frowned. He looked at Rose in a strange way - warningly?

'We're working on it,' he said.

'Best not delay,' said Crystal, grinning and looking meaningfully at Rose's waistline. 'Is your little girl excited?'

'Getting to be,' said Terry, quickly. 'Bit of a shock at first, wasn't it love? Having been an only child for eight years.'

'She'll love it,' said Crystal, 'and so will you, Terry. Your own little family - partly ready-made.' She put her hand on Rose's arm and gave it a squeeze. 'He's chosen well, sweetie. Lucky man.'

Terry asked Crystal about her new baby, as he called her beach bar, and at once they were away into the world of business and finance. Rose was left half-listening to a topic that seemed to be the same between Johnny and Kenny and Crystal and Terry.

After they'd had their fill of coffee, Johnny announced they'd have to go. Their plane was leaving soon after midnight and checking in would soon be starting.

'Quick flip to The Hilton to get our bags then off,' he said.

To Rose's surprise Kenny said he was leaving too - he'd only been with them about half an hour. She wasn't sorry. She didn't like the way he looked at her. It might have been flattering from someone more attractive but he was too much like a movie gangster. It wasn't just his physical looks that made her think that way but also the way he dressed. Under the black leather jacket was a black and white striped sweatshirt, worn with pale trousers. When he stood up and moved away from the table, Rose noticed his shoes, cream and pointed.

In the car park Johnny and Crystal gave Rose a hug, wished her and Terry well for the forthcoming birth, then they drove off in a hired Jaguar - Rose identified it by the leaping cat on the bonnet. Kenny also took his leave, but distantly, and drove off in a car similar to Terry's.

'Nice evening,' said Terry, turning to Rose with a satisfied smile. 'Nice people.'

'Strange bloke, that Kenny,' Rose ventured. 'Why does he dress like that?'

Terry laughed. 'You mean like a wide boy in a French film. Not a penny less than thousand quid those clothes would've cost. His shoes are always Hermes.'

'Just shows what money can't buy,' said Rose, giggling. 'Glad the others were different. Crystal seems really nice. She's even asked us to go to stay with them

Terry smiled at her. 'No reason why not - in time.'

On the drive home Rose was tempted to comment on Crystal's surprise that she and Terry weren't living together. She wanted to say much more but it would have to wait. It hadn't been a bad evening; not quite the chatty, funny occasion she'd hoped it would be though, with all that business talk, but at least she'd been seen, at last, as Terry's proper girlfriend. Terry was in a good mood but she couldn't risk spoiling it. If she said anything that would annoy him he'd just dump her at her place and drive off. He'd done so a few times. And she so wanted him to stay

When they reached her block he switched off the car engine in a decisive way, waited for her to get out of the car - it was getting a bit difficult - then he pressed the key to lock it and followed her up to her flat.

'Feel all right, do you?' he asked, closing the door behind them and gently propelling her into the sitting room. 'Not going to be like the last time we ate out?'

She smiled, touched that he'd remembered. 'I'm fine. I can't eat so much these last few days. Not so much room I s'pose.' She ran a hand over her belly.

'Not so much room left for me either. She becoming quite a substantial little madam. My mates were impressed. Johnny's convinced you're going to produce another little beauty like Carla.'

Rose beamed up at him, not just because of his words but the opening they gave her. And he was safely in the flat – he hadn't dumped her on the doorstep.

'Crystal can't understand why we're not together.

'Rose, how many times have I told you, I am trying.'

'That Kenny's in property? Can't he help?'

'Not property as you mean it. Why won't you trust me on this?'

'I do but I hate not being with you. And if we have to wait why don't we use the time differently? We can start being a family - go out at weekends.'

'We've been through all this. You know I don't want to do things by halves.'

Rose sat on the sofa and stared at Terry's back. He was standing by the window looking at the uninspiring view beyond the gallery - more dismal flats. Surely, with his friend seeing things her way he must start to realize he could be wrong. He hadn't been sounding or looking cross; so she took the plunge.

'Fay and Liz and Ellie - I can tell they think it's queer you haven't met Carla, and I noticed you didn't let on to Crystal. You want her to be with us, don't you? I sometimes wonder.' Her voice was suddenly tremulous. Terry turned and stared at her. For a second he looked irritated, then his expression changed. He sat down beside her and gently pulled her against him.

'If Carla doesn't take to me at once - and why should she after what she's been through, the social worker might turn awkward…try to delay things.'

'But Terry you've always said it's not their business. I've got rights as her mother. Now you seem to be saying something different?'

'I'm not. All I want is for you and Carla to be happily settled together for a few days, then I'll move in. If I knew the kid - was sure she liked me - it would be different.'

'I don't see it that way. I want her to get to know you. If you suddenly turn up and move in it could be more of a shock - that's the way the profs see it. I don't like them any more than you do but I think their right.' She kept her voice quiet and even but it was hard. A tear rolled down her face. She was afraid she'd really gone too far now but Terry didn't draw away. He was looking distant but not angry. Rose wiped her eyes with her hand and gulped hard. She had to be strong.

'Please come to Carla's play - at least do that for me, and her. I've told her about you, you know that. She knows the baby's got to have a father. She is eight.'

'Of course I'll come if I can. Yes, you're right, and that will be an easy way to start getting to know each other.' He turned to face her. 'Sorry to upset you, sweetie but I'm nervous about meeting Carla. I'm a bit ignorant about kids but I'll learn, I promise.'

The way he kissed her then made every word he'd said seem as if written in gold letters and underlined.

Chapter 7

'You can take her, get her ready in her costume. She'll love
that. You'll need to be here by five. It's got to be an early
evening show as most of the parents are working.'

Fay had been so enthusiastic. It felt awful having to say
'No' and that getting there for the start of the show would be
the best she could do. Terry hadn't been sympathetic. She
could go earlier, couldn't she? He'd meet her there - later.
She'd hoped she could budge him but it hadn't worked. She'd
pictured them turning up at Fay's in his car, then taking Carla
off to get her all dressed up. But, now it would be Fay
collecting Carla from school, rushing her home to feed her
and get her back to the school in time. Not at all the way Rose
had planned it but, at least, she and Terry would arrive
together, showing they were a couple.

She dressed with care, choosing one of the frocks Terry
loved, blue with big white daisies and tucks across the bodice.
Did the bit of gathering conceal or reveal her bulge? She
laughed at herself, turning to left and right and liking what the
mirror showed. She was proud of her shape. Proud to have
Terry's baby growing inside her. She had none of the fear and
uncertainty that went with carrying Carla. With so much
going on, her mum's death then Gran's months later, and not
well, herself, having strange bouts of bleeding, she learnt of
her pregnancy too late to resort to the obvious. With Carla's
probable dad unaware– she hadn't known how to contact him
or whether she wanted to - and with there being two possible
others…. No, she must stop it - stop thinking about the past.
Those awful times were as dead and gone as the rat she'd seen
in the gutter last night and nearly stepped on.

She checked her watch: Terry was late. He'd allow an
hour to get there, he'd said. They'd arrive with time to spare
unless the rush hour traffic did an about turn. When he did
arrive she couldn't conceal her agitation. He looked annoyed
and turned away so she found herself complaining to his back.
When she stopped, he turned to face her.

'What's the fuss? I left early for you. I told you to go on your own if my early wasn't good enough.'

'I wanted us to see Carla before it starts.' She sighed. 'Never mind, we'll meet afterwards. We can go back with her - take her with us. She needn't go in Fay's car.'

'Come on. You're making us late - talking.' He strode ahead down to his car and turned the engine on before she got in. He drove off jerkily, not the way he usually drove, and swore at every other driver on the road.

Rose sat, tight and quiet, hands locked together. She wanted it to be different, relaxed and chatty. This was Terry's chance to meet Carla, at last: it was supposed to be perfect.

The school hall was already packed. They went in with a few latecomers and were lucky to get seats. They only managed to sit together because someone shifted. From then on Rose started to relax. There was an air of anticipation and in seconds a tune was struck up on the piano, a jolly tune that made Rose want to dance. The pianist was a plump young woman with long fair hair: Miss Evans, a teacher, so the programme said. And there was Carla's name: Carla Davis *The Forget-me-Not Fairy.* Proudly, Rose pointed it out to Terry. He nodded, smiled at her for the first time that evening, and fiddled with the tiny camera that was on a strap around his wrist.

She felt proud to be beside him. He was wearing a suit and tie - straight from work he hadn't had time to change if he'd wanted to. She was pleased. Nice to see a man decently dressed. She looked around her. There were mums and dads and grandparents of all shapes and sizes and in all manner of dress; some looking as if they'd come from the office and some from the garage or building site. Lots seemed to know each other, turning round chatting, offering sweets, swinging spare babies onto laps. Suddenly emotional she reached for Terry's hand and squeezed it.

'What's that for?' he said, smiling again so it was hard not to forget where she was and twine herself around him.

'Everything. You being here, this….' she ran his hand over her bulge, 'specially this.'

The pianist stopped playing and a middle-aged woman walked onto the platform. She stopped in the centre and smiled at the clapping audience. '

'Mrs. Croft, the head teacher - she's lovely.' The woman sitting next to Rose, whispered to her elderly companion. Thanks, thought Rose, I ought to know that.

The Head introduced herself, which caused a little ripple of laughter - clearly she was popular - then she said, 'The show consists of a series of tableaux representing the twelve months of the year, each month represented by a flower fairy.'

There were murmurs of approval from the audience and a man called out, 'Nice change from wizards and Black Riders.'

Mrs. Croft joined in the ensuing laughter and Rose added to the ripple of applause, although not sure what it was about. Mrs. Croft continued,

'The idea was inspired by late Cicely Mary Barker's lovely *Flower Fairy* books. The children taking part are between five and nine years of age. Not all could be in the tableau representing their birth month but some are. You see, if we'd put all the children born in October in that tableau the stage would have collapsed...'

'Got to keep the January cold out somehow,' called a wag near the front and was rewarded with a burst of laughter.

Smiling, Mrs. Croft said, 'A for arithmetic, Mr. Green,' which set the audience off again. Rose squeezed Terry's hand hard and whispered, 'Our month – January, when we met.' He grinned at her, sideways, and returned the squeeze.

'Finally,' continued the Head, 'I'm most grateful for all the hard, creative work of parents and grandparents, indeed everyone who's helped towards producing this show.'

Yet more applause as Mrs. Croft left the platform. The lights went down in the artificially darkened hall and Terry's hand briefly joined Rose's. The pianist started to play a quiet, lilting tune and the curtains glided back revealing the opening scene, January, the first month of the year. Rose gasped at the backdrop painted with frosted leaves and berries and sparkling spiders' webs. A small girl walked on dressed in a red and green tunic with gossamer wings and announced she was *The Old Man's Beard Fairy*. She recited a short poem then was joined by four other fairies who danced with her for a minute to enthusiastic applause.

'It's lovely, isn't it?' Rose whispered. Terry murmured his agreement.

Every tableau was brilliant but the one Rose was waiting for was May. As March's Blackthorn fairy and her retinue danced off, Terry whispered,

'Sorry, not feeling good. Must get some air. I'll pop back in time for Carla.'

Luckily, sitting on the outside seat he disturbed nobody. Rose, staring after him, hesitated. Should she go after him? He'd been fine driving there - just irritable. No, she wasn't going to miss Carla. It was bad enough being late and not being able to help get Carla dressed up. She hadn't even glimpsed Fay. She'd be helping backstage, of course, with the in-crowd of mothers – the sort Rose felt she'd never belong with.

In a white filmy dress with gossamer wings and a wreath of forget-me-not flowers on her fair curls, Carla's entrance brought 'oohs' and 'ahs' from the audience. It wasn't Rose's imagination: they all loved her. Hearing Rose's intake of breath, the women next to her whispered, 'Yours, is she? She's lovely.'

Rose wanted to hug her. She was almost in tears as Carla spoke her few lines beautifully, danced a few steps, then left with her little entourage. She was sure the clapping was harder and went on longer for May than for the other months.

As the June fairy entered a man's voice, at the front, called, 'Happy birthday, June fairy,' and the clapping surged. Of course it would - this being June. A few hours difference and it could have been Carla's month - should have been but she'd come a bit early.

Rose turned to look for Terry but there was no sign of him. Should she follow him? Fay had told her that although Carla was the star of the May tableau she was also a background dancer in some of the later ones. She didn't want to miss any of her appearances. She sat rigidly, the feeling of euphoria ebbing away.

Terry returned as the September fairy flitted onto the stage. His face was shining and, even in the muted light, she could see it was flushed.

'You all right?' she whispered as he sat down. 'Did you see Carla?'

'No, might have a temperature, and yes, I did. She was lovely. Better go home. Not you, Rose, you must stay. You'll get back all right, won't you?'

He got up, mouthed what looked like, 'See you,' and quickly left the hall.

She hesitated, aware that one or two heads had turned but now, anxious, she hurried after him. She turned the wrong way, opened doors into classrooms: headed for a wide open door that must lead to the playground. Instead, she found herself in a glass-lined corridor with a locked door at the end. This was horribly like a dream about being trapped in a warren of tunnels. She felt a sob rising in her throat as she pulled and pushed at the unyielding door.

'Can I help?' A man stood in the open doorway behind her. 'If it's the Ladies you want it's the staff one by the entrance. Back this way then turn left.'

Rose recognized him. It was Fay's husband. She'd met him twice.

'Oh, I know you. It's Rose, isn't it,' he said as she approached. 'Glad you could come.'

'Have you seen someone leaving?' she said. Never mind the niceties, Terry needed her.

'Yes, a youngish guy left a few minutes ago. Roared off in a silver car.'

'Did he look all right?'

'I only got a glimpse. Bit flushed, he looked.'

'He's my friend, Terry. He's not well.'

'Well enough to drive off like Schumacher! Why don't you come back in? You won't want to miss anymore. Carla will be in the finale, then there's refreshments.'

'I don't know.' She felt torn - worried yet cross.

'You'll be a good hour getting home. He'll have sorted himself out by then. Come on. Slip in at the back. You won't disturb anyone.'

Bill was so kind and persuasive; no wonder Carla liked him. It would be awkward to say, 'No,' and he was right: Terry had been fit enough to drive. Bill smiled at her encouragingly and led the way back to the assembly hall. Quietly he opened the door just wide enough to allow her to slip in. Nobody glanced round as she sat in chair next to the door – Bill's chair. All eyes were turned to the stage where the November fairy, dressed to resemble a beechnut, was dancing off, followed by a retinue of which Carla was one. She wasn't in the December tableau, which included a glowing Christmas tree, but was back with the whole cast for the finale.

Rose stood up to clap and cheer, as did many others. She hoped Carla would spot her. The children trooped off after taking a second bow, and a woman came on and announced herself as a school manager. She looked about fifteen with long plaited hair and a filmy ankle length dress then, as the lights went up, Rose realized she was one of those exquisite-looking Indian women with the delicate bones of a child.

Good job Terry had gone, she thought, he might have fancied her. Then she felt guilty again, torn between wanting to stay for the refreshments the woman was offering, seeing Carla so she'd know her mum had come, and hurrying home to administer to her lover. She'd better stay for a few minutes to let herself be seen.

'Lovely, wasn't it dear?' said a woman walking alongside her into a big classroom where drink and food awaited them. 'Got a kiddie here have you?'

'Yes my daughter. She's the Forget-me-not Fairy -just. Born on the last day in May.

'Ooh, yes. Lovely, she was. My granddaughter was in April and Christmas. Didn't have a starring part. She's only little and a bit shy. Oh, there they all are. I'm supposed to help serve the little ones. See you later, dear.'

The woman walked to where the children were being

served refreshments away from the adults' buffet, but there was no sign of Carla. Maybe she was changing? But other children were swarming about still wearing their costumes. Hungrily, Rose eyed the array of sandwiches and cakes laid out on a long trestle table. She joined the queue. All around her women, mainly, were raving about the performance, boasting about their own child, a few generously praising another's. She wanted to join in but felt awkward, not knowing anyone. As she loaded a cardboard plate her arm was jogged and the food landed on the floor.

'What if that had been scalding tea...?' Her angry words died as she turned to find Carla beside her, still in her costume minus the wings.

'Sorry Mum, didn't mean to.'

Carla bent to retrieve the food but a woman behind Rose, said, 'Can't eat that, love,' and deftly kicked it under the table. All three giggled. Rose put her arms around Carla and kissed her cheek.

'You were a star. I felt so proud. I must get some more food then we can get together.'

Carla grinned. 'Auntie Fay forgot there'd be food and gave me a big tea to keep my strength up. Look, Mum, that's my friend over there. See you in a minute.'

She skipped off to join a girl who was waving to her from the far queue.

Couldn't wait to get away, thought Rose, and refilled her plate. She turned hoping to see Fay among the groups of parents sitting or standing about chatting and eating.

'Rose. Over here.'

Fay's voice rose above the chatter and she waved and pointed to an empty chair beside her. Relieved, Rose made her way to her, winding in and out of people. She must stop feeling she had no right to be there. That's how school had always felt for her.

'I'm so glad you could make it,' said Fay, 'and Carla's thrilled. Wasn't she brilliant? But what's happened to Terry?'

Rose explained, her eyes on Carla who was giggling with her friend.

'He even missed her piece so he must have been feeling rotten,' she ended.

'Shame. So they still haven't met. Bring him over one weekend. Nice for him if Bill's there, not just us women. Bill said how well you're looking.'

Rose smiled. She enthused about Carla's performance, then ate contentedly. Fay collected cups of tea for them both then talked about the wonderful Mrs. Croft and what she'd done for the school.

'I'll introduce you when I can get anywhere near her,' she said, smiling confidently, but Rose looked away. What did head teachers think of mothers who couldn't look after their children?

'Hullo Fay. You did your bit again, backstage, and Bill at front-of-house. What would we do without you both.'

A large middle-aged woman in a floral two-piece like curtain material, was suddenly standing beside Fay. Her gaze flickered over Rose as if she weren't there. Fay was drinking tea. She swallowed and put her cup down. She turned towards Rose as if about to introduce her but the woman gushed on:

'You're so public-spirited. All the work you do for the community: not to speak of those poor kids you take in. Lord knows what they've come from. They must think they've died and gone to heaven when they arrive at your place. Just the other day, I was saying….'

Fay stood up.

'Mary, this lady is Carla's mother.' Her voice was quiet but had the tone of a commanding officer. She turned, red faced, to Rose who was now on her feet, scrabbling behind her for her bag. Without a word or backward glance she was off, pausing only to blow Carla a kiss that was returned with a wave.

She cried at last, releasing some of her hurt and anger. Interspersed with her outbursts of sobbing were quieter moments when she sat clutching the phone, listening to the incessant bleeping of the engaged signal. The moment she got back she'd started ringing Terry's number. He should have stayed with her. He'd have shut that old bag up. They'd get Carla back and never again have anything to do with people like that.

How could he be talking for two hours even on business? Had he taken the phone off the hook so he wouldn't be disturbed? Being ill might make him do that. That was it - why he hadn't called her. He wouldn't have left like that for some silly little reason. He might be feeling awful. She should go to him.

Bloody summer. It was all down at Fay's. Here the sky was nearly as dark as midnight. She'd put on a jacket yet still shivered as she walked the half-mile to his block. Louts called out to her: 'Got the price of a joint, Babe?' and 'Fiver for a fuck?' She hated them with an intensity that made her think of gut-ripping knives. She'd carry one - never mind what the bloody pigs said. They never did anything to protect women.

The gate was unyielding. A number pad was let into the wall. She pressed every combination of numbers she could think of, half expecting an alarm to ring. Nothing happened. Terry's car was inside the courtyard with lots of others. He was in, then. She didn't know which side of the block his flat faced. She scanned the windows, some dark, some with lights on and curtains drawn, some with lights on and no curtains. She saw figures - just glimpses of people moving across windows.

She called out but her words were drowned by the screech of police car sirens, the roar of traffic, the singing from the pub down the road and the incessant ringing of ignored alarm bells.

Her voice rose to a desperate pitch. 'Terry, let me in. I must see you. Let me in.'

Her fingers fused onto the metal bars of the gate. She almost hung there, barely conscious of the pain in her hands. She only became aware that it had started raining when cold water, trickling down the bars, ran over her hands and under the cuffs of her jacket. She leaned her forehead against the gate and sobbed.

Chapter 8

It was strange, a scrabbling, scratching sound that made her
think of mice under the floorboards. She wanted to stop the
noise - maybe stamping on the floor would make it go away
but she was afraid to try. Suppose it wasn't a mouse but a
huge, unfriendly rat that might jump at her. She pulled the
bedclothes over her head and shut the noise out. Then it came
again, but was different, metal on metal - was it Mum's key in
the lock? Why didn't she come straight in? Maybe, she was in
a state…couldn't find the lock. Once she'd even tried to get
into the wrong flat. She might do that again - cause a row. The
nasty woman next door had shouted, threatening to call the
police and the council, who'd have her thrown off the estate.
Mum had shouted too, using all the words she hit Carla for
saying. Every bit of it she'd heard through the wall and had
gone outside to try to stop them.

      She'd better go now - help Mum before another row
started. She got out of bed and ran to the sitting room. As she
reached it a dark, hooded figure came through from the
passage, padding silently and slowly towards her. She began
to scream….

      A light flashed on and big male figure gathered her into
his arms. She went on screaming, pushing him away, and
crying, 'Help, help,' again and again. Then, above the man's
head, she saw Fay, who pulled him away and knelt beside the
bed. Carla felt her arms go around her. She relaxed into them,
shuddering and sobbing against Fay's chest.

      'It's all right, lovey. It was a nasty dream. I'm here, and
Uncle Bill - no one else. You're quite safe.'

      'Make him go away. Make him go away,' Carla gasped,
lifting her face to gaze beseechingly at Fay.

      'The nasty man isn't here. He's locked up in prison. It
was a horrible dream.'

      'I don't like men. They're nasty to Mum. I don't want
that Terry.' She resumed sobbing: Bill backed silently from
the room.

      An hour later Carla was asleep. A nightlight glimmered

on the landing and the door of her room was ajar. Downstairs, Bill perched on a stool at the kitchen table. Fay added sugar to cocoa in a large mug then she passed it to him. He wrapped his hands around it, stared at the frothy, revolving contents for a moment, then looked up at Fay who had crossed the room and put a hand on his shoulder, gently massaging.

'I'm so sorry. I know it was stupid of me but it was instinct - you hear a kid in distress and you go to it, just as if it was one of our own. I've set her right back.'

'No you haven't. Anyway, you didn't cause the dream, Bill. Maybe, it was all the excitement… or Rose suddenly going off. That was awful for her. I could hit that stupid tactless woman who upset her.'

Bill grinned. 'I'd like to see that.' He drank then put the mug down and gave a long sigh.

Still massaging, Fay said, 'Carla's been so different lately - much more relaxed. She really likes you. She needs to have a man about to show her they're not all bad. And she needs to meet this Terry - see that he's all right, different.'

'Yes, but I still need to keep my distance - only go into her room if she asks me - it's what we agreed and talked about with Liz. And I've messed it up.'

'Just a blip. It only happened because you're kind.'

She put her arms around him and drew his head gently back against her breast.

Liz sighed so heavily as she replaced the receiver that Dan glanced up from writing a tricky court report.

'That bad? It's not ten yet.'

'Feels like ten pm. That was Fay. Rose's appearance at the school play ended all too abruptly and unhappily. And Carla's had another nightmare.'

'Tell me, but first I'm putting the kettle on.'

'If the fire alarm sounded you'd first put the kettle on.'

'That sums me up. I'll be two minutes.'

Liz smiled at his retreating back. She picked up a referral sent by a primary school teacher. It concerned a small boy who was exhibiting serious withdrawal signs, not speaking, avoiding other children, eating like a bird. A priority case, no matter what else waited in her in-tray. She opened her diary. Lunch would have to be a sandwich eaten in the car.

'Here sweetheart - only don't tell your husband.' Dan put a mug of steaming coffee in front of her. She laughed and cupped her hands around the mug that bore the words: *Trust me – I'm a social worker.* Dan sat down at his desk and swigged noisily.

'That's better. Now, tell Uncle.'

Liz related Fay's account of the events leading up to Rose's sudden departure from the school.

'As she's so lacking in confidence this will be a big setback,' said Dan.' If I had to find a common link between clients it would be low self-esteem every time.'

'I must visit her,' said Liz, scanning her diary. 'Heaven knows how but I've got to fit her in somewhere and, preferably, today. I'm afraid her visits to Carla will stop altogether if she blames Fay. I really must talk to her.'

'Liz, this has got to stop. You're doing two people's work. Next team meeting you've got to say enough is enough, or I will for you.'

'And if neither of us does Hugh will. We had another row last night.'

'Is any job worth putting your marriage at risk?'

'Dan, stop it. You know as much as anyone this isn't just a job. I hate the atmosphere at home but Jack's safe and loved, and we've a secure roof - how can I put getting home to please Hugh before Rose's problems.'

'I'm only suggesting that you could be putting all this effort into your work at the expense of your own welfare. In the end who is going to be helped? Not you or the clients. Just think about looking after yourself - the bloody department doesn't.'

Liz sighed and took a gulp of coffee.

'Sorry I snapped. Hugh accuses me of thinking I'm indispensable. D'you think he's right?'

Dan smiled. 'No. Could I stand sharing this shoe box

with you if you were like that? You just seem to stand up for everyone but yourself.'

'So maybe that's what I've got in common with clients - low self-esteem.'

'Stretch out on the desk, sweetheart, and I'll psychoanalyse you. We'll really get down to it.'

Liz started to laugh but the abrupt arrival of Sheila ended her mirth. Hatchet-faced, her manager stared at her from the doorway.

'I wonder you've time for that. Perhaps you two could do with a few more cases.' She left as silently and abruptly as she'd arrived.

'That's it,' said Dan. 'You bring your predicament up on Thursday or I'll walk out. And that would break your heart - and mine.'

Rose had wrapped herself in a towel and, without bothering to remove her clothes, had crawled into bed, sobbing until exhaustion dragged her into oblivion. Then around two in the afternoon, the phone's incessant ringing activated her brain. She flung out her hand and knocked the receiver to the floor from where a voice said, 'Are you all right Rose? It's Liz. Okay if I call round - about four today?'

Rose retrieved the phone and said, 'Sorry - dropped it. Yes that's all right. See you.'

She hated Liz for not being Terry then, seconds after she'd rung off, he phoned. He couldn't talk, he said, but he was quite recovered and would see her around eight. She scarcely responded. Her voice wouldn't work properly as tears of relief poured slowly, warmly down her cheeks. She managed, 'Yes, yes. See you later.'

She unwound herself from the towel. Her clothes were still damp and her skin felt clammy. She stripped and, standing in the bath, washed herself all over with the handheld rubber hose attachment that the council had the cheek to call a shower. Towelling herself vigorously, she felt an unmistakable movement inside the rounded dome that had once been concave between jutting hip bones. Not quite a kick, gentler, but much more than a wriggle. She laughed delightedly and hugged herself and the contents of her swollen belly. They'd asked her at the clinic whether she felt anything and she'd said she did - vaguely.

'Oh well, she's small yet,' responded the last enquirer, a midwife, and Rose could have sworn a funny look had passed between her and the doctor. Well, she'd really have something to tell them next visit. No funny looks then.

She dressed in a loose, flowery shirt over trousers with an elastic waistband. Her face looked pale so she rubbed a bit of lipstick onto her cheekbones. As Terry hated her to wear obvious makeup she only used lipstick and eyeliner. She was lovely the way she was, he often told her. She might be hearing those words soon but first she had to go shopping. Hardly a morsel of food was in the fridge or the kitchen cupboard and she was hungry. And he'd be angry if he found she'd not been eating.

She chose the Burger Bar because she didn't want to be drawn into talking with Kev. He was nice but his teasing and banter were not what she was wanting today. She wanted to think, be serious. She couldn't have felt more different since Terry's phone call – what did that silly cow's remark matter and it wasn't Terry's fault he couldn't stay on to put her in her place. She'd been wrong to feel angry. He couldn't help being ill. He'd be right as rain tonight, arriving in his confident way, telling her what they were going to do - eat in, eat out or neither.

Sitting in front of a piled-up plate of food that Terry would disapprove of, Rose considered his promise about the flat and how Carla would leave Fay's and come home - to a real home. Soon she'd need to have no contact with Fay or Liz - they'd be out of her life forever. She had a sudden image of Carla hurrying home from school – not because school was awful but because home was lovely. Perhaps she'd run the last bit, pink-cheeked and smiling, eager for her tea and games with her little sister. On the heels of this happy image was a horrible one from ages ago– her own reluctance to go home even after leaving hateful school. It was never going to be like that for her kids. Already things were better for Carla; she wasn't pestered to say who her dad was the way Rose had been. One particularly nasty bully had kept on and on at her: *you must've seen him or don't you know which was your dad? Lots of them, was there? Is your mum a slapper?*

They'd fought in the end, scratching and tearing, tugging and punching until a male teacher pushed his bulk between them. The suspension they both got was the best resolution for Rose - she never went back, never went to any school again.

As she finished the greasy meal she felt a brief pang of guilt. She ran a consoling hand over her stomach and resolved that, on the way back, she'd buy fruit, milk, bread and orange juice. The market beckoned on this bright afternoon and, restored in mind and body, she wouldn't mind the banter.

'Fattening yourself up for Christmas,' Benji said, with a knowing wink. 'Few months away yet, darlin'.'

Everyone loved Benji. Brought over from Jamaica as a baby, he was more cockney than most born within the sound of Bow Bells. She turned away from his stall, giggling, arms full of bulging bags, and was nearly flattened by Brad.

'It's the titfer,' said Benji. 'He can't see anything above his plates.'

Brad pushed the brim of his baseball cap up. 'Sorry, darlin', didn't squash your tomatoes, did I? God, you're fruity today.'

Rose was surprised when Brad took several bags from her.

'Girls shouldn't carry things my mum used to say - or was it boys? Come on, I'm getting a coffee. Want one?'

He was off towards the coffee stall before she could reply. Giggling, she followed him. He bought two big cartons of coffee, refused her offer to pay, then, with difficulty, balanced the lidded cartons against his chest on top of the groceries.

'Park, I think. Nice day for it.'

Rose followed him the hundred yards to the little oasis that commemorated the dead of two World Wars. They settled

87

themselves on a bench that faced a circular flowerbed, ablaze
with patriotic colours.

'Been cleaned up,' said Rose, smiling around her.

'Community service lot's just done it,' said Brad.

And you? Rose wondered, grinning. Brad handed her
the coffee, first prizing off the lid. Again she was surprised;
he'd always seemed such a slouching, indifferent sort of guy,
wrapped up in himself.

'When's it due?' Brad's eyes were on her belly.

Rose slopped hot coffee onto her hand.

'I don't know why you're surprised - it's obvious -
suddenly. Pleased are you?'

Rose smiled and dabbed her hand with a tissue. 'Yes,
really, really pleased.'

'And the dad?'

'Just the same. He can't wait for her to arrive.'

'A girl. You sure?'

'Yes, they did a test.'

'Blimey.' Brad drank his coffee.

Rose looked at an elderly couple walking towards a seat
by the little rose garden. They were hand-in-hand. She
wondered if they'd been together years - fifty even, like
people she sometimes read about in the newspaper. Would she
reach that stage with Terry, even be a granny?'

'So who's the bloke?'

'Terry Brooks. Lives in the same block as you. Ellie told
me.'

'Oh Ellie knows it all, or thinks she does. She's right
though, I do know him - or of him. Seen you in his posh car.
Go out with him a lot, do you?'

'Three or four times a week. It'll be different when we
move in together.' Rose smiled, imagining it.

'That'll be in his place?'

'No - somewhere new for both of us - Terry's flat's too
small.'

'So how do all his mates fit in?'

Rose stared at Brad. He looked straight ahead, face
expressionless.

'I don't know what you mean. What mates?'

He turned, swiveling so his knee touched hers, a movement that rang bells. Now he was looking at her, his expression serious.

'Up to a few weeks ago I wondered if he was part of a gay club. Blokes of all ages go in there at all hours. They come in posh cars, bikes, walking - all sorts. I wanted to tell you 'cause I'd seen you with him - to warn you. I thought he might be stringing you along - you know - swinging both ways.' He paused, then looking away, said, 'I like you, Rose.'

She stared into the flowerbed, trying to sort out his words. They were a jumble in her mind: lots of different blokes, comings and goings at all hours; was Terry gay, swinging both ways? It was all rubbish. She began to feel angry. Brad was jealous - that was it. He fancied her. He couldn't compete with Terry - not with his scruffy looks, his tricoloured hair and shambling ways. If Terry had lots of friends it wasn't surprising.

'Rose, have I upset you? I knew I was wrong - once I saw you were pregnant. Guessed it might be serious....'

'It bloody is. You know my Carla's in foster care but not for much longer. Terry wants her out so we'll all be together - a real family. Don't that tell you everything?'

Rose's tone was aggressive. Brad's face tightened. He put his hand over hers but she pulled away.

'I reckon they're in a poker school. They've got money, by the look of most of them. It'll be something like that.'

'It ain't your business, Brad. My Terry's clever enough to be doing lots of different things. If he likes to gamble a bit, that's his affair. It don't leave him short I can tell you.'

'I'm sorry Rose. I'm pleased for you. You're nice. I've always thought so even when you first joined the group and were – like - stroppy.'

Rose grinned. She looked at Brad's shabby combat trousers and grubby sweatshirt. Who was he to judge anyone: a criminal record, according to Ellie, living off handouts or worse, and looking like a hobo. But what else was it Ellie had said? Oh, yes, his parents were dead. And he was young -

nineteen or so. He'd got a flat but not much else. He wasn't bad looking. If he did something with his hair and dressed better he'd probably pull. She'd never seen him with a girl. That would sort him out - a girlfriend, just as a proper boyfriend had sorted her out.

Comparing their lives she began to feel a bit sorry for him. Anyway she didn't want to go home yet - not to be alone. She'd put up with him a bit longer.

'Another coffee?' she suggested in a bright voice. He turned in surprise, stared at her for a second, then laughed.

'Not cross, then? You're a funny one. Yeah, coffee'll be fine. You strong enough to carry it?'

Liz glanced at her watch: four ten. How she'd managed to arrive at all, let alone only ten minutes late, was a miracle. An unexpected chance to meet a primary school teacher had bitten into her schedule but it had been a vital meeting. Her gut feeling that led her to enquire further was showing, sadly, that her suspicions had to be quickly and strenuously pursued. This visit to Rose now seemed an indulgence.

She looked out from the fourth floor gallery, waiting for Rose to respond, hoping there'd be fewer times she'd have this particular view. It was unlikely Rose would be offered a better flat - all that mattered was that it was somewhere else. In the yard below three boys played football with a tin can. A woman's voice rose from a lower floor, 'Just get out of my sight, will you, and get yourself a fuckin' job.' Then a baby started to yell.

Liz tapped on the door in case the bell wasn't working. No sound from inside, not even from the television. From the next flat the smell of frying wafted through the open slit of a window. No point in knocking on that door as Rose was still in the dog house with Mrs. Barnes, who'd called the police the night of the break-in. She'd taken the terrified Carla into her flat and berated the duty social worker for allowing such people to have children, as if he'd impregnated Rose himself.

Twenty-past four. Liz took a card from her bag, wrote on it, *Sorry to have missed you, Liz,* and pushed it through the letterbox. She had to go back to the office to write some letters and catch the evening post. She turned and saw a boy hovering near her car. As she reached the second floor he scuttled away. At least he looked too slight to have turned it into a three-wheeler, but if it still had wing mirrors and windscreen wipers she'd be lucky.

Terry came in beaming, arms full of cartons from the Indian Takeaway. He went straight to the kitchen.

'Sure you're all right? Feeling better?' asked Rose, from the doorway. There was barely room for two inside.

'Right as rain. Twenty-four hour something, I expect. Sorry, having to rush off like that. Did I miss much?'

'About half. I had a horrible time later. An old bag talked to Fay about all the poor kids she'd looked after, how wonderful she is and what awful homes they must come from. You'd have shut her up.'

'Silly cow, I certainly would have. You all right?'

'Yes, but I shouldn't be after that soaking.'

'How d'you mean?'

'I came to your place in all that rain. I was worried - thought you might need me. You'd better tell me how to get in. Give me the code that opens the gates.'

He turned then from spilling the contents of the cartons onto plates. 'Come here.'

She walked into his extended arms. He pulled her against him and kissed her on the mouth, briefly. He held her away from him looking her up and down, smiling.

'Didn't realize you cared, my little night nurse. Shame you got caught in the rain when I was all tucked up, but I don't need to give you the code - not now.'

'Because you're better?'

'No.' He grinned and twirled a tendril of her hair. 'Much better reason than that.'

'Then what do you mean?' Her voice squeaked with excitement. She knew that teasing look. He turned away and started putting plates on a tray.

'We'll eat then talk. Go and sit down like a good girl.'

91

She giggled and did as she was told. She'd meant to ask him about his visitors. Brad's words had returned to her mind a few times, but they seemed rubbish now. He was jealous - that was the answer. She'd always suspected he fancied her.

While they ate she struggled to contain really important questions. She marveled at her self-restraint. It must be something really special he was going to tell her that made him tease her a bit, keep her waiting. It was one of his games. Sometimes he was like it when they were making love. He'd know she was at boiling point but he'd suddenly stop and watch her writhe. She didn't care - ecstasy was only minutes away.

How could she have almost hated him yesterday? He'd been ill and she should have made allowances. No, it was those great gates she'd hated - cold, iron barriers shutting her off from him. So why wouldn't they matter anymore? It could only mean....

She ate fast, matching his pace, not talking but munching.

'Had enough?'

'Yes, more than.' She gathered up the debris of the meal and took it into the kitchen. 'Coffee?'

'Later. Come here.'

She sat next to him on the sofa, leaning forward to look into his face. 'Are you going to talk now?'

'Yes. Your Carla's a beautiful little girl, what I saw of her.'

'I know that. What else are you going to say?'

He grinned. 'What d'you want me to say? Let's go to bed? Watch a video?'

She pretended to hit him. He caught her arm and held it. 'All right, I'll tell you as you've been quite good. I've found a flat.'

'What! That's brilliant. Where? When do we move in? Why didn't you told me this before?'

'Hang on. I only got the offer this morning Things have to be sorted. Gordon, my mate who owns it, has got to get the tenants out first, and you've got to get Carla back.'

'She won't come back - not here - you know that. We'll have to move first.'

'All right, don't get agitated.' He stroked her hair, smiling at her. 'You can get things going with Carla, tell that social worker you're moving - probably in less than a month if I know Gord's tactics. But takes time, doesn't it, getting a kid out of Care?'

'I don't know. She was taken in under a thing called an EPO when they couldn't find me. When I said she could stay at Fay's I don't think they went to court or anything. It's hard to remember. The drink was fuddling my brain.'

'If she's only where she is because they haven't rehoused you, there's nothing they can do to stop you. You'll have done their job for them. Sooner we get on with it the better.' Terry put his arm around her, pulling her against him. He felt a bit clammy and his face was flushed. He was as excited as she was. She nuzzled into his shoulder, close to tears with happiness and relief. How could she have doubted him, had such angry thoughts and sobbed herself into exhaustion.

'Where is the flat?' she asked, tremulously.

'Walthamstow. Not ideal, but a start. It's smaller than we'd like but a jumping off point. We'll be together - all of us.'

She felt a momentary pang of disappointment. A more drastic move was what she'd hoped for. She hated this flat and the immediate surroundings, but there were some good things: the market, the public garden, Kev's Kaf and her friends. She wouldn't be going out to shop and find herself eating with Ellie, or being teased by Benji and his mates, or even seeing Brad. But anywhere, even Walthamstow, would be better than this filthy dump.

'D'you know Brad?' she asked.

'No. Brad who?'

'He lives in your block.'

'What's he look like?'

'Green and orange hair. Oh, but he nearly always wears a baseball cap.'

'Oh yes, scruffy-looking guy. Could be sitting in an underpass with a dog on a bit of string. Am I likely to know him 'cept by sight? How d'you know him?'

'He's a member of the Alco's group.'

'Not the sort for you to mix with - another reason for moving. Anyway, we've talked enough.' He stood up and pulled her to her feet. He slid a hand under her dress and over her belly, pushing her pants down. 'She's coming along very nicely, the little Sugar Plum Fairy.'

Rose giggled. 'Two fairies. Aren't we lucky? When can I see the flat - take Carla to see it?'

'Steady, Gord's got to do his stuff first. You're an impatient little thing.'

His hand slid to her crotch. She gasped and twining her arms around his neck kissed him urgently. He responded for a second then, abruptly, drew away, removing his hand.

'Can't have sex with a pincushion. Bit of attention needed in that department.'

He swept her up and carried her into the bedroom.

Chapter 9

They sat around the long table in the conference room for nearly an hour before Rose's name was reached. A third of the cases already discussed were Liz's. The ever-supportive Dan sat next to her, occasionally doodling on a notepad angled so only she could see it. Several times she had to suppress giggles; Dan was a natural cartoonist. His depiction of their manager as Cruella de Ville was worthy of Private Eye.

'This next one is a *Looked After* child - not *In Care*,' said Sheila. 'She's not a candidate for next week's review. We should be able to clear this up today. As I see it, we've been tying up an excellent foster placement because a mother insists on being rehoused – for a third time.'

Somehow, managing to speak in a neutral tone, Liz said, 'The little girl, Carla, is terrified to return to the flat where a burglar broke in when she was alone and her mother was out drinking.'

Why did she have to say this yet again? It had been discussed at so many meetings and at supervision.

'What's been done about the child's fears? Has she been referred to the psychological service?'

This question came from a student on placement. Liz was impressed.

'She's been seen three times which is miraculous considering the demands on the service. After each session her nightmares have started again so it's going to take....'

'Just a case of having to get worse before getting better,' interrupted Sheila. 'Liz, we can hardly wait any longer. It's now up to the mother to find a solution, surely?'

'She has,' said Liz, tonelessly, 'or rather, her boyfriend has. They're moving to Walthamstow in about a month.'

Sheila's face changed shape on Dan's notepad. Liz glanced along the table to check the accuracy of his drawing. The look was triumphant, implying that this was about power as much as it was about trying to eke out limited resources as fairly as possible.

For the student's sake Liz gave a brief resume/ of Rose's story and was relieved when the girl, Wendy, commented, 'Sounds a bit Mills and Boonish. What if the hero lets her down? Strange he hasn't got to know his sort of prospective stepchild.'

Briskly, Sheila suggested moving on to a more pressing case - one of Dan's. Twenty minutes later in *Any Other Business*, Liz firmly announced she would be reverting to her contracted working hours in a month's time, stunning all present except Dan, who wrote, *Brave girl,* on his notepad.

Liz turned from the bar holding a tall glass of orange juice and smiled with surprise and pleasure at a man standing behind her.

'Tim Lane, isn't it? We met at a conference, about a year ago.'

'That's right. You're Liz, a social worker. First time I've seen you in here.'

'Ditto,' she said. 'You don't live around here do you?'

'Not far - Camden. Muttley and I gravitate towards dog-friendly pubs and the inevitable canned music is at least quiet here.' He held out his hand to a large brownish-grey dog standing beside him. Muttley obligingly licked it.

'So you're not on duty with your sniffer dog.'

Tim laughed. 'I've a bit of leave, and Jane, my wife, is at work, Holly's with her granny and we two are skiving from domestic chores. How about you, Liz? What are you up to?'

'I'm definitely not on leave. I've just been into the Health Centre down the road, talking to one of the health visitors. Suddenly, a pub lunch seemed very inviting - a bit of normality. Are you going to join me?'

'Love to. I'll get a pint.'

Liz moved away to sit at a nearby table and one of the bar staff brought her ploughman's lunch over. She glanced around at the local traders congregating to eat. It was very much a locals' pub and she liked it that way. And, unusually, dogs were welcome provided, a notice said, they kept their owner under control.

Joining her minutes later, Tim said, 'I'm having the same, cheese and pickles. Might even have a pudding. Dead unhealthy by Jane's standards but sometimes I have to be a bit reckless.'

Liz laughed. 'I don't know about reckless - I see this as restorative, and don't I need it.'

'Life hectic? Sorry, daft question. It always is. Do you ever ask yourself why you do your job?'

Liz grinned. 'Daily. Do you?'

'Yes, and particularly since Holly arrived. I find I struggle more and more to be objective.'

'It's been the same for me since Jack arrived. We've always cared but, somehow the poignancy is greater - it's sharper, isn't it? And I get angrier.'

'Exactly. We wonder what it would be like if our kids suffered the horrors we see. It must stretch our professional training to the limits....'

'Worse for you,' said Liz, detecting a note of exasperation and weariness in Tim's voice. 'Always at the sharp end.'

Tim took a good swig from his pint, fondled Muttley who had rested his head on his knee then said, 'We're investigating something so nasty at present even the gov'nor's been reduced to tears of anger and frustration and she's a tough nut. Months we've been at it. These bastards are dead cunning in so many ways. Never shitting on their own doorsteps - sorry.'

Liz laughed. 'Tim, you're a gentleman. D'you think I haven't heard or said that? There's not an expletive that hasn't been thrown at me. Yesterday, walking up to a top flat, a little boy looked over the balcony and yelled, "Mum it's her from the welfare." Mum's reply was, "Why don't she bleeding fuck off." I got up there, expecting hostility, and found the kettle switched on for tea and I was greeted with a hug.'

Tim laughed. 'Inside your client is a human being - can't say the same for many of mine - well, they're hardly clients.'

Tim's food arrived and they ate in companionable silence for a while. Liz thought about the multi agency conference and how impressed she'd been by Tim's hour-long address, and the way he'd coped with challenging questions. The delegates had been a diverse bunch: police officers, social workers, psychologists, medics and, toughest of all, journalists.

A niggling doubt that had been busy in the back of her mind for weeks was creeping to the fore; could Tim help her to quell it? Had she the right to ask him when the poor guy was snatching a few hours away from the horrors?

'Saw a brilliant film the other week,' he said, suddenly. Then, after taking a good long drink, added, 'At the National, *The Chorus*, have you seen it?'

Liz admitted she hadn't, wondering when she last went to a film, but she was able to discuss the merits of other films they'd both seen. It was a relief to move off the subject of work but twenty minutes later, as they ate sponge pudding and fed the patient Muttley with crisps, the niggling returned. Finally she took the plunge.

'Tim, remember the talk you gave at that conference, titled: *Can we spot an abuser?*'

He smiled. 'I'm flattered that you do. First time I'd talked at such a big gathering.'

'You gave us plenty to think about. You referred to some research that implied an abuser could be profiled; then you gave examples from all over the world that refuted it, and - gosh - that caused a bit of controversy.'

Tim laughed. 'I really stuck my neck out but I believed what I was saying

'And do you still?'

'I try to keep an open mind. I respect the research that's being done but I worry that while we're looking for the peculiar we're missing the seemingly normal. Cunning is the trait I'd attribute to most abusers and it takes all forms. Think of the ease with which they once entered the so-called caring professions - still do but not quite so easily.' He paused, a bleak expression in his eyes. He finished his pint, then continued:

'Abusers come in all shapes and sizes. As you know,

98

Liz, the commonest abuse is within families. In some sections of society it's still the norm - albeit more hidden than it used to be - and I'm talking about the U.K. The abuse of children by women is still vehemently denied in many circles. There's little enough research into that. I was talking to a woman journalist recently and she got really heated, refusing to consider such a thing. Can you believe a journalist would be so naive?'

'Gender getting in the way of professional objectiveness. Tim, do you have any sympathy with abusers? No, don't look like that, I'm not being the do-gooder, love everyone, social worker.'

Tim had raised his eyebrows: now he laughed.

'I know. We should look at the 'why'. Plenty of my colleagues think we just need to hunt down and severely punish them, but I've met some pathetic abusers who hate what they do. I do have some sympathy with abusers who've been abused. Some of them respond to therapy but I'm pretty sceptical - we still know too little about their psychopathology. I'm getting more and more interested in the research side. Might even shift into that area. I'm hoping to get over to the States next year, to an international conference on that subject.'

'Your unit concentrates on a particular area of abuse, doesn't it?'

'Yes, the type that's a huge money earner. Appalling misery and degradation for the victims can mean millionaire lifestyles for the perpetrators. Some kid themselves that it's okay - they're not getting *their* hands dirty as they get their vicarious pleasure. And you can't imagine the difficulty of tracking *them* down, secure in their homes and offices.'

Liz stared at him for a second, then looking down at Muttley's brindled coat, stroked it and said,

'Tim, I can't say much - we both respect each other's boundaries, but I've a gut feeling about someone....' She tailed off, feeling an uncomfortable tightness in her throat.

In the moment's silence that fell between them her thoughts somersaulted confusedly. What was she doing sowing seeds of suspicion? Suppose her indiscretion led to someone's life being wrecked? And yet - if she kept quiet.... She looked up, meeting Tim's eyes. His expression was sympathetic.

He asked, 'Does this hypothetical person have a hypothetical name? Not that I'll remember the hypothetical source of the information with my awful memory.'

Liz leaned towards him and whispered two words. Not a flicker of a response showed on Tim's face. He looked down at Muttley who was now stretching out under the table. After a minute he looked up, smiled broadly and suggested, 'Coffee? Or something stronger? Brandy?'

She smiled. 'Coffee would be lovely. On me. It's black, one sugar, isn't it?'

Tim beamed. 'There's nothing wrong with *your* memory. And we only met for a few hours. Yes, lovely - the real goods, but I'm getting them.'

It had been beautiful on the common: one of those evenings when the world seemed to be wrapped in rich velvet, outlines and textures soft, yet colours dazzling. The sky carried a brilliant banner of vermilion dissolving into palest orange.

'Like a well-sucked iced lolly,' observed Hugh. This had sent Jack and Liz into peals of laughter. Jack, distracted from his relentless dribbling of a football, studied the sky for a second then said, 'I like that new sky, Mummy. I like it when the sun's going to bed.'

And bed's not only for the sun, thought Liz, anticipating a leisurely bath and early night but Hugh, unusually, was in the mood for a talk. Liz sensed this as he stacked the dishwasher then poured himself a whisky and sat at the kitchen table, watching her expectantly as she folded dry washing.

'What? You've something on your mind?'

'You.'

She smiled. 'Is that good or bad?'

'Better. At least I might now reclaim a bit of you.'

'Has it been that bad? I only added two days to my

week.'

'It's seemed like seven. It's not so much the time as the way your job claims your mind; here or there, you always seem to be thinking about it.'

'I do worry a bit - but not always. Depends what's going on.'

'I don't remember it being so bad when we met. You'd switch off - have fun, laugh a lot.'

Liz put the clothes in a wicker basket and sat down opposite Hugh, leaning heavily on her arms, resisting dropping her head onto them. She'd felt different out walking, revelling in the changing colours and patterns of nature, happily watching Jack's skill with a ball, grateful for Hugh's quiet company - he wasn't one to chat and ruin the spell of a magical evening. The moment she got home the heaviness had descended.

'Is it me, Liz - not just the job? Are we going wrong?'

'No. It isn't you. Only…sometimes, I think you resent my job.'

'I think it's crazy that you work over the river. There are plenty of jobs in south London. I think you've been unreasonable about that. And there's all the driving….'

'The drive home helps me to switch off from work, and if you remember I was pregnant when you inherited this house. After all the trouble I had getting pregnant, I was hardly in a state to seek a job change as well as moving.'

'Yet that was the ideal time - a complete change all round. I put up with it then, but why now - nearly five years on? Is it so unreasonable to ask you to make a change?'

'No, I think you've been very patient but I can't switch off as easily as you can. You design a house, finish the job and move on. You know social work isn't like that. We can be involved with a family for years….'

'Because you're indispensable, is that it? No one can take over from you and do as good a job? What about the cases you'll be withdrawing from - if and when they replace that selfish cow who never intended returning? *Take the maternity leave and run*: that was her motto.'

'I don't think I'm indispensable. I just know how bad changes can be for clients. Just as they're beginning to trust us we leave, and they feel they have to start all over again. It's not about me - it's about them.'

'For Christ's sake! You think you matter that much to them? You know damn well they badmouth the last social worker to the new one. You've heard it yourself.'

'Only because they're disappointed and feel let down. They don' mean it. And they aren't all like that. I wish you wouldn't stereotype clients.'

'Isn't that what you do? They're all so hard-done-by, all deserving hours of work, years of support that sees nothing but repeated patterns....'

'You sound like the tabloid press.' Liz interrupted him. 'I'm amazed you're not a Daily Mail reader.'

'Maybe it sometimes speaks with the voice of commonsense. The trouble is you see the best in everyone. God...after years in the job you're still so bloody naive.'

Liz looked away, clenching her hands together. She got up.

'End of discussion?' said Hugh, his tone tinged with sarcasm.

'End of potential row,' said Liz, tightly. She picked up the clothes' basket and walked out of the kitchen.

Chapter 10

Terry 's suggestion of a day out, looking at the flat, then driving into the country and having a pub lunch, had been made as he left the flat close to midnight. Disappointed at his early departure and wanting cuddles and reassurance after sex that had been brief and uncomfortable, Rose's sagging spirits had instantly lifted and they'd remained high.

She hadn't slept much: she'd been too busy mentally furnishing the flat. It would be lovely starting from scratch - not have any of the second-hand rubbish from this place. She wanted the sort of clean-looking furniture she saw in advertisements on the telly and lovely curtains, silky-looking. Together, she and Terry would plan and decorate the nursery. They were so lucky to know what the colour scheme should be - soft pinks and, maybe, cream. And Carla should have a say too …she was old enough to know what she liked. Then a really brilliant idea came to her, went to sleep with her and woke up with her.

She caught sight of her face in the spotted mirror on the hideous chest she used as a dressing table. She was smiling, unconsciously. Did she go about looking like that? Funny, but people did seem to smile at her lately -often complete strangers - and sometimes they'd speak. She remembered a saying of Gran's: 'Smile and the world smiles with you.' It seemed to be true but she'd had a couple of days of feeling frustrated that things seemed to be moving slowly, disappointed that she couldn't give notice to Housing until a moving in date was settled. She told Liz she'd be moving - at least she'd left a message at her office and the next step was to tell Carla, which could be today.

Before Terry could turn his key in the lock she leapt to open the door. He
took a step back, grinned and said, 'You going somewhere?'

She laughed and hugged him.

'Steady, you'll squash her,' he said, 'and her dad.'

At that she hugged him again and he lifted her up,

pretending to pant at her weight.

'What's all the excitement about?' He put her on the sofa and sat alongside.

'We could drive to Fay's and pick Carla up. She should see the flat too. It's going to be her new home.'

He looked away and gave a sigh. 'We can't go in, remember. Gordon hasn't got them out yet. We're only looking at the outside: boring for Carla. Anyway, there won't be time to collect her as well as doing other things.'

'Then let's forget the flat for today and take her out.'

'Isn't it a bit short notice? Anyway, it'll add two hours at least on the day and I haven't that much time. Things have changed since last night. I had an urgent call. I've got colleagues coming to a meeting later. No, don't look like that - it's work and I can't get out of it now. You should have said something yesterday. Come on, let's get going. And stop worrying. Don't you trust me? You must know I want us all to be together.'

In the car Rose fiddled with the seat belt. It pressed uncomfortably, reminding her that she was expanding and causing her to laugh.

'That's better,' Terry said. 'What's funny?'

'Me - like Tweedledum.'

'Can't be helped. But I do look forward to you being slim as a rail again.'

Rose went quiet. Although Terry seemed as keen on her as ever, attentive and complimentary, their sex was becoming more about foreplay than intercourse. Was he afraid he'd hurt the baby? But that time in the wood he'd shown no such concern. She didn't want it to be like that again, but she wanted the ultimate togetherness of full intercourse, the fusing of their bodies. That was when she felt they really owned each other - nothing and no one mattered beyond the pair of them. The playful dressing up, the anointing of each other with honey and licking it off, the pretence at coyness which led to Terry chasing her around the flat - it was fun if it led to full sex and if not....

'Penny for 'em,' said Terry.

104

'Oh, nothing …just dreams.'

They drove through many uninspiring streets, no better than Rose's familiar ones but then they turned into a nice quiet avenue. Higher Walthamstow sounded good too - something to tell Ellie.

'Nearly there,' Terry said. 'Number forty - on the corner.'

They drew up opposite a detached house. Terry prepared to get out.

'We'll walk down the side road where the entrance is.'

'Not the front?' asked Rose, unbuckling and shifting awkwardly.

'No, that's to the ground floor flat.'

He slammed the door and came round and yanked Rose up from the low-slung seat. Had she irritated him? She smiled up at him, hoping this showed her gratitude, and slipped her arm through his.

The house looked cared-for with new-looking paintwork. There were neatly clipped shrubs in the small garden. She wasn't pleased to see a flight of concrete steps leading to a front door at first floor level – the way to their flat. How would she get a pram up those? And the garden went with the ground floor flat Terry told her. Maybe she wouldn't have a pram but use one of those sling things. And they'd have moved by the time the baby needed a pushchair. There wasn't a garage, just a concrete parking area but Terry seemed pleased with everything.

A man on a bike passed them, lifting a hand in greeting. He was followed by two small boys pedalling hard and calling, 'Wait, Dad, you're s'posed to be teaching us.'

Rose turned to watch them. The father stopped fifty yards ahead and dismounted, watching his sons' progress. He was smiling and again lifted a hand. Rose waved back.

'D'you know him, Terry ?' she asked.

'No, just a friendly guy.'

Rose smiled. He'd have noticed she was pregnant. His wave showed that he saw her and Terry as kindred spirits, members of that huge family group who had Sunday outings, played games in parks, watched telly together. At last, after all those awful years, she belonged.

Terry drove in such a laid-back way it was as if the car was doing it all by itself. He sat back, almost reclining, fingertips lightly on the steering wheel, humming and smiling. He took his left hand off the wheel and squeezed Rose's thigh.

'Happier? Shame we couldn't go inside but Gord's confident he won't be long getting them out.'

'Doesn't matter. I've seen where it is. I like it.'

Never mind the flat, she thought, it had to be better than her present one. And there were lots of open spaces around for Carla to play in - Whipps Cross and Epping Forest, where Terry was heading, along with other Sunday drivers in cars packed with families.

That was a point: how would they all fit into this car. Terry would change it, of course. There was no room for a car seat and a carrycot, or whatever was safe for a baby to travel in, and certainly not a dog. She'd like a dog: it would make her feel safe when Terry was away or working late. The flat was small - too small with only two bedrooms because the third had to be a living- room, but at least it was a start.

'Where will you keep your stuff?' she asked.

'What stuff?'

'All your electrical stuff. You said it was dangerous for Carla to be near it.'

'It'll have to stay at my flat. I'll still have to do some work from home. I can't give the flat up straight away.'

'But you will when we move to a bigger place?'

'Of course. I'm not made of money. Can't keep two places going."

She wished he hadn't said that, and in such a cold tone. Did he think she was taking and taking – not giving anything? But it had been his suggestion to move now, not hers. And he'd made the quick decision. She went quiet. He continued to squeeze her thigh until a complicated-looking junction demanded both hands on the wheel. He swore at another driver as he turned into a road that led, he told her, to the forest.

'I've never been here before,' she said, 'nor has Carla.'

'You've not been anywhere,' said Terry. 'Most of your life spent in London and what've you seen? We'll change that.'

They parked and walked a short way until, out of breath, Rose sank thankfully onto a strategically placed seat.
'Never mind,' said Terry. 'Once little Sugar pops out you'll soon get slim and fit.'
I'll need to, thought Rose, picturing the outside stairs

'Shame we can't have the ground floor,' she said to Terry's back. He was walking around, hands in pockets, idly kicking at clumps of turf.

'No chance - Gord's brother lives there. Changing your mind, are you?' He turned, looking at her, unsmiling.

'No, course not. I don't mind waiting for the right place. I want Carla back and all of us to be together. You'll be part of her new start.'

He crossed to the seat, bent and kissed her, then ruffled her hair. 'Good girl. Let's get a bite to eat, then off home. Time's money in my game.'

She knew then they wouldn't spend the whole day together. She couldn't begrudge him the work - it helped to provide for these outings, the meals, the clothes, presents for Carla and, soon, a new flat, but she hated the bits of days and nights left to her to get through alone.

Fay put groceries into the trolley that Carla pushed. Unlike many of the deprived children Fay had known she made no demands as they went along the aisles. Her 'goodness' seemed unnatural. The few tantrums she'd thrown had reassured Fay she could express her anger but since hearing about the baby she'd gone back into her shell. She'd even started squirreling food away in her room - something she'd done when she first arrived at Fay's and had no faith that she'd be fed regularly Was she still furious with Rose? If only she'd talk about it. Fay resolved to talk again soon with Liz. She was always helpful, but she had other clients - all too many.

At the checkout a young woman ahead of them was trying to empty her trolley onto the belt but her small son

107

insisted on putting the groceries back into the trolley. Fay, caught the mother's eye, grinned and said, 'We could do with a bit of help here. Would this young man lend a hand?'

She put a plastic partition a couple of feet behind the woman's groceries. The child turned and looked from Mum to Fay and back again.

'Would you help the lady to empty her trolley, Carl?'

'Carl! That's nearly my name, 'said Carla. 'I'm Carla.'

The boy smiled and moved away from his mother to stand beside her and together they slowly filled the conveyor belt, while his mother finished emptying her trolley with Fay's help.

'Lovely bit of co-operation,' said the checkout assistant, beaming at the children.

While Fay and Carl's mother packed Fay's groceries, Carl and Carla stood side by side staring at twin babies in a double buggy held by an elderly woman.

'We've got a baby,' said Carl.

Carla stared at him then looked at Fay who was chatting with his mother. She'd discreetly told her that Carl, aged four, had played up a bit since their new baby had arrived: his nose a little out of joint he needed a bit of special attention.

Carla went to take the laden trolley from Fay, who held on to it, saying,

'We're going to have a cup of tea and a cake - that'll be nice, won't it?'

Carla said nothing but followed the adults and Carl to the railed-off café area.

'Have you got a brother or sister?' Carl asked Carla.

She stared at Fay, her mouth tight.

'Carla's mum is having a baby soon,' Fay said.

'Our baby's quite nice. You can come and see her, can't she, Mummy?'

Carl's mother and Fay exchanged an understanding smile.

'I expect so. It depends where Carla lives.'

To Fay's surprise, Carla said, 'I live in Chestnut Close with Auntie Fay.'

Carl's mother beamed. 'Ah, now I can place you. I've seen you around. My big son, Jamie - he's nine - has some new roller blades thanks to you, Carla. He's watched you tearing around the park. Now, I think this calls for a special cake each.'

Fay looked at the younger woman with the appreciation of one whose prayer has been answered.

Chapter 11

'Liz, come to my office, please.' Sheila's voice sounded even tighter than usual. Not waiting for Liz's response she walked smartly down the corridor, pin heels tapping.

'Oh God, what have I done?' Liz said looking at Dan.

He raised his eyebrows skywards, grinned and said, 'I doubt if even He can tell you.'

As she reached the door, he said, 'If you're not back in twenty I'll come and rescue you.'

Inside Sheila's office she heard a male voice speaking quietly. She tapped on the door. A full minute later, Sheila responded in an imperious tone, 'Come in.'.

A man Liz didn't know was standing by Sheila's desk. He was in his forties, she guessed, and kindly looking.

Sheila said, 'This is D. S. Ingram from CEOP. He's brought some pictures to show us. Some are not very pleasant. I'm wondering if you'll recognise any of the subjects. When you've finished send the others in, one at a time.'

D.S. Ingram smiled. 'My name's Bob...I didn't catch yours.'

Just managing to refrain from saying, 'You weren't given the chance,' Liz smiled, volunteered her name and shook his proffered hand. She looked at the desk: sheets of paper were spread all over it.

Indicating them with his hand, Bob said, heavily, 'My boss wonders if any of these unfortunates are known to Social Services. You may have heard of him - D.I Tim Lane.'

His tone gave nothing away: part of his training, or was he genuinely unaware that she and Tim knew one another? This thought lasted a fleeting moment then much darker ones entered her mind. Apprehensively, she approached the desk.

Rose walked into the tiny patch of garden, a rectangular piece of grass edged with flowers, the pride and joy of Ellie's husband, second only to his love for football.

'And where do you come?' asked Rose, laughing.

'A poor third,' said Ellie, cheerfully. 'I'll show you his

tomatoes.'

'Wow. What about his giant marrow?'

Giggling, Ellie said, 'Sadly he ain't got one. If he had I wouldn't share it, not even with you.' She opened the door of a tiny greenhouse.

'Lovely smell.' Rose smiled, wrinkling her nose as she glanced inside.

'Sun warmed tomatoes,' said Ellie. 'Those and his runners I don't have to buy for a few weeks.'

Rose wandered around, admiring the brilliantly coloured Busy Lizzies and Begonias.

'We need a ground floor flat and garden,' she said. 'We can't be upstairs for long - not once the baby's walking. I don't want the life for her that Carla's had.'

'Does Terry realise how you feel?'

'Course. He agrees with me. It's just a temporary place 'til we get Carla back. We talked on the phone last night, me and Carla, and she told me about a new friend who's got a baby sister. She sounded quite excited, asking me when the baby was coming and how did I know it was a girl? Her friend's mum didn't known 'til hers arrived.'

'Great. And Terry - she knows about him?'

'Yeah, of course, Ellie. I told her before her play that the baby's dad might be coming but she wasn't – like - interested. Since then, I've told her how he was taken ill and was disappointed not to meet her.'

'But he still hasn't met her?'

'Only 'cause he wants it to be perfect after that disappointment.'

'Oh well, it's your business. Let's talk about something else, or, better still, you sit in the sun and rest. You look tired. A bit panda like. I'll bring us out a drink. What'll it be?'

'Vod and ton?' said Rose which sent Ellie away giggling.

A tricky moment had passed thank God – this was not the time or place to get ratty with Ellie. Rose sank onto a sunbed and lifted her face, eyes closed, to the afternoon's sunshine. Soon the smell of real coffee drifted into the garden.

111

'I like that,' said Rose when Ellie returned and put a tray with mugs, milk, sugar and a cafetiere on a low wooden table. 'What - the coffee?'
'Hm, I love the smell.'
'And the taste, I expect. Once I started buying the real stuff I couldn't face bottled, but Ron'd drink distilled cow dung if I gave it to him.'
Rose giggled. 'And yet he likes home grown veg.'
'He's a funny mixture, my bloke,' said Ellie, fondly.
'Terry likes proper coffee. I'll get one of those things for the flat - start as we mean to go on.'
Ellie smiled. 'Ain't it furnished?'
'Part, Terry says. He's taking care of all that, bringing some of his own
stuff. I'm sorry we can't furnish it ourselves. I got lots of ideas but they'll have to wait 'til we get our own place - really our own. You'll visit us, won't you? I wish we was going to be a bit nearer, specially as it's just a temporary move.'
'Lord, Rose, it's only a few stops up the line. I could baby sit sometimes. Might find I got a maternal instinct.'
'You have, Ellie. You just pretend to be tough. You always talk to kids in the street and they like you.'
'I've nothing against kids - just don't fancy carrying one about inside me. Oh, I forgot the biscuits. Hang on.'
She returned with a plateful of custard creams and sat down alongside Rose. They drank and talked companionably, until Rose succumbed to the soporific effect of being in a sun drenched garden. She dozed a few times while Ellie chattered about her plans to set herself up as a mobile hairdresser, specialising in elderly and housebound clients. She'd have to save up for a vehicle, that was the problem.
'Can't you get a job in a salon for a bit, then set up on your own,' asked Rose, stifling a yawn.
'Not with my record. Twice sacked for having hangovers or being downright pissed - and that time was after our lunch break.'
Rose giggled, wondering what hairstyles Ellie had achieved in a drunken state. She closed her heavy eyelids to

picture them and awoke to hear Ellie exclaim,

'It's four o'clock. I'd better get something for tea.'

'Ellie, not more food.'

'It's for that lump when he comes in. Just a quick trip to the market. You can stay here if you like, Rose. Stay for the evening and eat with us. You'll manage something by then, surely.'

'Thanks but I better get moving. Terry might come round.'

Parting from Ellie ten minutes later, with difficulty she gave her a fond hug.

'Who's got the bigger belly now?' said Ellie, laughing.

'Thanks Ellie, I've had a lovely time. I ain't going to let it go about needing to have a garden.'

'No you keep him at it. You going to alcos on Friday?'

'Might as well. It'll be my last one - I hope.'

'See you there, then.'

Climbing the four flights of stairs to her flat, Rose realised she'd have but one floor to reach when she moved. And they'd only be there a few months - Terry had promised her that.

She dumped her bags on the table and made for the phone in the bedroom to check for messages. The doorbell rang. She stopped. It wouldn't be Terry - he never rang. Could be Ellie - not likely as they'd parted only minutes ago. She opened the door. Liz stood there. Strange - she usually phoned first. Perhaps she'd left a message like the other day when Rose forgot she was coming.

'Sorry, Rose. I did ring a few times but I expect you were out.'

'That's okay. Come in.'

What the hell if Terry arrived while Liz was there, though it wasn't likely this early. Soon, she and Terry would be calling the shots.

Liz looked tired, not her usual bright-faced self.

'Cuppa?' Rose suggested as they moved into the sitting room.

'No thanks.'

Rose sat down and Liz sat opposite her on the small sofa. She bent forward to put her bag on the floor and stayed like that, not relaxing the way she usually did. Probably she wanted to talk about the coming move - preparing Carla for it - that sort of thing. She'd always wanted Rose in a better place - had understood Carla's fears. Social worker though she was she was pretty okay.

'Rose, have you a friend nearby?'

Funny question. 'Ellie,' Rose said. 'I've just left her.'

'Yes, of course, you've mentioned her. It's just that I've something to tell you Rose and I'm afraid it will be a shock - nothing about Carla, she's fine...'

'Well, what then? The council have found us a flat? Bit late in the day.'

'No, it's about Terry. I'm afraid he's been arrested.'

'What? Was he speeding? He can drive a bit fast but he's a good driver.'

'It wasn't a driving offence, Rose.' Liz hesitated, biting her lip and looking anywhere but at Rose, then said, 'He's been trading pornography over the internet.'

'What? That's rubbish. He's in business - financial stuff. He wouldn't do that.'

'I'm afraid it's on his computer. I'm so sorry Rose. I hate having to tell you this.' She was looking at Rose now, her expression saying more than her words.

'It ain't true. Can't be. Anyway, if it was, lots of men like that sort of thing. It's not against the law. You can buy dirty videos in sex shops - you don't have to go as far as Soho...'

'It isn't adult porn, Rose.'

'You're saying it's kids? He'd never get mixed up in anything like that. He loves kids - can't wait for the baby to come.'

'Rose, he sells child porn. His arrest is already public knowledge. He was arrested at his flat last evening, along with others. I was afraid you'd hear about it on the radio, or from local gossip.'

'But you got in first. Always wondered about him - you

114

and Fay. You're wrong - all the fuckin' lot of you - someone's set him up. Bloody jealous people round here - can't bear to see anyone get on....'

'Rose, if it's on a person's computer it is very strong evidence.'

'It bloody ain't. I've seen it on the telly - the police taking computers away and planting stuff in them. That's what's happened to Terry.'

'I'm so sorry, Rose. This is awful for you.'

'Awful for Terry, you mean. I got to see him. Where is he?'

'It's best if you don't. If there's a court case we'll all do everything to keep your name out of it. He never did meet Carla - the closest he's come to her was seeing her in her school play...'

'What are you saying - Carla might have been hurt by Terry? Don't talk like that to me. He's done more for me than you or any of your bloody kind.'

Rose stood up. Shaking visibly she stumbled and grabbed the arm of the chair. Liz leapt up to steady her, putting an arm around her shoulders, but Rose pushed her so roughly she nearly fell.

'Get out. Don't ever come here again or go anywhere near Carla.'

'That's not possible Rose, I'm Carla's social worker.'

'Not anymore. I don't want you poisoning her against Terry.'

'Rose, there'll be no need to mention Terry if she never has contact with him.'

'So you're saying he's guilty - a danger to Carla? You all think alike. Don't give anyone a chance.'

Feeling as if her legs were going to collapse, she sat down and clenched her hands tightly in front of her chest. It was all she could do to keep them off Liz.

'You've done so well, giving up the smoking and drinking and taking more care of yourself. Try to hang on to that.' Liz sat down again.

'And who did that for me? Not you. It was Terry who

115

put me straight. What have you ever done? Taken my Carla and left me in this dump.'

'I'm sorry we haven't been able to find you a decent place to live....'

'Are you? D'you really care a fuck? Funny... the person you think is a pervert is the only one who's helped me.'

'I'm so sorry. We all wanted it to work out well for you, truly we did...'

'So you come round here repeating filthy lies about Terry...'

Struggling against sobs Rose lost the fight and dropped her head into her hands. She felt Liz's arm go round her shoulder. For a second she tolerated this then anger gave her strength - she jerked away and got up. Liz stepped back.

'Get out. Get out of my sight. I never want to see you again.'

Liz picked up her bag and moved towards the door, then turned.

'Will you let me contact Ellie? I don't think you should be alone.'

'Get out,' Rose shouted. 'Go on or I'll throw you out.'

Liz opened the door but still hesitated, looking at Rose as if she didn't know what to do next. Rose lumbered towards her. Liz left, closing the door after her.

As if shock had affected her sight, Rose blundered around the flat, bumping into furniture as incoherent thoughts tore through her mind.

The police must have broken in to his flat and put stuff on Terry's computer. One of the gambling friends was getting back at him for cleaning him out. Someone he'd annoyed was settling a score, or someone he'd known years ago was filled with vicious envy of his position. Maybe it was an old girlfriend who'd done this to him. He never spoke of past affairs - it was as if she, Rose, had come into his life and blotted everyone else out. That was it - vicious jealousy.

If she could find whoever had done this to Terry she'd be capable of murder.

No cruelty would be too extreme. As long-drawn out as

possible would be the torture. She'd do life for it - gladly.

'Rose, are you in there? It's me, Ellie. If you're there, let me in.'

If Ellie had come to gloat she' d get her face stove in. The knocking on the door was persistent. At last Rose mustered enough voice to shout, 'Sod off. I don't want you or anyone. I s'pose that bloody Liz told you.'

'No, it's the talk of the place. Rose, I'm your friend: I want to help. You shouldn't be alone. Come home with me for the night.'

'I want to be alone. I don't need no one. Go away.'

'You don't want to be alone. You can't be. You've had a horrible shock.'

Rose forced herself to open the door then, knowing Ellie would go on until the bloody woman next door knew more than she did.

'I'm so sorry.' Ellie put her arms around Rose, after shutting the door. Rose didn't resist. She half-collapsed against Ellie's capacious breasts and began to sob.

'It ain't true. It's bloody lies. My Terry's not like that.'

'You come and sit down. I'm going to put the kettle on.' Gently and firmly, Ellie led Rose back to the sitting room. She sat beside her on the sofa, stroking her hair and telling her it would all be sorted out, then she went to make tea.

She returned with steaming mugs and urged Rose to drink.

'I'll fucking drink but not this muck.' Seconds later Rose drained the mug.

'That's more like it. Keep your strength up, gal. No running back into booze.
You got Carla to think of. You'll need her more than ever after this.'

'You saying I won't be with Terry? You think he's guilty?'

'No. We only know he's been arrested, and half a dozen others. It's been on the radio. My Ron heard it in the van, driving home and a neighbour told us more – he watched it all happening. He was working there, painting the outside of the flats. He recognised Terry. But you know what the fuzz are like round here - arrest you if you a piss in a milk bottle, only it could take time getting sorted. Come home with me for a bit - just 'til you're over the shock. You don't want that old bitch next door tormenting you, or anyone else in the block.'

Rose stared at Ellie, realising how serious were her concerns. She was a true friend - the only one she'd ever had. She put her head in Ellie's lap and sobbed with relief that she had someone to help her, someone who'd stick by her, someone besides Terry.

Chapter 12

It wasn't easy to concentrate. At the best of times Liz disliked board games. Not competitive she didn't have to try to lose Mayfair to Jack; didn't even have to apply *Granny's Rules*, which always made the youngest player the winner. She grinned. What message was Monopoly giving to a nearly five year old? She could imagine what some of her politically correct colleagues might reply. One had criticised Cluedo as trivialising murder, although her own ten-year-old child obsessively played violent computer games.

Frances, a local friend and frequent baby sitter, commented quietly to Liz that, while Jack was ecstatic that he'd won, he would have been endearingly unperturbed if he'd lost.

'That's it, then,' said Hugh,' bankrupted by my own son.'

'You can have all my money Daddy,' said Jack.

'Not this time, darling. If I get desperate I'll come to you. I think I'll have a drink, though. Coffee, girls?'

'Me too, please,' said Jack and followed his father into the kitchen

Exchanging grins, Frances and Liz packed the game into its box.

'He's so sweet and funny,' said Frances, fondly.

'Hugh? I'm not sure about that,' replied Liz, and they dissolved into giggles.

'Are you sure you want to baby sit tomorrow, Fran? It's a bit short notice.'

'Yes, that's fine. Anyway, it's time you two had a night out. Mind you, if Brad Pitt rings meanwhile, I'll have to cancel.'

'What's wrong with you two? If I didn't know better I'd say you'd been at the whisky.' Hugh put a laden tray on the coffee table.

Hours later Liz sat on the edge of the bed, staring at the face reflected in the mirror opposite as if puzzling over who it was. Panda eyes, hollows under the cheek bones, tightness around the mouth. At this rate she'd soon be finding grey hairs in the tawny mane - Hugh's name for her thick, brown hair. She stood up and examined her body. No stretch marks to tell of her hard-won childbearing, breasts still taught and high, but her shoulders and hips looked bony. She heard Hugh coming back from the bathroom and hastily pulled her nightdress over her head. She didn't want him to see her naked in strong light - not looking like this. She hastily switched out all but the bedside lights.

'Nice day,' commented Hugh, getting his pyjamas on. 'Glad you asked Fran round.'

So much easier than us being alone, thought Liz, like tomorrow night - out with two other couples, never just us. She got into bed and pulled the duvet up to her neck.

It was chance that she'd caught Rose at home. For days the answering machine was the only response to her phone calls. Rose and Ellie were just leaving, each carrying a plastic bag.

'I'm sorry to just turn up,' said Liz. 'I have tried to phone.'

'She ain't at home,' said Ellie, belligerently. 'She's staying with me. We came to get some things. We're off now.'

'That's a good idea. I'm glad you're not alone, Rose.'

Rose scowled at Liz and made to walk away.

'I need to talk about Carla. Could we do that for a minute.'

'What's there to talk about?' asked Ellie. 'Rose doesn't want anything to do with you.'

Liz saw the curtain twitch beside the next front door. Rose had seen it too. She turned back to her own front door and unlocked it.

'You'd better say what you have to indoors,' she said with a glance at Ellie, who was looking furious and said sharply,

'We want to get on, don't we? Get some shopping.'

'I'm sorry,' said Liz, 'but this won't take long.'

She followed Ellie and Rose into the flat and they all sat, upright and uncomfortable, in the living room.

'Rose, there's been quite a breakthrough for Carla. She's

made a new friend, a boy with a baby sister, living close to Fay. Carla's been asking questions about babies and showing a real interest.'

'Oh, yes. So what's this about?' said Ellie.

Looking at Rose, Liz said, 'Fay and I wondered if you could visit Carla. Give her a chance to talk about the baby, make some.....'

'More to the point, what about Carla coming home?' interrupted Ellie. 'She could talk to Rose all she wants then.'

'She won't come home here,' said Rose, now glaring at Ellie.

'Then it's time you got a new place. Months they've strung you along.' Ellie turned a furious face to Liz. 'If you'd found her a place she wouldn't be in this mess. You social workers are all talk. And what happens to the bloody so-called refugees? They get houses, benefits, the bloody lot, while the likes of Rose are dumped anywhere.'

'I feel as sorry as anyone about Rose's housing problem but we can't dictate to the Housing Authority - just make as strong a case as possible....'

'Not fucking strong enough. Thanks to your lot, Rose was on the verge of moving in with a bloody perve....'

'Shut your fucking mouth. My Terry's innocent.' Rose was clenching her fists. She could easily take a fling at Ellie, thought Liz, but that second Rose turned her wild gaze on her.

'It's your lot that's framed him, you and the pigs.'

'Rose, there were pictures on his computer. How they got there is up to the police to find out.'

'They'll say what suits them. Half of them's perverts. Don't you read the fucking papers?'

Rose's voice lost strength. She dropped her head and sat bowed, rocking slightly.

Gently, Liz said, 'A police officer, a nice woman, Andrea Grant wants to talk to you so we'll need to know where to find you.'

At once Rose's head shot up. 'What's she want to talk about. I'm not saying anything against my Terry. He's done nothing wrong. Never even met my Carla.'

121

'That's what she wants to hear - from you. Once that's settled you shouldn't need to be involved. For Carla's sake and yours and the baby's, it's best to distance yourself....'

'What d'you mean? You think I've done with Terry? He'll be out soon and we'll be together.'

Ellie put a hand on Rose's arm. She flung it off.

'Rose, you need your Carla with you. They can't keep her if there's no reason. You tell them the truth - that Terry never met her, let alone touched her. I'm a witness to that - to what you said just now.' Ellie was now staring challengingly at Liz.

'Let's talk about Carla, Rose. She wants to see you. She doesn't know what's happened to Terry and doesn't need to know. Will you ring Fay and arrange something?'

Liz received a look from Rose of unnerving loathing. Somehow she'd have to see her alone. Ellie's presence made further talk impossible.

'Will you be here for the next couple of days?'

'Dunno.'

'Let me know, will you? The idea is to keep the police off your back as much as possible. If you cooperate they'll leave you alone.'

If looks could slit throats.... With that unpleasant thought Liz left.

Her tossing and turning awoke Hugh at around two o'clock.

'What's wrong? Aren't you well?'

'I'm okay.'

'You can't be.' Hugh switched on the bedside light and sat up. He looked tired and cross.

'You're worried about something. For Heaven's sake tell me what it is, then we might both get some rest.'

Liz shifted up the bed. She wanted to talk, describe yesterday's visit she'd been reliving, but she was afraid mention of her work would lead to a row. They'd been so tetchy with each other lately. It would be so easy to turn away, bury her face in a pillow. She stared ahead, silent and alone.

'I can't stand this. You're never with me. It's as if you're miles away. God, that pal I had whose wife was having an affair - he described this sort of thing.'

Liz nearly smiled. 'I'm not having an affair.'

'I know, but d'you see what I'm getting at? It must feel a bit like that.'

'I'm sorry. I have been thinking about work far too much, but....' She found her throat had gone tight. Tears pricked her eyelids.

'Yes. Go on.' Hugh's voice was rough with impatience. 'Talk about it for once. Christ, I'm your husband not the bloody News of the World.'

That was enough for Liz. She could stem the flow no longer. Tears coursed down her cheeks.

'I feel so awful - as if I've shattered someone's life.' She reached for a tissue from the box by the bed, and dabbed at her eyes. 'I gave a man's name - the partner of a client - to a police officer who's a member of a special unit, CeeOPS. He's now facing charges....'Her voice failed.

Still sounding impatient Hugh said,' Go on. Charges for what?'

She struggled. 'Being part of an internet child pornography ring.'

Hugh turned round so he was nearly facing her, his expression saying it all.

'You regret grassing on evil scum like that?'

'It's not as simple as that. The police were already on to him. Only it might have accelerated things.' Liz grabbed another tissue. 'Hugh, imagine you have nothing - no proper family, little education, brought up by a drunken mother. Suddenly, you're being treated as if you matter - you're someone. You've a man in your life who's promising you the earth - a home, a family, security for your expected child and the one you've already got....'

'And she's your client.'

'I know it had to end like this but I so wish it hadn't....'

She really sobbed then. Hugh put his arms around her. Gradually she regained control

'I so wanted her to have a break. She's got a lovely little

123

girl in foster care and she's worked hard on cracking her drinking, but she did it for him - the lover, because he gave her hopjle.'

'Which shows how hopeless such people are - not doing it for the sake of the child, or children.'

'You don't understand. If you think you're worthless you need something, or someone, to convince you you're not. The agencies who've been involved with her haven't been able to give her that. If we had she might not have needed this man.'

'So you're blaming yourself.'

'No. I just feel what's been done over the years has been pretty worthless for Rose.'

'Liz, you're the one with all the experience, training in psychology and the like, yet you can't see how bloody hopeless it is to endlessly pour resources into people who won't help themselves.'

Liz began to sob again. Hugh held her, stroking her hair. When her sobs subsided she said, 'This girl once said, "You're the first one I've felt I could really talk to - say anything to. You won't judge me," but what use was that? They need one-to-one support. They're often as vulnerable as their children.'

'But the child is really the first-line client - you've often said so. D'you think such parents should have their own personal social worker also? In an ideal world that would probably be right but who the hell, in this one, would pay for it? For God's sake darling, don't blame yourself for the system.'

Liz gave a small smile. 'Hard not to - I'm part of it - a rotten, failing system.'

Hugh sighed. 'Remember there are some rotten people who won't be helped. Maybe, the system fails some because it's spending too much time and money on the no hopers. Now you're going to tell me I sound like the rag press - dividing people into the deserving and undeserving but, before you do, I'm going to make a very large pot of tea.'

Suddenly Liz giggled. She put her hands on either side of Hugh's face and gazed at him. 'It's the contrast too that makes it so sad.'

'How d'you mean?'

'With this – with what we've got.'

Hugh smiled, kissed her gently then said, 'Something we mustn't lose sight of.' He was looking at her in a way she hadn't seen for far too long.

'Thanks for the sympathy but I'm not sure now about the tea,' she said and kissed him far from gently.

Rose agreed to see Andrea Grant on condition that it was at Ellie's house and Ellie was present.

'You're right gal, you need a witness,' said Ellie grimly, but she admitted the young policewoman with a friendly greeting and, even, offered her a cup of tea or coffee.

Rose frowned. How could she turn this into a bloody social call? It was a wonder she didn't invite her into the garden, where she and Rose had been soaking up the sun

Andrea Jones got down to business straightaway, declining a drink and choosing to sit on a hard, upright chair. She was young, Rose observed, and good looking.

'I just need to know if your daughter ever came into contact with an individual called Terry Brooks.'

'No. My social worker knows that. Why d'you need to ask me?'

'We don't want to involve you more than we have to, unless you want to be involved - give us information.'

'I can tell you you've got it all wrong. He's decent - wouldn't harm anyone.'

'I see you're expecting. Is it his child?'

'What d'you mean? Of course *she* is. Terry's thrilled to bits. Is that someone who harms kids? I wouldn't be surprised if you've set him up - covering up for one of your own....'

'Rose, a photo was found on his computer - one of your daughter.'

'I don't believe you. How would you know, anyway?'

'Social services identified the child as yours.'

'I knew that fucking Liz was behind this. I bet she supplied the photo.'

'I can show it to you. It's not nasty.'

125

Looking at Ellie who seemed unable to meet her gaze, Rose clenched her hands together, struggling to keep control of her anger. Why didn't Ellie speak up for her?

'Here.' Rose took the offered photo, not a proper glossy one but printed on ordinary paper. She nearly smiled. The photo showed Carla in her Flower Fairy costume, poised on the stage, delivering her lines. Typed underneath were the words: *Waiting in the wings - one for the future.*

'What's wrong with it? It's lovely. That was the one time Terry saw my Carla. Didn't even meet her properly then. He was taken bad.'

'It's the caption that concerns us - the writing underneath....'

'I know what a fucking caption is. That's what we was all doing - waiting. Months we've been waiting to be together and now what've your lot done to us.'

'I'm sure this is awful for you - a terrible shock. I have to say this to you, Rose - we must be sure you won't be letting your daughter near Terry Brooks.'

'How can anyone be near him? He's banged up.'

'He may be granted bail. It really is best if you don't see him.'

'That's my bloody business.'

'Perhaps you'd better go' said Ellie and stood up. Rose saw her exchange looks with P.C. Grant who then looked at her almost pleadingly and said,

'Take care of yourself and your daughter.'

'Yeah, both of them.' She patted her bulge. 'This girl's my Terry's and he loves her, so you lot fuck off.'

Ellie and the police officer walked into the hall. Rose heard the door being opened and quiet murmurings, then words clearly said by Ellie,' Don't worry, I'll try to talk some sense into her.'

'Cup of rosie, I think,' she said, returning to the room.

'Stuff your tea, I'm off.' Rose got to her feet. Ellie moved to the doorway as if to stop her.

'Get out of my way. What sort of friend are you? "Talk sense into me." What d'you fucking mean?'

126

'Rose, sit down. It meant whatever the woman wanted it to mean -talk you into keeping your distance - that sort of thing. You want them off your back, don't you?'

Rose sat - her legs gave her no choice. She was still furious.

'You don't believe my Terry's innocent. You was always funny about him - asking questions.'

'I was interested. You must see it was a bit odd that he never met Carla.'

'It's not odd - it was always too difficult. If he was a perve he'd be all over her, not wanting to wait 'til he could put a decent roof over our heads.'

'He had months to get to know her if he'd wanted to. You said he wanted to wait 'til Carla was back with you - didn't that strike you as odd? Why didn't he meet Fay and Liz - get their confidence?'

'Because we didn't want their fucking interference. I'm all right now. Why should we have to prove anything to them? Why are you on their side? You've always said they was bloody useless, not finding me a place.'

'I did - still do. If they'd re-housed you, you wouldn't have thought of moving in with Terry.'

'Why not?' Rose stood up. 'What difference would it have made? You're still saying he's no good, not to be trusted with kids. I'm not taking l this.'

She left the room and thundered up the stairs. Ellie followed and found her flinging her possessions into bags. Nothing she said prevailed upon Rose to stay.

'At least let me help you with your stuff,' she called from the front door, but Rose lifted one hand with the middle finger pointing skywards, and stomped away.

The flat smelt musty but she'd only been away four nights. It was the disgusting fumes from all over the block, penetrating the walls, the rotten window frames, coming up through the floorboards. What had that silly cow said who'd brought her here? Lucky!
One of the best blocks built since the war, just before they

went mad with tower blocks. All doors opening onto galleries, just like a street of terrace houses. Just like the old days of standing on doorsteps, hobnobbing with neighbours.

She'd tell her a few things now if she met her. Housing officials don't live like sewer rats, don't live in ghettos with disgusting smells, don't have to hear shouting and violent rows and have their ears blasted by Eminem and his bloody like.

Well, she wouldn't have to stand it much longer.... She stopped in mid thought: things *had* changed. She couldn't bear it, couldn't go back to loneliness. Couldn't bear the thought of losing the chance to move, of facing single motherhood again, of not having a partner to support her. But it couldn't happen like that: Terry would get sorted out. He was clever. He had money - plenty for a good Brief, but how long would it take?

The thought of waiting was unbearable. A terrifying blankness seemed to be stretching ahead of her and her mind felt as if it were being stuffed with cotton wool, filled with impenetrable fog.

She rushed to her bedroom and fumbled on top of the dresser for a small china pot. Taking a key from it she reached up with difficulty and unlocked the top door of the great, ugly wardrobe. Her fingers close around the bottle she thought she'd never need again.

Chapter 13

It would be sensible to take the car, Fay decided. Her friend, living opposite the school, often said, 'Use my drive. I'm at work. You won't block me.' For once Fay decided to accept her offer. It was getting late and, anyway, the last day of term always meant plenty to bring home, precious works of art, books and sports gear. She hadn't reckoned on a traffic hold up because a lorry had spilled planks all across the road. It would be quicker to walk but she could hardly abandon the car. Shame Rose hadn't phoned back. Fay told the school Carla's mum might collect her, but she'd confirm it. She'd waited as long as she could for the call then, when it hadn't come, she phoned the school office but there was no reply. With Rose being so unreliable she couldn't chance that she'd turn up, and she'd sounded a bit odd – maybe unwell or could she....

A tap on the window startled her. A policeman stood by the car. She wound the window down.

'Sorry, we've got to wait for lifting gear,' he said. 'School pick up, is it?'

Fay nodded.

'Then best to go back and round the avenue way. I'll see you out.'

Carla laughed at first, struggling with rolled up pictures, collages, and a cardboard model of The London Eye, made after an exciting school outing, but, as they hurried into unfamiliar streets, she became irritated with her burden.

'Help me, Mum. I'm squashing my paintings. Some are real good - my teacher said. I've got one for you. Where are we going? Why are we going this way?'

'I can't carry any more than I've got, lovey. We're going to have a lovely tea.'

'Where? This isn't the way to Auntie Fay's. We've come a long way from hers. We wouldn't get the train - why are we going to the station?'

Oh, dear, sharp as a needle was Carla. Where did she

get it from? Not her mum with her dozy brain.

'We're going to see my friend. You'll like her. She's called Ellie. Here we are. Just a little tube ride.'

'You hate the tube – you like buses. Does Auntie Fay know where we're going?'

'Course she does. Let's get the tickets.'

Good thing it wasn't quite rush hour. At least they could sit down and Rose needed to. As the train rattled off, she felt a surge of relief that also brought a feeling of physical weakness. She'd be all right. A good tea was waiting - she'd taken trouble. They'd eat then she'd have a rest and they'd talk - get things sorted.

Carla was looking around, reading the adverts above their heads and, when the train stopped, swivelling to see where they were and who was getting on and off.

'Why do we have to change?' she asked, when they got up to switch to the Victoria line. 'Where are we going?'

Carla was looking at Rose with suspicion.

'I told you - we're going to have a lovely tea.'

Carla followed her docilely into the train, but Rose felt uneasy, dreading her reaction when she saw familiar landmarks.

'My drawings are all crumpled,' she said, frowning. 'We should've taken them home.'

How that word hurt. Wanting to refute Fay's as home but even more anxious to avoid a row, Rose squeezed her arm and said, 'I expect we can iron them.'

The short journey passed in silence. Rose had no idea how to chat to her daughter. Why couldn't Carla help? Make it easier for both of them. Fay had got it wrong that she wanted to talk about the baby. She didn't seem to want to talk about anything.

'Here we are. Up we get.'

Outside the station Rose attempted to take Carla's hand, causing her to drop her model. Carla picked it up without a word. They walked towards the market where once Rose would have heard friendly greetings and funny comments: now she wasn't sure. How much had spread around? At Ellie's she'd lain low - not gone out: had refused to read a paper, watch telly or listen to the radio. If Ellie tried to tell her something, she instantly shut her up. Swiftly, she decided to avoid courting trouble and turned into Brand Lane. It would add a few hundred yards to their journey but they wouldn't see anyone who knew them. It was a safe but eerie route, skirting an area where a number of Bangladeshi families lived their shrouded lives. The women moved like solid black ghosts, only their eyes showed through slitted cowls. The men never met your eyes. Were they afraid of contamination? Today Rose and Carla saw nobody.

'Where are we going?' asked Carla.

'I told you - to have a nice tea.'

'But where? Not going to the flat?' There was tremor in Carla's voice. The eyes that stared at Rose were wide, frightened.

'There's nothing to be afraid of sweetie. We'll have a nice time. We can talk about the baby …the things we'll need to get for her. You'll like that won't you?'

'I'm not coming with you. I want to go to Auntie Fay's.'

Carla stopped and pulled her school bag from Rose's shoulder.' Mum, take me back.' Her voice was tremulous.

'No, we're going home. You belong there with me. Come on. Stop playing up. You're not a baby.' Rose's voice had risen. She put a detaining hand on Carla's arm, tightened it as she tried to twist away.

'Let go, you're hurting me. I want to go home.' Tears poured down Carla's face. Softening, Rose relaxed her grip. At once Carle threw her hand off and sobbing loudly ran back the way they'd come, dropping papers and scraps of cardboard from her disintegrating model.

Rose tried to run after her but managed only a few yards. Pain and breathlessness forced her to lean against a wall. A black-shrouded woman, coming slowly along the street, stopped beside her.

'Aren't you well?'

With supreme effort Rose replied, 'Out of breath.'

131

'Want to come into my house and rest? Only a bit along the street.'

Rose was scared. She couldn't see the woman's face, only her eyes. What was her expression? What was she thinking?

'I'll be all right. I was a bit silly, thinking I could run.'

There was a smile in the woman's voice as she said, 'Not a good idea in your condition. Not long to go, eh?' She put a gentle hand on Rose's shoulder.

'I live really close,' Rose said, 'but thanks. I gotta go - tea's waiting.'

She walked away but not towards home. It was like following a paper chase but the trail stopped short of the station. She picked nothing up. She couldn't bend and why should she?

There was no sign of Carla outside or inside. She stood for minutes, confused with worry and anger. Finally she bought the cheapest ticket and went through the barrier. Would Carla have known which platform to go to? There were people waiting but no Carla. She'd probably got the train. She was a bright girl, streetwise beyond her years. She'd been noticing all the stops on the way - she'd have got the right train.

Rose wasn't going to ask anyone if they'd seen her - what a fuss that would cause. She'd best get away. A bit more walking and she'd be facing the right way to take a train just one stop. No point in wasting the ticket.

Rose began to think about her position. She supposed she should let Fay know what had happened, but she hadn't told Fay she was bringing Carla home. She'd probably done the wrong thing. Liz would be told and they'd all talk about it, criticise her, especially since Terry's trouble.

Terry - he'd help her, tell her what to do. He'd be at his flat. They couldn't have kept him banged up. It wasn't what they did anymore. And why should anything have changed between the two of them? She was carrying his child. He had rights, whatever the bloody pigs said. She had to go to him.

The police car, with siren screeching, arrived as Rose

did, fearful yet drawn by the racket. The mob, banging on the iron gates, throwing paint onto the bars and shouting, 'Come out you fucking, cowardly perve,' made no attempt to run. They turned, baying, towards the police, challenging them get on with the job of arresting decent-living people like them, while releasing filthy scum to go back home and harm their kids.

A police van screeched to a halt alongside the car, spilling out policemen carrying truncheons. Scuffles were breaking out as Rose left. Sobs wrenched painfully and loudly from her chest, which felt so tight she could hardly breath.

She had to get home without seeing anyone she knew. This meant twisting and turning through a myriad of streets, getting lost, retracing her steps and coming close to exhaustion. She stumbled when she at last reached her staircase, grazing her knees, trailing blood along the passage. She nearly fell through her door, went to the kitchen and dabbed her knees with kitchen paper. It was the best she could do - she had no plasters - she'd just have to bleed. Her rescue remedy sat on the draining board. She seized the bottle and drank the vodka as if slaking her thirst with tap water.

Carla had no money for a train ticket. She'd heard bigger children boast about getting round the barriers but if she got caught she'd be handed over to her mum. She needed a mobile phone. All the other kids at school had them. She didn't even have enough money for the public phone. If she stayed here her mum might catch up with her. Crowds were surging for the trains: she'd have to lose herself among them - there was no other way. She edged towards a barrier. Could she sneak through, behind someone, as if she was their kid?

'Now then, what are you up to?' A man in uniform glared at her. 'Can't hang around here. Are you going through or not?'

She couldn't speak. Her throat felt tight. His manner frightened her.

'What's wrong, love? Lost, are you?' A big black man had appeared by her side. His uniform was the same as the nasty man's. His kindly tone was her undoing. She felt tears again trickling down her cheeks.

'Come on, tell me what's wrong?'

Gulping hard, Carla said, 'I can't get home. I got no money.'

'Where's home, love?'

'Near Chiswick - at Auntie Fay's. I want to go home to her. I don't want to go home with Mum. I don't live with her anymore.'

Carla saw the man exchange a worried look with his mate. Wasn't he going to help her? Would the nasty man stop him? She felt so helpless. The tears were pouring now.

'Ah, there's someone who'll help us, darlin'. Mary, over here would you, please.'

A young policewoman, standing a few yards away, turned towards the man, smiling.

'Do anything for you, Jim.'

'Young lady in distress. Got a bit lost. Wants to go to Chiswick.'

Mary smiled at Carla.

'Your office okay, Jim? Quieter there for phoning. Come on, love, we'll soon have you sorted out and safely home.'

As she was putting files away and hoping she might, with luck, leave in another five minutes, Liz's phone rang. Turning from a filing cabinet, she picked it up and heard Fay's voice.

'I'm so sorry, Liz. I assumed Rose wasn't going to pick Carla up from school after all, so I went by car and got diverted. When I got there I found Carla had gone - a bit early - with Rose. I drove home assuming they'd be heading that way, but there was no sign of them. I know she has every right to see Carla but...I'm afraid she 's taken her home. I've phoned her number three times but there's no reply. I've left messages on her answer phone.'

'Fay, I'll go there now. I'll ring you as soon as I know anything. Try not to worry.'

'Thanks. Once again you'll be late...Oh, my Lord....'

Fay's voice had tailed off, as if she'd turned away from the phone.

'Fay, what is it?'

'A police car's stopped outside.... Carla's getting out with a policewoman. Oh, heaven's, I'll have to go. I'll ring you as soon as possible.'

'Fay. I'll hang on here for your call. I'll come over if you need me.' Feeling sick with concern, Liz put the phone down and stood motionless beside her desk. She looked at the clock. It was six ten. God! She'd phoned Hugh at five thirty to say she hadn't left and could be another hour. She'd be rather more than that.

It had been a hellish day taken up with writing reports, and trying to convince a health visitor that reporting unexplained bruising on a ten month old might upset her relationship with his parents but how much more upsetting if the child had died. Three times the wretched girl had noticed bruising and ignored it and now the child was in hospital.

It was the hospital social worker who'd reported the matter to the Duty Officer and as it had occurred on Liz's patch it was referred to her straight away.

The door opened. Sheila stood in the doorway.

'The police called a while ago - on my direct line. They've picked up Carla Davis. She ran away from her mother and got stranded in the underground. I had several calls all at once, or I'd have told you. They're taking her to Fay's - for the time being. Of course the mother has every right to take her.'

Liz stared at her. 'Fay's just phoned me. She's been worried sick. Wouldn't it be safer if all such calls were handled by the Duty Officer?'

'The child was safe, and I had other more urgent matters going on. I think certain calls are more appropriate for the team manager. Now, I must get on. I can't leave just because it's after hours - lots more to do.'

And nor can I leave, thought Liz, with a disturbing feeling of savage anger. Yes, you're damned right. Rose has every right to take Carla.

Fay's call came minutes later. 'I feel awful about this.

If I'd got to the school a bit earlier I might have stopped Rose taking her - persuaded her to come back here.'

'Hardly your fault, Fay, especially if Rose made sure of being early. I'll have to see her - try to convince her it's best for Carla to stay with you a bit longer. This is when we could do with a Care Order. Of course, when Rose started to cooperate about the drinking and agreed to leave Carla with you, we had no grounds.'

They talked for several minutes, then Liz spoke to Carla.

'I'm going to see your mum, Carla. No, I don't think she'll be cross. She'll be pleased you're safe. I'll see you soon. 'Bye.'

Fay came on the line again. 'I couldn't say anything earlier as Carla came in - she's gone upstairs now, but the teacher who saw Rose briefly thought she'd been drinking. Not enough for her to intervene and stop her from taking Carla, but she said there was a kind of reckless look about her.'

'Almost inevitable, I suppose, her prop having gone. I'll try to see her now. Thanks so much, Fay. I'll ring you later.'

Liz sat down at her desk: whom should she ring first, Rose or Hugh?

She dialled Rose's number three times. Twice the answering machine came on but the third time Rose answered. Her voice was slurred.

'Who is it? You there, Carla?'

'It's me -Liz. Carla's safe and at Fay's. I wonder - can I come over?'

'No, you fucking can't. I told you I don't want to see you ever again. I want my child and you've no right to stop me. You and your lot framed my Terry.'

'That isn't so, Rose. All we want - any of us - is to keep children safe....'

'What d'you mean? You think my Carla won't be safe?'

'Terry's out on police bail. It's important you don't have contact until it's all been sorted out....'

'Don't you fuckin' tell me what to do. As soon as we can we're moving in together. His name will be cleared whatever you and the fucking filth think. And I'm having my Carla with me…you can't stop me.'

'Rose, will you promise not to let Terry near Carla. It'll be part of his bail conditions not to be around children. You wouldn't be helping him.'

'Stop telling me what to do. I know my Terry….'

'Rose, this is important. I want to come over - talk about Carla….'

'If you or any of your lot come near me you'll get a bottle in your face.'

The line went dead.

Liz sat staring at the clock on the wall opposite her desk as if willing the hands to move backwards. Going to Rose's now would be a waste of time. Clearly she wouldn't cooperate, yet it would have to be attempted soon. How soon? Carla was safe for a few hours. It had sounded as if Rose was in no fit state to go out. She longed to discuss this but all her colleagues had left. She'd have to talk to Sheila for what that was worth.

'Still here?' was the greeting she received.

'I think we need to go for an EPO in view of Rose's refusal to even consider Terry might be a sex offender. She won't agree to keep away from him.'

Sheila stood up, looked at the clock and checked it with her watch.

'Let's dissect the term: *Emergency Protection Order.* It's hardly an emergency now the child is back with the foster mother. Who does she need protection from? Her mother, or a man on strict conditional Police Bail?'

'Possibly both if Rose is drinking again.'

'Do you really think this Terry will risk jeopardising his case by making contact?' Sheila gave a little laugh. 'Then we come to the word: *Order.* Is it likely to be granted on such slim grounds?'

'It would be touch and go, but I have the confidence of local magistrates. I've applied for EPO's before and never had one refused.'

'Well. I think this one would be. Maybe, you're over-reacting. Distance yourself and look at it again.'

'I think you've made valid points Sheila, but I know Rose. Her behaviour's childish and erratic. Her needs will come first, and for her to have care of Carla in her present state would undo a lot of Fay's good work.'

'Well, we'll talk about it tomorrow. If anything drastic happens meanwhile the Emergency Duty team can get on with it. Now, I have a home to go to, don't you?'

Chapter 14

It was a strange letter: no address, no *Dear Rose* or *Darling* or anything -just straight into: *I don't want you to get involved. We must think of the baby and our future together so keep your distance until all this has been sorted. Don't try to ring me and definitely don't call round. Once it's all over we'll go on as before - the four of us.* And that was it: typed and with no signature.

It came by post - posted locally. He was protecting her and still cared about her -about all of them. It was going to work out all right. The police would be shown up for what they were - scheming liars. She longed to ignore his warning not to call but she'd phoned his number many times but there was never a reply - not even from the answering machine. Could she blame him when so many people were out for his blood? She could imagine the vitriolic messages he'd get.

She'd have to do what he wanted. She had an obligation to him - she was carrying his child. Suddenly, the enormity of what they were both facing hit her. She could be facing the birth alone. Might have to bring his baby back here where everyone would know. Why couldn't they go on with the plan to move? Why did that have to stop?

She had to talk to him. For hours she agonised over what to do. One minute not doubting the wisdom of his instructions, and the next angry that he was telling her to keep away and really saying nothing about himself.

She thought of Ellie and wished she could talk to her. Would she change her mind about Terry if she saw his note? She could do with her support now more than ever. After several swigs from the vodka bottle, she knew what she must do. She'd go round to Ellie's and chance another row. She couldn't stand being alone any longer.

She dreaded going past neighbouring doors. Only when she was well clear of the building could she relax, walk normally and hold her head up. After a few hundred yards she was struggling, her breathing was loud and her chest felt tight.

The weight of the baby was getting too much - how could she stand it for another three months? Then she began to think of the birth, the plans she'd had. Terry would be with her massaging her back, holding her hand, the way it was with the father on the video he'd got her. Only, would he - now?

Tears threatened. She gulped them back. She wasn't going to show her fears to Ellie.

She arrived at the house and rapped the door with the brass knocker. There was no sound of hurrying footsteps. She rapped several more times. It was a lovely day - Ellie was probably in the garden, but there was no way to it except through the house. The threat of tears was again imminent. She'd geared herself up for this meeting: she couldn't bear to just go away. Go where? To that horrible pit of a flat where the sun never penetrated?

As she turned to leave, the door was opened a few inches. Ellie stood behind it, her head wrapped in a towel. As if she'd seen Rose only yesterday, she laughed, flung the door wide and said, 'Sorry love, I was doing me roots.'

She stood back so Rose could get into the narrow hallway, then she closed the door.   'D'you need to finish them?' asked Rose.

'No, all done. Let's have a cuppa.' She gave Rose a hug, stared at her for a second, then looked away.

'You been drinking.' Her words were not said in an accusing way - just flatly, but Rose felt meek as she followed her to the kitchen.

'Sit down. You look done in. Hope you're eating, and for God's sake stop the drinking.' Ellie switched the kettle on and put tea bags into two large mugs.

Rose sank into a chair and rested her arms on the table. She could still feel her heart pounding. 'I've lapsed. I know it's all wrong but it's the only way I can stop thinking.'

'You'll do that all right. Like Dave the Rave says, your brain'll end up pickled. I think of his words every time I buy piccalilli. Puts me off buying it but my Ron likes it.'

As ever Ellie could raise a smile from Rose. Thankfully, she stirred sugar into the tea Ellie put in front of her.

'I'm scared Ellie. I don't want to be alone. I want my Carla back. I tried to get her back - pretended I was bringing her here but she ran off. Got taken back to Fay's by the police'

'You can bring her here,' Ellie said, enthusiastically. 'It'll be lovely. We've only got the two bedrooms but - 'til you get sorted and Carla gets a bit confident....'

Her kindness made Rose dissolve into tears at last. Ellie got up and pulled off several sheets of kitchen roll.

'Here, have a fistful,' she said. Rose took them, blew her nose and mopped her eyes. Ellie stood behind her, gently rubbing her shoulders.

'I want to show you something.' Rose rummaged in her bag and pulled out Terry's letter. 'You see, it'll be all right. Terry's not going to let us down.'

She took a large gulp of tea and she her face wore a broad smile as she watched Ellie return to her chair, sit down and start to read. Any doubts Ellie had would now go.

Ellie read the few lines slowly, then handed the letter to Rose without looking at her.

'Well, what d'you think?' demanded Rose, suddenly strong.

Ellie gave a long sigh. 'More tea?' she offered, still not looking at Rose.

'I want to know what you think.'

'I think you must be careful. Look after yourself - don't get dragged in.'

'That's what he means. He don't want me to be involved in this wicked, bloody case. That shows what he's like - just thinking about me and the baby. When it's all over we'll go on with our plans. It's all there, isn't it.'

'Yes, I s'pose it is. What if he's convicted, Rose? Will you still believe in him?'

Rose stared at her. 'He won't be. He can't be. Even if the pigs have planted something, someone'll grass on them. He's got important friends who'll see things are done right.'

'You haven't been reading the papers, or watching the telly, have you?'

This was true. For days Rose still hadn't switched on the

141

radio or the television. When she passed a news stand she shied away.

'What are you getting at?' Her tone was aggressive.

'The so-called important friends have been accused with Terry. The police have been watching them for months. It's big, Rose. It includes tourist sex. Children can be selected from photos before the holiday starts. Bookings are made all over Thailand and the Far East....'

'You believe all that shit? You can't see it's what the papers make up? They're covering up for what they do - the fucking police, the reporters....'

Rose was shouting. The door opened to reveal Ron, Ellie's husband in his work overalls, a bemused look on his round, kindly face. Rose stopped abruptly.

'Problems? Hullo Rose. Glad you're back.'

Calmly, as if she and Rose had been having a woman-to-woman chat, Ellie said, 'I suggested Rose could bring Carla here 'til she gets sorted. That all right, love?'

'Course it is. Poor mite should be with 'er mum.' Beaming at Rose he moved his bulk round the table and sat down beside her.

'Took your boots off, did you?' asked Ellie, getting up and pouring him a mug of tea.

'Don't I always, lover? Got standards, my wife. Surprised she don't line the kazi with paper before I sit down.'

Despite her anger, Rose giggled. She liked Ron, and for all Ellie's moaning about him, she was sure she wouldn't be without him.

He drank his tea thirstily then wiped hit mouth with the back of his large hand.

'Be nice to have your little maid here. We can keep her safe here - away from that lowlife. Gawd knows what he must've promised you to take you in like that. I'd like to string him up by his goolies and that would be too...hey, what's wrong, love?'

Ellie had reached across the table and prodded his arm, mouthing 'Shut up' but, already, he'd said too much. Rose leapt up, grabbed her bag and pushed herself painfully between the back of Ron's chair and the cooker. Ignoring the couple's pleas for her to stop she slammed her way out of their house - forever, as far as she was concerned.

Too angry to cry, she muttered aloud as she walked at a pace defying late pregnancy.

'Fucking traitors. What sort of friends are they? Fucking bloody hypocrites.'

She walked blindly, oblivious of passers-by stepping off the pavement, staring at her curiously or warily. If anyone had detained her she'd have hit out so it was as well that Brad called her name from across the street. For a second she hesitated, then hurried on but he called again from behind her. He was following her.

'Rose - stop. I want to talk to you.'

He drew level with her and took hold of her arm. She turned a furious face to him but he smiled and didn't loosen his grip.

'I been looking for you - been to your place several times.'

'Why? What d'you want?'

'Nothing. I thought you might need a friend.'

'Why? What's in it for you.'

He grinned. 'Not what you think. Not turned on by pregnant women. Rose, come and have a coffee.'

'No, I'm not going near the Kaf or the market.'

'We don't have to. Come on, over here. We're not known in this one.'

He gently propelled her towards a café a few yards on and across the road.

She found, suddenly, she didn't want to resist. The tears that had been held back by anger were nearly surfacing. She pulled back at the doorway, conscious of her appearance, but then allowed him to push her on.

She looked around. There was nobody she knew. He bought the coffee and sat opposite her, stirring several spoons of sugar into two beakers.

'Where've you been?'

'Ellie's for a bit. I'm back now. Nowhere else to go.'

143

'You could come to my place....'

He stopped, looked away then thumped himself in the chest. 'Sorry. I'm a bloody fool. As if you'd want to go anywhere near....'

'Terry's?' Her tone was truculent.

'I mean - too many reminders. Upsetting for you.'

'I don't want to be near anyone from around this dump. All talking - sure Terry's guilty.'

'Not much talking about him - not since yesterday.'

'Why, what's happened?'

'Bloke in the same block's been arrested for crack dealing. That's what they're all talking about now. All pretending they didn't know and half them on it themselves.'

'And you?'

'Have been but not any more. Can't afford it.' He looked around shiftily, then back at Rose.

'It'll be a nine minute wonder now, this business with Terry. Who knew you were going out with him except me and Ellie?'

'Loads of people, thanks to the gossiping cows in the flats. They know this baby's his, or they guess it right. I know they watched us. I bet they knew every time we went out.'

'Stick two fingers up at 'em, I would.'

'I got my Carla to think about. Don't want them saying bad things to her.'

She drank her coffee, watching him over the rim of her beaker. He wasn't bad looking, really. He'd even cleaned himself up a bit since she'd last seen him.

'It's been like The Bill in my place - police swarming everywhere. Bloody silly when you think half east London's on crack. They've always known it. Suddenly, they want something to do so they crack down....' He grinned and Rose found herself giggling. 'Rotten crack, darling - even by my standards.'

'I think you should be one of those stand-up comics - do the clubs and pubs. I've always thought you funny.'

'Funny you should say that. I've joined a gig; doing a bit of entertaining - singing, guitar playing, joke cracking. Local places, not up West - not yet.'

Rose beamed at him. 'That's great. You tell me where you're performing and I'll come and watch you.'

'I will - like a shot. We practise at my place sometimes, but that's a risk thanks to that perve. Men going into a flat - got to be up to no good.'

Instantly Rose's mood changed. 'That's exactly what you thought about my Terry.'

'I know. And wasn't I right? I'm no saint Rose. Anyone born round here is practically born into crime, but messing with little kids is...hey, where you going?'

Rose had got up. She stood glaring at him for a second then rushed from the café.

At home she collapsed on her bed after taking a large drink of vodka. Soon the soporific effects of the alcohol would assuage her pain but, meanwhile, she sobbed uncontrollably. Nobody understood - was on her side. She was alone and desperate for Terry's reassuring presence, or at least another note from him. He needed her surely, as much as she needed him. After nearly an hour she was feeling no better so she dragged herself to the kitchen and drained the last drop from the vodka bottle. She had to get more but first she'd tell that bloody Liz to bring Carla to her. She couldn't stand the loneliness and it was the bloody Social Services duty to restore her child to her. She couldn't stand the hassle of getting the child herself - stroppy little brat she'd been the other day. But she wasn't really like that. They'd changed her but she'd soon get her back into shape - she was her mum and that still meant something.

'What's wrong? That new referral - the pregnant heroin addict?' asked Liz. Dan was frowning.

'Yes. Clare, the hospital social worker, rang just before you came back. Another heroin addicted baby - born yesterday and nearly died.'

'Oh God.' Liz's phone rang. 'Liz Allan here. How may I help you?'

The response was scarcely intelligible but Liz

recognised. Rose's voice, slurred though it was. Her speech was so full of expletives it hardly made sense but Liz got the gist of her demands.

'Rose, I'll come to see you. We'll need to make plans. I can't bring Carla back while you're in this state....' She held the receiver away from her ear, wincing.

'Christ, that could be seriously damaging,' said Anne, the team's secretary, sifting through a filing cabinet on the other side of the room. She grinned and left, carrying an armful of files.

Rose raved for several minutes then stopped abruptly. She'd either dropped the receiver or rung off.

Minutes later Liz's phone rang again. Apprehensively she picked it up.

'Ellie here, Rose's friend,' said a robust voice before Liz could speak. 'I don't like social workers - bloody useless lot - but I got to tell you about Rose. She won't accept that Terry's a perve. I know it's awful for her but she's got to think of that poor kid. I still blame your lot for not finding her somewhere decent to live - she might not have met him if you had. I said she could stay with me - her and Carla, but she won't 'cause we won't go along with her whitewashing of that lowlife....' She paused as if she'd run out of breath.

'Thanks for ringing,' Liz said. 'Rose has just rung off. I'm afraid she's been drinking - wasn't making much sense. I want to see her but she won't have it.'

'Not surprising. Don't you tell her I rang. She'd never speak to me again - probably won't anyway.'

'That's a shame. She needs friends.'

'Well, I done my best - can't say the same for you lot.' The phone went dead.

Liz stared ahead, clutching the phone for a second, then replacing the receiver clumsily, got up and hurried to a metal tray above the filing cabinets.

'I'm going for it Dan,' she said, selecting some forms. 'If Sheila objects I'll go over her head.'

'What we discussed this morning?' said Dan. 'It won't be thrown out. The courts do some bloody silly things but they can't argue against this.'

Chapter 15

It wasn't just drink Rose wanted - she had to be near people. She didn't mind being alone when her brain gave up thinking, but now it wasn't co-operating. Her legs scarcely worked but they got her to a pub in The Green. The market people wouldn't be in there. Probably no one she knew. When she stopped drinking she lost all her old drinking mates. If she went back to old haunts they'd be there but what would they think of her? How much would they know? She couldn't go back. She'd be letting Terry down. Better to be here where she was unknown - just seen as a great, pregnant lump.

The packed bar was hazy with cigarette smoke. She didn't like the way the barmaid looked at her - suspicious like, as if she thought she'd had enough, but she passed a double vodka and tonic over the bar. Rose picked it up and looked for a chair. The only space left was on a window seat. She perched uncomfortably.

As she drank two men, seated at the bar, turned to stare at her. She stared back. One said something to his mate that set them both laughing. She looked away and drank again, swiftly. What the hell were they staring at? Not her stunning looks judging from her reflection in the mirror that morning. Hardly her figure - that disappeared weeks ago.

'Got a bun in there, darlin'?' said a voice to her left. She turned. Beside her stood a grizzled man, probably in his seventies. 'One, is it?'

Even with the stench of stale smoke all around she could smell him. He was disgusting. A great guffaw went up from the two younger men who'd been watching her from the bar.

'Too late, Grandad, someone's given her one already.'

There was more laughter and people all around were looking at her.

'Leave 'er alone,' said a woman's voice but Rose could only see men.

'Someone didn't. Room for one more, is there?'

Rose threw the glass to the floor. It rolled on the carpet.

'You're scum.' she said, and got up, grabbing her bag.

'You'll pay for it if it's broken,' called the barmaid.

Outside, Rose's bravado fled. Suppose one of them followed her. She didn't care anymore what Terry had written: she had to go to him. It would be for his good as much as hers. They'd be holed up together, looking after each other, showing the world they didn't care what the papers, the pigs, or the neighbours said or thought. If she was with him it would show she trusted him. Who better to know her man than the mother of his child.

The streets were unfamiliar and dark. There were pools of blackness between the outdated streetlights. Litter was strewn everywhere. To her left someone was retching in a doorway. A motorbike roared past, so close she felt a tug as if from its slipstream.

She was panting, her chest heaved painfully. The weight of her abdomen pushed into her groins. She'd probably give birth at Terry's. That thought made her want to laugh aloud but she hadn't the breath. She had to reach him. He'd keep her safe.

The pavement ran out: she was stepping into a void. She cried out and flung her arms wide to grab something but there was nothing to grab. Her forehead hit the concrete a fraction before her abdomen. Intense pain engulfed her for a second before she lost consciousness.

For three days she had only a vague notion of where she was. Concussion was a minor result compared with the blood loss, but it made her so muzzy-headed she retained only scraps of information about her accident. The really awful one stayed with her, tormenting her even while she slept, giving her terrifying dreams about searching for something - she wasn't sure what, and she never found it, but continued to race through dark, dripping tunnels getting increasingly frantic.

Sedated and transfused she lay in the women's surgical ward - thank goodness not in maternity - gradually becoming aware of fellow patients but not communicating with them, or anyone except to answer questions in monosyllables or not at all. The nights were horrible. She moaned and cried out so much a fellow patient told her to shut up, and she wasn't the only one in pain.

She wanted Terry but was scared to call his name.

'Are you sure there's no one we can contact?' asked a pink-faced, bespectacled young doctor - a question put to her numerous times, and with increasing urgency as if not naming a Next of Kin was shaking the hospital to its foundations. She glared at the man who looked like a kid dressed up for a fancy dress party.

'No - I keep saying I haven't got anyone.'

'You under stand what happened? The placenta became detached - that's why you lost a lot of blood and needed a transfusion. And we had to do a little operation - because it didn't all come away. I'm so sorry. The father…might he want some say…you know, in arrangements?'

Rose had been slumped in a chair beside her bed - now she shot upright. 'How many times do I have to tell you - I'm not in touch any more. It's my business. I've told that chaplain bloke I don't want any… arrangements. It's no one else's business. I thought you were a doctor not a bloody social worker.'

Already Rose had refused to see the hospital social worker. She should see her, they said, she could arrange counselling, services, surely Rose would need a bit of support at home?

A week after her admission they traced her medical records which revealed she had a daughter. Now the social worker had a reason for resisting Rose's refusal to see her. Her approach was firm but gentle.

'I wonder if your little girl is worried - not having seen you or heard from you. Did she know about the baby?'

'Course she knows.' Rose stopped. Carla was expecting there would be a baby. How could she understand that now there wouldn't be a little sister. Rose stared at the social worker, whose expression was full of concern. She covered Rose's hands with her much warmer ones and gently squeezed. She was older than Rose and wore a wedding ring.

She was all right then - married - looked after; so nothing in her life to worry about.

'We all want to help you. You've had a horrible time. Won't you let me arrange a bit of practical help for a few days? And would you let me tell Carla's social worker so she knows where you are - in case the little girl is worried? She won't say any more than you want her to.'

Rose nodded. She had to think of Carla now. As she thought of how Carla might react her own disappointment began to sink in. Minutes after the social worker left she cried for the first time since she'd been admitted.

'That social worker shouldn't have upset her like that,' said an indignant student nurse and drew a withering look from the ward sister.

'We've been worried sick that she's shown no emotion - expressed no grief,' she said. 'Thank goodness something's caused a reaction at last.'

Minutes after receiving the call from the hospital social worker, Liz managed to ring Fay.

'Oh no. It must have been a bad fall for her to lose the baby at this stage.'

'It was partly the fall, but there could have been other problems. The placenta came away - she could have bled to death. A motorist nearly ran over her and called an ambulance. She lost a lot of blood.'

'That's so awful. She must be devastated about the baby.'

'She's said very little. Wouldn't name Terry to the staff - hardly surprising. I'm so worried about her going home. I know her friend Ellie would have her but I don't think she'd agree. We had to go for the E.P.O in view of her attitude. And then we couldn't find her.... Oh. God, I've yet to talk to her about that.'

'That's going to be a difficult one. I don't envy you that, Liz. What should we do about poor Carla? She's even been getting quite chatty about the baby.'

'I'll come to see you as soon as possible. First. I must find out if Rose wants us to tell her or if she'll do it herself.

151

The ward will let me talk to her on the phone, in privacy I hope.'

Unable to stand to stand the torture of sleepless nights, veiled questions from the staff, and curious glances from fellow patient, in borrowed hospital clothes Rose discharged herself. It wasn't an official self-discharge - she couldn't face that, arguing, signing a form, threats of dire consequences to her health. She just walked out. She had to see Terry - couldn't be without him any longer. He was her life. Only she could tell him about the baby. She couldn't let him get the wrong idea. She hadn't neglected herself. If there was a problem the staff should have discovered it. He'd be desperately disappointed, she was sure, and they'd need to love and reassure one another. She'd go to him whatever he'd said.

She had just enough money for a cab. It was surprising her bag hadn't been pinched while she'd lain in the road.

She wondered if people had walked by - on the other side, or had thought she was a mere bundle of rags. The driver who'd called an ambulance wanted no fuss so Rose couldn't ring her up to thank her. It would be a woman, of course. A man would probably have accelerated on.

Handing over the fare to the cab driver, she suddenly felt dizzy. Her hand missed his and several coins fell into the road. She couldn't risk bending. She looked at him and saw concern in his eyes. He smiled, showing white teeth in his black, round face.

'Been poorly, love. You get on inside. I'll pick it up.'

She could have cried at his kindness. The dizziness passed and she walked normally into the yard. It was dead quiet. Not even a curtain twitched as she went along the gallery. She felt weak. Tackling the stairs had left her breathless so she went straight into the bedroom. Her reflection in the mirror on the hideous wardrobe shocked her. Of course the dust coloured sweatshirt and baggy skirt didn't help. She'd do herself up a bit before seeing Terry. Tomorrow she'd go when, with luck, she'd have had a decent sleep. It had been too noisy to sleep in the hospital. It hadn't just been the racket from other patients, snoring and muttering, but bloody inconsiderate nurses yacking and crashing about as if they were working in a supermarket.

She'd have a drink to help her get off, but would she find anything. On the kitchen draining board was one vodka bottle with a few swigs left in it. She carried it to her room, drained it, and sank down on the bed. Within minutes the phone rang. It was the hospital social worker. How the hell had she got the number?

'Rose, we were so surprised to find you'd left. You need to rest a bit longer.

'I told you I don't want help. Leave me alone. I was trying to rest.'

'Sorry if I've disturbed you. There's another concern too - you should still be having antibiotic cover. You'd have been sent home with them if you'd waited. Sister's here - she wants a word....'

Rose put the phone down. Bugger the antibiotics. Alcohol was sterile, wasn't it? She could always go to the Indian doctor if she felt queer. And Terry would help her.

She slept until nine o'clock and awoke hungry and cold. Christ it was cold for summer. She'd forgotten to switch the water heater on so had a brief cold wash then dressed carefully. A flowery dress Terry had chosen would be right, and strappy shoes that she hadn't been able to get her puffy feet into for weeks. They'd washed her hair in the hospital so that was just about all right, but her face needed some help - cheeks chalk white, eyes like a panda's. While she got ready she allowed only Terry to fill her thoughts. He was her lifeline and he'd be there for her as she would be for him.

She avoided familiar streets taking twice as long to reach Marlow Court. Only as she stood at the gate did she realise she had no means of contacting Terry and letting him know she was there. She'd phoned five times but no one answered. She stared through the railings remembering that awful rainy night when she'd needed him so much. It couldn't be like that again. No, it wasn't going to be. Someone was walking across the courtyard, a middle-aged man in a long coat. He got into a large black car and swiftly manoeuvred it to point at the gates. As it neared them there was a gentle creak and the gates moved inwards. The car slowly emerged and Rose rushed past it and into the yard. The gates closed silently behind her. She turned and gave a thumbs up sign.

Where now? She had no idea how to find Terry's flat but to her right was an important-looking door. Two steps led up to it. It was painted dark blue and the surrounding wood was gold. To the left was an entry phone with name slots alongside, but none said Terry Brookes and one was empty. She'd try any name. Someone must be in. She pressed the six buttons in turn, including the unnamed one, but no one responded. She began to panic. What else could she do? She'd find Terry's car. She moved away and scanned the courtyard. On both sides of the building there were garages and parking bays, mostly empty, but no sign of the long silver car.

'What are you doing here?'

She turned to find Brad standing yards away, a guitar slung from his shoulder.

'Brad, help me. I've got to find Terry.'

Brad stared at her. 'Something's happened - you look different.'

Rose sobbed as she blurted out her story and was hardly aware of Brad putting his arms around her, letting the guitar slip to the ground.

'I've got to tell him. I need him, Brad - he'll need me.'

'He lives in that block - they're joined together but, sort of, separate.' Brad indicated the building she'd just tried to enter.

'I tried there - pressed all the buzzers. Terry's name's not there.'

'For his own safety, I expect. Rose, I'll take you into my block. I think there's a way through. There's a service or fire door that might not be locked. Have to be careful. Not s'posed to use it.'

Still with an arm around her Brad took her into the left hand block. The entrance hall was smaller than she expected and not grand. It was carpeted and clean but plain.

'The lift, I think,' said Brad, and summoned it.

'It's coming,' said Rose, impressed. Brad grinned.

'I'll drop my guitar first,' he said pressing the third floor button.

'You been practising?' asked Rose.

'Going to.'

'You stopped for me. Why did you bother?'

'Why not? I like you.'

Brad unlocked his flat and led the way through a tiny hall into a sitting room.

'Should you be doing this, Rose? You look shattered.'

'I got to. I owe it to Terry to tell him myself.'

Brad put his guitar down on a sofa strewn with clothes: clean or dirty Rose couldn't tell, but something stale was polluting the room. Most of the floor space was covered with piles of C.D's, magazines and newspapers.

'Cuppa?' Brad offered. Rose shook her head. From the cluttered sitting room she glimpsed a kitchen that looked more like a garden shed.

'Is Terry's flat like yours?' asked Rose. Brad grinned.

'Shouldn't think so, would you? Never been in it. It'll be the same size but mine's a different shape. It's one the developers couldn't change. Wanted me out and paid lots of the controlled tenants to go but I think they'd run out of money when they got round to me. The other block - Terry's - was gutted.'

'What's a controlled tenant?'

'Someone whose agreement goes back years - to my grandparents in my case. I lived with Mum and Dad so they couldn't force me out when they died.'

'So you got two bedrooms?' asked Rose, remembering one of Terry's reasons for not letting her move in with him.'

'Not as you'd know,' Brad said, grinning. 'There's no bed in there, just stuff belonging to my parents. Haven't got round to sorting it. Only two years since they died.'

Rose came close to smiling. Terry would never live in a dump. She pictured streamlined spotlessness. When he went

155

back to her place for the first time he'd cleaned it from top to bottom - didn't ask her, just collected cloths and cleaning stuff from the cupboards and got on with it. He didn't reproach her but she knew he didn't expected to see it in a disgusting mess ever again.

'Feel up to it? Ready?' asked Brad. Rose nodded, thinking of what was ahead with both dread and longing.

Brad led the way along a corridor and up two staircases. The second one was narrow and uncarpeted. At the top was a door painted with the words, Fire Exit. Emergency Use Only.

'I reckon this is an emergency,' said Brad. 'Hope the bloody door isn't alarmed.'

It wasn't and yielded to several shoves from Brad's shoulder.

'Can't see a frail old person getting out of here if there's ever a fire,' he said, chuckling. Rose didn't think his mood was appropriate. She followed him down more stairs and along corridors, then he stopped in front of a white door, plain except for spy a hole, a brass number: twenty-two, and an empty brass name holder.

Nervously, Rose whispered, 'How d'you know it's the right flat?'

'I just do.' Brad pressed the bell. Rose stopped breathing . No response came from inside so Brad pressed the bell again. Forced to breath, Rose said, still whispering, 'He could be out.'

In a normal tone Brad said, 'Can't have gone far. On bail, remember.'

He cocked his head on one side, and frowned. Quietly, he said, 'I heard something,' and pressed the bell a third time. Now Rose heard something, a very quiet shuffle.

She called, 'Terry, please open the door. I've something to tell you.'

Not a sound came from inside. Rose stood on tiptoe to look through the spy hole. She screamed and stumbled. Brad steadied her.

'He's looking. I saw an eye - I'm sure I did.'

'The shit,' said Brad and looked through the hole into

156

blackness.

He rapped hard on the door. Rose was sobbing now and clutching his arm.

'Terry, you've got to come out. I've lost our baby. Our lovely little girl...she's gone.'

Brad drew her to him, trying to still the awful shaking.

'D'you want me to break the fucking door down, you shit? Haven't you the decency to see this poor girl?'

More silence. Brad let go of Rose and put his weight into the door. It didn't budge

'He can't be there,' Rose gasped between sobs. 'He'd come out - I know he would. I must've imagined I saw someone. He wouldn't do this to me.'

'P'raps you're right,' said Brad. 'Well, we've tried. You look terrible Rose. You've got to rest. Come on.'

But Rose was not going to give up. She pressed the bell and started to call, 'Terry, come out, please come out. I've lost our baby. I've got to see you.'

Her voice went higher and louder as she repeated her plea until she was shouting. Brad took her arm and tried to pull her away but she clung to the door handle.

'D'you want the janitor to come? He will, you know, and you'll get chucked out.'

She stared at Brad then let go of the handle and slumped against him, sobbing, the fight leaving her. He swiftly took advantage of the moment to half pull, half carry her to his flat, talking to her all the way, trying to comfort and encourage her.

'P'raps he was out, or had someone with him. We can try another time - when you're a bit stronger.'

He threw everything off the sofa and collapsed onto it pulling her down beside him. He couldn't be going to...not with her in this state....

'Christ, I'm done in and so are you. You're having that tea now - that's an order.'

Carla was playing with her local friends but expected home for tea, Fay told Liz and suggested an early visit giving them time to talk in private before Carla was delivered home.

'Rose is so erratic, Fay. Sally, the hospital social worker did her best but Rose refused help. We don't even know where she is. At least she agreed to us talking to Carla.'

'So she spoke to you?'

'No, that was through Sally. I think poor Rose has other things on her mind…'

'Terry…yes. Poor girl. Her world's collapsed. You don't think she'd do anything…silly…harm herself?'

'Lord knows. What can we do Fay when she won't allow us near her? I know she can't stand me but she won't see anyone.'

'And we know who'll get the blame if anything does happen,' said Fay. 'Ah, sounds like a Carla's back. I'll just go to the door.

Fay left the room. Liz heard her call thanks and good bye to Carla's friends then she returned, preceded by Carla who beamed at Liz.

'We've been in the park. Jamie can skate nearly as good as me.'

'Lucky boy. I expect you've helped him. Auntie Fay's been telling me how you went to the zoo.'

Carla giggled. 'I said Jamie shouldn't stay near the monkeys in case they thought he was one and he told me I wouldn't ever be in a zoo 'cause I look like a stegosaurus and they're extinct.'

Laughing Fay and Liz exchanged delighted glances, which quickly faded as they remembered their sad task. Liz waited until Carla was settled in an armchair, then said gently,

'Your mum's not been well, Carla. She had a fall and had to go to hospital for a few days.'

Looking at Liz, Carla's eyes were full of concern. 'She's better? Out of hospital?'

'Yes, but the fall meant she lost the baby. I'm so sorry, Carla.'

The child looked from Liz to Fay and back again, as if giving time for the news to sink in, then she gave a big sigh and said, 'I was wanting to see Mum's baby. I shan't see her now - ever. Carl and Jamie have a nice baby and I wanted Mum's to be like theirs. Poor Mum. When can I see her?'

Carla's calmness, and matter-of-fact acceptance of Liz's news nearly fazed the two women - it was outside even their range of experience.

'As soon as possible,' said Liz. 'Mum's still a bit tired.'

'We could go to the zoo,' said Carla. 'That would cheer her up.'

Fay's outstretched arms were empty only for a second. Carla snuggled into them while Liz took the initiative and went to put the kettle on.

Chapter 16

The sheets smelt - ugh! Of what she couldn't tell - just sour and disgusting. Rose pushed them down to her waist and saw she was fully dressed. Brad hadn't taken advantage of her then. She grinned. For all her misery she could still see the irony of her situation - lying yards from her lover in the bed of a man he despised, whose flat was filthy yet had been a haven when the lover's door had been shut against her. She looked around at the dark furniture, maybe dating from Brad's grandparents' time. The bed couldn't have been theirs - it was a futon and not very comfortable. On a low shelf near her shoulder was the only photo in the room. It showed a middle-aged couple, arms around each other, making silly faces at the camera. Brad's parents she supposed

Brad appeared beside her and put a mug of coffee on floor. He drank from another one and sat down on his bed.

'Sleep all right?' he asked.

'Not bad,' she lied. 'Did you.'

He grinned. 'Not bad. I'm used to sofas. Toast and eggs all right for breakfast?'

Rose sat up and reached for the coffee. 'Yes, fine,' she said, impressed. 'Nice of you, Brad.' She drank gratefully, even enjoyably although, of course, it was the bottled sort.

'That's what friends are for. I got some good mates - stood by me when I got busted. One's in the band with me.'

'You didn't get your practice - that's where you were going.'

'It's all right. I'm meeting them today. You can stay here, Rose, as long as you like. You look a bit flushed - like you got a temperature.'

'I'm all right. 'Spect it's the hot coffee. I'm quite hungry.'

'I can take a hint,' said Brad, grinning, and as he left the room Rose wondered how she could stomach anything cooked in that kitchen but she was really very hungry.

Two hours later, Brad regarded Rose with concern and suggested, 'I think you should call in at that doctor's as you insist on going home. It's on the way.'

'You can't just call in. You gotta make an appointment.'

'If you're really unwell they got to see you. I'll come with you.'

'I want to try Terry again,' said Rose.

Brad looked away.

'What? You seen him?' demanded Rose.

'No, just the car going out - ten minutes ago.'

'He was in, then - all the time.'

'No, not necessarily. He could've been out. I looked for his car last night - you were sleeping - but I couldn't see it. He's got a garage but he doesn't always use it. It was shut - always is - so I couldn't tell.'

'And what about lights in his flat - did you see any?'

'Yes, there's always a light that comes on when it gets dark - must be on a time switch. It means nothing.'

'We should've tried again. Why didn't you wake me?'

'Rose, you don't know how you've been. You were muttering. I think you were feverish. I still want you to see that doctor.'

The receptionist's attitude was frosty. Before replying to Brad's request for an immediate slot for Rose, she looked pointedly around the crowded waiting room.

'We have emergency slots but this isn't one.'

'Don't care about that,' said Brad. 'This girl's not well - you can see that.'

The woman glared at him. 'All right, I'll see what the doctor says, but you'll have to wait.'

'Don't care as long as we see someone.' Brad led Rose to a chair on which sat a child engrossed in a comic. Putting on a friendly voice Brad asked him,

'Going to see the doctor are you?'

The boy looked up. 'No, my mum is.'

'Then you don't need that chair if you're not ill, do you?'

The boy looked uncertainly at the woman sitting next to him. She glared at Brad.

'You gotta cheek,' she said, then glared even harder at her son as he stood up.

'Thanks,' said Rose, sitting down.

'Yeah thanks. Got some manners - from somewhere,' said Brad.

The receptionist called out, 'The doctor has agreed to see you, Miss Davis.'

'Of course,' said Brad. 'That's his job.'

Hostile eyes viewed them, clearly seeing them as queue jumpers. Wanting to ask them who they were looking at, Rose felt too ill to bother. Saliva was pouring into her mouth making her swallow frequently and her legs and feet began to feel ominously cold. Five minutes later she made it to the toilet in the nick of time. She was violently and noisily sick.

'All right, you can go in,' said the receptionist, when she emerged, shakily. Brad, who had followed her and waited outside the toilet door, ignored the people tut-tutting around him and picked up a magazine with half the pages torn out. Rose hesitated at the surgery door, glancing back at him and wishing he'd offer to go in with her, but he was glaring at the mother who had dragged her son back onto the chair the moment Rose vacated it.

'You are naughty,' said Dr. Sevingha, as if addressing a child. 'You discharge yourself from hospital, without any medication, and now you have a temperature. It's not too high but you need an antibiotic. I'd tell you to go to the hospital pharmacy and pick up what's waiting for you but, as you need to go to bed, I'll give you a prescription and they'll dispense it next door. I'm sorry for what's happened but you must cooperate with us.'

Rose emerged looking cross. 'Bloody cheek. I didn't come here to get ticked off,' she muttered.

'You were lucky to be seen, young lady,' said the receptionist.

'Selfish little cow,' said a woman holding a snuffling baby on her lap.

'Come on, let's get out of here,' said Brad. 'You never know what you'll catch in these places.'

The first thing Rose wanted was a bath but it would take at least twenty minutes for the water to heat. Brad made her take her tablets then rest on the sofa while he checked how much food she had in the fridge and cupboards.

'Hardly anything,' he pronounced. 'I'm going shopping. Better make me a list.'

Rose groaned. The last thing she wanted to think about was food. Vodka was her greatest need but she knew Brad would argue. She suggested a few basics and after Brad left she picked up the phone and rang Terry's number. There was no reply. She'd write him a note and Brad could deliver it or push it under his door. Once that was done she felt a bit better. He can't have been in his flat, yesterday - he'd never have left her in such distress.

In the bath Rose, placed her hands on her empty, flaccid belly and cried. She hadn't really looked at herself until now. She supposed she'd had a bath in the Old London but couldn't remember. For ten minutes she derived comfort from the warm water. If there's been an endless supply she'd have stayed there forever.

Brad returned and unpacked the shopping. When Rose appeared wearing her dressing gown, he sniffed and said, 'Lovely scent. Want anything to eat, Rose?'

She groaned. 'Don't mention food. I'm going to lie down. Will you deliver this – somehow?'

She picked up the envelope from the table and handed it to him. He glanced at the name on it, looked at Rose for a second as if he about to speak, then put it in the tatty canvas bag that nearly always hung round his neck.

'I'll come back later - see how you are. Have you got a spare key for me in case you're asleep?'

'Yes...no, Terry's got it.'

'Right. I'll get on now. Got to practise.'

'You won't forget my note.'

'No, see you later.'

'Yeah. Thanks.'

Rose went into her bedroom and sank onto her bed, lifting her feet that felt like lumps of concrete. She'd never been so tired. Sleep took over rapidly despite the turmoil of thoughts churning in her mind.

It was late afternoon when Brad returned. After the bell rang once, waking Rose, she heard him trying the door handle while calling her name. She lay for a minute wondering if she'd ignore him then, in case he had news of Terry, she went to the door and unlocked it.

'Did you give him my letter?'

'Not even inside the flat yet,' Brad said, grinning. He glanced back along the gallery. 'Best let me in. Next door's watching and listening.'

He closed the door behind him then followed Rose back to her bedroom. She got into bed - the safest place to receive news. Brad sat on the edge.

'Well, did you?'

'I didn't hand it to him. I pushed it under his door. I thought it safer than putting it in the block's mailbox in case his post is being read.'

'What d'you mean? Who'd be reading it?'

'The pigs, the Press, any old snooper living in the block.'

Rose frowned. 'You think he's guilty, don't you? You've always been funny about him.'

'I admit I thought it was strange - all those people going to his flat...'

'How did you know they was going to *his* flat? You're a snooper.'

'I knew because the janitor talked. He was sure it was a poker school he was running. I just thought he was a bit strange. That's why I tried to say something to you.'

Rose still frowned, still sure he'd condemned Terry the moment he was arrested. Ironically, Brad was her only link with Terry, and, in the absence of any vodka, she was desperate for a cup of tea.

'As she won't accept you, Liz, we'll have to get someone else to take her on - ideally from mental health, but they're as overworked as we are,' said Sheila, presiding over the team meeting.

'Sally hoped she'd accept practical support from the community team, but she's isolated herself and that really worries me. She's lost Terry, lost the baby, is drinking again - Lord knows what she might do,' said Liz.

'And eight months ago she did: she took an overdose, drank and nearly lost her life,' said Dan, not even needing to look at the summary in front of him. 'And who has kept her on the straight and narrow? Terry. And what happens to Carla while she looks for another Terry?

'Aren't we rather condemning this girl? Taking it for granted that she'll regress, not giving her a chance to prove herself?' asked Selma.

'Sadly, she has already regressed,' said Liz. 'Then there's the denial of Terry's activities.'

'But he hasn't been tried yet?' said Selma indignantly. 'We're condemning the man before anything's been proved against him.'

'Do remember, in Family Law the burden of proof is different, and suspicion may be enough to take certain steps,' said Sheila.

'Well, of course I know that and I think it's appalling. There should be the same burden of proof as in any other court.'

'So why have you come into child protection? Is it to glean information to strengthen your argument? Are you an undercover journalist and not Selma Mason, Social Worker?'

Despite the laughter that followed Dan's words, there was tension.

'I must remind you that you work to the rules of the Children Act and subsequent legislation,' said Sheila. 'If we think a child is at risk, or could become at risk, we have a duty to act on probabilities.'

'Which is why Rose's denial of Terry's sexual preferences is such an important issue. We need to think about what it tells us about Rose as well as what it might tell us about Terry,' said Liz. 'Rose is so immature. She grasps at dreams, going from lover to lover. She can't trust herself - depend on herself - so how can her child depend on her?'

'Try telling that to the bloody magistrates,' said Dan. 'Half the stuff we know about clients would be laughed out of court as pseudo psychology.'

'Then there's Carla's view,' Liz continued, grinning. 'She doesn't trust her mother.'

'But if they'd been re-housed it might have been different,' said Selma, drawing a furious look from Sheila and a remonstration.

'We haven't time to discuss what might have been. We're considering the probabilities or otherwise of getting a Care Order.'

'And keeping the poor woman's child in a nice middle-class home, meeting the stereotypical ideal,' said Selma, looking meaningfully at Liz

'Oh for God's sake leave your class prejudice out of this,' said Dan.

Liz grinned. 'I'm not sure that Fay would agree with your classification, Selma.'

'What we have to decide is: although the EPO was granted - and clearly Liz's report satisfied dear old Sands – will the same considerations justify going for a Care Order?' said Dan.

Sheila looked annoyed. Dan was pulling the meeting into some order - her job. Thank God for Dan, thought Liz.

'The reasons were the denial that Terry might be an abuser, Rose's drinking starting again and taking Carla away without any prior discussion, terrifying the child. Then there were Fay's observations of Carla's behaviour - nightmare's starting again, clinging behaviour....'

'Yes Liz, because the poor kid was being taken back to that flat,' interrupted Selma.

'For God's sake, if we'd succeeded in rehousing Rose what guarantee would that have been that she'd have changed her behaviour? Why is Carla terrified of that flat? Because her mother left her night after night to go out drinking. There's the strongest danger that will happen again.' Dan was clearly angry.

Brenda, an experienced social worker in her late forties, a listener more than a talker at meetings, then spoke up.

'Are we in danger of holding back just because the

magistrates might chuck it out? There's always that danger when we're dealing with probabilities. We can't prove something that *might* happen. I've got faith in Liz's ability to put a well-reasoned case....'

'Here, here,' said three out of six people around the table.

'And she's got the approval of our lawyer,' Brenda continued. 'And Carla's wishes would be paramount in the guardian's report. Let's just pray that dear old Bob Sands is sitting, if the day ever comes.'

'If only the general public knew the knife edge we walk on to get a kid into care - but no - we're snatching them off the streets, dragging them from their beds....'

'Dan, we've no time for the soapbox,' said Sheila. 'Plenty more to get through.'

'Sorry it's not something stronger,' said Liz, bringing a tray of tea and coffee into the office. 'You did say coffee, Brenda?'

'Yes, please.'

'Three requests - one my own - and I can't even remember. God, I don't know what's happening to my brain.' Liz put the tray down and handed the mugs around.

'Overload, 'said Dan.

'Plus stress,' said Brenda. 'It's hard to switch off however professional we try to be.'

'That's just it. I know our first responsibility is to children but it doesn't stop us wincing as we drive nails into the parents' coffins.'

Dan grinned. 'Elegantly put, Liz.'

They all drank for a moment. Brenda sat in a spare chair alongside Liz's desk and looked appreciatively at the wildlife posters relieving the monotony of sickly green walls.

'Wish there was room for another desk in here,' she said. 'You'd have me wouldn't you?'

'Like a shot,' said Dan. 'Hell next door, is it?'

'I can't open my mouth nowadays without being accused of having some *ism* or other. I had my head snapped off this morning for mentioning my neighbour's blind granny and her guide dog. I should have said, "visually impaired senior citizen".'

'And her canine carer, no doubt,' said Dan, grinning. 'I know whose words those were. What kills me is the way these kids come out of training, knowing it all, correcting our terminology, and sure we're eaten up with every sort of prejudice imaginable.'

Brenda laughed. 'Who could be more prejudiced than that chippy young Eastender who thinks you can't empathise with clients if you don't live alongside them? God, where's the girl's imagination? They're all hidebound by rules, these younger ones.'

'And who, nowadays, would have the guts to climb through a loo window to get access to a child?' said Liz.

'You, was it?' asked Brenda.

'No, our former boss - aided and abetted by Dan.'

'And she nearly got stuck and ripped a good skirt. Good job she was pint size or we might have needed the fire brigade. That was a few years ago when we were basic graders together. You've got to respect spunk like that.'

Brenda laughed. 'The sort you'd follow into the firing line. We don't hear about the Denise's - just the types who won't go into dirty houses for fear of catching something. In my last job a colleague got a post in a hospital team - thrilled she was, then backed out - afraid of infection.'

'There's nowt stranger than ignorance,' said Dan.

'And speaking of which,' said Liz, 'if Rose had moved into a flat with Terry, I wonder how long she would've been blind to Terry's sexual interests.'

'The old story,' said Dan. 'You love someone so you're visually impaired as to their naughty little ways - no don't laugh....'

'Then don't make me,' said Liz. 'You're right - the Knight's armour couldn't be tarnished. We've got to get that Care Order. Not until Terry's locked up can we be sure of Carla's safety'

'And then only until yet a new lover boy comes on the scene,' said Dan.

'Hopeless old cynic,' said Brenda.

'Prejudiced through and through,' said Liz and dodged a flying missile - a paper dart made out of Local Authority headed paper, of which Dan kept a useful stock.

'Late again' had been Hugh's greeting to Liz. It irritated her. Did he think she enjoyed battling with rush hour traffic, missing time with her son? Surely, her reverting to part time hours had made things easier for him.

When Jack was asleep, the dishwasher stacked, and Hugh had poured his customary thimble-full of whisky, she asked,

'You want me to give up, don't you? I think you've turned into the sort of man who is jealous of his wife's job.'

Hugh sighed. 'That's not true. I know the job means a lot to you - I accept that, and I know you can't fit it neatly between nine and five....'

'Eight thirty.'

'All right. I just hate the way you come back shattered.'

'As I would if I were a doctor, or a lawyer or a police officer. And if you worked in a City practice you'd come back shattered. You'd be late sometimes because clients needed to see you after hours. It's easy for you to moan when your work's under this roof, you don't have to travel and you are your own boss.'

'Don't you think that has its drawbacks? I don't get a regular salary whether I work my arse off or just sit on it - I have to work damned hard.'

'Right, we'll get an au pair, because, whatever you think of my job, I do bring home a regular wage. Clearly, you've had enough so why can't you be honest?'

'It's not that. I just hate the way it's taken over your life. I appreciate your being part time, but what's that? Cramming five days work into three. I'm not angry with you - just the bloody system.'

'Are you sure, Hugh? I can't do any more than I have done - they won't warrant fewer hours. Your attitude is just adding to the pressure. Give up private practice, get a job

169

outside and I'll be the dutiful housewife. Then I can have a turn at nagging you for being late home, having out-of-hours meetings....'

'For Christ's sake, you're distorting things. I just want it to be a bit easier.'

Hugh left the kitchen, exercising restraint by not slamming the door. Liz, several times more tired than when she arrived home, sat at the kitchen table and tried to make sense of their argument but failed. Should she have given up work for at least five years? If Hugh had worked for a firm she probably would have, or worked part-time with the help of an au pair, but being at home with Hugh working under the same roof had never appealed. This scene happened all too often. She was sick to death of it. Something had to change but what? Her brain felt too addled to think anymore. She'd think about it tomorrow, then, remembering Scarlet O'Hara's famous last lines, dissolved into a mixture of laughter and tears.

Chapter17

Rose hurried to the door the moment the post hit the floorboards. She extricated a brown envelope, recognisable as coming from social services, and threw it into the bin. Then she scrabbled through the rest - flyers for double-glazing, garden landscaping, cheap car tax - scrunched them up and threw them after the other rubbish. Howling, she fled back to bed.

'Give it time,' said Brad, arriving in late afternoon with a loaf and a pint of milk. 'It's been dead quiet. Not a sign of him.'

'You said he couldn't go anywhere.'

'He can't, well not far. He's got to go shopping - no, I doubt if he's doing that.'

'Why not?'

'For safety - people are out for his blood, Rose.'

She pictured the baying mob, the paint thrown at the gates.

'Has there been another demonstration - people trying to break in?'

'No, the police clamped down hard, but that's made people very angry.'

'You did give him my note?'

'Yes, of course - well, not to him - I told you, I put it under his door.'

'You telling the truth?'

'Yes, why shouldn't I? Want a cuppa?'

No, she wanted vodka. 'Yes, all right.'

Brad went into the kitchen. 'Want anything to eat?' he called.

'No, not hungry.'

She'd had nothing but a cake and some crisps, probably at breakfast time. She had little appetite - different from when she was pregnant. That thought made her tearful. Brad came in with her tea and found her sobbing into her pillow. He rubbed her shoulder for a while, then she felt his weight on the mattress beside her. She curled into a tight ball, hedgehog-like, only she had no protective spines. Brad lay still, not touching her.

After minutes, he asked, 'Anything I can do?'

She straightened up and wiped her face on the duvet cover.

'Drink your tea while it's hot.' It was a command but said like plea.

She sat up and drank.

'You can come to my gig tonight. Might cheer you up. Only down the Green - at The Eagle.'

'I want to send another note to Terry or try to see him again.'

"Don't trust me, do you?'

'I want to see him. He was out last time - he must've been. Let me try again, please, Brad.'

He sighed. 'All right. We'll go to my place, then on to the gig, but you mustn't make a scene.'

'I won't Brad, I promise.'

She spent at least an hour getting ready, taking more trouble than she had for ages - well, since Terry was arrested. Getting into jeans she'd been unable to zip up for weeks brought on a little weep; so she had to reapply mascara and eye liner. She rubbed blusher on her cheekbones. It gave her face an instant lift and emphasised her eyes - wonderful eyes, Terry'd often said. A filmy pink blouse with a scooped fringed neckline contrasted well with dark blue denim. It was one of Terry's first presents to her.

'Great,' enthused Brad when she emerged into the sitting room. He had been immersed in car racing on the telly but leapt to his feet and bowed. With mock civility he offered her an exaggeratedly crooked arm and pretended to swing an imaginary umbrella, as ever reducing Rose to giggles.

At the sight of Marlow Court's huge metal gates, Rose's confidence dropped. They seemed to symbolise the barrier that had arisen in her relationship with Terry. Although they slid open at Brad's touch it seemed as if in mockery. Brad caught her arm and firmly led her to his block.

'No point in trying his entry phone,' he said. 'It's not

working.'

'How d'you know? You've spoken to him.' The latter
was said accusingly.

"No, I haven't. Why won't you believe me? I saw the
janitor this morning and he told me.'

Brad unlocked the door into his block and led the way to
his flat. Rose wrinkled her nose at the smell of stale curry and
beer and....

'You been smoking pot,' she said, sniffing hard.

'So what? Got to have something - no booze - no bird.'
He was looking at her, eyebrows raised questioningly.

Rose looked away from him, grinning. Nor will you get
one living in this filth she wanted to say, but she couldn't risk
it. He was her link with Terry.

'Got to change,' said Brad. 'Then we'll try Terry.'

'I'll find the way. You needn't come.'

'No, best not, in case we bump into the janitor. I got
more right there. Help your self to anything - watch telly. I'm
off for a shower.'

Miracles, thought Rose and picked up a music
magazine. After scanning a few pages without interest she put
it down and listened. Water was rushing from beyond the
dingy bedroom. She got up, silently closed the bedroom door,
walked across to the hallway and let herself out into the
corridor. Now, which way, left or right? Maybe right - yes, up
a staircase and along another corridor - but more than one
corridor? A door opened ahead and a woman came out. She
looked forty, was heavily made up and dressed like a classy
hooker - as Terry might say.

'Lost, are you? Not seen you around.'

Rose swallowed. 'Um, no I'm a visitor. Just having a bit
of a walk while he's in the shower.'

The woman grinned. 'Say no more darlin'. Enjoy
yourself.'

She walked away, disappearing round a corner.
Nervously Rose followed. It was the only way to go and at the
turn was a door she recognised, a narrow, cupboard-like door.
She opened it and saw the second staircase. The fire door at

173

the top yielded to her third push and she was through - through into Terry's block. She felt excited. So close now but she could still go wrong. They'd gone down, hadn't they, then along? Down just one floor? She hurried and felt her breathing increase. She stumbled on the last stair and grabbed the rail just in time. The numbers were wrong - thirty-one, thirty-three - and on the other side, thirty-two, thirty-four, thirty-six.... Oh no, the wrong floor! She turned round and saw the numbers were getting lower to the right. Twenty-eight, twenty six....She was there - at the right flat - number twenty-two.

She stood listening but the sound of her breathing intruded. She leaned close to the door. No sound inside - or was there? A chink or clunk of something - a bottle perhaps - being put down? Afraid of getting no response she hesitated then, more afraid of losing this opportunity, she pressed the bell and stood away from the door, to one side. Footsteps approached.

'Who is it? Stand where I can see you or go away.'

She obeyed, full frontal, smiling. 'Please let me in, Terry.' She tried to keep the desperation put of her voice. 'I want to see you so much.'

There was silence. He'd unlock the door, surely. She'd hear the lock turn and maybe a chain being unhooked. Still silence.

'Terry, let me in. I must talk to you.' Her voice rose. She couldn't help it.

'Rose, you mustn't come here. You're doing no good. I'm sorry about...everything going wrong but you're not helping.'

'I've lost our baby...and you don't care.' She began to sob.

'I do care. I was really upset but I can't do anything about it....'

'You can - you can let me in. I want to be with you.'

'Stop it, Rose. You're not helping either of us. Just go away.'

'Terry, I want to be with you. I hate what they've done to

you. I want to be with you…like we said we'd be.'

'That was then. It's different now. You've got to stay away. That's the way you can support me. Stay away if you care about me.'

She heard footsteps walking away, heavily, emphatically. It was as if he'd slammed a door in her face. Now she was crying loudly, helplessly, wanting to lie down on the floor and curl up.

'Oh Christ. You'll get me chucked out. You promised you wouldn't make a scene.'

Brad was beside her. She turned her ravaged face towards him, imploring him to help her.

'We've been here before,' he said, roughly. 'I'm not getting myself chucked out for that shit. Come on, you're coming back with me.'

Rose was too helpless to resist. Crying had exhausted her. Brad led her, stumbling, back to his flat, his hand clamped on her arm all the way. He almost threw her inside the hall.

'How could you? The bloody janitor's already suspicious 'cause of my questions about Terry. I don't want to be linked with that fucking perve. And doesn't this tell you what he really is? Not even willing to open the door and face you.'

'Stop it. I don't want to hear it…'

'No, 'cause you won't face the truth.'

Brad shut and locked the door behind them.

'I got to go in five minutes, and you're either coming with me or going home.'

'I want to go home.'

'Right, but you'll have to go alone. I'm nearly late for my gig.'

Then Rose noticed his gear - spotless cream jeans, a scarlet shirt made of something silky, a studded belt on his hips and no baseball cap. His hair was still streaked with colour but - blimey - he'd washed it. And he smelt good. He walked into the kitchen and she sank onto the sofa, wishing she could lift her legs and stay there. As she couldn't - he wouldn't risk leaving her – she might as well go with him -

anything would be better than returning to the pit whatever she'd said. Her bag was on the floor. She leaned down, took out her compact and examined her face in the mirror.. She looked a mess. She'd have to wash all the streaks off and start gain.

They were good, *The Potboilers*. She had to admit they had something, but ignorant about all kinds of music, she couldn't find any words to say what it was. The stamping, clapping audience agreed, it seemed, for they shouted for more, and the landlord beamed and said the next drinks were on the house. A cheer went up and the group downed their guitars to take well-deserved advantage.

After being waylaid several times by gig groupies, from teenagers to grannies, Brad arrived beside Rose, pulled up an uncomfortable-looking stool and sat down. His mates had dispersed to join their girlfriends. Rose had already met them. They were all around Brad's age and spoken for, temporarily anyway, so would they think she was Brad's girl? She hoped not but was pleased he'd come over to her after his performance. It made her feel a bit important. Tonight, in The Eagle, he was a celebrity.

'You're good Brad,' she said. 'It's a great gig. Who's writes the words?'

'Malc, mainly, but we all chip in a bit. You feeling better, Rose?'

'Yeah, a bit. Glad I came.'

'Not drinking? I'm sticking to tonic water whatever the guys say.'

Rose covered her glass with her hand. 'Yeah, same here. They got to understand.'

'Going to Alco's Group tomorrow? I still got no choice.'

'S'pose so. Bit of a drag but it'll be nice to see Ellie.'

Brad had no idea she and Ellie had fallen out and she had no intention of telling him. It was none of his business. He'd even said Ellie wasn't much of a pal as she hadn't been to see Rose. She didn't refute this - let him think what he wanted.

'Take care of yourself, won't you, Rose. You're not well

176

yet. Must take some getting over.' Brad stretched out a hand and stroked her arm. She didn't pull away - he was being kind but she didn't want his sort of concern. She'd only come with him to try to push the rest of the day out of her mind and postpone returning home, to solitariness.

'I'm all right, Brad. I don't want to talk about it.'

'Sorry.' Brad removed his hand. 'Why don't you join the girls? They're a laugh.'

'Why'd they want me?'

'Why not? Malc's Hestor suggested it. Didn't like to see you sitting on your own.'

'I'm all right, Brad. I came to hear you.'

'If you're sure. Thanks for coming anyway. Not sure when we'll stop - p'raps when the landlord stops paying us - then we could go on somewhere. George has got his own place....Looks like we're off again.'

Brad stood up responding to a signal from George.

'See you later, Rose.' He joined the group on the little dais and they started to tune up. Once they were well under way, Rose went to the bar and claimed her free drink, vodka and tonic.

'On your own, love?' said a man standing next to her.

'My friend's the base guitar player,' said Rose. She'd noticed the man earlier. He was well dressed, in a navy suit, and handsome in a lean-faced way. He was tall and thin, fortyish, she guessed. It was hard to tell men's ages. Terry looked younger than thirty-five, having a round, boyish face but his fair hair was already receding. She must stop it - mustn't think about him anymore today.

'Good, he is. Strong member of the group,' said the man. 'Boyfriend, is he?'

'A friend,' said Rose, guardedly. She turned and went back to the seat she'd left but someone was sitting in it.

'I was sitting there,' Rose said. 'D'you mind?'

'Yes, I do,' said the woman, a hard-faced thirty something blonde. 'It's my usual seat.'

'Well you can get out of it, it's mine tonight.'

'I'm not moving. I'm a regular. Sit on that stool if you

177

must.'

'Now then there's no need for that, Zara. This young lady's been here all evening.'

Rose looked round - it was the man who'd been beside her at the bar. He smiled at her and she bridled. Young lady!

'Well, I ain't fucking moving for you. And you'd better not lay a finger on me, Jason.'

'As if I'd want to. Still hoping are you?'

The girl gave him a paint-strippng look. Jason grinned and looked towards the bar where the landlord was watching them. In a normal tone, not attempting to speak above the sound of the band, he said, 'Bert, over here please.'

To Rose's surprise the landlord, obviously a lip reader, came out from behind the bar and across to them.

'What's up mate?' he asked.

'The usual, Bert. This stroppy cow's pinched this young lady's seat and won't give it up.'

'I wouldn't mind pinching her seat myself but we can't have that, can we? Up you get, Zara, or out - and remember, I've the right as landlord.'

To Rose's surprise the woman got up, gave Rose a look of pure venom, told them they could stuff themselves and left.

'Sorry, love,' said the landlord to Rose. 'You get on with enjoying yourself. I'll find you a chair, Jason - more comfortable than that stool.'

Cleary Jason had some clout here. Rose was impressed. Bert returned with a chair and apologised again for Zara's behaviour, then said their next drinks were on the house. Rose was bemused. Why did he have to do so much? The nastiness wasn't his fault.

'I didn't mean to make a fuss,' she said and sat down.

'You didn't make a fuss, I did,' said Jason. 'Mind if I join you?'

'No, course not, and thanks. What's her problem, I wonder.'

'Stood up, most likely. Never mind her - what about you - not from this manor?'

'No, you a cop?'

'No, just act like one. What do I call you?'

'Rose.'

'Very appropriate too. Lovely name, lovely girl. Tell me all about yourself.'

Rose hesitated and sipped her drink, looking towards the group. She caught Brad's eye. He frowned and shook his head. She turned to Jason and told him as little as possible - she wasn't from these parts but very close, was between jobs and her daughter was staying with her aunt.

'I'm a businessman,' said Jason. 'Divorced with two kids. Your glass is empty, Rose. Let me fill it up.'

He filled it several times. Rose found herself telling him more about herself but not mentioning Terry, just that she'd been let down by a boyfriend recently. She was enjoying all the attention but her head felt a bit funny - not used to steady drinking anymore. Near to midnight the gig was playing its final piece and, every time Rose glanced in his direction, Brad glared at her. Let him glare. She had a right to a bit of spoiling after today and he should remember how he'd gone of on one, earlier.

'How you getting home?' asked Jason. 'Boyfriend taking you?'

'I told you he's not my boyfriend,' said Rose. 'Just a friend.'

'Then he won't mind if I drop you off. Can't go out in this. You haven't even got a coat. See the rain running down the windows?'

It was. Rose accepted the offer and without a glance in Brad's direction left with Jason.

Chapter 18

No doubt pleased with his boosted earnings, the landlord added twenty pounds to the agreed fee and asked The Potboilers if they could give him a regular slot. Brad said they'd ring him in a few days after checking their schedule, but was the first to give a whoop of triumph when they were clear of the pub.

'Good man, Brad. Can't appear too keen,' said George. 'Gotta seem in demand. Coming back to my place?'

Brad hesitated, not sure if he wanted to be the only one without a partner. They'd all be smooching, smoking pot and drinking too. He'd hoped Rose would be with him, either to go on to George's or back to her place.

'Didn't any of you see Rose leave?' he asked.

'I saw her with that Jason Flynn,' said Jodi, George's girlfriend. 'I don't know if she left with him.'

'Who is he?' asked Brad.

Jodi looked behind her then said quietly, 'You don't want to know. And if you did you'd keep quiet.'

Fearful of being sick, Rose was relieved when the car drew up. For once the sight of her flat would be welcome. Getting out of the car was hard; her head was muzzy and her legs were like sticks of jelly, nearly collapsing with the weight of her body.

'Steady. Hold on to me,' said Jason. She did, having no choice. The alternative would be to fall into the gutter. She let him get her up to her door then she spent minutes finding her key. Rain ran off the overhanging roof where the guttering was broken, turning the gallery into a stream. What a dump he'd think it was.

'Don't have to wait. I'll be all right,' she said, wishing the door would keep still and not move away when she tried to put the key in the lock.

'Can't leave you like this. Must see you indoors,' said Jason and took the key from her. 'There - no problem. In you go.'

He pushed the door open. She ricocheted off the jamb, painfully banging her elbow. He steadied her and closed the door behind them.

'That hurt,' he said, fumbling for the light switch. She said nothing, biting back tears.

He turned on the light and propelled her forward as if in his own place.

'Where's your bed? Looks like you need it.'

She didn't need to answer him. He picked her up and carried her through the open door to her bedroom.

'No, I don't know who you are,' she protested.

'Yes, you do. I'm Jason and you accepted a lift from me. Don't worry, I'm not a serial killer and I've never needed to rape a woman, yet.' He put her on her unmade bed and stood looking down at her, smiling.

The only light in the room came from outside and from the hall. Rain was spitting against the window. It wouldn't have been much fun walking home. Brad and his mates didn't have a car amongst them. She supposed she should be grateful to this stranger.

'You can have some coffee,' she said in a slurred voice. 'I don't think I can...'

'No, I'm sure you can't. You were drinking like there was a drought. Still, you got a gut for it.'

Rose said nothing. The room was moving, making her dizzy. She wished he'd go away. She gave a sudden shiver.

'Your clothes are damp. Better get out of them and properly into bed. You do that while I'll make the coffee. I'll find everything.'

She waited until he was out of the room then, with difficulty, undressed and put on a nightdress Terry had bought her. It was made of cotton sprigged with rosebuds. She mustn't think of Terry. He'd be shocked to see her like this, but if it hadn't all gone wrong she wouldn't be drinking. She got under the duvet and closed her eyes. That made it worse - the room moved faster.

Jason returned carrying two mugs of coffee. Rose shook her head, painfully, so he put one mug on the bedside table and drained the other. Through drooping eyelids Rose watched him. He was dark and mysterious-looking in the dim light. He looked at her and smiled, showing white, perfect teeth.

'You're very pretty Rose. Shouldn't be alone, a girl like you.'

He leaned towards her and cupped her face in his hands. 'Ever tried crack? Makes you feel better than alcohol.'

She stared at him. 'No, I don't do drugs.'

'You do. What's booze if it isn't a drug? You need it - that's obvious.'

'I don't. I been off it for months.'

'Not tonight you weren't. Was it 'cause you were alone - no one to keep an eye on you?'

'No. It's got nothing to do with you.'

'I think it has.' His voice had gone cold. 'You let me pick you up. You made it my business.'

'I didn't pick you up. You gave me a lift 'cause it was raining.'

He stood up and removed his jacket, then his tie.

'I can't,' she gasped, a feeling of nausea creeping upon her.

'You can.' He shed his clothes rapidly and stood beside the bed, fully erect, looking down and laughing. 'Got no choice by the look of it.'

He turned away for a second, taking something from his trouser pocket - a condom she guessed, then he got onto the bed and kissed her hard on the mouth. She gagged and he stopped.

'Okay, let's try something else.'

His hand was on her crotch, fingers probing, his mouth playing around her nipples. She was aroused but didn't want to be. She was being disloyal to Terry. But he'd told her to go away. He hadn't been there for her.

Jason's weight was on her, his hand pushing her legs apart, his chest grinding against her breasts as he thrust into her. He was a dark object above her as he raised himself to thrust harder. She was whimpering but he continued until he climaxed, saying, 'I needed that,' as if he'd just downed a stiff drink. He rolled off her, took a packet of cigarettes and lighter from his jacket pocket.

'Change your mind? Want one?' he said, with a strange smirk.

'No.'

She lay still, silently loathing him.

'Wonder what you're like when you're sober. D'you put a bit more into it? Can't judge you on tonight's performance.'

He sat on the edge of the bed with his back to her, smoking. Even in the dim artificial light she could see he was thin, his spine was knobbly. Terry had a wonderful body.

'I could do something for you, Rose. Put on a bit of weight and do yourself up a bit and you could become an earner. I got a club up West and I'm always looking for new talent. Got a kid, you said? Well, they cost a bit to keep.'

He turned to look at her. She closed her eyes. The illegal smoking in the pub hadn't bothered her but now the smell was aggravating her feeling of nausea. She gulped several times and pressed her hands against her breastbone, pushing against tightness and pain. She had to get to the bathroom but her legs weren't responding. Suddenly, she was violently sick over the side of the bed.

Jason leapt up, grabbed his clothes and rushed naked from the room. Seconds later Rose heard rushing water and exclamations of disgust. Sweat streamed off her as she sat with her head hanging above a pool of vomit. Jason appeared in the bedroom doorway fully dressed.

'You didn't tell me you were bleeding, you little tart. I'm off. Thanks for your wonderful hospitality.'

Brad was bored but every now and then a particular concern entered his mind and dispelled his boredom. The stories being related around him were distant rumblings - too familiar to warrant attention but the information he'd picked up concerning Jason did warrant it. He had a duty to pass it on, privately, to Rose.

There was a flurry of interest as Ellie arrived, full of

apologies for being late. Dave seemed unimpressed with her explanation and was about to hurry on but Brad took the opportunity to enquire about absent members.

'We should start with that,' said Joe. 'You know - like Parish notices.'

No one did know but agreed they should be kept up to date about members.

'Apologies from Brian and Jean,' said Dave, looking annoyed, 'but nothing from Rose. Let's get on.'

'She's not been well,' Brad.

'Tell me later,' said Ellie, in an undertone.

An hour later, in Kev's Kaf, Ellie's eyes widened in dismay at Brad's news.

'I didn't know any of this. We fell out - couple of weeks ago, perhaps, and all about that Terry. She wouldn't hear a word against him.'

'Nothing's changed there, only he won't see her.'

'He's got some sense. It wouldn't do his case much good if his relationship with Rose came out. It's obvious why he took up with her,' Ellie said with customary conviction. 'That's the way any Court would see it - he was worming his way in with a single mum....'

'And growing his own,' Brad said. 'She's in a bad way, Ellie. She came to my gig last night and went home with a crack dealer - he's notorious but nobody shops him. He runs a few girls and it's said he's got a protection racket going.'

'No wonder no one shops him,' said Ellie. 'She'll never get that little girl back at this rate. What can I do? She's probably still angry with me.'

'We could try going to see her together. I went earlier but there was no sign of her.'

'Best leave it 'til tomorrow. You free in the morning?'

Brad grinned. 'Too free for the likes of the Obscurity.'

Ellie looked bemused. 'The what?'

Brad laughed. 'Social Security. They're going to stop my money if I don't get a job soon.'

'Don't the gigs count as work?' asked Ellie, with a sly

grin.

'Christ no. Can't let them find out about those. Whatever I do I'm going on playing - it's cash in hand.'

'Well I won't shop you. I guess they'll be onto Rose now there's no baby,' said Ellie, sighing heavily as she stirred three full spoons of sugar into her cappuccino. 'We must do something, Brad - those bloody social workers are useless.'

'I think they try but she won't let them near her,' said Brad, reasonably but Ellie was having none of it. At once she was on her hobby horse.

'And why won't she see them? Because they've left her in that dump while they're re-housing all the illegal scum. And because they took her little girl away. It's their fault she ever met that perve.'

Brad avoided her gaze as he drank his coffee. Maybe the picture was a bit more complicated than the one Ellie saw. He remembered seeing Carla trying to help her mother along the street - blind drunk Rose had been. That was all of a year ago. He still felt bad that he hadn't helped, but he hadn't been much different himself in those days.

Aware that Brad had called - indeed his loud knocking and calling brought Rose out of her stupor - she made sure she appeared to be out, no radio or telly on, no lights, and she moved about like a ghost. The mess in her bedroom was disgusting, dried vomit on the side of her bed and on the rug and - oh Christ - the sheet was bloodstained. They'd said at the hospital it might happen - didn't always stop after a few days. It was that Jasper's fault for forcing her. She didn't give him any encouragement, she was sure, only she couldn't remember much about it. Her head was thumping but she cleaned up; after all lying down didn't help and the stench could start her throwing up again. Frequently she slumped - once with her head almost in the mop bucket.

Gradually, the events of yesterday returned to her conscious mind. Terry's rejection kept replaying, reducing her to helplessness. She'd never loved anyone the way she loved him - nothing could stop that feeling. He made her feel safe, cared for and valued. He hadn't abused her - hit her or used foul language. She'd felt she was someone for the first time in her life.

How could she go back to how she'd always been when she'd seen a different way of living? But she had gone back. She'd been with an abuser, known to her for a few hours. She was back where Terry had found her - in the gutter.

Chapter 19

'Why doesn't Mum come to see me? Is she still poorly?'

Fay turned from the washing up to face Carla who was sitting at the kitchen table. For a good twenty minutes she'd been making a birthday card for Fay's son, William.

'Your mum isn't very well but better than she was. Shall we go to see her?'

.   'But she's at home, not in hospital. That was ages ago. I'm not going to the flat. I want her to come here. Has she phoned? Did she get my card?'

'I don't know. We'll try ringing her again.'

Fay turned back to the sink remembering the care Carla had put into the Get Well card she'd made for Rose. Strange how, whatever her deficiencies as a mother, Rose had somehow produced a kind and caring child. It made Carla's situation the more poignant.

She asked for so little - a phone call, an occasional visit. Responsibility had been put on her so young, she was still learning to be a little girl. Was Rose learning to be an adult?

'We'll try your mum's number now, shall we?' Fay said more brightly than she felt. She pulled off her rubber gloves. Carla leapt up and scampered to the hall phone. Instantly, Fay regretted her suggestion. The last time Carla had dialled Rose's number she'd heard only slurred, unintelligible words. Gently, Fay had taken the phone from her and tried to make some sense of Rose's monologue. It was all about the fucking social services and how Rose was going to get Carla back. In the end Fay was forced to say 'Goodbye, talk to you soon,' and put the phone down.

'Mum was drunk, wasn't she,' Carla had said - a statement, not a question.

Fay hurried into the hall to find Carla was already holding the receiver to her ear.

'It's ringing,' she said, and it went on ringing until the answer phone came on with its recorded message. 'Mum, it's me, Carla. Are you all right? When are you coming to see me? I ain't seen you for weeks. Lots of love.'

Fay took the phone from her. 'Never mind, darling. We'll try later. Now, I'm going to ring James's mum - see if we can all do something nice together.'

The phone rang and rang, then went dead. Rose had turned the volume down on the answering machine. If there were going to be abusive calls she didn't want to hear them, let alone share them with the neighbours. She was sure the woman next door listened with a glass to the wall.

Rose pulled the duvet over her head. Then the banging and calling started. It was Brad. She looked down at herself - she hadn't bothered to undress. Brad would go on at her but she didn't care. She might as well let him in. She was hungry.

Brad put his foot in the door as Ellie appeared behind him.

'What are you doing here?' Rose stared at her furiously.

'I been worried about you. Brad's told me what's happened. I'm so sorry.'

Rose turned away and, unable to close the door on them, went inside. They both followed her.

'You don't look well, Rose,' said Ellie. 'Have you been eating?'

'Not as you'd notice,' said Brad and went into the kitchen.

Ellie grinned. 'Knows his way around,' she said.

'Meaning what?' said Rose.

'Nothing. All right if I sit down?'

'Up to you.' Rose remained standing.

'Awful news about the baby,' said Ellie, sitting on the sofa. 'I'm really so sorry Rose.'

Rose stared straight ahead. Silence was like a closed window between them. After minutes Ellie said,

'You can come back to us any time. It's not going to get...' her words tailed off as Brad came into the room carrying a tray.

'Toast,' he announced. 'I could only find bread. And tea.'

188

Realising her gut felt as if it was devouring itself, Rose sat in an armchair and allowed Brad to wait on her. After a few minutes of munching and drinking hot tea, she even felt quite warm towards him. She ignored Ellie.

'You've stopped coming to Group and people keep asking after you, 'said Ellie.

'Yeah. Wouldn't if they knew.'

'Knew what?' said Ellie.

'Don't pretend,' said Rose scornfully. 'Brad will have told you.'

'The Group wants people back who lapse, Rose. They'd welcome you.'

'Yeah, make them feel smug.'

'No, it would show them it's a struggle but can be done. Think how cross you were when you first came to Group - furious with Social Services just as Brad was with Probation. You weren't given much choice, but now you'd come willingly 'cause you know it can work.'

'You think I'm drinking all the time?'

Rose noticed a swift look pass from Brad to Ellie.

'There's bottles lined up in the kitchen like a platoon. And think of the way you knocked it back the other night. You pretended you were drinking fizz.'

'For Christ's sake, what right have you got to lecture me - smoking pot and God knows what else....'

'And as you've brought up drugs, perhaps you should know that you let yourself be brought home by one of the most dangerous pushers in the East End. And Jason isn't just a coke dealer, he's also a pimp.'

'Think he was trying to recruit me, do you? That's what you think of me? Well, you can get out.'

Brad put down his mug and stood up, clearly waiting for Ellie to do likewise. She sat tight.

'Rose, you won't want to hear this but I've come across a couple who knew Terry's parents when they were running a garage in Brentford. They sold up and went to live in Spain about ten years ago.'

'So what? They're dead.'

189

'No Rose, they're not.'

'I don't believe you. Terry's an orphan - he told me.'

'Then I don't know who sends this couple a card from Malaga each Christmas.'

Ellie stood up. 'Maybe you should ask yourself if he told you any other lies. It's not going to get easier for you, Rose....Look, you can still come to my place at any time.'

'Why should I want to do that?'

Ellie sighed, made as if to approach Rose, then turned and joined Brad at the door.

'See you,' said Brad and they both left.

Back from a picnic in the park, Carla was in high spirits. She had won every roller blade race against James who had gone into a sulk.

'I wish I could swim like you,' she'd said, when they were saying their goodbyes. Instantly, James forgot his sulk. Magnanimously, he'd replied that if she kept practising she could end up nearly as good

One to tell Bill Fay smilingly reminded herself as she chopped vegetables for supper. The phone rang. She put down her knife, rinsed and dried her hands and walked unhurriedly to the hall. It was probably a sales call - they usually came as she was preparing for, or cooking, a meal. Carla, whom Fay had assumed was up in her room, had already picked up the receiver. She turned huge, frightened eyes towards Fay, dropped the phone and ran to her.

'What is it, sweetheart?' Fay held the trembling child close, thinking, Oh God, not an obscene call. They'd never had one, hadn't heard of any made to friends or neighbours, but there was always a first. Carla burst into tears.

'All right, lovey. Let me hang up the phone then we can talk.'

Still holding Carla close Fay edged to the hall table.

'It's Mum. She says she's coming to get me and you can't stop her. I don't want to go. I want to stay with you.'

'You will. I'll talk to your mum, if she's still there. You go into the sitting room and keep Jess company, there's a dear.'

In spite of the state she was in, Carla did as she was told. Fay retrieved the phone.

'Rose, are you there?' There was no reply, just a buzzing noise, then a barely recognisable voice said,

'I'm coming for Carla. She's mine and she should be with me. I'm coming now.'

The line went dead. Fay glanced at her watch. Too late to ring Liz - anyway was it one of her working days? She'd have to ring the emergency duty team. She checked on Carla who was curled up with the cat, thumb in her mouth and no longer crying.

'You'll be all right, Carla, I promise. You can't be taken away from here. I'm just going upstairs.'

Carla looked up and gave a small smile, 'Mum was being silly, wasn't she? She was drunk again.'

Fay nodded and left the room. In her bedroom she rang the Emergency Duty Team, thankful to offload her anxieties and to hear that every effort would be made to contact Rose.

Where could she go to find company? She'd lost Brad and Ellie, she was sure. They wouldn't see things her way so they were showing her they were against her. They were no better than Social Services - yes, they pestered her but for what? To tell her what to do - what she couldn't do - that she couldn't have Carla. They lied to her when they said they'd been upfront - sending her letters when they couldn't find her and when she refused to see them. They were liars and torturers.

Such angry thoughts crowded her mind, jostling with painful longings. She wanted her baby - her Carla - her only baby now. She wanted Terry beside her, telling them to leave her alone - he would look after her. They were all the same, the police and social workers, ruining people's lives. Drink was now her only friend. It stopped the pain, stopped her thinking, helped her to go into a strange world where sharp edges were rounded and hard surfaces sagged and swayed. Sometimes it was a funny world in which there was more laughter than anger. The hurt started again when she was forced to leave it. She had to make sure it was always there for her - if she bought nothing else she had to have her means of escape.

Two days of peace, no phone calls from Rose, and a happy family day to celebrate William's twenty second birthday. Fay and Ron hosted an early lunch after which came a trip to Battersea Park. The day was rounded with a special tea with Carla importantly carrying in the birthday cake.

The screaming came around one o'clock. Fay's feet hit the floor with jarring force. She was beside Carla in a second, holding her shuddering body close.
When she felt her relax she laid her back on the pillow, gently stroking her forehead which felt damp and cold.

'You're safe, darling. It was a nasty dream.'

'I don't want him to come back,' Carla whispered.

'He can't. He's in prison - for a long time. He'd done lots of burglaries.'

'Not just him - all the others. I don't want them to come back.'

'Were they all in your dream?'

'Yes. The one who beat Mum kept coming in, shouting.' Carla began to cry.

'I'm sure he's gone right away,' said Fay.

'The police...took him away... but he'd hit Mum a lot.' Carla managed to get the words out between great, wrenching sobs.

'Did he ever hit you?'

'No. He kept saying ...he was going to... but he didn't. I was so frightened.'

'No need to be anymore. You're safe.'

'Mum won't take me, will she? You won't let her?'

'She can't, Carla. Your mum needs lots more help before she can have you to live with her. She's had a setback.'

'It's always happening. Mum says she's not going to drink anymore...she always starts again.'

'But she was better, for months, then she had an upset.'

'Did she want the baby more than me?'

192

'She wanted both of you.'

Fay gently dabbed Carla's face with a tissue, then tucked the duvet around her. A voice from the doorway attracted their attention. 'Meow,' it repeated.

'Jess! Have you come to see Carla?'

Carla sat up, leaned forward and held out her hand to the approaching cat.

'Can he stay? Can he sleep here?'

'Yes. Just make sure he has plenty of room.'

Carla's face creased with laughter. 'Auntie Fay, you know he always wants the whole bed.'

'Well, he's a V.I.P.C.'

'Very important pussy cat,' Carla translated, giggling as she relaxed back against the pillows.

'Warm drink?' Fay suggested.

'Please. I expect you need one as well.'

Chapter 20

'New Zealand!' Liz stared at Hugh. 'You mean emigrate?'
He laughed. 'No, just go for six months, maybe a year.
A job and house swop. Remember cousin John - Dad's
cousin? He was over for our wedding.'
'Of course I do. We always write at Christmas. He was
really nice. Strange he's never married.'
'His fiancée died in a light aircraft accident years ago.
He's never got over it.'
'Awful. Poor man. Go on - what's his suggestion?'
'You know, like me, he's an architect in a one man
practice - in Christchurch, South Island. Before he gets much
older, he says, he wants to come over for long enough to see
relations, get in contact with old friends, visit old haunts - that
sort of thing.'
'How could it be a job swop if he's gallivanting?'
Hugh smiled. 'He wouldn't be - not all the time -
anymore than we would, but we'd have weekends and
holidays for exploring. What an opportunity, Liz - no worries
about the house, Jack starting proper school there, not here...'
'You mean we'd go that soon? What about my job...?'
'No, I realise we'd need a bit more time, but what d'you
think? Will you even consider it?'

'You'll break my heart, Liz. You realise that. As I was saying
to my wife...'
'Oh God, Dan, don't make me feel any guiltier than I
need to.'
'We're past masters at guilt,' said Dan. 'Stock in trade.
That student we had on placement is applying - Wendy,
wasn't it? No experience but really bright. We shouldn't even
look at inexperienced people in this job.'
'She was reasonably mature,' said Liz. 'And attractive –
that'll compensate you.'
'Not compared with you, Liz. I suppose you might come
back.'
'Somehow, I doubt it. If I do return to social work it'll be

south of the river.'

'How about Battersea Dogs' Home? You be their could adoptions' officer.'

'Thanks, Dan, I'll bear that in mind.'

Grinning, Liz tidied her desk.' I just pray that I and the new person overlap. I must do a proper handover. It's going to be so hard if I have to leave clients in a vacuum. It should never happen.'

'Not your fault if it does. You've given enough notice. November you're going, aren't you?'

'Yes. You ready to go?'

'Sure.' Dan shifted a pile of papers into a drawer and locked it. Liz took a compact and lipstick from her back and swiftly repaired her makeup.

'That for my benefit, darling?'

'No - Tim's.'

Together they left the building and walked the few hundred yards to the pub they regarded as their local. To snatch a sandwich and a drink there at lunchtime was a rare treat - lunch break was usually spent seated at their desks, munching between phone calls. Tim, who had suggested meeting there, was standing at the bar chatting to the landlord.

'Great you could make it,' he said and shook hands with Dan, whom he knew only through Liz. Both men wanted to treat Liz so she sat down with two glasses of tomato juice in front of her. She was pleased they hit it off at once, both having a similar sense of humour, or sense of the ridiculous. An easy, relaxing forty minutes passed: talking eating and drinking, Liz wished they'd done this more often.

'I can't believe you're going away for a year,' said Tim. 'I'm eaten up with envy. Maybe I could do a job swop with someone in another country.'

'Like Queens, or the Bronx, or Chicago?' said Dan, grinning.

'He watches too much trashy television,' Liz said. 'Aren't there lovely jobs in the police force looking after wildlife? I'm sure I've seen a programme....'

She could hardly refuse to join in their laughter.

'Speaking of wildlife,' began Tim, in an undertone, 'a certain person, recently arrested, was also arrested nearly eleven years ago. His partner, a single mum of a small boy and girl, alleged he'd been taking indecent photos of them. There wasn't concrete evidence to back her allegations - the kids' stories were not considered sufficient, but it would be different today.' He paused, looking from Liz to Dan and back again, as if gauging the impact of his words.

Dan reached across the table and squeezed Liz's hand.

'Funny how that gut feeling is usually worth heeding,' he said. 'Most valuable tool in the job but you won't find a word about it any social work manual.'

'And the only guts we come across are spilt ones,' said Tim.

Liz grinned and shuddered.

Back at the office a piece of encouraging news awaited her. A note from Sheila informed her that four people, including Wendy, had been short listed for her job. Dan was right - in an ideal world only experienced people should be considered - but not much was ideal about social work. She smiled wryly, remembering Hugh's prediction that she'd be working within a month of arriving in New Zealand. Working she might be but it was more likely to be sheep-shearing than doing social work. A complete change was what she needed.

Rose's dilemma crept into her mind. What chance had she of moving to the other side of the world; what choices in life did she have? Her upbringing of Carla was a repetition of her own. She was the carer, never the cared for. No wonder she grasped every bit of attention men offered.

Dan interrupted her thoughts. He came into the room, grimfaced. In the pub he'd been hilarious. He picked up his briefcase.

'What's wrong?'

'It looks as if little Tom Ryder's being abused. The play group leader has reported seeing bruises on his buttocks on two occasions.'

'God! He's in a foster home isn't he - with the Willis's?'

'Yes. I'm off Liz. Can't leave this one overnight. And I'm

certainly not waiting for the bloody paperwork. I'm sure that stops plenty of referrals being made.'

Her sympathetic gaze followed him. If anyone could handle such a situation it was Dan, but it was every social worker's worst nightmare. There was no greater outrage than a child being abused in a 'place of safety'. She could imagine the repercussions if abuse were proved; the agonising over how such people came to be approved as foster parents and the guilt if some indicator had been missed.

And she was getting out, leaving a dear and trusted colleague to face the possible flack while she looked forward to beautiful scenery, a pleasant climate, and living in a country with one of the lowest crime rates on Earth.

But Dan, like anyone with a decent education and qualifications, had choices. If anything indicated the great divide in society it was choice. She remembered Dan's affectionate reminiscence about his retired father.

'If you've got to go round the bend in the course of your work, make it an S bend and get decently paid,' his father had suggested several times, but his attempt to persuade Dan to take over the family's plumbing business hadn't succeeded.

What choices did people have who'd been abused, deprived of an education, scorned by society? Opportunities tended to fall to the already fortunate.

This line of thought led her back to Rose. Of course she didn't *have* to drink, sleep around, keep company with drifters and abusers, yet what other blue print had she been exposed to since babyhood? That was a huge part of a social worker's task - trying to help clients see another way, a chance to break out of the system that, often, had enmeshed them since childhood, but it could only succeed if the clients saw a glimmer of hope, and found some motivation. For Rose that hope had been offered by Terry. He'd been the motivator. Would Rose seek another man, pin all her hopes on him?

At first Liz thought she'd got along reasonably well with Rose. She'd listened patiently while Rose vented her anger against the world at large, the Social Services and, sometimes, Liz personally. Knowing something of Rose's personality and her background she had no expectations of sudden changes. All she hoped was for Rose to see, in time, that she didn't have to be trapped in the system to which she'd been raised. If her self - esteem could be raised by beating the alcoholism and taking more control of her life, then she might see the worth in herself.

Rose's plight had always particularly touched her. She was more alone in the world than anyone else she'd ever known. To have the one person taken from her who was her sole relation was surely one of the cruellest blows ever dealt her? It had been an agonising decision - one of the hardest Liz had made. Would Rose ever understand why it had to be taken?

Part 2

Chapter 21

Only dimly aware of sounds, sirens screeching and engines roaring, voices calling but no intelligible words, Rose teetered on the edge, then slipped into the chasm of unconsciousness as the paramedics wheeled her into A. and E.

'Christmas Eve! Bloody hell - she might have waited until tomorrow when I'm off, or made a decent job of it,' said a young doctor. 'Haven't we got enough to do looking after the really ill?'

'That's a bit rough. We don't know the poor girl's story,' said the senior paramedic. 'All we got from the neighbour is her name, possible age, and she's known to Social Services.'

'Do we need to know more?' asked the doctor, lifting his hands in a gesture of hopelessness.

'God, Jon, five minutes in the job and you're already a bigoted old cynic. Where d'you want her?'

'Nowhere, preferably. Oh, Christ, put her in cubicle five. It's just emptied. After that it's the corridor.'

As Rose was lifted onto a bed, the paramedic handed a bottle to the doctor and said, 'Paracetemol. We've no idea how many she's taken, and there were empty Vodka bottles everywhere.'

The doctor's attitude changed. 'Bloody hell. God knows what she's done to herself. And if she hasn't already she may show it in the next weeks.'

Carla sat on the end the bed proudly watching Fay and Bill eating the breakfast she had prepared for them.

'And you haven't even opened your stocking,' said Bill. 'You are a kind girl.'

Carla smiled. 'I thought we'd do that together.'

'Lovely idea,' said Fay. 'And breakfast in bed - what a start to Christmas. Hmm, lovely brew, Carla.' Fay took a long drink from a mug like a mini chamber pot.

'I'll get my stocking,' said Carla. 'Yours are outside the door. I'll bring them in too.'

'Sure you won't need help? Forklift truck perhaps?' said Bill, and was rewarded by giggles and a hug.

'If only Rose would ring,' whispered Fay after Carla had let the room. 'You saw the lovely card Carla made for her - well, no reply - nothing from her.'

'And she can't be in any doubt you wanted her here for Christmas - a letter and God knows how many phone calls. Any news from the social worker?'

'Not for a couple of weeks. Poor woman's still settling into the job. Ssh …' Carla was struggling into the room, her arms full. Fay put down her cup and got up to help her.

'Carla, those stockings would fit a giant.'

Fay was on tenterhooks, which she managed to hide behind joviality. She expected Carla to say something about her mum, but not a word. She was sure she was thinking of Rose. Occasionally a bleak look would come into her eyes and she'd be quiet for a moment.

With the children, William and Annie, Bill's parents and Fay's widowed mother present, the house was full to bursting but a bed was still available for Rose.

Washing up with Bill after lunch, his mother and mother-in-law marvelled at the change in Carla. Last Christmas she'd been with Fay just a few days and they remembered her timidity and how she'd refused to join in with anything.

Overhearing, as she came in with more dirty glasses, Fay said,

'She and William are going to the park for an hour. He's dug out his old skate board from the shed and has bet her a box of Maltesers he won't fall off. It's fantastic that she's confident enough to go with him. And it'll be good for her to get some air.'

As if Fay hadn't spoken Bill's mother asked, 'And what if the mother takes her back - what then? All the good you and Bill have done…probably wasted.'

'She can't. Not without permission from Social Services. Carla's officially In Care,' said Bill.

'And any good experience is better than none,' said Fay, 'however brief.'

'Sad, the mum couldn't be here,' said Rene, Fay's mother. 'What chance did Rose ever have in life, I wonder.'

Bill's mother sniffed. 'Same as many people, I expect, no better, no worse. It's up to every one of us to make the best of what we have.'

'Some of us are a bit more fragile than others,' said Rene, and to Fay's relief a discussion was forestalled by her daughter calling,

'The Queen's speech is about to start. Come on.'

At five o'clock came the cutting of a beautiful cake, shimmering with frosted fir trees and lighted red candles, then there were more presents. Carla, triumphant at having won her Maltesers, snipped the small gifts from the branches of the Christmas tree and handed them around, then tackled the parcels stacked around the base.

Soon the room was littered with wrapping paper and string and Jess was protesting about the disorder and that there was nowhere to sit - at least that was William's translation of his high-pitched meowing. Giggling, Carla scooped the cat up and sat with him on her knee while they all watched the video: *The Lion, the Witch and the Wardrobe*, a present from faraway Liz.

The ringing telephone was not a serious interruption. Plenty of people ring up on Christmas day, thought Fay, reaching to answer the phone in her bedroom, where she was snatching a five minute break. Worries about Rose had, at last, been pushed aside in the busyness of the day - a day that had passed happily, with no more than mild and brief disagreements between slightly competing and very different grannies.

'Hullo, Fay here.'

'Fay, it's Dave Grey, from E.D.T. No panic, but I have to keep you informed. Rose is in hospital. She's overdosed on booze and paracetemol and is in The London.'

'Oh no. Is she going to be all right?'

'She's not in immediate danger but the damage might

not show for a while. You know it can be a lethal combination. I agonised about ringing you, then I wondered if you might have been expecting to hear from her, or see her.'

'Not expecting - just hoping. When did it happen?'

'Yesterday. I'm amazed the hospital bothered to call, nearly twenty-four hours on. I recognised the name at once - from about a year ago - one of Liz's clients. A neighbour hadn't seen her and called the police. Quite a hostile neighbour too - I remember - but she probably saved her life, again.'

'I hope you haven't had too many calls like this. Have you been busy, Dave?'

'No, amazingly this was the only call; so I've had a pretty good Christmas.'

They talked for a few minutes then Fay sat on her bed absorbing the news, wondering what, if anything, she should tell Carla. The last thing she wanted to do was spoil her day. She'd see what happened in the next few hours.

'Who was on the phone?' asked Carla the moment Fay entered the sitting room.

'A man called Dave.'

Carla made no response but at bedtime asked if her mum had phoned.

'Love, I'd have told you if she'd phoned. Unfortunately, she's not well. I didn't want to worry you and spoil your day because she's all right - just needing a bit of care.'

'Cause she's been drinking?'

'Yes.'

'She's unhappy. I expect she's lonely.'

'She has friends, Carla. Lots of people want to help her.'

'I helped her but I couldn't make her better. Would she get better now if I went to live with her?'

'No, she needs specialist help. I expect she'll get it now.'

'I'm scared of her when she drinks. She acts all funny. I wish she could have been here today.'

'I know - it would have been lovely to have you together.'

Carla snuggled down, pulling the duvet up to her chin.

'I like Christmas. Shame it's only once a year. Thank you for a lovely time Auntie Fay. Will Uncle Bill come and say goodnight?'

'Yes, of course. Sleep well sweetheart.'

They kissed and hugged.

'Thank you for giving all of us a lovely time, Carla. How am I going to keep my big boy off that skateboard?'

Carla giggled. Fay left the room, making sure the door was ajar so light penetrated from the landing. Carla still needed this reassurance.

Bill was lying on their bed, fully dressed apart from his shoes.

'Is she okay?' he asked, quietly.

'Yes. I told her Rose isn't well. She wants you to say goodnight.'

Bill sat up, looking pleased and surprised.

'That's a real breakthrough.' He got up and stretched, yawning. 'If I'm whacked, how must you be? Thanks for a lovely day, darling. You coped brilliantly.'

'I did have a bit of help, and I know you weren't just trying to impress your mother and mine.'

'Watch it, gal. You may need me again.'

Gently, he pulled a compliant Fay close to him and gave her a brief hug and kiss.

'Sorry, that will have to do for now. Can I cope with all these ladies needing my attention?'

Rose's reaction to finding herself in hospital was one of dismay then fury. She hated the staff, lumping them together as one interfering, manipulative body that had thwarted her attempt to achieve oblivion. Worst was finding out that the person who'd alerted the police was her hated neighbour. She'd always wanted to get rid of Rose so why did she mess up this opportunity?

She didn't just feel resentment - she demonstrated it. She pulled drip needles out of her arm, spat out pills and refused to drink bland fluids. Twice she tried to leave. The second time she was trailing a tube still attached to her arm. A night

204

security man grabbed her and tried to reason with her. She hit him, straight in the eye, but he still managed to hold her until help came along.

'You are still in danger. We cannot let you go for your own safety,' said a house officer.

'Bugger my safety. That's what I don't want. Let go of me. I gotta get out of here.'

Heaven knew what they did to her then, but something made her mind go all muzzy. It was assault, wasn't it? And holding people against their will was an offence. She'd sue them.

Dimly, she heard someone say, 'She's got energy - energy can amount to will. We've no choice.'

What were they saying? Choice about what? To let her go? No they hadn't a choice. She struggled to get out of the bed but something was stopping her. Her legs had lost strength. They'd drugged her - she was sure.

'You understand about the Section, don't you Rose? It had to be done for your protection.'

'You drugged me, didn't you? That's illegal.'

'No, you succumbed to the failure of your own body. Everything was explained to you but you wouldn't listen. If we hadn't taken the steps we did, we'd have been negligent.'

'But what about what I might want. I gotta record now - I'm a mental patient.

The psychiatrist smiled. 'You won't believe me but it gives you a chance to have a spell of rehabilitation in a beautiful place - in Dorset. You hate it here, I know, but Down House is like an old-fashioned luxury hotel - once it was a mini stately home.'

'A looney bin! I'm not going to no looney bin.'

'It's a rehab: place for people who have drug or alcohol problems. There's nothing compulsory about it. All kinds of people go there. And, honestly, it's five star of its kind.'

'And how am I going to afford that?'

'Not your worry. For a few people there's funding available. It's a great chance Rose - please take it.'

Rose liked Doctor Harris. For a start he was good looking, and he could make her laugh. He didn't blind her with science or lecture her - not like the silly woman who'd gone on about her liver and what paracetamol could do to it. Silly cow - didn't she realise Rose wanted it to do its worst? Rose told her this, vehemently, and she'd replied'

'You wanted to give yourself long and lingering death, did you? The major organ of digestion and purification in your body slowly breaking down, like a failure in a sewage system? I've seen it happen and it's one of the worst things I've witnessed.'

'It wouldn't have been like that anyway, only that bitch next door interfered,' said Rose furiously.

'Be thankful that she did. It wouldn't have been the quick end you wanted - not with the combination of drugs and drink you took. And if she hadn't got help quickly it might have been like the one I'm trying to describe to you.'

'Right, I'll make a better job of it next time. What d'you recommend?'

Rose reckoned the look the doctor had given her should have finished her off there and then. She hadn't come near her since.

Anything Doctor Harris suggested she was prepared to try but when she told him this he looked disappointed - not what she expected.

'Rose, you need to do this for yourself - for the sake of the life you've got ahead of you. You're young and - pretty.' He looked away for a second. She grinned. Was he embarrassed? When he looked back at her his face was quite expressionless. He continued,

'You have every chance now of making a life for yourself. Get well, build your health up and you'll find the rest will follow.'

'Like getting my Carla back and getting somewhere decent to live? Part of the package, is it?'

'You know we can't do that for you, but it's something you might achieve for yourself. You're a bright enough girl - if you'd only give yourself a chance ....'

He walked away, sighing. Was he fed up with her? She couldn't blame him. Poor bugger - he certainly earned his money. There'd been two new people in overnight, screaming and carrying on. She'd got hardly any sleep. A spot of rest in the country couldn't be worse than this.

Chapter 22

She hated the journey. Ellie and Ron's only vehicle was his van, which Ellie had
scrubbed out but still it stank of paint and turpentine, and smells that Rose couldn't identify.

Ellie had found out where she was via the local 'grapevine '. She'd told Rose this a bit evasively. She'd brought in flowers and grapes and magazines, and chattered so much there was no room for Rose to say anything. In a way, Rose was grateful - the visits made her seem more normal, like other patients who had visits from family and friends, but she felt awkward as well.

Ellie had said nothing about their rows. It was as if she'd forgotten them, but Rose hadn't. She didn't regret what she'd said to her - it was deserved, but she dreaded having to repeat her words. Whatever she had against Ellie, she had to admit she seemed to be her only a friend. If Ellie knew where she was, so did a few others - Brad, for example, but he didn't come in. It was Ellie who collected her clothes, washed and ironed them, and persuaded Ron to provide transport.

Ron drove and Rose, at Ellie's insistence, sat beside him. Ellie talked incessantly. After a few miles of tedious driving on the M3, Rose fell asleep, only to be prodded awake from behind when Ellie wanted a response to a question or to point out some boring sight.

Her spirits sank lower and lower. They were going miles from London - much further than she'd expected, right to the coast in Dorset. Names on signposts meant nothing to her. She's heard of the New Forest and Bournemouth but they were places as alien to her as Iceland.

'Not far now,' announced Ellie, 'we've just bypassed the "ancient capital of Wessex."' She giggled as if she made a joke.

Nearly an hour passed while Ron took two wrong turnings under Ellie's directions, then he gave an exclamation of triumph. To the left, off a narrow lane, was a pair of tall iron gates. Important looking with scrolls picked out in gold paint, they barred the way onto a long, disappearing drive. On either side of the gates was a sign: Down House

Ron stopped the van - he'd had instructions he said in reply to Ellie's question:

'How the hell do we get in.? It's bloody Fort Knox.

Rose shrank into the seat and wished she'd refused this 'wonderful opportunity'. The gates reminded her of the ones outside Terry's block.

Ron got out, pressed a pad in the wall and the gates opened allowing them to progress along the tree-lined drive that seemed miles long. Rose closed her eyes. She didn't want to arrive.

'God, look at that! Impressive, or what,' shrieked Ellie.

Rose forced her eyes open and saw a huge red house with lots of chimneys, and great pillars on either side of the front door. It was a studded door, a bit like the one to the Community Centre but the similarity ended there. This thought nearly caused her to laugh.

First out again Ron approached the door. It opened and a man walked down the wide steps and greeted him, shaking his hand. Then both men turned towards the van.

'Time to get out, Rose. Looks like you'll be to the manor born. Come on, can't get out until you do unless you want me to scramble through the rear.' Ellie prodded Rose's shoulder.

Ron took Rose's borrowed case from the van and reluctantly she shook hands with the man, Tom Buchan, an administrator he told them, then they all followed him in through the imposing entrance.

'There's a reception room here,' he said, opening a door just inside the outer hall. He stood aside while they went into a small comfortably furnished room. Piles of magazines lay on a low table and a large display of realistic-looking artificial flowers stood on the sill of the one window.

'You've had your explanatory leaflet, haven't you, Rose?' Tom asked. Rose nodded.

'Right, then you know the drill. You'll have a chat with the medical team then a guided tour, but first a cup of tea?'

He looked from one to the other, clearly including Ellie and Ron in his offer.

'Don't mind if I do,' said Ron, 'unless you've something stronger.'

Ellie frowned at him but Tom grinned.

'Make yourselves comfortable. Tea coming up.' He left them and Ron was the first to sit down.

'Cheeky devil,' said Ellie. 'You're not the patient.'

Within minutes a young girl arrived with a tray of tea and biscuits.

'What no Jeeves?' said Ron. 'Off today is he?'

'Excuse me?' said the girl in a foreign accent.

'Ignore him,' said Ellie, and helped the girl to pour and serve the tea. After she'd left, she commented, 'Not bad is it Rose? Better than you expected.'

Rose said nothing. She hated the place already. Ellie's incessant chatter filled the next fifteen minutes then she was collected by Tom and a nurse and had to say 'Goodbye'. She was tearful, wanting to go away with them, hating to see them go.

'We'll visit you,' said Ellie. 'We'll come really soon.'

Not soon enough. Wiping her eyes with the back of her hand, Rose followed the nurse into a huge inner hall. Tom walked behind – cutting off her retreat? A vast staircase and several doors led off the hall and they went through one into a bare passageway.

'I'm leaving you in good hands,' said Tom. 'See you soon.' He closed the door behind them and disappeared.

For thirty minutes Rose was asked questions about her health. How long was she in hospital, why had she been admitted, what drug was she on, how long had she been drinking? Her inquisitor, a middle aged doctor had reams of paper in front of him which, Rose was sure, held all the answers. All the information would have been supplied by the hospital. She felt irritated - sure she was being put through a test. The nurse, Lily, was present throughout. Once Rose glanced at her and saw she was stifling a yawn. She linked arms with Rose's as they left the room. Rose pulled away, seeing this gesture as patronising.

'I'm going to show you your room now,' Lily said and led the way back to the great hall. They mounted the massive staircase, moving upwards beside dark panelling on which hung paintings of old fashioned looking people. Noticing Rose gazing up at them, Lily said, 'People who once lived here.'

'What alcos and drug addicts?' said Rose, surprising herself as she and Lily giggled and exchanged their first connecting look.

In the bedroom her humour left her. Whatever squalor she and her mother lived in they'd always had separate rooms. She'd never shared with anyone other than a boyfriend. There were three single beds here. But the room was far better than she'd expected. Pretty floral curtains hung at the windows and matched the duvet covers, and the dark panelling had been painted cream and ended a third of the way up the walls. The rest was papered with a pale green swirly pattern. There was a view across the park through latticed windows that only opened six inches - Lily told her - so no chance of jumping out. The furniture was plain and clean looking, and two pictures hung on the walls - scenes of old-fashioned children, little girls in bonnets and pinafores, and boys in knee breeches, playing with hoops and a dog.

'Nice, isn't it? The bed near the door is free,' said Lily. 'Your roommates are Carol and Jen and Jen's also your mentor.'

'What's that mean?' asked Rose, suddenly suspicious.

'For a few days she'll help you to settle in. She's been here a month. She's nice.'

Rose looked away from Lily's encouraging smile. 'I don't want to share a room. I shan't sleep.'

'Sorry, but everyone shares. It's a big house but only has twelve big bedrooms. There are two tiny rooms for people going through severe detox: but they move in with others once they're through the worst. Look, Tom's had your stuff brought up. Let's unpack, then I'll take you to meet some of the others.'

A simple, friendly suggestion but unwelcome. She

didn't want a stranger handling her clothes. She positioned herself so all Lily could do was hand her coathangers from the small empty wardrobe beside her bed. Every garment she took from Ellie's suitcase had a link with Terry. She felt increasingly fragile and dissolved when Lily commented, 'What pretty stuff. Lovely colours. Goodness - cashmere!'

She sat on the bed struggling to regain control.

'It's okay. Best let it all out,' said Lily. 'D'you want to talk?'

Rose shook her head, grabbed a tissue, dabbed her eyes and blew her nose then a got on with the job.

Five minutes later she was on a tour of the house that ended with meeting other residents in a huge lounge. There must have been twenty people present, the majority men. Among them was Jen, her mentor. About the same age as Rose, she had a friendly, freckle-sprinkled face, framed by curly brown hair. She leapt up from her chair and extended a hand to Rose, who shook it tentatively.

'Hi, I'm sort of your minder for a few days,' she said, giggling. 'Goodness knows why they chose a scatty twit like me. Where d'you live, Rose?'

'Hang on,' said Lily. 'I want Rose to meet everyone. You'll have plenty of time to chat a bit later.'

They moved on. No one else's name stayed with Rose, and only one face impinged - that of a thin, neatly-dressed older woman who looked her up and down, unsmiling, and said, 'I hope you'll take advantage of being here. For some it's quite a privilege.'

Her meaning was clear: Rose was the wrong type. She would not fit in.

'And this is Bob, from Surrey,' said Lily, hastily, gently propelling Rose on.

The introductions over, Rose was left to sit next to Jen. Exhausted, all she wanted to do was close her eyes and drift away but Jen was a talker. Perhaps half an hour passed, during which she was told Jen's life story but heard none of it, then she stood up.

'Got to rest - lie down for a bit,' she said.

'We're not supposed to go to our rooms except to sleep,' said Jen.

'Yeah, well, that's what I'm going to do,' Rose replied. 'See you.' She walked a bit unsteadily towards the door.

'Right little madam, that one,' said the snooty older woman who had looked so sniffily at her. If Rose was meant to hear her words she didn't care - she was too weary and demoralised to respond.

She found her room more by luck than from memory. She stretched out on her bed but was feeling too irritable to find the oblivion she craved. Why the hell did people think they were all so interesting? She wanted to shut off from problems not be loaded with other peoples'. For just a few minutes she lay still then curiosity sidelined weariness. She got up and went over to the huge multipaned window. The view was mesmerising: a great expanse of parkland stretching away for miles then seeming to dissolve into sky. Clumps of trees relieved the bareness of the grass - huge trees, some dark and woolly-looking, others bare of cladding so their intricate shapes could be seen. A few familiar-looking birds flew amid the branches - pigeons, she realised, more streamlined than their London cousins. If she had to stay here, then outside might be better than indoors. Plenty of space to escape into and get away from unwelcome company. How strange - hadn't she been craving company recently? Yes, that was true but where had it got her? She'd been let down too badly to trust anyone ever again.

The door opened. 'There you are,' said Jen. 'Nice view, isn't it? We're lucky to be here, aren't we? It's just a mile from the sea. Sometimes you can glimpse it.
We need to go down now. The evening groups are starting.'

Rose stared at her. She sounded so upbeat.

'Don't worry,' said 'Jen. 'They'll let you take your time. You won't be put under pressure - not for a few days, anyway.'

Reluctantly, Rose followed her from the room. It seemed she had little choice.

Jen was right, she wasn't put under pressure but she still

hated being there. The leader, a counsellor called Greg, tried to draw her out, gently, from time to time but she resisted, avoiding eye contact and shaking her head. She looked all around the room while others were talking, noting the dark panelling that seemed to be everywhere. That was depressing in itself. She found herself observing the other members surreptitiously, although not listening to their stories.

Of the ten members six were men and three of them tried to dominate the group but Jen challenged them several times, accusing them of doling out unasked for advice. And what the hell qualified them to do that?

Rose had no idea how the session ended. All she knew was a voice in her ear was saying, 'Wakey, wakey. Suppertime,' and Jen's hand was on her shoulder giving her a gentle, if unwelcome, shake.

Chapter 23

Fay had far less contact with Wendy, Liz's successor, than she'd had with Liz. She'd visited a couple of times and seemed to get on with Carla. All Fay could conclude was that with Rose in rehab: and Carla safe, she had to concentrate on other cases. Carla and Rose were probably the least of her worries - and thank goodness. Also, she was newly qualified and paired with a mentor, who probably had some horrific problems to contend with.

What Fay wanted to know was how the social workers would feel about Carla visiting Rose.

'When will I see Mum again?' was a regular question, and Fay was stumped for a positive reply.

'Let's find a lovely card to send her, or you do one of your beautiful drawings,' was a response that always brought a smile to Carla's face and kept her busy for a while, but the question was being asked almost daily.

It could surely only do good for Carla to visit Rose in a peaceful setting and see how much she'd improved - if she'd improved?

Carla's nightmares had become more frequent just prior to Christmas. They were lessening but still very upsetting. After each one her drawings changed, showing scenes of darkness and with strange shapes. Drawing and painting had become her favourite pastime next to skateboarding with her friends.

Her teacher was excited by her ability. She'd asked Fay to encourage her to enter a competition entitled 'My Best friend', run by three local schools. Carla's drawing of Jess won second prize and she was photographed beside her picture for the local newspaper. Several people, wandering around the hall where the entries were on display, commented that Carla's was by far the best and should have been the winner. Fay agreed and wondered if the winning entry found more favour because it depicted a person - a granddad. Technically, she was sure Carla's was better.

She sent Rose a photocopy of the newspaper cutting and

Carla excitedly awaited her response. None came.

Rose stayed in her room as much as she could get away with which was very little. As Jen had told her bedrooms were just for bedtime. Every time she disappeared someone came to fetch her.

'I'm surprised I'm even allowed in the toilet alone,' she complained many times.

She could walk in the grounds for short periods if she wanted to be alone, they told her, but learning to socialise was part of the therapy. She was sick to death of hearing that. And who'd want to be outside in a biting wind? She began to hate her mentor, Jen, who regularly told her she had to mix with the others and she'd soon find most of them were really nice.

Lily was less tiresome but a bit bossy. At least she was a nurse and had some right to be. She took charge of Rose's medication, dolling it out from the surgery, as the former gun room was called. Jen had told her that as if it were funny. Sick, Rose thought. Pity there wasn't a gun in there so she could put an end to her misery.

Mealtimes were the worst. Only people going through a hideous drugs detoxification were excused. The others sat at a huge table after helping themselves to food set out on a long sideboard. It was good food and there was plenty but Rose had no appetite. She ate like a sparrow, which was noted and commented on, as was everything she said, every move she made - she was sure of that. At least in hospital nothing was expected of her.

The thirty odd residents were a mixed bunch - all ages, shapes colours and classes - which made Rose feel slightly better. There were other Londoners, in fact they comprised most of the group. Three, in particular, Rose noticed: a publican, Bert, from Bermondsey, who seemed to be the joker in the pack and the snooty older woman, Helena, from Holland Park, who looked down her beaky nose at nearly everyone. No one liked her.

A girl called Beth, born in Lewisham, around Rose's age wanted to make friends but she didn't encourage her. She was too nosy. She was single, a career girl who'd been making a success of her dressmaking business, designing the clothes and selling them in an exclusive boutique in Cheltenham, but drink got in the way. What the hell had she got to drink for? Nothing had happened to Beth to compare with losing a lover, a baby and a daughter to the bloody Social Services.

The Down House regime was strict: daily group sessions for up to ten people, and individual therapy three times a week and a talk by an outside speaker twice a week. The first talk on the day after Rose's arrival, was called, *How alcohol can damage us.*

'Don't want to go,' Rose grumbled to Jen. 'What's the point. Isn't this place s'posed to make us feel better, not worse?'

'We have to go,' said Jen. 'I know we'll have heard it all before but the person giving it is a well-known research doctor – she could be a bit more interesting than most.'

She was right on both counts. Rose didn't need to be told what damage drink could do to the liver but was gripped by the before and after slides of various organs, particularly the ones of the brain. What had she done to her brain in years of drinking? She was forgetful – at least she was aware of it, but was it irreversible?

The speaker was uncompromising, sparing nobody's feelings.

'We're only just beginning to realise the extent that young teenagers are drinking, and the younger they start the more likely they are to end up as alcoholics.' She showed a short video of groups of drinking teenagers, some as young as twelve, then a slide of a reeling, heavily pregnant woman.

'The child of an alcoholic mother is very fortunate if he or she is not damaged in some way. The results of drinking heavily during pregnancy may be a brain damaged child, with other physical defects which may show in bones, kidneys and the heart, and in neurological disorders. Many babies don't get that far – twice as many miscarriages occur in alcohol dependant women compared with non or moderate drinkers.'

There were gasps from several women in the audience

217

and an older women, sitting next to Rose, whispered,' Good job there aren't any pregnant residents.'

'How does she know? There might be – there's young girls here,' replied the woman on her other side.

'No, I heard the speaker discreetly asking Lily, before she started,' replied Rose's neighbour.

Little more was heard or seen by Rose. Grateful for the semi-darkness, she huddled into herself, her mind teeming with memories and images of her first pregnancy. She'd started drinking, hadn't she – before Mum and Gran died? She was drunk when Carla was conceived – she must have been, not to be sure, not to really remember. But how could Carla be so perfect if this woman's words were true? She was exaggerating, making herself more important than she really was, the way doctors do. Her Carla was beautiful and bright and so would Terry's little girl have been. She'd given alcohol up completely the moment she found she was pregnant – Terry had seen to that. She began to feel angry. This woman had no right to come here and upset her, making her question the past. She closed her eyes, trying to visualise happier times but, relentlessly, came an image of a nurse staring at a scan, asking Rose about her eating and drinking habits, then calling a doctor in who'd said, 'The baby's quite small but seems fine. Make sure you look after yourself.'

She had looked after herself and been looked after. Her throat tightened and she felt tears welling. She swallowed hard and clenched her hands tightly together. She only drank later because of the shock. She'd stumbled, hadn't she? That's what had caused her to lose the baby. So why had they hinted there might have been a problem anyway? Bloody know-alls.

She started as lights went on and clapping told her the lecture had ended. People were murmuring all around her, mainly being complimentary. She walked away from the exiting group. Never mind a nightcap - something Carol was suggesting – the sort of nightcap she could do with wouldn't be on the night drinks' trolley.

It was still hard for Rose to talk in the Group. It had been different at Alcoholics' Support. She'd had Terry behind her, encouraging her to stick with it. She had something - someone to work for. She'd proudly told the group about her boyfriend, but what had she to tell this lot? Her Terry was a suspected perve and her daughter was In Care?

'Rose, one of the reasons for coming here is to unburden yourself and seek support from the others. You won't be judged. We look at what's happened to you – try to link cause and event. Most people here share one common feeling - they can't risk trusting anyone. Our job is to show that trust can be built, slowly, brick by brick,' explained Mary, her personal counsellor, at their first meeting. She was a plain, earnest-looking woman, around forty. Her mousy hair hung lankly, looking as if it needed the attention of a good stylist. She was wearing a wedding ring

How did you get a man? Rose wanted to ask her, then her thoughts drifted back to Terry. She cried in that first session and Mary said she could see how deeply unhappy she was. Bloody clever of you, thought Rose.

There was nothing to aim for so what the hell was she doing here? She likened it to prison, only she wasn't a prisoner. So why stay?

After a few days she found a way of achieving a little privacy by making sure she went to bed before her roommates, and if she wasn't asleep when they came in, she pretended to be. Carol frequently told Jen to be quiet. Eventually, she got the message but still talked in a whisper until she received a protracted snore as a response, then she shut up.

Rose started to taste her food - really taste it and even ask questions about it.

'I take it you don't cook,' commented snooty Helena who, probably against her will, was sitting opposite Rose one lunchtime. 'All packet stuff I expect.'

To Rose's surprise, Bert, sitting next to her, said, 'Why d'you suppose that? Maybe she just don't like cooking. All right for some - having their food cooked for them.'

This was clearly a dig at the woman. She loved talking

about her cook/housekeeper, usually in a derogatory way.

Thank God, we're not in the same therapy group, Rose thought and gave Bert an appreciative smile.

One afternoon, waiting for the tea to appear, she overheard Helena and two cronies talking about the cost of rehabilitation at Down House.

'You realise we subsidise the people paid for by the State. Our taxes are going towards the cost of such residents,' complained an overweight, blue-rinsed woman.

'I well know, Theresa, and not just when they're here. We pay for their Benefits. How many have ever paid National Insurance but we have to, and what have we ever got from the State? We pay for their drugs because they can't be deprived of their heroin, and they buy their alcohol with their social security payments,' said Helena.

'Can they get heroin on the NHS? I don't think so,' said the third woman. 'They get a substitute – methadone, I think. Why not let them suffer doing without it– why do it the kind way?'

'Yes, it's disgraceful. The whole system is wrong. The State panders to them – gives them social workers, therapists, doctors and not a penny do they contribute. There'll be a good number here of that sort.' Helena turned to look straight at Rose as she finished speaking.

Rose stared past her, determined not to show she'd overheard. A clatter of china on the approaching tea trolley took the attention of the Three Witches (Rose's label for them), then came clucks of dismay and disapproval. The young girl carer nearly tipped the trolley over as she wheeled it onto the thick carpet. No longer interested in tea, Rose swiftly got up and went out through the French windows, oblivious that she was coatless.

It was a dark afternoon: nothing in the view across the park to cheer her up. She sniffed: cigarette smoke – ugh. Thank God she hadn't weakened in that respect. She glanced sideways and, at the end of the terrace, saw Bert almost concealed by a great vine or something growing against the house. Smoking in the house was completely banned and smoking at all was only just tolerated. Trust Bert not to care. There was a glow as he drew on his cigarette. She walked towards him.

'Can we go on meeting like this?' he said, removing his cigarette and beaming at her.

She giggled 'I didn't know you smoked.'

'Course I do. Got to 'ave some vices. Don't you?'

'I did – heavily - but patches stopped me.'

'Best introduce us then. P'raps this Patch bloke could do something for me.'

'You daft thing. You don't want to stop, do you?'

'Not particularly. What you doin' out side without a coat? It's bitter.'

'Just had to get away. Can't stand some of them women. You'd think they owned this place.'

'I know who you mean, darlin'. Think I'm dead common. I don't give a stuff and nor should you. Got to learn to laugh at such people. And we're all 'ere for the same reason – booze, the great leveller. You think about that, gal, when they're bein' hoity-toity.' Bert gave a great drag on his cigarette, then exhaled a cloud of smoke, turning his face away from her.

'Remember, they got a story to tell same as us. They got their reasons same as us. You got anyone out there for you, Rose?'

She hesitated. 'Friends.' To forestall further questions she asked, 'And you?'

'My wife. She's the Guv'nor now. I was lucky, see. They gave her the licence or we'd 'ave lost everthing. She's a wonderful woman, my Greta.'

Bert had someone - probably everyone did except her. There'd been no news from Terry but how could there be? He'd have no idea where she was. He might be worried sick about her but too protective to try to get in touch, until all that dreadful stuff was sorted out. She could write to him, tell him all about Down House, and perhaps even make him laugh. Then a vividly painful memory flashed into her mind – his words: 'Stay away if you care about me.' She'd been so hurt.

There'd been no words of comfort for her. Maybe that's what he was showing her by staying away –that he did care, so didn't want to drag her into all the awful mess.

Bert had finished his cigarette. He threw it down on the stones and ground it underfoot, then gave a satisfied grunt and breathed in deeply. Rose took it that he was about to start talking again and probably would ask questions. She gave an exaggerated shiver, wrapping her arms around herself.

'You get yourself inside, love,' said Bert, helpfully. 'You'll catch your death like that and there's better ways of goin'.'

She laughed. 'And if I stay you'll tell me.' She walked away along the terrace and in through the French windows.

The Three Witches stared at her. She stared back, lifted her chin and stalked past them.

After two weeks she found she was becoming more relaxed. Maybe it was just because she was safe - cocooned. Having meals provided and hot water always available - these were some compensation for loss of freedom and having to put up with a structure to her day. She was even finding sharing a room was less of strain. It was helping her to get to know Carol, much quieter than Jen, and even to see that much of Jen's irritating smothering stemmed from her own neediness. Adopted by an undemonstrative couple, she confessed she'd never experienced hugs and cuddles. She grew up wondering if her parents really loved her, or was she just the optional extra that rounded them into a neat family.

The second Saturday Ellie and Ron turned up. Visiting was allowed in the afternoon but Rose was surprised – she wasn't expecting them. She was touched that they'd come so far for a short visit.

'Brad sends his love. Hope you don't mind but I saw him in the market and he was asking after you,' said Ellie after hugs had been exchanged.

To her surprise Rose was pleased. 'Say "hello" from me, will you. He's not a bad sort.'

'Doing all right too,' said Ellie. 'There've been posters

around the market advertising his gigs. He's just worried the Social will rumble him.'

Rose giggled. 'No change there.'

To avoid seeing other people's visitors, Rose had been about to go outside and was dressed in a coat and boots that Terry had bought for her. Thank goodness Ellie had seen them several times at Alco meetings and didn't comment beyond saying,

'About to escape, were you? We'll come out with you. Be nice to have some proper fresh air. Not much about back home.'

They walked in the park for a while. The weather was calm with a hint of sunshine. Ellie puffed a bit. She was bundled up in a mock fur coat, with tight leather trousers and high-heeled boots. In the lounge at teatime she discarded her coat to reveal a pale pink angora jumper that, in Rose's opinion, turned her breasts into udders.

She felt amused but also embarrassed by Ellie, whose loud comments on the paintings, the panelling and the park, were heard above everyone else's chatter.

'Don't you think yourself too grand for us when you come out,' she said. 'You could get used to living like this.'

The ghastly Helena had no visitors and sat scrutinising everyone else's. Ellie and Ron seemed to be drawing her disapproving gaze more than most. When tea arrived Ron trotted out his Jeeves joke which raised a few laughs but only a sniffy look of contempt from Helena.

'Who's that?' said Ellie, a shade too loudly. She was looking towards the doorway of the lounge. 'He's tasty.'

Rose turned in her chair and caught a glimpse of a tall figure in a tweed jacket, walking away into the hall.

'Shame - missed him,' said Ellie. 'Bit of a younger Harrison Ford.'

'Someone's visitor I s'pect,' said Rose. 'No point in getting excited - no one here is worth a glance.'

Ellie gave her a questioning look and seemed about to speak. She moistened her lips, then looked away and said nothing. She drank her tea and gazed around the room as if she'd lost interest in Rose, but Rose wasn't fooled. She knew Ellie had been going to talk about Terry.

Now she felt agitated. Had Ellie got news of him - even seen him about? If so why didn't she say so, only quietly?

Ron started to ask Rose about the treatment and how she spent her time, but in a minute Ellie interrupted to ask after Carla.

'Haven't heard,' Rose lied.

'Then you should of. Those social workers should keep you informed. I could get on to them for you.'

'No, don't.' The words came out more sharply than Rose intended. Several people glanced at her including Helena. She scowled at them.

'All right, I won't interfere,' said Ellie. 'Didn't mean to upset you.'

'It's all right. Only I got to concentrate on getting okay. If there are any problems they'll get in touch.'

'Course they will,' said Ron, shooting Ellie a reproving look. 'Looks like more tea's coming round and those yummy cakes. Get you something can I, girls?' He stood up.

Rose smiled at him gratefully. Whatever Ellie said or thought of him, he was a lot more tuned in than she gave him credit for.

After Ellie and Ron left, Rose retreated to her room and wept. The visit had been a funny mixture, a nice surprise, funny at times but an overall strain. And now guilt, anger and self-pity overwhelmed her. Her yearning for Terry and all he'd promised her was undiminished. She felt angry that everything had been snatched from her; even her only child was less hers than she'd ever been. She should have phoned or written to her, but what could she say? *Mum's in a treatment centre because she's an alcoholic.* Carla was no fool and pretty streetwise. She'd had to be: from the age of four she'd been more carer than cared for. She'd write or, better still, phone when she had something cheerful to say. God knew when that would be.

Parked in a lay-by, munching fish and chips, Ellie and Ron were unusually quiet together. They had been both encouraged and disappointed with the visit. Rose was looking better - they agreed on that. She had a little colour in her cheeks and they'd seen a bit of her old sparkiness. Quite funny she'd been when describing the group therapy that she didn't think much of, but Ellie thought she was still pretty uptight.

Ron was the more optimistic. 'She's coming on a treat,' he enthused.

'Until I mentioned Carla,' said Ellie. 'She'd have flared right up if I'd gone on.' '

'You were daft there. She needs to get over all that - put it behind her.'

'What, forget her kid? And what about the trial - we know it'll come to that. She'll have to face it then."

'Yeah, and when will that be - a year or more? For God's sake, Ell, she's got to bury her head in the sand for a bit. That's probably the only way she can cope. Thank God you didn't say anything about that perve. We both know 'e got what was coming to him but I reckon she'd still say it was all wrong and the bastard didn't deserve it.'

Ellie gave a deep sigh. Ron knew what it had taken for her to keep the latest news about Terry to herself. When she heard on the local grapevine, then on the news, that someone had got into the yard of Terry's flat, waited for him to come out then given him a good beating, she'd been elated. She felt no shame that she'd relished all the gory details. It was a shame the bloke hadn't succeeded in cutting off his balls. Now he'd be kept in custody for his own safety and a pity that was.

She scrunched up the chip paper and put it in the door pocket, then she leaned her head wearily against Ron's shoulder.

'I have to say Ron, when it comes to understanding people you're far from being just a pretty face.'

Chapter 24

Having ventured out-of-doors with Ellie and Ron, Rose decided it wasn't a bad place to be. She had to tell a member of staff where she was going, and for how long then, provided she stayed within the grounds, she could go out alone. To leave the grounds she'd need to have two companions with her, one to stay with her if she had an accident and one to run for help.

This was a strictly enforced rule as Rose realised one day when a recently arrived girl didn't come to group therapy. She wasn't seen all day and the staff seemed agitated and preoccupied. At the supper table, Bermondsey Bert, who was proving to be brilliant at gleaning information, announced that the miscreant, Sylvia, had been brought back from the local pub.

'Pissed as a newt and causing trouble,' he said, beaming around at everyone. 'Upstairs now, throwing up. Silly cow. If I'd known she were going to the boozer, I'd 'ave gone with 'er.'

A few people joined in his laughter and then he became serious.

'No. Silly not to tow the line. One trip outside the premises on your own and you get a warning - second time and you're out on your arse.'

'Some people don't deserve to be here. It's wasted on them,' said Helena. 'They should be thrown out without a warning. They are taking up a valuable place.'

'Here, here,' was the response from many around the table. Rose was surprised. She thought most of them would be more tolerant.

'I waited weeks to get in here,' said a woman called Martha. 'I was desperate.'

'You get in faster if you pay,' said Bert, looking hard at Helena. 'Money helps queue jumpers every time.'

Helena ignored the obvious gibe.

Watching and listening, Rose wondered where would she go if she got thrown out? She couldn't bear the thought of ever going back to the flat. Trouble was if you got out of council housing you never got back in, unless you were homeless - like on the street – or an asylum seeker. She'd talk to Ellie if she ever visited again. She had a few contacts. Maybe she'd help her to find somewhere private but cheap. But she didn't want to think about the future. She wanted to stay in a magical present, where a day stretched endlessly and the future was constantly pushed away.

That was the attraction of certain drugs, she supposed. Drugs she'd been attracted to but could never afford. Through buying drugs Brad had got through every penny his parents left him, then into debt. Strange to think she'd been saved from that by her poverty. Ironically, she was now on free, prescribed drugs that were supposed to make everything look brighter but they hadn't so far. The doctor told her she had to stay on anti-depressants - they'd help her to become more positive. She didn't believe him and grumbled to her therapist who sided with him.

'Think of them as a crutch while you heal. Once you're better you can discard the crutch. I'm hoping our talks and the exercises will help you to get there,' she'd said.

'Penny for 'em,' said Bert 'You're miles away, Rose.'

'No I'm not, I'm here.' Her positive response surprised her. She even laughed.

'That's better. You're a lovely girl when you laugh,' said Bert. 'Coming to the film tonight, are you? Be my guest?'

Rose grinned. It was film night on Tuesdays, in the gymn, but she'd always gone to bed. Tonight she'd give the film a go. It was a musical – really old but still popular - South Pacific.

'Yeah, I'll come.'

Jen, at the far end of the table gave a little cheer and there were murmurs of approval from a few others.

'Of course, we might upset Helena if we sit in the back row,' said Bert, 'but she can't be with me every time.'

Did Helena's mouth give a little twitch - the mere hint of a smile? Just in case, Rose smiled at her but Helena's response was a slight incline of her head. Ah well, if anyone could crack her ice it would be Bert, the good-hearted, Bermondsey bloke.

She began to walk outside every day. Even if it was cold she put on one or two extra layers and braved the elements as she never had at home. It made all the difference knowing a fire in each downstairs room would restore her circulation. Shame they weren't huge, blazing log fires - just pretend gas ones. Some rubbish to do with Health and Safety, Bermondsey Bert told her, or maybe, people like them couldn't be trusted not to strew logs around and burn the place down.

'Promise you won't go far. Remember the rules.' How many times had she heard those words?

She noticed more and more on her walks: frosted twigs on starkly bare trees, spiders' webs hung with sparklers, and leaves on coloured bushes looking as if they'd been dipped in icing sugar - good enough to eat! Frost was a temporary decoration on the landscape. More permanent were the snowdrops, like tiny lights gleaming beneath the isolated stands of trees and fringing woods.

Birds twittered despite the cold and sometimes a song arrested her. She'd stop and listen, seldom able to see the chorister and never able to identify it. Late in the afternoon large flocks traversed the sky but why? Did they meet in numbers to keep warm overnight? The biggest birds in the park were dark and noisy. She wondered if they were crows. They were pushy and bossy - horrid to smaller birds

The unpleasant thought crept into her mind that they were like her tormentors at school. Their raucous caw-cawing became words: 'Your mum's a slag,' 'Your mum's a soak.' 'You smell - you're disgusting.'

One morning, when her mind was cluttered with these hateful memories, she saw a deer. It was no more than a hundred yards away, staring at her, causing her to stop in mid thought and track. They seemed mesmerised by each other - held fast in a suspension of time, then the creature gave a leap as if taking off into flight. It was suspended for seconds then touched down and moved across the grass with the grace of a dancer. The last she saw of it was of flash of white rump as it disappeared into a wood fringing the park. She laughed aloud. Was it 'mooning' her?

'Nice to hear that.'

She started. A human voice seemed out of place here. It came from behind her, to the left. She turned and saw a man standing by a group of three great trees. How long had he been there? Had he been watching her?

He walked towards her, smiling, and she remembered the glimpse she'd had of a man on the afternoon of Ellie and Ron's visit. This was the same person, surely, although his clothes were different. He was wearing a sand coloured short coat over dark cords pushed into Wellingtons. He looked as if he belonged here.

'I saw a deer,' said Rose. 'It stared at me for ages, then ran off, flashing its white bum at me like it was mooning.'

The man laughed He was only a few yards away now and she could see his lovely smile - perfect teeth in a tanned-looking face. Ellie was right - he *was* like a younger Harrison Ford only better looking – tasty.

'There are plenty of deer around but you're lucky to see one. They're such shy creatures. You like to commune with nature?'

'Don't know - only just started. It's all a bit strange still but better than being in the house.'

He smiled. 'I agree. Suddenly you're with thirty odd people - complete strangers - and you have to live like a family.'

'You're not ….?'

He grinned. 'Yes, I am.'

'But I haven't seen you - well just once. I thought you were a visitor.'

'I probably was then - checking the place out. I arrived last night as an inmate.' He held out a hand and said, 'I'm Adrian Shawfield.'

She shook hands with him. 'I'm Rose Davies.'

"How long have you been here, Rose?'

'Um…in my third week. I hated it for the first week. Felt a fish out of water.'

229

'And now?'

'It's beginning to make a bit of sense - what they're trying to do for us. Which reminds me - I s'pose I'd better get back for my group.'

'Yes, I must too. Better not be late first time. My mentor will be looking for me. Are you in the Red group?'

'No, the Yellow. Daft names. Who's your mentor – or tormentor?'

Adrian laughed. 'Chap called Bob. Seems nice.'

Shame it's not me, Rose thought as they walked towards the house. Adrian was tall but matched his stride to hers. He told her he lived in Wiltshire and guessed she lived in London.

'How did you guess?' she asked and they both laughed.

'I lived up there for several years for college and then work. Ah, here comes Bob looking a bit worried. I expect he thought I'd escaped.'

Rose was sorry they couldn't go on talking. Shame they weren't in the same group - she'd learn more about him, but he'd also learn about her... no, better to be in different groups. She'd hate a nice guy like him to know her life story. She'd struggled to write it all down for her counsellor - an essential exercise she'd told her. It had made her cry a lot. It was like having to relive the really awful times - nights when Ruby, too drunk to stand, was brought home by the police or a man - just any man from the pub - who always told Rose to go away. There'd been plenty of them. She'd described school and how seldom she'd gone. It was so awful she didn't care how much schooling she missed. She'd described Mum's and Gran's deaths and her pregnancy with Carla, but skimmed over the last years, not mentioning Terry and her miscarriage. If the counsellor knew already, from her medical history, she could bring it up.

As she walked into the group therapy session, Jen said, 'You look good, Rose. Got a bit of colour in your cheeks.'

'Thanks. I s'pose I feel better too.'

Overhearing, Paul, the therapist for the session, commented, 'Not a bad starting point - how I'm feeling today.

Everyone happy with that?'

There were murmurs of approval.

The group therapy went well - maybe a bit too gentle and chatty for the therapist who looked slightly irritated at times, but whose group was it? Rose felt more confident - better able to face people. She

At lunchtime she looked for Adrian, hoping they could talk again. She was irritated to see him sitting next to Helena. Yes, she would latch onto him. She even put a hand on his arm once or twice. Probably saw him as more her class.

Adrian glanced along the table and waved at Rose. That took the smile off Helena's face. She stared at her coldly. Rose stared back, making sure that Helena dropped her eyes first.

'Going to this bloody talk this afternoon?' asked Bert, from across the table.

'No choice,' said Rose. ' And we'll have seen and head it all before. I'd rather go to sleep.'

There were murmurs of agreement and sympathy but everyone turned up at the lecture room, a few yawning exaggeratedly and nearly all grumbling.

Brian, a therapist, met them at the door and told them they'd be favourably surprised - this talk was unique. Unconvinced they shambled in.

Seated in the space beneath the screen were two men, one looked in his fifties and the other quite a bit younger. Casually dressed, even scruffy, they sprawled in their chairs and didn't seem to notice the arrival of their audience. Brian walked forward and with warmth and enthusiasm, introduced them as Fred and Steve. At that point they turned and, still seated, stared vaguely above the heads of their audience, then they began a strange duologue: What were they here for? Who were all these people? Were they supposed to be here? What day was it? Who were they? Did they know each other?

'They're effing mad,' said Bert.

'Bloody barmy,' said someone further back.

If the men heard they gave no sign and continued their duologue for several minutes, by which time most people in the audience were in agreement with the complainers. A couple of people at the back muttered and shifted as if about to leave, and Brian's voice was heard quietly trying to placate them. At that moment the two men changed their style. They stood up, bowed and introduced themselves.

'Forgive us for that little performance but we were showing you the people we once were - almost brain dead. We didn't know who we were half the time. We had no motivation except to drink and drug ourselves to the eyeballs. I was using heroin and Fred was the alco. If you can stand it, ladies and gentlemen, we're going to tell you how we rediscovered ourselves,'

Steve, the younger man was speaking. He smiled around at his audience and a few people clapped. Rose was one of them. She liked the look of the chap. He had a cheeky smile that stripped a few years off his probable age. He was cadaverously thin in contrast to Fred who had a beer gut.

Taking turns they told how they became addicts, then the long haul out of addiction. They did this by a series of clever sketches that had the audience in pain with laughter one minute and in tears the next. Rose was particularly impressed by Fred who acted being a prison officer, telling Steve wouldn't even bother to scrape him off his shoe, then he was a consultant, brutally telling Steve (acting as Fred) that he'd incurably damaged his brain by his thirty years of heavy drinking. Finally they showed homemade videos of fellow addicts doing cold turkey, being aggressive, even violent. It was powerful stuff - nothing had been censored.

Questions took place for half an hour, then they all went for tea and Steve and Fred moved among the residents, chatting. There was plenty of laughter and even Helena seemed drawn by the relaxed and friendly atmosphere. She seemed to talk to Steve for ages. Adrian was standing beside her but not appearing to say much.

Selfish cow, thought Rose. What right had she to monopolise younger men.

'All right darlin'?' asked Bert sitting down next to her. 'Best talk I been to. Worth a dozen from them professionals. Makes you think, don't it? Nearly killed themselves and now

232

see where they are - Fred's in amateur dramatics and getting
known, they've both got jobs and go all over the place
lecturin' - in schools, colleges, prisons, and bins like this.'

Rose giggled. 'Is that what you think - we're a load of
nutters?'

'Well, not you and me, darlin'...Oh, how you doin'?'

Fred had appeared in front of them. Bert stood up,
offering him his chair which he accepted. Bert perched on the
arm of Rose's and she was soon included in the banter that
started between the two men.

'You a Cockney sparrow, darling?' asked Fred. 'Anyway
you're a lovely little bird - oh lawd, I'm being politically
incorrect. Don't report me will you?'

'Course she won't,' said Bert. 'She's a mate - a right cup
of Rosie Lea.'

Rose laughed, enjoying the attention. Once, she
noticed Adrian looking at her. He smiled and gave a little
wave. When she next looked in his direction, he'd gone.

An hour later and well after their scheduled departure
time, Fred and Steve left after shaking hands with everyone. It
was a prolonged and moving farewell.

Rose felt wrung out. She didn't want to chat anymore as
everyone else was doing, she wanted to think - ponder on the
situation of the two speakers. They'd had rotten starts in life,
just as bad as hers: Fred spending time in various Children's
Homes when his mum had several breakdowns and Steve
abused by his stepfather. And that wasn't the half of it.

She wandered away from the lounge and into the great
hall. A door with the sign *Library* above was ajar. She'd never
been in there. Curiosity and the wish to hide for a bit
propelled her forward into a dark room with a slightly fusty,
unused smell about it. Cabinets full of books lined three walls
and three small sofas faced the fireplace - otherwise it was
bare. She looked towards the window and started: a figure
stood looking onto the park, one hand resting on the crimson
velvet curtain. It was Adrian. Clearly he'd not heard her come
in as he didn't turn round. She wasn't sure what to do. Did he
want to be alone? Maybe he'd come in to get away from

everyone as she had. As she dithered, he turned and started too, then smiled.

'Wanted to get away, did you?'

'Yes, but I'll go somewhere else.'

'Only if you can't stand my company.' He grinned. 'Don't go on my account, please. I was only thinking over what we've heard.'

'Same here. They was so good - made me think.'

'I'm really lucky - hearing those two on my first day. Let's sit down. Might as well make use of the peace and quiet.'

They sat facing each other after Adrian had turned up the gas fire. He looked different from how he'd been that morning. His skin looked paler and his expression was serious.

'You all right?' Rose asked.

'Not brilliant. It's probably these detox pills. They're said to be up-to-the- minute wonder pills with minimal side effects but I don't know.'

'I'm lucky,' said Rose. 'I started them in hospital before I came here.'

'I shouldn't react badly. This is my second time in rehab, so I and my body should know the ropes. I went to a place in Surrey two years ago. I was all right for a few months afterwards, then I started to drink again.' He sighed heavily. He really didn't look well.

'D'you have a family Rose?'

'I've a daughter, Carla. She's eight. No one else.'

'Hard for you being away from her and....' He paused, looked away, staring at the fire, then said, 'I've two daughters, Becky's thirteen and Rachel's fifteen. They're disgusted with me, but my wife's the one who's really suffered – trying to minimise the damage. No, I've put them all through hell.'

Adrian looked so sad Rose wondered if he'd break down. He sat hunched forward, hands crossed, hanging between his knees. Without looking at her he said, 'Did it strike you how much those two, Steve and Fred, talked about the people they'd hurt and disappointed?'

'Yes. It was really sad the way Fred spoke of his mum

234

dying and he was too drunk to be there.'

'Eventually we have to face the guilt,' said Adrian and sighed. 'God knows I've plenty to feel guilty about.'

'I s'pose we all have stuff we'd like to forget,' Rose said. 'I feel terrible about Carla. She's happier now, with Auntie Fay, than she's ever been and that's because she's away from me. I used her - made her my carer.'

'It sounds as if you've been too much alone.' Adrian was again looking towards the fire and that made it easier for her to reply.

'I've not seen Carla's dad for years - he doesn't know her.'

Adrian turned to her, giving a gentle smile. 'Must be really hard being a single parent. God knows how but somehow we've hung together as a family. That's what makes me so ashamed. My wife must have felt alone although I was always around - too much around.'

'Oh, there you are. You okay? I've got you booked in for a session before supper.' Brian's voice sounded from the doorway, loud and intrusive.

Adrian looked up and stared at him for a second as if he hadn't understood.

'Sorry, am I late?'

'No, but we might as well get started. If you'll come with me.'

Adrian got up wearily, like an older man. He smiled at Rose.

'Thanks for listening. Be seeing you.'

As he passed her he lightly touched her shoulder. She stared after him, wishing she could follow. She didn't even know him - had talked for a few minutes - yet she felt she might have gone on talking. She felt irritated with Brian for interrupting them.

There was no sign of Adrian at supper. Strange. His mentor, Bob, was talking to Sylvia, the girl who'd sloped out to the pub. He was laughing so he wasn't perturbed about his charge being absent. Pity Jen hadn't been like him. She would be leaving in a couple of weeks and seemed okay about going.

Rose wondered how she'd feel when her time came, then pushed the thought away. She wasn't ready to leave the cocoon.

Chapter 25

The morning post brought a surprise for Rose - a cylindrical shape parcel wrapped in brown paper. She scrutinised the address but didn't recognise the handwriting. The parcel was feather light and nothing moved inside when she gave it a little shake. Noticing, Martha suggested it might be a school photograph. They were on the verge of going in to breakfast but Rose turned back and hurried upstairs to her room. She sat on the bed and carefully slit the paper open, half expecting to find a joke present – the sort of thing Ellie might send. The cylinder was of plain cardboard with a plastic lid, secured with selotape. Could it contain a scroll of some kind? She resisted opening it for a second and pictured what might be inside: a proclamation of Terry's love for her? She almost laughed aloud. She'd done as he'd said - not attempted to contact him so how would he know where she was? He could be no part of her present (in both meanings of the word) and that wasn't his fault, but he was still going to be her future.

She removed the lid and found, taped to it, a small piece of paper. Written on it were the words, *Open with care. Photo of the original which is being framed. All the best, Fay.* Controlling her excitement, carefully' she withdrew the rolled photograph and gently flattened it. She gasped and stared for minutes. It was a beautifully sharp image of Carla's prize-winning drawing. Only when a drop of water fell on the precious object did she realise she was crying. She'd never replied to the letter Carla had sent her, enclosing the cutting from the paper, yet Fay had gone to this trouble for her. She sat staring at the photo for ten minutes, then hunger growled in her stomach and regrets were pushed away. She dabbed her eyes and put on some concealing makeup. She'd face the others proudly - she had something to be really proud about.

'All right? Was it something nice?' asked Martha as Rose placed her bowl of cereal on the table and sat next to her.

Rose smiled, almost a secretive smile.'

'Well…aren't you going to tell me?'

'Better than that, I'll show you.' She reached under the table for her bag, a soft capacious shoulder bag that Ellie had given her. She drew out the photo.

'My little girl's drawing. It won a prize.'

Martha wiped her hands on a paper napkin before taking the photo.

'It's lovely. How old is she?'

'Eight last May.'

'Wow. She's good. Can I pass it round?'

Rose nodded happily and ate her breakfast while the photo was handed round and enthused over. Only Helena seemed unimpressed, glancing and not commenting. When it reached Bert he had, of course, to praise it in his inimitable way.

'I've seen a good many pussies in my lifetime but none as pretty as this.'

After the laughter subsided, Martha said,' Show it to Adrian. He's an artist. I know because we're in the same group.'

An artist! Rose had seen him as a vet or a well-off farmer.

'Where is he?' she asked. 'He wasn't at supper.'

'He's been in and out. Just had tea and toast - nothing else, then left. Not too well, he said.'

Rose looked at the dismal sight of rain lashing the windows. However much he liked nature he wasn't likely to be outside in that.

'Quiet bloke,' said Bert. 'Poncy name. Seems all right, though. Opened up in the group, didn't he Martha.'

'Yes, but he found it hard. Seems such a nice person. How do such people get into this state?'

'Well, you're a nice person,' said Bert, grinning. 'Don't you ask yourself the same question? Then there's a lovely guy like me...ouch!'

Martha had thrown a piece of toast at him. The ensuing giggles and deteriorating behaviour brought paint-stripping looks from Helena at the other end of the table.

As soon as she'd finished eating Rose left the room.

Adrian would be in the library, she was sure. Pity she hadn't discovered it as a retreat. She might have been left alone a bit more. She wouldn't have been routed out of a public room, open to anyone, as she was from her bedroom. Strange that few people used it.

The door was ajar. She walked in expecting to find an even darker gloom than yesterday's as the window looked onto a part of the terrace that was overhung with greenery, now dripping and lashing against the latticed panes. Instead, brightness radiated from the fake logs and beside them, sitting in an armchair and reading a newspaper, was Adrian.

'Hope I'm not intruding....'she started to say, but he turned at once and smiled, putting the paper down.

'No, of course not. Come and get warm.' He half rose as she walked forward. She sat opposite him, suddenly feeling a little shy, so she was pleased she had a reason for being there. She took the photo out of her bag, relieved it hadn't got creased or smeared in its passage around the table.

'I've had this in the post. It's of a drawing my Carla did.'

He got up and took the photo from her. After a few minutes of studying it intently, he asked, 'How old is your daughter? Sorry, you probably told me....'

'That's all right. She's nine in May.'

He positively beamed. 'This is remarkable. It would show real promise if done by an art college student.'

He sat down beside her then, holding the photo in front of them both.

'See how she's managed to get the impression of texture - you want to sink your fingers into the cat's fur. And it has expression - benevolence. It's delightful.'

'D'you really think it's good? Martha told me you're an artist so I wanted to ask you.'

'I'm a failed art teacher. Failed in that I've lost two jobs through my drinking, but I know talent when I see it.'

He continued to hold the photo and scrutinise it. 'Has she had any special tuition?'

'No, just the usual drawing classes at school - and just an ordinary school, but her teacher encourages her. She won

239

second prize with this in a schools' competition.'

'Hmn, I wonder what the winner submitted. Where does this skill come from...is it...?' He stopped abruptly, looking a bit embarrassed.

Rose grinned. He'd remembered something of yesterday's conversation.

'Can't be from me,' she said lightly. '

'Who knows what we get from distant ancestors. My father's a farmer and wanted me to carry on from him but I knew what I wanted to do from an early age. He was bitterly disappointed. My mother backed me, which caused strife between them. My sister, thank God, married a farmer and that helped a bit. She's a *chip off the old block* - pro hunting and shooting. You can imagine what they think of me, now.'

There was no hint of self-pity in Adrian's tone, but nor did he sound proud of himself.

'Enough of me.' He handed back the photo. 'You've something precious there, Rose, I'm really pleased for you.'

She smiled and carefully put the photo away.

'Thank you. I want my Carla to have every chance. I was dragged up by an alcoholic mother but she's not going to be.'

'Good for you. If it weren't for my wife, my daughters would have had a terrible time. She's worked tirelessly to keep us all going. There, back to me again - sorry.'

Once again, just as Rose was beginning to feel she could really talk, there was an interruption.

'Group therapy time. Come along everyone, please,' called a counsellor from the hall.

'Bother,' said Adrian, 'I'm feeling comfortable. We could have our own group
therapy here - but can two be a group?'

Rose laughed and stood up as he did.

'Thanks, Rose, for showing me the drawing. If you get any more I'd love to see them.'

'I will and thank you.'

Walking into the hall, they almost collided with Helena who ignored Rose and put a proprietary hand on Adrian's arm.

'See you later,' he said, and Rose was sure he winked at her.

Receiving a letter was an unusual happening for Carla. Seeing the expression of anticipation on her face, Fay fervently hoped it was from Rose - an acknowledgement of receiving the photo, perhaps. The post mark was indecipherable and she'd seen little of Rose's handwriting, but Carla's reaction as she opened it told her it was just what the child had been waiting for.

'Mum loves my picture. She's shown it to lots of people and a proper artist too.

Look, Auntie Fay, read what he said about it.'

Smiling with a happiness that must have nearly matched Carla's, Fay read the brief letter then handed it back to Carla after hugging her.

'One artist praising another – "a clever, talented girl". How proud your mum must be. I'm so pleased, darling.'

'When will the real picture be ready?'

'In about a week. The framer was busy but he's so good I didn't want to try elsewhere. It's worth getting it done by an expert.'

Carla beamed. 'Can we take it to Mum - give her a surprise?'

'That would be lovely. I'll find out. Now we'd better get some supper on. Bath first or last?'

'Last,' said Carla, laughing. 'That's Uncle Bill coming in. I'm going to show him my letter.'

The next morning Fay rang Wendy to tell her the good news about the letter and Carla's request to visit Rose. She was pleased with the response. Wendy said she'd talk to the staff at Down House and, she hoped, to Rose. If she received a positive response, certainly Fay could take Carla. She'd love to go but time was always limited. She'd have to fly as she was due in the Family Court shortly.

Poor kid, thought Fay, replacing the receiver. Busy as ever. She wondered about Liz, now away three months. Was she missing her job? There'd been no mention of a job in her

Christmas card. Fay hoped she was just having fun - she'd earned it.

Rose walked further than usual. She knew she'd reached the edge of the grounds because she came up to dark green-painted railings and she'd been told green was the colour used to mark all the boundaries - except walls, she supposed, but they were obvious. Beyond the railings were fields as far as she could see and then, she'd been told, the sea. She'd like to go there. Maybe, several of them could go together. Adrian would, she was sure. She'd hoped to see him this morning - they'd walked together a few times and she'd learnt a lot more about him. He was on probation he'd told her and her look of shock made him burst out laughing.

'No, not officially - from my wife. She's had enough of the drunken me. We've stayed under the same roof but that's been about it for nearly a year. If I don't come good this time, we're over.'

He'd changed the subject then, telling her about his freelance work and how he'd never wanted to teach but finances forced him to. He'd found it soul destroying. For every talented student there were twenty just killing time - having fun before facing the awful prospect of work or going on to more 'important' studies.

She'd half listened but her thoughts were on his earlier revelation. What sort of a woman would ditch such a man? He was everything any woman could want - good looking, funny, kind and a listener. He really listened. He didn't say, 'What you should do...' or 'Why don't you....' He just listened. She hadn't told him everything - she couldn't - not even to a man who seemed to find a redeeming feature in everyone.

She followed the railings, walking under beech trees spangled with frost. Beyond a clump of bushes a dark shape moved and she heard a strange noise - a kind of snort. She stopped. She'd heard of sightings of big cats in the country. What sort of noise did they make? Would one be more afraid of her that she'd be of it? Whatever sort of creature it might be, it was safely on the other side of the railings so she walked

on but warily. The bushes ended and there was the dark shape
- staring at her. She giggled. What a fool! It was a horse. The
darkness came from a rug that covered it from shoulder to
rump. Where there was no rug was a lovely dark golden
colour and the hair that grew from its neck was almost blonde.

They regarded each other for minutes. The horse gave
another funny little snort and Rose said, 'You're beautiful.'

'I think so,' said a light voice from beyond the bushes
and Rose saw a young woman approaching. She wore a long
mackintosh, like a highwayman's coat, and boots. She was
smiling at Rose as she walked up to the horse and put her
arms around its neck. The horse stood like a rock, apart from
curving its neck a bit, still watching Rose.

'It seems gentle,' she said.

The girl smiled again. 'She is. You can stroke her if you
like. I'll just put her headcollar on.'

She put a leather contraption with a rope attached onto
the horse's face then led her up to the railings. Rose
approached gingerly, explaining, 'I ain't never been close to a
horse except for police horses when they're on the road and
I'm on the pavement.'

'Right, give her this,' said the girl handing her a polo
mint. 'Take your mitten off or it might get slobbered on. Put
the mint on your palm with fingers flat -- like this.'

She demonstrated and daintily the horse took a mint.

Tentatively Rose did as she was shown and felt the
horse's warm, whiskery muzzle brush her bare hand. She
smiled with pleasure and the girl returned her smile, warmly.
She looked really nice with tawny brown hair pulled,
appropriately, into a pony tail.

'Now you can stroke her. She loves being scratched
under her mane.'

She demonstrated, running her fingers under the pale
hair and scratching around the horse's ears.

'She's lovely. I never thought horses could be so gentle.
What's her name?' asked Rose. She ran her hand down the
horse's neck. Her skin felt soft and warm.

'Her full name is Bridport Briar Rose, only we just call

her Rosie.

Rose burst out laughing . 'That's my name - just Rose - nothing posh like hers.'

'Mine's Nick. Come and talk to Rosie whenever you like. Look, take these. Give her one when you see her and you'll have a friend for life.'

Rose took the offered tube of mints and put them in her pocket.

'Thanks. I promise I won't eat them.

Nick laughed. 'We're off for a ride now. See you again, maybe.'

She led Rosie away, watched by Rose for a few minutes. Nick would know she was a resident at Down House - anyone inside the green boundary, other than an employee, had to be, yet the girl was so friendly.

Retracing her steps to the house Rose considered that the day had started really well.   When she joined the others in the hall, waiting to go into their Therapy Groups, she was reproved gently by Lily for being late.

'Sorry, I got talking to a horse,' she said.

Everyone laughed and Adrian said, quietly, 'That's why I didn't see you. You were enjoying superior company.'

Chapter 26

Wendy was told that visiting could be on Saturday or Sunday afternoons then, briefly, Rose spoke to her, saying she'd love to see Carla but couldn't see the point of talking to any social worker - what was there to discuss?

'Do go, Fay,' Wendy said, relaying this to her. 'Yours is the more important visit,' so Fay then completed the arrangements. They'd drive down, have lunch on the way and join Rose for tea.

For the first time Fay felt sufficiently confident to enthuse about the plan to Carla. There'd be no repetition of past disappointments.

'Where is Mum staying? Not a hospital, you said, so what is it?' Carla asked.

Not an easy one to answer, but an honest answer was needed, and needed often. They'd had this conversation a few times.

'It's a place where they help people to learn to manage without drugs and alcohol. A beautiful house in lovely grounds, not far from the sea.'

Carla beamed. 'Can we go to the sea? Mum would like that.'

'I don't see why not. Let's think about what we'll take for your mum -- your lovely picture ...'

'And some sweets,' said Carla. 'A big box of Dairy Milk, some Turkish Delight and Maltesers.'

Fay laughed. 'Funny - all the ones you like.'

Rose was looking forward to the visit. It would be good to show Carla off to everyone, but specially to Adrian. She borrowed Bert's mobile phone to ask Fay to bring some of Carla's drawings. It was after nine in the evening so she couldn't talk to Carla who was fast asleep. It seemed bedtime was at eight and, of course, at Fay's routine would be all.

'Come and meet Rosie,' she suggested to Adrian the following morning. They were walking on frost-crackling grass towards the far end of the park.

'Isn't one Rose enough?' he said, grinning. She giggled, loving his teasing, and felt in her pockets for the Polo Mints.

'You seem better, Adrian - not so many off days.'

'You're right. I do feel better. Not so many days when I just want to curl up and die.'

Rose stopped and turned startled eyes to him.

'Did you really mean that?'

'Sometimes - well, I don't know how far I'd go really. Could I do that to my family?'

They walked in silence for a while then Rose said, 'I did.'

Now Adrian turned startled eyes to her. 'You really tried?'

'Not sure if I did it deliberately or I just shoved anything into me that was around, but I was furious afterwards and wished I'd done a proper job. It's only since I've been here I've been pleased I didn't kill myself.

'So what's made you feel different?

'Dunno. P'raps it's being safe and, like my counsellor Mary says, everyone's accepted here. And most of the people are nice. That Helena ain't - she looks down her long nose at the rest of us - well, all except you.'

Adrian grinned. 'She's in my group. I can't say much - as you know what we say is confidential - but, believe me, she's had a very hard time.'

'Probably got what she deserved.'

Rose, I don't think you're unkind.'

'She ain't very kind to me. Looks at me as if I'm scum.'

'Well, as I said I can't break confidentiality but I wonder if it's your looks she can't cope with.'

'You mean she sees me as a tart?'

Adrian put a hand on her shoulder and gently turned her to face him.

'Why should anyone think that? You're a very pretty girl, and funny. You make me laugh and that takes some doing. Only…Helena might see you as someone who was once a threat.'

'That's silly. I didn't know her 'til I came here.'

'I know. I didn't mean you, literally, but you could remind her of someone young and lovely....' He took his hand away and looked into the distance.

Rose stared at his profile. Had he really called her 'young and lovely'? He couldn't have meant it - not about a too thin, old-before-her-time, ex. alco! She felt a giggle coming on but it caught somewhere in her throat, almost turning into sob. She must have made some sort of noise because he turned questioning eyes towards her, then a loud, shrill sound forestalled any comment he was going to make and both of them burst out laughing. Rosie was making it clear she was getting impatient.

'This way,' said Rose, not sure if she was grateful for the interruption. Might he have said more? No, she was being ridiculous. She walked ahead, past the clump of bushes and right up to the horse without a moment of doubt that she'd be warmly greeted.

'You seem confident,' said Adrian.

She smiled. 'First horse I've ever touched. Do you like them?'

'Yes. I rode a bit as a kid but not like my sister. She's horse mad, like my youngest. She keeps a pony on the farm for Beccy.'

Rosie daintily accepted the Polo mint and rubbed her head against Rose's arm.

'She's saying thank you.' Rose stroked and patted the mare with increasing confidence and gave her another mint.

'Sorry, can't really offer you one, Adrian, as her owner gave them to me for Rosie.'

He laughed, 'No, that wouldn't be right at all.'

Walking back, Rose told him of Carla's forthcoming visit.

'We could come here - meet Rosie. Don't think Carla's ever been close to a horse. She could draw her.'

'Nice idea. I'd like to meet this young artist. I'm not expecting a family visit. They might just turn up but I doubt it.' He sounded sad.

'Share mine,' said Rose, then remembered Fay would be

there and, probably, Bill too: 'Auntie Fay' and 'Uncle Bill' - so normal sounding. Adrian didn't know Carla was In Care. Would he have to know? Fay wouldn't tell him. Would he think worse of her if he knew?

'Come on, you two, you're going to be late.' Bob was calling from the terrace. 'How can you stand these cold mornings?' He gave an exaggerated shiver.

'Best not to ask,' said a voice from inside the open French window - Helena's. Rose shot her a furious look.

At lunch she received a look of contempt whenever she glanced in Helena's direction. What was the vicious old bag thinking - that she and Adrian were carrying on? Jealous, of course - probably wanting a younger man.

An hour and a half of hearing about and learning relaxation techniques caused considerable merriment and a light-hearted atmosphere prevailed in the lounge at teatime. Bermondsey Bert was teased for piling his plate with butter-oozing crumpets when he was on a strict, gut-reducing diet.

'It's all that bloody relaxing,' he said. 'Worn me out. Gotta build up me strength.'

He sat next to Rose and munched shamelessly, egging her on to match his pace.

'She can,' said Carol. 'She needs to eat more but you're a disgrace.'

Bert grinned. He wiped his mouth with the back of his hand then, still eating, picked up a newspaper someone had left on the arm of the sofa and dripped butter over it as he perused the front page. A minute later he flung the paper to the floor and shouted,

'I'll tell you what's a disgrace - filthy, bloody paedophiles getting away with making fortunes out of exploiting little kids.' He glared around as if expecting someone to refute this.

'Not another awful case? Every week there's something,' said Martha

'No, it's that same one from last year - the East End lot. They've arrested a contact in Bali - maybe even a woman's involved. Important business bloke, owns clubs and hotels,

248

seems to be the main provider of sex holidays and 'is wife's thought to be the procurer of the kiddies.' Bert picked up his mug of tea from a low table in front of him and took a long, noisy drink. Bob leaned forward from his chair and retrieved the paper. His colour turned grey after a minute's reading.

'God, they should be strung up and castrated,' he said.

'Preferably without an anaesthetic,' said Martha.

'One bit of good, 'e's shopped the rest of 'em,' said Bert. 'Named that Terry bloke as the key one this side. 'E'd denied it all, remember? Eh, steady gel, that's my tea.'

Rose had leapt up, jogging his arm and nearly falling over the table. Adrian, as ever sitting near Helena, called, 'Rose - are you okay?'

She ignored him and left the room with Bert's words following her: 'Going to be sick, I shouldn't wonder. That's what we all feel hearing about such scum.'

Fay put the phone down and stood beside the hall table staring at the coloured glass in the door panel yet not seeing it. After knowing Rose for over a year the phone call shouldn't have surprised her. Rose had renounced the world; she would talk to nobody, not her roommates, her therapist, her doctor - no one. She wanted Fay's and Carla's visit to be cancelled. If they turned up she wouldn't see them.

Lily, who had phoned, expressed puzzlement and disappointment - she had no idea why Rose was suffering such a setback.

'She's been doing so well. And she was getting excited about your visit. Could she have received bad news - not been able to tell anyone?'

Oh, you're so near the truth, Fay thought, but said, 'Who knows? Well, I'll have to break it to her daughter. She'll be so upset. If there's a change of heart please let me know at once.'

Politely Fay fended further queries. She felt it wasn't her place to enlighten Lily. How unrealistic had she been to hope that with Rose cocooned in her world of therapies and support, the latest revelations about Terry wouldn't reach her? That was what was behind this, she was sure.

How many times had she had similar calls? They'd usually been from Liz, telling her Rose was in hospital, or paralytic or just not traceable. Seldom had Rose called to say the visit was off – normally she just didn't turn up. How was she going to break the news to Carla who couldn't wait for the weekend to come so she could proudly hand over her picture to her mother?

She went to the kitchen and rummaged in the fridge for something for supper. It was hard to engage her mind on planning a meal when she was rehearsing words in her head and rearranging them. 'Mum's not well,' meant 'Mum's drunk again,' to Carla. It would be so tempting to lie - to say, 'The car's broken down,' 'Uncle Bill's got to work.' 'There's a flu bug going round in Down House.' At times she'd been a bit economical with the truth but had never gone as far as to actually reinvent it. She wished Bill was there to talk it over with, but he'd appear with Carla – he was picking her up from a birthday party. And that could be poignant for her, if she thought about her own last one, but was she crediting the child with an adult's reaction? She'd be having too much fun with her friends to become reflective.

At six- twenty Carla and Bill arrived home – Carla clutching a bag of party goodies which she emptied onto the kitchen tables, a large marzipan dice, a slice of birthday cake and a bag of sweets.

'You can have them all, you and Uncle Bill. I've eaten too much,' she announced, beaming at them.

'So you won't want any supper?' said Fay.

'Um, not sure.'

'Was it fun?'

'Yeah. We played lots of games. It was a bit babyish 'cause Carl's only little. We big ones were really there to help. Shall I go and change?'

'Yes, there's a dear.'

Once Carla was upstairs Fay told Bill about the cancelled visit.

'We'll do something special,' he said, at once. 'See which of her friends we can take and go to the coast, or a theme park – whatever she wants to do.'

Fay smiled. Dear Bill, always to be trusted to come up with a practical solution – fill the gap with activity.

Carla returned in jeans and a sweatshirt and with Jess in her arms.

'He wants his supper,' she said, gently putting the cat on the floor. She took his food from the larder, put it in his dish then topped up his drinking bowl. Politely, Jess meowed his thanks before eating. Carla giggled, pulled a chair up to the table and said perhaps she wasn't as full as she'd thought she was.

It wasn't until just before Carla's bedtime that Fay felt she could break the news. She'd been so buoyant all evening.

'Sorry Carla but there was a call from Down House, where your mum is. She's not so well. It's best if we don't go this weekend.'

'But we'll do something really great,' said Bill. 'Alton or the seaside – nice for walking in the winter, no crowds and if your friend James comes he can bring Harry. Dogs are allowed on the beach at this time of year.'

Carla looked from one to the other.

'Drinking again, is she?' Her voice was toneless.

'No, just not too good, She's been doing really well,' said Fay. 'I'm sure she's really disappointed.'

Carla got up from the table, pushing aside the board on which she and Bill had been playing highly competitive dominoes.

'I'm going to bed,' she said, and left the kitchen.

Bill sighed. 'Best go after her, love?'

'No, I'll leave her for a bit, then I'll go up.'

'Has Rose been naughty, d'you think – slipped out to the pub?'

'No. It's a mystery to the staff but I'm pretty sure what's caused her set back.'

Fay sat down opposite Bill cupping her hands around a mug of coffee.

'You mean the latest about Terry and the gang. You're right, I'm sure. You usually are.'

Fay grinned and stretched her hand across to squeeze

251

Bill's arm.

'I must be unbearable at times. Always right.'

'Yes, but this isn't one of them. I'll tell you when you're unbearable.'

Ten minutes later Carla appeared in her dressing gown, carrying a well-wrapped parcel. She set it down on the table in front of Fay.

'That's for you Auntie Fay,' she said in a serious tone.

Fay fingered the edge of the package then looked up at Carla.

'But that's your mum's picture – your prize-winning drawing,' she said.

'I know. I want you to have it. You and Uncle Bill.'

Fay looked at Bill who was staring at the parcel, lost for words. No help there.

'But your mum will be so disappointed,' she said.

'No she won't. She didn't know I was going to give it to her.'

'But, really wouldn't you like her to have it? We can take it another time...there'll be another....'

'No,' Carla broke in, her tone firm. 'It's yours now.'

She walked to the door, hesitated, turned and said, 'Uncle Bill, Harry'd like the beach much more than Alton Towers.'

Chapter 27

'If you're ill you must be seen by the doctor. There's no other reason for staying up here. It's not helpful to you, Rose. Won't you tell me what's wrong?' Lily's voice was firm but kindly.

'I don't want to see anyone.'

'I'm sorry but you have to stick to the rules here. We don't do room service.' Lily smiled as if she 'd made a joke. Silence came between them like a shutter. After minutes, Lily sighed, got up from the chair beside Rose's bed and walked to the door where she paused.

'Will you talk to Mary? She might agree to see you up here?'

Rose wanted to pull the clothes over her head and shut everything and everyone out; only the fear of being asked to leave made her give a grudging nod.

As Lily left the room Rose turned her face into the pillow but minutes later she heard the door open and footsteps approaching the bed. There was a scraping of chair legs on polished boards.

'Rose, it's Mary. I think something's upset you very much in the last day or two.'

The tone of Mary's voice encouraged Rose to turn towards her. If she'd learned nothing else about this earnest-looking, plain woman, she had found her to be kind, to give her whole attention - to want to know how she really felt.

'I ain't told you lots of things - things I should've. I feel ashamed you see. You know lots about me but not the worst things.'

'I sensed it was still hard for you to talk -there were things you couldn't say. But it can be harder to carry so much alone than to share it. No one will judge you here, Rose.'

Rose didn't doubt Mary's genuineness. It was probably a quality in all the counsellors but, somehow, it came over more powerfully from her. Reticent people opened up when it was Mary's turn to take the Group. Not that they'd included Rose, but now...alone with Mary....

She sat up, drew her knees up close to her chest and wrapped her arms around them. Without making eye contact - it was easier that way - she began by describing her first meeting with Terry.

Mary sat quietly, only speaking when Rose clearly needed a response. Half an hour passed like a few minutes. Towards the end Rose talked about Terry's arrest.

'I thought it was the real thing - love and a proper family. I wanted it all so much, I'd have lived with a child abuser - brought Carla into danger...I couldn't see there was anything queer about him, like always putting off meeting Carla...'

She broke down, sobbing. Mary passed her a box of tissues and as her sobs abated said, 'Rose, the danger lies with the cunning of abusers. You had no reason to suspect Terry. His distancing himself from Carla was a clever tactic.'

'But I wouldn't face it... wouldn't believe it even when he was arrested. It couldn't be my Terry.' She looked at Mary, beseeching her to understand.

'Wouldn't believe this could be the man you'd known...that's a pretty understandable reaction,' Mary said. 'He would have shown the best of himself to you.'

'It's been in the papers again. Others have been arrested and some have grassed. They were all talking about it in the lounge. I couldn't stand it. I can't face them.'

'I understand. What's happened has been shattering for you.'

'There's nothing in the future for me. Everything was about Terry, what he was going to do for us, what we were going to do together...It's just blank now.'

'You can't see a different future yet. You're still so shocked.'

'What's the point of trying anymore ...ever again.'

'It will be about trying for your sake, not Terry's. You've heard this many times, Rose, but it can't be said too often: we need to beat the alcoholism for ourselves.'

'That sounds selfish. Shouldn't I be doing this for my Carla? I've harmed her.'

'We have to learn to care for ourselves - to heal - before we can really care for others. Mostly we resort to drink because of personal unhappiness, a sense of not being good enough, or to hide from something. You've been dealing with those problems.'

It was long after Mary had gone that Rose realised how much she'd used the word, 'we'. Was she an ex: alco - that rather dowdy but sweet woman? It didn't seem possible.

She still wanted to stay in her room although she felt a bit better. In the end hunger forced her to get up and dress. As Lily said, there was no room service.

At supper Bert greeted her effusively. 'Come on darlin' and sit next to me - your Uncle Bert. I've missed you. Feelin' better?'

'A bit, thanks.' She sat down and glanced along the table. Adrian, as ever next to Helena, smiled and mouthed, 'Good to see you.'

To Rose's astonishment Helena nodded and smiled at her. Uncertainly, she returned the smile then looked away. How strange. How out of character.

'Come to the film won't you?' asked Bert. 'Funny French thing.'

'Dunno.'

'Come on - do you good.'

Rose stuck her fork into a crusty slice of steak pie. She didn't want to talk. By now her hunger was painful.

Despite the chink of cutlery on china and general chatter one voice could be heard above the rest - Sylvia's. Nicknamed 'the runner' by Bert she was a rebel. Most of the residents, who had waited weeks or months for a place at Down House, disapproved of her, seeing her as undeserving. She'd broken the rules within hours of arriving and risked being thrown out. And she was brash and noisy. Rose was indifferent to her. If she wanted to flaunt herself in flimsy, low-cut tops in winter, showing a crevasse of cleavage, that was her business. It certainly didn't impress Adrian who looked pained and was stiffly polite whenever she was near him. But Helena was

255

giving her acid looks.

Carol caught Rose's eye from across the table and winked.

'If anyone can squash the silly cow it's Helena,' she said approvingly.

After supper Rose looked around for Adrian. He'd left the room before coffee arrived. She hesitated at the library door, which was shut, but Carol and Bert, coming up behind her hustled her along to the film. After twenty minutes of sub titles and no sign of Adrian, she fell asleep.

Undressing with Carol and Jen (unusually because she was normally first up to bed), she was pleased at Jen's observation: 'I wish I was slim like you, Rose. I'm not fat exactly but I don't go in and out at just the right places the way you do.'

'Thanks,' said Rose slipping a cotton nightdress on, one Terry had chosen.

'What d'you think of that tarty Sylvia?' asked Carol of both of them.

'Not much,' said Rose.

'Not much,' echoed Jen.

'She's a spoilt brat,' said Carol, who was less discreet than Jen. 'All she says in Group is she likes the effect of drugs and the taste of booze, and her dad threatened to cut off her allowance if she refused to come here. The rest us - we've all had a reason to drink, losing parents, splitting up with a spouse or partner, going bust, but she's got a charmed life.'

'That Helena can't stand her. She's even laying off Rose and giving her withering looks to Sylvia,' said Jen, getting into bed. 'I can't understand why she was horrible to Rose, can you Carol?'

'Yes, I suppose I can up to a point - Rose being young, pretty and blonde, but now we've someone else with those assets. And she's confident, brash, sexy - makes it clear she'll get all she wants out of life. Sylvia's everything Helena hates and fears.'

'But why?' asked Rose.

'Well....' Carol looked towards Jen. 'It's just among us -

okay? I wouldn't gossip outside of here.'

Both girls nodded but Jen's expression was sceptical.

Carol got into bed but left the light on. Rose smiled. It was a bit like a schoolgirls' story - talking in the dorm.

'Helena was married for years to an army officer. He retired, youngish, as they do and had a high-powered civilian job that took him abroad a lot. On one trip to Germany he didn't come back. He'd fallen for a young tart - as Helena put it - and rang her to say he was moving in with her. Helena was devastated. A year later he wrote to say he'd had enough. He wanted to come home and be forgiven.'

'She didn't take him back?' exclaimed Jen.

'Yes, she still loved him. Their son was also in Germany but hadn't seen his dad in a year. He was relieved for his mum's sake and collected his dad in his car but on the way to the airport they were killed in a crash caused by an unlicensed teenager.'

'Christ,' said Rose. 'That's one of the worst things I've heard.'

She and Jen were staring at Carol in horror.

'That's not the end of it. Within a year she got a letter from the tart telling her she'd had a baby boy and needed money.'

'Was the baby Helena's husband's?' asked Jen.

'So the tart claimed. Helena agonised over it then sent her some money. She hoped she'd see the child one day but they disappeared. She's never heard another word.'

'So she's left not knowing if she has a grandson and with her family wiped out,' said Jen. 'Not surprising she's sour and bitter.'

Carol got out of bed and turned off the light. There was an exchange of 'Good night' then quiet. No one felt like chattering. Rose pulled the bedclothes up to her chin and mulled over the horrendous story. No wonder Adrian tolerated Helena - he'd hinted she'd had hard time. And Carol being in the same Group would know all about him as well as Helena, maybe more than he'd talked about on their morning walks. She couldn't question her - she'd be giving too much away -

257

but she wanted to.

She slept at last but awoke around two o'clock having had a horrible, confused dream. It didn't seem to have a story but she was afraid of something. She was in a dark place, hiding, trying to keep still. It could have been a cave; it was so pitch black, the place was frightening in itself, but outside was even worse.

The shapes of cupboards and beds, just discernable, reassured her. It had been a dream. She remembered saying to Carla, 'It's only a dream,' as if dreams were nothing. It was right to make them seem unimportant to a child, a health visitor had told her that. She should sympathise and reassure but emphasise they weren't reality. Easier said than done, particularly when Carla's worst dream that had been about a real event.

If she fell asleep she might slip back there, into the dark place that was so horrible. She closed her eyes and made a picture in her mind of the park and the deer she hadn't seen again. Adrian appeared - his face close to hers, smiling that kind, beautiful smile that was as much in his eyes as on his lips. She smiled back at him. A throb began in her lower belly. Her hand inched over the flatness and her fingers grazed the line of springy hair. She nearly laughed aloud, snatched her hand away and turned on her side, drawing her knees up. She had to remember there were two other people sharing the room with her.

Despite opening up to Mary, Rose found she could only give a slimmer version of her story to the Group. She told them she'd been upset because she'd once known a guy who'd seemed wonderful and had turned out to an abuser. There was instant sympathy and outrage but would it have been the same if she'd given them the full version - her denial, her fury with everyone, her taking Carla away and terrifying her? She couldn't bear to think of the muttered whisperings that might take place away from the Group in private.

As it was there'd been speculation that she's suffered abuse as a child – sexual abuse. She learnt that from Jen.

258

Suddenly, everyone in the house was really nice to her. Across the table, or sitting in the lounge someone would pat her shoulder, squeeze her hand or just smile in a way that said: 'So awful for you.'

Adrian said nothing about her absence. He was as he always had been. Their walks resumed. They didn't always set out together but invariable met in the park. Rosie received regular visits and even whinnied sometimes when she spotted them.

One morning when there was no sign of Adrian, Rose was feeling low. Jen had finished her term of rehabilitation and had left the day before. Rose had got used to her and had come to really like her. She'd had a rotten early marriage, no children and in her thirties was unsure what she wanted to do with her life. But she seemed ready to leave Down House. She laughed a lot during the silly ceremony with its ringing of bells, chanting and clapping. She seemed excited more than sad which Rose was sure she was going to be when her time came

Rosie rubbed her head gently against Rose's arm as if in sympathy and the tears started to trickle. Where could she go when she left here? Ellie hadn't visited again. Was it because of the latest revelations about Terry? Perhaps she was too disgusted to visit - maybe wondering if she was still protesting Terry's innocence. She'd been so naïve, so trusting, yet what clues had there been? Had others seen what she couldn't? But what? She stood leaning her head now against the mare as the flow of tears gathered momentum. Thinking about Terry couldn't raise images of horror - there'd never been any. It had been lovely: all the outings, the gorgeous clothes he bought her, the way he made her feel. The person she'd experienced couldn't become someone else in her memory.

'Rose?' She stiffened at the sound of Adrian's voice and turned her face into Rosie's mane. She felt in her pockets for a tissue but failed to find one.

'Will this help?' She turned then to see Adrian holding out a handkerchief. 'Please take it. I'm sorry you're so upset. Is there anything I can do?'

She wiped her eyes and blew her nose, scrunched the handkerchief up and put it in her pocket.

'I'll wash it for you,' she said, at last meeting his eyes.

'Chuck it,' he said. 'I've loads. Is it to do with not getting that visit? Sunday, wasn't it? Your daughter was coming.'

'In a way, but I stopped her coming. I couldn't face her - or anyone.'

She gave Rosie a farewell pat then moved away from the railings.

'I'm so sorry, Rose. D'you want to walk a bit further?'

'Yes, but I ain't much company.'

'You are. You don't have to talk, and you can tell me to shut up at any time.' He put his arm through hers and smiled his lovely crinkly-eyed smile that made her feel like melting.

They walked in silence for a while but it felt comfortable. Rose glanced at Adrian's profile - definitely superior to Harrison Ford's. How could his wife ever bear to leave him? But it had only been a threat. Finally, she couldn't resist asking,

'Have you had any visitors? Your family p'raps?'

'No. And no phone calls. They could be on another planet.'

'D'you mind not seeing them?'

'It's funny but in away it's a relief. I can concentrate on why I'm here. And Mel must be so relieved to have me out of the way.'

'Don't you worry that she might not have you back?'

'Yes, but I've got to concentrate on being the person she once knew.'

'You're so lucky - you got someone to get better for.'

He stopped walking and half turned, facing her.'

'You've your little girl. But aren't we supposed to do it for ourselves? Convince our selves we're worth it? That's the really hard bit. And it seems selfish.'

'Mary tried to explain it to me but why should I ever think I'm worth anything?' Rose felt her throat constrict and the tears started again.

'It's more than your upbringing, isn't it? Something

recent. I'm not probing, Rose, but if you want to talk....'

'I do...I do.' She was crying hard. She could hardly get her words out. Adrian's arms went around her and he stroked the back of her head. Her face was against his chest.

'It's all right Rose. Say whatever you like.'

Was it the tone of his voice and its sincerity that made her want to talk - to even reveal the things she was so ashamed of? She lifted her head and looked at him. He smiled and continued to hold her, gently rubbing her back.

She looked down again, her head leaning against him.

'I had an affair with a man...Terry. I thought he was going to be the answer to everything...we'd be a proper family. He said he wanted that too, me, Carla and the baby....'

'His baby?'

'Yes.' She was unable to continue for a minute and all the time held her. At last she said, with a struggle,

'He wasn't what I thought. He's one of the people they've been talking about.' She lifted her head and looked in the direction of the house. 'They were all talking about him - and others.'

'You mean the internet porn case? That's terrible for you.'

'And terrible *of* me. You see I wouldn't believe he could be like that. I made myself believe he'd been framed. I didn't want it all to end - all the lovely things we was going to have and going to do. I couldn't bear to lose it all.'

'That's so understandable. At last a real family life was in reach. No one could blame you for that.'

'I do. I was going to let my Carla live with him. He might have done awful things to her and the baby. There might have been things I didn't want to see 'cause I couldn't believe he could be that sort of person. You hear of women like that...turning a blind eye, refusing to see what others can.'

'Rose, you can't torment yourself over what might have happened. You've enough to contend with getting over the drinking and you might still be recovering from the birth.

When was it?'

'It wasn't. I mean not as it should have been. I lost her - around five months. I was drunk and I fell over in the street...' She sobbed so hard she was shuddering against him and his arms closed around her even tighter.

'I'm sorry - telling you all this,' she gasped, blotting her face with his handkerchief.

'Why? Aren't friends meant to listen to one another?'

'Can you want to be my friend after what you've heard? I'm not sure if I've even got a girl friend anymore. My friend Ellie hasn't visited since just before you arrived.'

'Have you asked her to?'

'No, haven't thought of that.'

'Ring her or write. Now, we'd better get back before a search party arrives.' He let go of her but took her hand and continued to hold it for several minutes. His hands were bare - he never wore gloves. She wished her hand too were bare so their skins could touch. Despite the cold she knew his hand would be warm.

'Talk whenever you want to, Rose. It can't help to carry this alone.'

'You understand, don't you - how hard it is to tell everything in the Group. I've said a bit but I'm scared of what some of them will think of me if I say any more.'

'That's a shame. I think they'd understand.'

They walked in silence for a while; back towards the house that Rose hoped would recede so they'd never reach it.

Adrian said, 'Rose, there's an outing tomorrow, a minibus trip to Lyme Regis. You'll come, won't you? It might do us both good.'

She looked up at him and smiled - really smiled for the first time that morning, 'Yes, I'll come - of course.'

Chapter 28

'Be careful. Don't do a Louisa Musgrove on me,' called Adrian, hurrying up the steps to take Rose's hand. 'These steps are lethal after rain.'

Clutching him, Rose descended gingerly to the lower Cobb, the precariousness making her laugh with excitement. Minutes later, safely beside him and gazing out to sea where a few fishing boats bounced on the waves, she asked,

'Who's Louisa Musgrove? An old girl friend?'

Adrian grinned. 'A Jane Austin character. Had a fall from the Cobb that had far reaching results.'

'I saw one of her things on telly once. It was good. You know so much Adrian. All that stuff about fossils and how this is called the Jurassic Coast and about books.'

He laughed. 'Yes, what I know about many things you could write on the back of a matchbox. Oh look, the others are walking back. I reckon a teashop beckons.'

She didn't want to catch up with the eight others who'd made the minibus trip to Lyme Regis. She'd had Adrian to herself walking, or struggling, along the beach, giving up attempts to talk against the wind. In the lea of the cliff he'd told her about ammonites he and his children had found and the many and varied fossils that had been discovered over centuries. It hadn't been boring. And the way he talked about dinosaurs made her picture them trundling along the beach or lurching out of the sea. She'd even looked warily behind her as they retraced their steps and that set them both laughing.

Martha, waiting for them, called them intrepid explorers.

'All the others want is to be in the warm,' she said. 'Shall we join them?'

'Let's,' said Adrian. 'I fancy a teacake. How about you Rose?'

She grinned. Goodness, what did she fancy!

The outings had to be staggered as the bus carried only ten passengers. Most of the younger residents had chosen to attend a modern dance class, which left Rose and Adrian as the youngest members on the trip. Helena had a cold and was confined to her room and Bermondsey Bert had boasted he would show the kids how to boogie and take his outing tomorrow. Rose was relieved when she saw the composition of the group. Nobody present ragged them for walking away, along the beach, and no eyebrows were raised when they sat together on the bus.

'We've saved seats for you,' said James, an elderly man, as they entered the tearoom. 'My, what rosy cheeks, ladies, and I should say, ruddy, for Adrian.' He stood up as they approached a round table and pulled chairs out for them.

He had such nice manners. Rose took to him the moment he arrived and often wondered what it would have been like to have a grandfather.

Soon they were enjoying teacakes oozing butter and japonica jelly, and drinking several cups of revitalising tea, and Rose was loving the cosiness and friendly atmosphere. She looked around the room at its pretty flower-sprigged curtains, silk flowers on the tables and windowsills, and dark bentwood furniture. Watercolours of seascapes relieved the whiteness of the walls between black beams.

'This is lovely. Bet it's old,' she said

'It is. Nearly as old as me,' said James, making Rose giggle. 'I've been here before - with my grandchildren. That was before I let the drink get a grip of me – before my wife died.'

'Awful to lose someone like that,' said Adrian. 'Were you married long?'

'Nearly reached our fiftieth – a few months off. And now look at me – a disgrace to her memory.'

'Not true,' said Rose stoutly. 'You're getting better, really working on it.'

'Sweet of you, but I'm old enough to have known better. Life's much harder for you young things than it was in my day.'

'Thanks for the "young things,"' said Adrian, grinning. 'I'm forty-two, and I should have known better, specially with two kids to set an example to. What sort of role model of family life have I been? Okay, I'm sober now and intend to stay that way but what of the residual damage to my kids?'

A young waitress arrived with a fresh pot of tea and, to Rose's relief, chatted for several minutes. The trip was for fun not talking about painful memories and regrets. They got enough of that at Down House. Thank goodness that discussion wasn't resumed when the waitress moved away

The drive back was fun. Apparently it was traditional to sing, and sing they did: old wartime songs, songs from shows - one Rose joined in lustily, 'I'm gonna wash that man right out of my hair,' and half the busload, including her and Adrian, stood up and jigged in the aisles. The poor driver had no control over them.

They were back all too soon.   'Looks as if you've enjoyed yourselves,' said Lily, greeting them in the hall. 'Rose, Mary's put you in for a session straight after supper – all right?'

All right? What choice did she have? She'd have loved to say, 'No, this is a fun day. You can stick you're therapy.'

Mary smiled warmly as she went into the room.

'You look so well, Rose. The sea air has done you good.

'It was lovely. To be honest I didn't want to come back. Not that this is a bad place, but I s'pose I felt normal out there.'

'And here is a reminder of not so normal?'

Rose grinned. 'Yes, I s'pose so.

'That's a really good sign. You're reaching the stage where outside is less frightening.'

'Yeah, and I didn't feel different from other people – it was as if I was a just any tripper. I didn't feel people were looking at me as if I was some kind of freak.'

'It's encouraging to hear that,' said Mary, smiling. 'I think it shows you're moving to a state of readiness for the next stage...'

'What's that?' Rose's tone was suspicious. 'You mean leaving here?'

Mary looked at the open file lying on the arm of her

chair. 'Nearly five and a half weeks since you came. We'll spend some time on what you plan to do in the last few sessions, or earlier if you feel ready.'

'I'm not. I got to find somewhere to go. I aint0' going back to that flat.' Her voice rose with anxiety.

Mary looked uncomfortable. 'I don't want to push you but we'll need to talk about your leaving – it's only just over two weeks.'

'Yes, but not now. I'm not ready.'

'Right, not now – whatever you like, Rose.'

Rose was alarmed by the sudden hostility she felt towards Mary. She looked at the carpet for several minutes wondering if anger showed in her face. It was idiotic – it wasn't Mary's fault that she couldn't stay here forever but she wanted to be the judge of her readiness.

'You're not feeling very happy now, Rose. Would it help to talk about it?'

Rose looked up. Mary's face was full of concern and she gave Rose a gentle smile of encouragement.

'I still feel scared. I don't know what's going to happen to me.'

'Going to happen to you.... Yet you've taken charge of yourself in that you've beaten the drinking.

'It's other things.'

Again a long silence. How could she say she wanted to be with Adrian. She'd probably be kicked out immediately.

'I don't want to be on my own,' she said at last.

'It sounds as if you want someone who'll make you feel safe.'

'I thought that's what I'd got with Terry – I was so bloody wrong.' Her voice wavered.

'You're afraid of forming another attachment that could go wrong.'

'There aren't any bloody guarantees, are there.'

'No, not for any of us. So we need to practise protecting ourselves. Build up our own strengths – take more charge. And it's about learning to be kind to ourselves, to give ourselves credit for our good points.'

'What good points? I couldn't even care for my Carla. I shouldn't have had her. I only wanted the last one 'cause she was part of being with Terry. I wouldn't want her on my own.'

'You're afraid of repeating the past. Rose – that's understandable. Have you discovered anything in yourself since you've been here that will help you in the future?'

Rose was thoughtful for a moment then she gave a little smile. 'I can be funny – and I've been told I'm good company.'

'Good. So you've plenty to offer. You socialise now, you join in much more and you are open with me and in the group. That's progress, Rose. And keep working on your confidence. Do you remember we talked about the child Rose, the little girl who didn't have the care and attention she needed, and the adult Rose – together in the same person?'

Rose nodded.

'Don't forget that little girl. Nurture her. Others won't, so the adult Rose must do it. That little girl will need the adult Rose in the future.'

'Is that why I couldn't look after my Carla 'cause I was needing to be looked after?'

'Was that how it seemed?'

'I s'pose so. I relied on Carla, then Terry came along. Once he left I knew deep down I couldn't cope with the baby on my own. That's why I didn't cry much at losing her. And I s'pose the drink dulled my feelings.'

'It was your help when you felt sad or frightened.'

'I think I looked on it as a friend I could call up anytime. I didn't want to be an alco – not after all those years with Mum and seeing the way she died but I couldn't see any other way to cope.'

'And now I wonder if you can see other ways.'

'Yes. I can make friends. That's something I've learnt here.'

'Great. Rose will you do a little task over the next few days – write down the things that worry you about leaving here, and the positive things that will help you. Then we can do some work on them, together.'

Rose nodded. It couldn't be worse than the 'lifeline' she'd had to write soon after she arrived. That had dredged up such awful memories.

'And don't forget,' Mary said, 'there's a support network out there as well as your friends.'

Speaking of which… thought Rose, and felt in her pocket for some coins.

After two false tries, she heard an encouraging ringing which ended with Ron's voice, saying, in an unfamiliar tone, 'Mix'n Match, painting and decorating, or Hair at Home. Please say which service you require?'

Rose giggled. 'Neither, thanks, I'd like to speak to a real person – my friend Ellie.'

At once the phone was picked up and Ellie cried, 'Rose. This is great. I was even thinking about you.'

They talked – or Ellie did – for minutes, with Rose trying to get a word in occasionally, then the pips went and Ellie screeched, 'We'll be down at the weekend. See you.'

Rose walked into the lounge beaming.

'Good news?' asked Adrian as Rose passed his chair. She smiled and explained.

'I'm so pleased,' he said, getting to his feet. 'She was probably just waiting for that call. Maybe I should make one.'

He felt in his trouser pocket and produced a mobile phone and, with a wink at Rose, went out through the French windows into the blustery night. She watched him walk away along the terrace, the phone clamped to his ear and the upbeat feeling she'd been carrying since leaving Mary seemed to drop away.

'Fancy that bloke, don't you,' said Sylvia, sitting nearby. She grinned nastily. She'd spoken in her normal loud voice and several pairs of eyes looked up from books and newspapers. Rose didn't meet any of their glances. Ignoring Sylvia she walked to the drinks trolley, mixed herself an Ovaltine, then walked as far from her as she could and sat next to Carol, who muttered,

'Don't take any notice of that little cow. She's cross

because she doesn't impress Adrian. You should see the way she tries to flirt with him in the group. Makes a right fool of herself.'

Rose grinned, instantly cheering up.

The sea air, wonderfully invigorating when she was wrapped in it, now seemed to have zapped her energy. Adrian didn't return to the lounge – maybe he was feeling the same way. She sat quietly, nodding and smiling now and then as if listening to the chatter going on around her but her thoughts were about the strangeness of attraction: Adrian being so different from Terry – he of the pinstriped suits, shiny ties and rather pointed black shoes and Adrian, casual in elbow-patched jacket, ancient Barbour, or duffle coat. Unlike Terry he had plenty of hair, thick dark stuff with a wave to it, and he'd never lose it, she was sure. Nor would he *run to fat* – Gran's scornful prediction for thick-necked young men. But she shouldn't think that way – making comparisons, or thinking about Terry at all. She had to close that book and never re-open it.

At ten o'clock she went up to bed, first soaking for at least twenty minutes in
scented foam – a farewell present from Jen. She loved the big, old-fashioned bathroom with its free-standing tub. Relaxed almost to the point of falling asleep, she relived the walk along the beach, and Adrian holding her safely as she negotiated the tricky steps. She could have stayed there forever but she wanted to be in bed before Carol and the new girl appeared. As she towelled herself she considered her reflection in the long mirror opposite the bath and felt pleased that her shape had returned to normal and weight had been gained in the right places. In bed, every time she closed her eyes, Adrian's face was before hers. She smiled –if she'd been a cat she'd have purred.

Chapter 29

It was warmer: no frost crunched underfoot and the sun was lurking teasingly behind clouds that Adrian described as cumulus.

'You know so much,' said Rose. 'To me they're just clouds.'

'But you spotted them and said, "Look at their shape." I reckon you've an artist's eye.'

'Don't be daft. I just don't see such things in London. And you make me look at things. What you said once, " the stark, cleanness of winter," has made me see things differently. Trees without leaves do have their own beauty.'

'That's when I like to draw them, when I can see all the intricate shapes of twigs and branches,' Adrian said.

And women, wondered Rose, is that how you like to draw them - unclothed? It was an exciting thought causing a flush to rise in her cheeks.

Adrian took in a great gulp of cool air, looked at his watch and said, 'Fancy a glimpse of the sea? If it weren't for the hill and the trees we'd see it from here.'

'But we'll have to go over the fence – out of the grounds,' said Rose.

'Does it matter? You're leaving soon and I don't care if I get chucked out.'

'Adrian, you must care. That's not what you've always said. You want it to work – really work this time.'

'For what? Mel's not visiting this weekend. I'm not seeing my children. I'm really glad that phone call worked for you, Rose, but mine didn't.'

'But it's against what we've been told – we have to want to heal ourselves for our sakes.'

'Yes, hearing that is one thing but believing it is a bit harder. Oh, Rose, I'm sorry, I do think that's right but I'm just having a blip, I suppose.'

'I'm sorry, Adrian. You're doing so well – everyone says so. Don't wreck it.'

He smiled. 'I won't, and that's a good word. I still

want to see the sea but I'm not going to lead you astray – you go back.'

'No, I'm coming too. How do we get out?'

'You're sure? Come on then, we'll climb over the fence. Good job it's post and rails here.

Getting over was easy but still Adrian held out a steadying hand as Rose swung over the top rail. The hill sloped gently but undemanding though the walk was, Rose was puffing slightly when they arrived at the trees that defined the summit. Adrian smiled and said, 'You could go to the gymn every day. You'd soon get fit.'

Fit for what, she thought, and in two weeks? No, she didn't want to think about leaving – that stretched away into the distance like the landscape in front of her: a large expanse of grassland dissolving into an even larger expanse of bluish, greyish....

'The sea,' she exclaimed, and turned to Adrian as if for conformation.

He laughed. 'It is indeed – the same one that we saw at Lyme and Chesil, only the seagulls might be different.

'Of course, I've been hearing them. And look, the sun's coming out. Thanks, Adrian, this is lovely.'

'Nothing to do with me,' he said, smiling.

They stood in the companionable silence that Rose had come to recognise as important between friends. With Adrian there was never the need to fill time with chatter. She had never felt so comfortable with anyone, male of female.

'In almost all weathers the fishing boats go out,' he commented, and pointed to three tiny bobbing shapes on the horizon. 'A hard life, but every fisherman I've met has said there's no thinkable other way for him. Gives credence to the saying: the sea's in the blood.'

'I remember a poem – crikey, the only poem that's stuck since school – all about "the lonely sea and the sky" and "the wind's like a whetted knife." D'you know it, Adrian?'

He beamed. 'Yes, I learnt it as a kid - Masefield's Sea Fever There are some great lines. "And all I ask is a windy day with the..."'His words were drowned by a thunderous roar. With a cry of terror Rose threw herself against him. He steadied her and held her fast as the noise continued, each thunderous roar underpinned by the next.

'It's okay. You're quite safe,' he said, his face close to hers. Rose was sobbing heavily but managed to gasp in response,

'It's thunder. We're not safe.'

'No, it's gunfire. We're close to the army ranges where they train and practice. I'm so sorry Rose, I didn't give it a thought.'

She pulled back an inch and stared up at him. 'It's not thunder? You're sure?'

'Yes, quite sure. It's heavy stuff – mortars, perhaps. Here...' He let go of her with one arm, produced a handkerchief and gently mopped her face.

'Poor girl, you were terrified. You are safe – trust me.'

Tears were still coursing down her cheeks but they were tears of relief. There was a lull in the firing and Adrian said, 'Don't cry, you're safe, honestly.' Then he kissed her, on her wet cheeks as he might comfort a frightened child. As if she had no control over her body Rose felt herself arch upwards, her mouth seeking his. Their lips met in a kiss so passionate that Rose felt she would melt into him, fuse with him and cease to be a separate being.

At last Adrian drew back, staring down at her with an expression of perplexity as if something had happened but he didn't know what it was. She smiled and let out a huge sigh of happiness. He returned the smile, but shakily, then looked away towards the silvery horizon.

'I'm sorry, Rose.'

'Why? I'm not. That was lovely.'

'Yes, it was...it's just that...' his words were drowned by another burst of gunfire. He took her hand and, with a reassuring smile, led her away, through the belt of trees and down the sloping field towards the boundary.

He was hurrying her a bit. She wanted to talk and prolong their return. He glanced at his watch, then at her.

'Should just make it before they send out the blood

hounds – oh, there's one.'

He pointed to the boundary fence. Leaning on it was the comfortable figure of Martha. She spotted them and waved and as they drew nearer she called, 'Advance warning – they're about to send a search party. No one saw me slip away – we've been together, haven't we –the three of us?'

Safely back over the fence, the three fused in an impulsive hug, giggling over their conspiracy.

The day was packed with activities: a visiting speaker, Group and individual therapy for Rose – an extra session to start the preparation for her leaving. It was all rather unreal, as if things were going on around her but she was just an onlooker. Her mind was elsewhere, reliving every word spoken, every move and gesture of Adrian's on the walk. There were things Adrian wanted to say, she was sure, and now they'd have to wait, leaving her in a state of excitement mixed with frustration. She'd felt a mixture of relief and irritation at Martha's presence. If she hadn't been there Adrian would have said more, she was sure, but at least she'd forestalled any telling off they might have got.

'You mention the sadness of leaving new friends,' said Mary, looking up from the sheet of paper on which Rose had scribbled the pros and cons of leaving. There was a long pause. Rose was thinking of Bert's recent departure – he so optimistic and happy. He'd swung her round in his arms as if she were a child and told her she could have as many soft drinks on the house as she could swallow if she ever visited The Compass, then he'd given her a smacking kiss on both cheeks.

'You've had a lot of loss lately and things happening you want to forget, but what about the mo

'How d'you mean?'

'We can carry good experiences on with us. What we get from friendship can stay with us. Some of the friendships forged here go on and on. But it strikes me the what's really worrying you is where you're going to live.'

'I'm not returning to that awful flat – not for a day.'

273

'So you've found an alternative.'

'I don't know. I think so. I'll know when I next see you – on Monday.'

'Good. I'll see you then.' Mary stood up. 'Enjoy your weekend.'

Oh I shall, thought Rose and nearly collided with Sylvia as she entered the corridor.

'Watch out. Cat that got the cream, are you?'

Rose frowned after Sylvia's retreating figure. What the hell did she mean? Was it so obvious? Anyway, why should she care? Sylvia was jealous – rich, spoilt brat – jealous of a poor eastender! That was worth a laugh.

She saw Adrian the usual amount for the rest of the day. He was as friendly as always but she was disappointed not to find him in the library after lunch and supper. Probably having therapy – it happened at all odd times. She'd talk to him tomorrow, before or after Ellie's visit.

She didn't care about Ellie's loudness or Ron's jokes: she was accepted now, part of the place. Helena was occupied with a visitor yet smiled vaguely at them and others chatted to them. Martha commented to them that it was lovely to see how Rose had blossomed.

'That's what Rose's do,' said Ron. 'A winter flowering Rose – special.'

Adrian turned round in his chair and smiled, then he got up, mouthed, 'See you later,' and left the lounge. Rose was disappointed: she wanted Ellie and Ron to meet him. Maybe, it was hard for him – alone again, no visitors. Ellie had noticed him, of course. She'd kept nudging Rose and smiling significantly, inclining her head in his direction.

'Oh, by the way, Brad sends his love,' said Ellie. 'Came up to me in the market and asked after you.'

'That's nice. Still doing all right, is he?'

'Yeah, really well. Ron and me went to one of his gigs a while back. Good it was, even Ron got up and jigged a bit.'

'Ron grinned. 'And we didn't touch a drop – neither of us.'

'What you done about the flat?' asked Ellie. 'You can't go back there.'

'Nothing,' said Rose. 'What can I do?'

'Give notice,' said Ellie.

'But I gotta live somewhere.'

'Yeah, with us. You can stay as long as you like. I told you that before.'

'Yes, but ...'

'No buts. I came over a bit strong p'raps – didn't understand what a terrible shock it all was for you. I'm sorry, Rose.'

'No, I should be saying that. You tried to help and I threw it back at you.'

'No matter. You write to the council and I can collect your stuff, if you like, then you needn't ever go back.'

However bossy and pushy Ellie was, she was a true friend. Her words affected Rose deeply, bringing her close to tears.

'None of that,' said Ellie. 'Now, we want to take you out.'

'But you done enough driving?'

'I ain't done any. Now where shall we go? Weymouth or Swanage – nice bit of dry pub lunch?'

Rose smiled. 'I don't know anywhere around here – you decide.'

If the invitation could include Adrian it would be perfect. It had poured with rain earlier so they'd missed their walk. She longed to be alone with him but a group lunch would be second best. She couldn't ask him, of course, this was Ron and Ellie's treat to her.

In the pub in a little place called Corfe Castle, Rose looked happily around at the rustic interior and the log fire. She'd enjoyed a steak and ale pie and nearly matched Ron's appetite. He told her she'd end up tubby like him and Ellie.

'She needs feeding up,' protested Ellie, 'though you've put on some weight already and it suits you. I'm looking forward to you living with us. Help me keep Ron in order.'

275

Ron grinned and shook his head. 'Oh no, darlin,' you'll be my little harem, girls doin'my bidding.' He gave a great guffaw of laughter that drew amused glances from other customers.

Nice place, thought Rose, not snooty. 'How d'you know this place,' she asked.

'We've been to Dorset a lot,' said Ellie. 'We know lots of nice little B and B's, don't we Ron? You must come with us sometime.'

Rose smiled her appreciation, her mind on the possibilities of keeping in touch with the area. Adrian lived just over the border, in Wiltshire, and if his marriage broke up...No, she shouldn't think like that.

'Penny for 'em,' said Ron.

'Oh, just thinking about the future.'

'And you got one,' said Ellie, 'you and your little one. We'll get her out of Care in no time.'

Rose stared at her. 'I don't know... Well, it should be easier now I'm dry and...I've accepted what's happened...you know what I mean?'

'We certainly do, and we'll back you all the way, won't we Ron?'

'Course we will. Bit of pud now, Rose? Fill up the corners?'

She burst out laughing and rubbed her hand over her comfortably full stomach.

Waving Ron and Ellie away in the late afternoon, Rose watched the van until it disappeared around a curve in the drive. It had been so different from their last visit when she'd wondered if she'd see them again or would even want to. They'd all come back to Down House for tea in the lounge and, apart from the absence of Adrian, it had been a happy time. Even Helena had asked them if they'd had a good lunch. Funny she was still there – she'd arrived at the same time as Bert. Maybe she was buying more time.

Rose felt compelled to find Adrian and tell him all about her day. She went through the huge doors and into the hall where visitors were collecting their coats and saying their goodbyes. Unnoticed, Rose slipped into the library and there he was.

Chapter 30

He stood up. He was holding a pencil and open sketchpad. He shut it, grinned and said, 'Escaping from the hordes, I'm afraid. Not very sociable.'

'You want me to go?'

'No, of course not. I just couldn't face all those visitors. How did it go for you?' He sat down again on the small sofa, putting the sketchpad on the space beside him.

'Great.' She sat opposite him. 'We went out for a lovely lunch and, best of all, Ellie says I can stay with them.'

'I'm so pleased Rose. You won't have to face that awful flat. I could picture it clearly from your description – and the neighbours. It'll make it so much easier for you.'

She swallowed. 'Leaving you mean? Yes, a bit.'

'Are you scared?'

'Not as much as I was.' She looked into the fireplace. She had to say more – let him know how she felt. 'I'll… miss you. You've helped me so much.'

'You've helped me – no don't shake your head, it's the truth. You've given me company, made me laugh, help me put things more in perspective. I'll miss you too.'

'Do we have to…miss each other?' She still looked at the fireplace. 'Ellie comes to Dorset for holidays. She said I could come too.' Suddenly feeling bolder, she looked at him. 'We could meet.'

He held her gaze for a moment then looked away, his expression serious.

'It would be lovely, but….' He sighed. 'I'm very fond of you Rose. It wouldn't be fair to you or to Melanie.'

'But you don't know if you're ever going back to her, and, anyway, we're friends, aren't we?'

'Yes, of course we are…only, I found yesterday really disturbing. I wanted to go on kissing you. I resented having to come back here.'

She smiled. He was going to make it easy for her.

'That's how I felt. We feel the same way.'

'But it isn't right. I can't cheat on Mel. I've put her

through so much.' His tone was gentle but his words were piercing. She willed him to look at her and, as if reading her, he did. His expression was sad now.

''Cause you haven't wanted anyone else?'

'Because it would be wrong.'

'And 'I've looked at other women and appreciated them, like any man, but I've never seriously thought any more than that. Yesterday, I found I wanted more. When I was holding you I wanted to make love to you and, I think, you felt the same way.'

'I did. I love being with you. You treat me like a decent person.'

'Because you are. Life's chucked some hard things at you, Rose – things I've never had to endure. What sort of blueprint were you given at birth?'

'What d'you mean?'

'I mean a sort of inherited pattern of how to live. You didn't want it to be like that.'

'I didn't have to repeat everything that happened to me – do the same damage to my Carla.' Her voice was becoming unsteady

'Rose, when another way seemed possible you went all out for it, but it was being offered by the wrong person.'

'There'll never be a right person,' she said and, feeling tears welling, swallowed hard. She wasn't going to give way and feed off his sympathy.

'The right person has to be oneself. That's what they've been trying to tell us, Rose, haven't they? Only it's so damned hard. Like struggling into a suit that doesn't quite fit.'

She stared at him, and despite her yearning, almost laughed at the picture of all the residents trying to struggle into a new, person-shaped garment.

'Rose, I think you nearly smiled. I hope so. I don't want you to be unhappy. I'll always be grateful for the company you've given me. I shan't forget.'

His smile was so lovely. She longed to sit beside him, lean her head against him and relinquish all her fears onto him but he was right. She had to rely on herself. Her brain told her

279

that but her body and mind so longed for something else.

'I shan't forget you. Adrian. I've learnt more from you than anyone.'

He smiled. 'If my former pupils had all been like you I might have loved teaching.' He picked up his sketchpad and pencil, glancing at the clock above the fireplace.

'What were you drawing?' she asked, both to delay him and because she really wanted to know.

He grinned. 'I'll show you when it's finished. I'm going to have a bath before dinner – water's hottest now. See you later.'

After he'd gone she could no longer stem her tears. Everything he said made sense but it was going to be so hard, relying on herself, avoiding unhelpful relationships, learning how to discern between people, and above all, learning to say 'No.' And all the time longing to be taken care off.

'Hullo, I was looking for a particular book.' Martha came into the room, looking happy. Her daughter with her little boy had visited her, travelling from Kent, an awkward journey. She was always good-humoured but Rose could see a new sparkle about her.

'Had a happy time with your friends, did you? They seem good fun?' Martha was perusing the bookshelves as she spoke, then she looked at Rose and her expression changed.

'Oh, Rose dear, you've been crying. I'm so sorry.'

'It's all right. I did have a good time.' Rose wiped her eyes and blew her nose.

'But it's hard when people leave,' said Martha. She walked across to an armchair and sat opposite Rose. 'I don't see my daughter and grandson very often, but I'm going to stay with them when I leave here. Might even move closer to them. What about you, Rose? You've said how much you hate your flat.'

'Ellie says I can stay with them. I'm going to write to the council and give them notice.'

'I'm glad for you. It won't be long now – 'til you go. You'll be missed.'

At that Rose felt the tears well again.

'Are you afraid to go, Rose?'

'I'll be sad more than afraid. I've made some good friend.'

The tears were flowing now. Martha moved across, sat beside her and put her arm around her shoulder.

'It's one in particular, isn't it? It's been lovely to see the way that friendship's grown.'

Rose turned and stared at her. 'You don't think it's wrong – that we've got close.'

'No. It's what you've both needed. Adrian's told me how lonely he's been – for months. You've given him more confidence.'

'Me? That's rubbish. He's done that for me.'

'He's told me. He said you make him laugh, remind him life can be fun, not all doom and gloom.'

'But I'm not that sort of person. My life's a disaster. I can't see it getting any better.'

'That's not how he sees you, Rose. Look, don't think we discuss you, only one day he was angry –unusual for Adrian. Helena had said something about the time he spends with you, and that people were talking. He told her he valued your friendship and if you were a man she'd not be implying anything, and he didn't care about gossip. A less polite person would probably have called her an evil-minded old cow. He was very restrained but later, he let rip to me.'

'When was that?'

'Couple of weeks ago, less maybe, just before you had that upset.'

'That's why you came to meet us, isn't it, to shut people up? That day we went outside the grounds.'

'Yes.'

Rose leaned her head on Martha's shoulder and sobbed more from gratitude than grief.

'You look pleased. Won the lottery, have we?' asked Bill.

'No, can't have – we don't do it.'

Fay laughed. 'Nearly as good – a letter from Rose. She leaves Down House in a few days and isn't going back to that awful flat.'

'She's being rehoused?' Bill's tone was a mixture of incredulity and concern.

'She's going to her friend, Ellie. She has a spare room and Rose is going to rent it.'

'Just one spare room.' Bill looked thoughtful'

'I know what you're thinking. Here, read the letter.' Fay took it from her apron pocket and handed it to him. As she spooned tea into the pot and unhooked mugs from the dresser, she took several glances at Bill and smiled. His concentration as he read the one page was more suited to the study of a lengthy, serious tome.

Fay put his mug of tea in front of him and he laid down the letter and looked at her with a smile that told all.

'You're right. There's no way she can have Carla back until she finds something bigger. And all she says is she's looking forward to seeing her.'

Bill nodded but still looked concerned. 'If she and Social Services reach an agreement, there'll be little we can do. She's obviously cured so she might get sorted quite quickly. God, Fay, the longer it takes the better, for Carla's sake.'

'I know. She's so happy. We've been at this point before – a few times – but never after this length of time. Weeks or months it's usually been, not a year and a quarter.'

Bill stood up and put his arms around Fay. 'You've been so marvellous, always trying to see the parent's side a well as the child's, but it's got to have taken its toll over the years.'

'You mean the grey hairs and the multiplying lines?'

Bill grinned. 'I mean inside - the pain and sadness. I don't think we can do it again. We'll see Carla through whatever she has to face – no question of that – but then, I think, we've got to stop.'

'Carla will have a home for life here, Bill, if that's what she wants. As for more foster children - that probably wouldn't be considered. We're middle aged - over the hill. There may be people of our parents' ages having children, even by IVF, but isn't there an upper age limit for foster parents? I don't think they'd let us start all over again.'

Bill's lost his serious look and laughed. 'Wouldn't they be guilty of ageism? Contravening the new legislation?'

Chapter 31

'Spend your last few days having fun,' said Carol. 'I'm going
to. I don't want to look back regretting not having done
things. Come to Pilates, have a massage and aromatherapy.
We might never get the chance to try so many things again.'

Rose smiled complacently. Carol was right and she'd be
better filling her days with activity instead of brooding. It
surprised her how fond she'd grown of Down House as well
as of significant residents. The great, gilt-framed pictures no
longer seemed gloomy but interesting. The dark panelling was
overdone but, in some places, gave a cosy effect. Her
favourite room was the library, of course, although she never
picked up a book. Best of all were the grounds. She'd never
have believed she could happily spend so much time outside
and not just because of her walks with Adrian. She recognised
how much she was now really looking around, wondering
about different kinds of trees, why some held onto their leaves
and others shed theirs and faced the winter brazenly naked.
They were the ones Adrian loved to draw. She'd learnt that
not all big black birds were crows – some were rooks, or
jackdaws, and the latter, sensibly, wore a grey headscarf to
distinguish themselves from the others. She hadn't seen the
deer again but she'd never forget it.

She'd miss the park so maybe she'd explore open
spaces in London – places she should have gone to with Carla,
feeding ducks and playing ball. So much they hadn't done
together – so much she'd never done as a child.

'You look so much better,' said Doctor James. 'You've
gained weight so you must be eating well. How do you think
you can keep this up when you go home?'

Rose grinned. She'd have to watch her weight in
another way - on Ellie's cooking.

Given an excellent report by the doctor she was free to
leave. Ellie and Ron would be collecting her at the weekend
but first she had to face her leaving ceremony., and before that
there were some farewells to attend to.

'I'm going to say goodbye to Rosie,' she told Adrian, as they left the breakfast table.

'A private occasion, or may I come along?' he asked.

Rose laughed and stared unflinchingly at Sylvia whose expression revealed she'd overheard. Grinning nastily, she said, 'I'll come too. You'll need a chaperone Adrian.'

'Thanks, but I'd have one in Rose if you came, and we're fine alone, thanks.'

She flushed, gave Adrian a venomous look and walked away.

Rose giggled. Never before had she heard Adrian put anyone down. They went out through the French windows onto the terrace. At once Rose's hair was tugged by the wind. She pulled up the hood of her anorak. Adrian, as always, was bareheaded. She commented that he never seemed to feel the cold.

'Raised on a farm I had to be tough. Whatever the weather, animals had to be seen to. Orphan lambs were my speciality which stood me in good stead when the girls were little.'

She laughed. She could picture him with an armful of baby – competent and gentle. How lucky Melanie had been then. Did she ever think back to the times when he was a support and a full partner? At least she'd had that time – something to remember.

She noticed how the wind ruffled his hair, such thick hair with just a few strands of grey. Terry was rapidly balding.

'I miss the children so much,' Adrian said, 'but I can't blame Mel for keeping them away – it's probably as much their decision as hers. You must be longing to see Carla.'

'I am.' Her response was truthful. She missed her but it was different since she'd been at Down House. It wasn't a desperate feeling, that painful feeling of need as if Carla was her source of security.

'Will you collect her on your way back – from her aunt?'

Rose stared at him. Of course, he didn't know the whole story. She'd tell him. She didn't want to pretend any more – didn't need to.

'Fay is Carla's foster mum. After Terry was arrested she was taken into Care. You see, I wouldn't accept anything they told me about him. They were afraid I'd let him meet Carla. It was awful of me but I couldn't let go of my dream.'

Adrian was looking ahead, his expression thoughtful.

'But once you knew for sure you wouldn't have let anything happen to Carla. And I can understand how you clung on to hope. What opportunities had ever come your way before you met Terry?'

He reached down and squeezed her mittened hand.

'You'll be fine now, won't you? No more alcohol and good friends to help you. You'll have Carla back in no time.'

'You don't think badly of me?'

He stopped and faced her, smiling gently. 'Who am I to judge you, Rose, or anyone. I've never been in your situation. We have to let go of the past and carve our own future but can those we've hurt let it go? That's my worry - can my family forgive me?'

And can mine, thought Rose. What damage had she done to Carla?

'Look, Rosie's owner is with her,' said Adrian. 'Better hurry before she leads her away.'

They ran the last few yards which made them laugh like children.

'I've come to say goodbye,' called Rose.

'So you're off,' said Nick, smiling. 'Well, thanks for all the attention to Rosie. She'll miss you.'

Rose laughed. 'Not me – the mints. I've run out so I've a crust for her today. Is that all right?'

'Yes, she won't grumble.'

Rose flattened her hand and the mare daintily took the crust, specially saved from yesterday's breakfast.

'You're really confident with her now,' said Nick.

'Yes, I'll have to watch it when I see a police horse,' said Rose.

'You could be accused of bribery or enticement,' said Adrian .'We don't want to read about you in the Nationals.'

They all giggled and Rosie gave a little snort.

'Oh, she's so lovely,' said Rose hugging the patient mare who was still leaning over the fence expectantly.

'Come on Rosie, work to do,' said Nick and slipped the headcollar on.

'All the best Rose,' she said. 'Nice to have met you.'

'And you. And thanks to both of you.' Rose's voice was quite thick. She watched Nick lead Rosie away. Just before they disappeared behind a large stand of trees, Nick turned to wave.

'Nice girl,' said Adrian.

'Yes, she didn't mind about me being at Down. Treated me like any ordinary person,' Rose replied.

'Which you aren't. No one is ordinary.'

Rose grinned. 'You know what I mean. She didn't behave as if I was some out-of-control soak who might corrupt her horse.'

Adrian laughed. 'I was a bit like that before I arrived. I even had the shakes some mornings. Thank God for the pills.'

'You've never seemed like that to me.'

'You've never seen me at my worst – not a pretty sight. James has the shakes sometimes. We share a room and he can be quite bad some mornings.'

'Poor James: he's so nice. What's he ever done but love someone too much.'

Rose stopped. That's exactly what she had done. Perhaps was doing it again.

As if reading her thoughts Adrian took her hand and led her on, back to Down House, talking all the while about some of his most bizarre students. Perhaps safely filling what might have been too risky a silence.

She cried. She couldn't help it with so many people hugging her and wishing her luck. James, ever the gentleman, shook her hand and gave her a peck on each cheek. Martha pressed a piece of paper into her hand.

'My address and my daughter's. Do keep in touch.'

There were lots of other requests to 'Keep in touch'

but not the one she wanted. Adrian stood a little way back, joining in the clapping but saying nothing. The ceremony over, everyone dispersed to their Groups, leaving Rose standing alone, gazing at the empty doorway. She waited a moment, struggling to keep back tears, then left the room and, instead of joining her Group for the last time, went upstairs where she flopped onto her bed and let the waters gush.

At midday Lily appeared.

'Hi, your friends have arrived. They can stay for lunch if you like. I've checked with cook. Three people have gone sick so there'll be plenty.'

Rose wondered if she could face the dining room again, but didn't Ellie and Ron deserve a meal *on the house* with all they were doing for her?

'That's kind. And thanks Lily, for everything.'

'It's been a pleasure, Rose. You've done well. Any help needed with your stuff?'

'Thanks but it's all packed.'

'Okay. I'll get it taken down to the hall. You go on and find your friends.'

The meal wasn't the ordeal Rose had anticipated. Ron and Ellie soon had everyone around them collapsing with laughter. In his customary place but no longer next to Helen, who had left at last, Adrian frequently smiled. As they all left the room he appeared beside Rose and whispered, 'A minute of your time – in the library?'

It was a struggle not to embrace him. She beamed and nodded. After he'd gone through the library door, she said to Ellie, 'See you outside - in a minute.'

'Yeah, I need a pee too. See you in the van,' Ellie replied loudly and winked at her

Adrian was standing by the fireplace. He felt under a cushion on the sofa and produced a wrapped package about eight by ten inches. He smiled as he handed it to her.

'What's this?' she asked, holding it carefully although it felt stiff and unbendable.

'Wait and see. Please open it later. Sorry the paper's

brown and not covered with roses as it should be.'

She laughed. 'Thanks Adrian. I'll treasure it, whatever it is.'

'And I'll treasure the times we've had.' Gently he took the package from her and laid it on the sofa then he drew her to him in an enveloping hug. She longed to kiss him but something told her it wouldn't be right. But it was so hard to be restrained, to accept this was the last time she'd feel him against her, smell his masculine freshness. After a minute he released her, turned and picked up the package, handed it to her then, with his arm around her shoulders, gently propelled her into the hall. He didn't remove his arm until they were on the steps, then he kissed her on each cheek.

'Take great care of yourself, Rose.'

'And you must too. I'll never forget you Adrian.' She gulped, turned quickly away and walked down the steps to the waiting van.

'In the front,' called Ellie from the makeshift rear seat. 'Place of honour.'

Rose got in.

'Seat belt, darlin' ' said Ron and started up. Rose looked towards Adrian who responded with a blown kiss and stood waving until the van turned along the drive and he was lost from view.

As Ron drove along the tree-lined avenue a large vehicle came towards them. Both drivers slowed to pass each other, and the women in the Landrover smiled and waved. The pace was slow enough for Rose to see there were two young girls with her. The one sitting beside her had auburn hair and the one behind was dark. The glimpse was enough to tell her who they were.

A few miles on Ellie commented, 'You're quiet, Rose. Hard to leave Harrison, is it?'

'Shut up Ellie. Give the girl some peace,' said Ron. 'What's in the package, Rose?'

Relieved to have this diversion, Rose carefully opened it to find two pieces of cardboard held together by selotape. Ron glanced sideways. ' Scissors,' he suggested, 'in the door pocket.'

Rose found them and slit the tape. Parting the cardboard she gasped; she was looking at herself. Her cheek was brushing Rosie's head, her mouth was smiling and, somehow, Adrian had caught laughter in her eyes. It was a drawing but with added colour. In the bottom left hand corner in copperplate writing were the words: *Adrian's Roses.*

'I can't believe it. And all from memory 'cause I never sat for it.'

Leaning over the back of the seat to see, Ellie squealed with delight and Ron glanced sideways again, putting the van into a wobble.

'Pull over,' commanded Ellie.

Grinning, Ron obeyed, pulling into the next gateway. Gently, he took the drawing from Rose and held it against the windscreen.

'Blimey, that's you to a tee but I didn't know you had ears on the top of your head, and a fringe and great long face.'

Ellie smacked his head. 'It's lovely – you know it is.'

'Course it is. Only joking. Lawd, the bloke must've studied you Rose. It's a brilliant likeness. Worth framing this is. I could do it for you.'

'Delicate bit of carpentry like that? You sure, Ron?'

Rose wished Ellie would stop disparaging him.

'Thanks Ron. I know you'll do it right.'

'It's done in pastels,' said Ellie. 'I've watched painting programmes on the telly. Gawd, he knows what he's doing. Might be famous one day and you'll be worth a fortune Rose. His muse – that's right isn't it?'

Now really emotional, Rose's laugh broke on a sob. She took the picture, covered it with the cardboard then fumbled in her pocket for a tissue, but out came a recognisable hanky. Dropping her head and straining against the seat belt, she couldn't repress her sobs. Ron's arm went around her shoulders. 'It's all right love. Must've been a great friendship.'

Part 3
Eleven months later.

Chapter 32

Liz looked at the relentlessly grey sky and thought of the previous February when she and her family had been surrounded by magical scenery in an equable climate. She had nearly an hour to pass before meeting Dan and any other colleagues, who might be free, for a pub lunch. She shivered and turned up her collar. Kev's Kaf was yards away and looked bright and welcoming. It was empty but for two elderly women who smiled at Liz as she passed their table.

'Don't get the wrong idea, love,' said one. 'In half an hour the place will be heaving. Just a bit early.'

'I'm not surprised it gets busy,' said Liz. 'Nice place.' She sat down at a table with a view of the street and looked around. The café was pristine with real cloths on the tables and even a real flower, a white chrysanthemum, in each vase. A menu in a wooden holder told her that there was a variety of light snacks and drinks as well as more substantial meals but who was there to take her order? As that thought struck her the curtains behind the counter parted and a young woman appeared. Smiling, she looked at Liz then exclaimed, 'Is it? Liz, is it really you?'

'Oh Rose, is it really you?' said Liz. They both burst out laughing and Rose came out from behind the counter, a neat figure in black trousers and crisp white blouse. Her hair was short, curling against her head, boyishly. She looked younger than Liz remembered.

'What can I get you?' she asked.

'Just an ordinary coffee, please, and will you have something and join me?'

'Yeah, I'll have the same. Just as well we're not busy and the boss is out.' She disappeared for a few minutes returning with two cups of coffee, milk and sugar on a tray. She carefully set everything on the table then sat opposite Liz.

'How long have you worked here? Milk? Sugar?'

'Both please, but I should be serving you.' Rose giggled. 'I been here ten months, and I do two cleaning jobs. It's expensive having a kid in foster care.'

Liz drank for a second. 'Good coffee. I needed this. I'd forgotten how dreary February could be.'

'Been back long?

'A month. We stayed on a bit and had a holiday with my husband's relation. He gave Hugh the job out there – made it all possible'.

'Sorry to be back?'

'No, but I'm glad we went. It was a wonderful experience. And such a lovely place.'

'I know. Carla's shown me all the lovely postcards you sent her- mountains, waterfalls, amazing animals. The sort of stuff you see on the telly. That was nice of you, Liz. She really liked them'

She drank her coffee in one long gulp, gasped and grinned. 'I needed that. First drink since breakfast. Kev, my boss is always saying, "Help yourself gel. Keep your strength up," but I forget.'

'Good boss, is he?'

'Brill. Took me on the moment I got back. Are you working around here again?'

'No, in south London. I start next week – in a hospice.'

'Gawd, a bit different. Had enough of the likes of me?'

Liz grinned. 'I've had enough of the huge caseloads – never really doing the job properly.'

'You did a proper job on me.' There was no anger in Rose's tone and she laughed. 'I was pretty hellish, wasn't I? Horrible to you.'

'You were having a horrible time. You had to show your anger somewhere.'

'I couldn't see what was going on around me – I was blind. It took me months to accept it all.'

'Not surprising, it was a shattering blow. But you look so well now, Rose. It's great to see you like this.'

'Thanks. You look pretty good yourself. Is that tan real or can I buy it somewhere?'

Liz laughed. 'Real, but fast fading.'

'I got a tan last summer – first time ever. Fay and Bill

have a caravan now and they took me to Devon and it was a really hot week. It was a bit of a squeeze but we took it in turns to sleep in a big tent. Carla wanted to be in it all the time – she liked it more than the comfortable van. We're going to the New Forest at Easter. Carla can't wait to see the wild horses.'

Liz smiled. This casual drop-in visit was turning out to be really special.

'Tell me all about Carla.'

'She's grown, and filled out. She loves drawing and painting and swims like a fish. She's staying with Fay and Bill. It's her choice. I'm not upsetting her life again. She's been there over two years - probably the best years of her little life.'

Liz felt a surge of emotion. Instinctively she reached across the table and squeezed Rose's hand.

'That's brave of you.'

'Trouble was I wanted her for the wrong reason – to look after me.'

'Never having been really cared for yourself it was hard for you to be any other way – you had no real childhood.'

'Yeah, 'til Terry came along I didn't know what it was like to feel looked after – well, p'raps a few times with Gran- but never with Mum. Terry was like the guy of my dreams.'

She drank her coffee and was silent for a moment, looking thoughtful.

'You tried to warn me Liz. I realise now you saw things I didn't but, then, I hated you for the action you took.'

'I know. It must have seemed so harsh at the time – like kicking you when you were down. I hated having to do it.'

'But you were right. I'd have gone back to Terry like a shot given the chance. You had to protect Carla. I never thought I'd be grateful to you, Liz, but I am now. It's funny how awful things can lead to good. I've met really good people through awful happenings. There was some lovely people in rehab: – some I'd never would've met outside. I know you tried to get me to see things differently but it took a real shock before I could....' she tailed off, swallowing hard

After a minute Liz said, 'Awful things happened here. Hasn't that been hard for you returning to this area?'

'It's funny but it's been all right. Not returning to that awful flat and staying with Ellie was the only way I could come back. And I'm still there. Friends are everything.'

Liz smiled. 'You're so right. I missed mine while we were away, and Jack, my little boy, is thrilled to be back near his grandparents.'

'Lucky kid. That's what me and Carla needed – a family, only not the way I thought it was going to be. Ellie kept on and on about getting Carla back. We fell out about it. She started again when I came back here. She thought with me being sorted it would be easy but she reckoned without Carla....' She tailed off again. The two women had taken her attention. They were standing up, preparing to leave.

'Sorry, must take their money.' She moved over to the counter, attended to the women then returned to Liz. From the doorway one of the women said, 'See you on Saturday, love. You're singing at The George aren't you?'

'Yeah, see you there.' Rose waved at the departing pair.

'What's this? You're a singer?'

Rose laughed. 'Only with a gig – nothing grand. My mate Brad heard me singing in the bath and said I'd be okay with backing. We do the pubs –'bout once a week.'

'But that's great. It must be fun.'

'It is. Kev would have us here only it's too small. He's great - always gives me time off for engagements.' She giggled. 'There I go – sounding like a real pro.'

'It sounds as if you've got some really good friends.'

'You're right. Didn't give them a chance at one time. I was angry with everyone. Hated everyone's guts.'

Laughing, Liz said, 'And not least mine. Oh, Rose, I'm so pleased the way everything's turned out for you.'

'I'll be turned out if I don't get busy,' Rose said. 'More coffee?'

Liz glanced at her watch. 'Thanks but I'd better not.'

The door opened and several lunchtime customers
entered. They all greeted Rose by name. They were a mixed
bunch, some in overalls, some in suits and of all ages.

''S'cuse me, work to do,' said Rose, getting up.

.How would she cope with them on her own, Liz
wondered? She got up and walked to the counter. Rose was
halfway through the door into a back room delivering a lunch
order to someone invisible to Liz. As she turned back, Liz
said, 'You've enough to do. Should you be on your own?'

'It's okay, Kev's back. He always works with me
although he's the boss.'

'Well, I'd best be going. Is this correct?' Liz put the
money for the coffees on the counter and, surreptitiously, a tip
in a gratuity box. 'Thanks, Rose, it's been so good to see you.
I've really enjoyed it.'

'Same here. I hope you'll come in again.'

'Give my love to Carla, will you?'

'Sure I will. Bye Liz.' Rose followed her to the door.
Simultaneously they turned to one another and hugged.

It was beginning to rain. No umbrella, of course! Having lived
in the driest part of New Zealand Liz had nearly forgotten
what rain was. She laughed, lifting her face to the splattering
drops. Despite the rain, or maybe because of it, pale wintry
sunlight, brightened the sky as it edged its way around the
clouds that were slowly shedding their burden.

Fifteen minutes later she was in the tiny crowded office
wondering what had made it tolerable for nine years, and the
answer was, of course, around her – her colleagues and above
all, Dan.

The structure had changed. Sheila had been moved
sideways into an administrative job and Dan had resisted
promotion to the disappointment of many colleagues, but the
new team manager was proving to be a kindly, experienced
man. Strong enough to challenge ridiculous whims and
fashions and resilient enough to ride with those he had to
accept, he had gained the respect and affection of the team.

Could she have moved back into her old job quite

happily, Liz wondered? No, she'd made the right decision. She wanted and needed more time with Jack and Hugh; she wanted to do a better job all round. Her time in New Zealand had been a repairing stage, and a rediscovering of a relationship she'd been in danger of losing. How few clients ever got such chances in life; and how wonderful to know that one, despite so many difficulties, had turned her life around.

'Who was your friend?' asked Kevin, turning the notice around on the door so it read: *Closed 3p.m. until 6p.m.*

'Liz Allan, my Carla's old social worker.'

'Didn't look that old to me.'

'Old as in ex. You know what I meant,' said Rose, giggling.

'Thought she was a real friend the way you said goodbye – like a proper buddy not a bloody social worker.'

'You know Kev, even a bloody social worker can be a real friend.'

The End

Printed in the United Kingdom by
Lightning Source UK Ltd., Milton Keynes
140664UK00001B/93/P